THOROUGHLY Kissed

S0-AGH-590

KRISTINE GRAYSON

Published by Sourcebooks Casablanca, an imprint of Sourcebooks, Inc.
P.O. Box 4410, Naperville, Illinois 60567-4410
(630) 961-3900
FAX: (630) 961-2168
www.sourcebooks.com

Originally published in 2001 by Zebra Books, an imprint of Kensington
Publishing Corp., New York.

Printed and bound in the United States of America
VP 10 9 8 7 6 5 4 3 2 1

For my niece, Kathryn MacNally, with love.

Chapter 1

EMMA LOST CLEARED THE LAST OF THE WINTER DEBRIS from her yard, put her dirt-covered hands on the small of her back, and stretched. The air had a sweet, fresh odor, and the sky was a warmer blue than it had been a month ago.

Spring had finally arrived—and not a moment too soon. Sometimes she questioned her sanity, moving to Wisconsin from Oregon. Oregon, at least, had had winters like those she had grown up in—wet, chilly, and rainy. Nothing like the hip-deep snow she had had to endure, the layers of ice beneath it, and temperatures so far below freezing that they barely registered on the thermometer the house's previous owner had glued to the outside of her kitchen window.

And even though she had been a member of the modern era for the last ten years, there were still things she didn't completely understand. Like wind chill. The concept was clear enough—it got colder when the wind blew. But she had no idea how anyone would be able to measure how much colder, or why they couldn't build a thermometer that incorporated it.

She'd asked one of her colleagues at the university, and she had looked at Emma as if she were crazy, a look Emma should be used to by now. If she told most people her history, they all would think she was crazy, or at least delusional. They would have no idea that she was telling them the truth.

She didn't even try anymore.

An angry yowl sounded from her front door. She turned, just as she was expected to. Her black cat, Darnell, sat behind the screen, his ears back, his green eyes slit. When he realized she was looking at him, he put a paw on the screen door.

"No such luck, pal," she said. "You have never been an outdoor cat, and I'm not starting the habit now."

Darnell's ears went even flatter, if that were possible. His eyes flashed.

"You're twenty years old," she said. "And I don't care that the vet just gave you a clean bill of health, you wouldn't survive a day out here. Sometimes I wonder how I do it."

Darnell huffed at her, then butted his head against the screen.

"One more time," she said, "and I'll close the door. You won't even get the fresh air."

He moved his head away from the screen so fast he nearly fell over. Then he wrapped his tail around his paws as if he had no interest in leaving the house.

She grabbed her pruning sheers off the pile of tools she had placed on her brick stairs, then headed for the tulip bed. The previous owner of this house had loved flowers—especially spring flowers, especially bulbs. She had so many tulips on the south side of her house that it looked as if she had moved to Holland. The daffodils were planted around back—just as many if not more.

The tulips and daffodils were nearing the end of their season and needed to be deadheaded. Not that she minded. She would be working near the lilac bushes, which were just beginning to flower. The lilac scent was heavenly.

Before she started to change the flower garden', she would have to wait to see how many more surprises the warm weather would bring. She had rented the house last fall, when the University of Wisconsin hired her as an associate history professor. Her specialty was the Early Middle Ages in England, commonly known as the Dark Ages—the years from 500 to 1100 AD— but she'd been teaching everything from survey classes of the whole medieval period to graduate seminars on everything from the Roman Conquest to the Crusades.

But it was her lecture series—England in the First Millennium—that made her one of the most popular professors on campus. Her popularity, and her book, *Light on the Darkness*: *England from 450–1000 AD*, a pop culture bestseller, which had inspired the university to ask her to teach in the first place, convinced Mort Collier, the chairman of the history department, to recommend her for a permanent position.

To celebrate, she had bought the house. She loved it. Her refuge in a world that was too modern for her. She had friends here—a lot of them, actually—but none of them knew who she was—or why she specialized in the Dark Ages.

And she would never tell them.

Imagine, sitting with her girlfriends at Mother Fool's Coffee House, sharing lattes, and explaining that she taught about the Dark Ages because she had been born in them. That would go over well. Just about as well as telling them that when she was twenty years old, she kissed a young man named Aethelstan and went into a magically induced coma for the next thousand years. Then, when she woke up, it was to find herself in a glass coffin in the back of a decrepit VW microbus, facing Aethelstan's lawyer—the pretty, petite woman who later became his wife.

And she could have him. Emma shuddered as she always did when she thought of Aethelstan. He had lived those thousand years—aging slightly, as all mages did—and becoming a person she didn't know. She liked him now, but she couldn't imagine being attracted to him—or wanting to kiss him.

Then again, she didn't want to kiss anyone again. Ever. For any reason. Too risky.

She knew the spell that had put her in the magical coma had supposedly ended ten years ago, but sometimes magic was tricky. It didn't always do what people expected. And sometimes it came back. So Emma protected herself, and her lips. She didn't need a real man with real problems and real needs. She had Darnell. He was cranky enough for one lifetime.

A UPS truck drove by and stopped in front of a house down the block. Emma set down her shears beside the tulips and hurried to her brick sidewalk. Sure enough, the UPS truck had stopped in front of the house at the corner. She slipped her dirty hands in the back pocket of her jeans. She hadn't expected that. The house had been empty ever since she had moved into the neighborhood last fall.

She kept an eye on that house because it was a companion house to hers. Both had been designed by Frank Lloyd Wright who had spent much of his life in the Madison area. Apparently, he had designed the houses for sisters who wanted to live in the same neighborhood. Emma's sister had died young, and the next owner had remodeled the house—leaving the Wright exterior, which blended so beautifully with the lot, and meddling with the interior. But the other Wright house was just as it had been when it was built—furniture and all.

Emma had wanted to go in it since she'd heard that, but the owner was out of the country. No one knew when he was coming back.

The UPS driver opened the back of the truck, and grabbed a huge cardboard box. He staggered with it over the curb and toward the front door of the sister house. Then he leaned on the doorbell.

The door opened, but Emma couldn't see who was inside. She walked to her lilac bushes, and hoped that the branches would hide her just enough to prevent her neighbors from knowing how nosy she really was.

The box disappeared out of the UPS driver's hands, and then he went back to the truck, peering inside it as if he were facing a herculean task. After a moment, the door to the mystery house opened, and a man came out.

Emma caught her breath. He was gorgeous. Broad-shouldered with a narrow waist that tapered into long muscular legs. He had hair so blond that it could rightly be called golden, and his features seemed, from this distance at least, to be perfect. Women these days would call him "movie star handsome" but an old term from her past rose in her mind. He was *wulfstrang*—powerful enough to defend anything.

Then she shook herself. It didn't matter how good-looking he was. She wasn't going to allow herself to be attracted to anyone, for any reason. The last time it had happened cost her a thousand years of her life.

Darnell yowled from the house, and she shushed him

over her shoulder. Obnoxious cat. He had originally belonged to Aethelstan's wife, Nora, but then became enamored with Emma, and cried for her when she wasn't with him. Nora had given him to Emma and, at the time, she'd been very happy to have him. She still was, if truth be told. But she didn't like the yowling or the jealousy. And that cat was jealous of everyone.

The blond man with the broad shoulders took a box from the UPS man, who then took one of his own. They carried the boxes into the house. The blond man seemed to have no trouble with the box's weight, while the UPS man staggered yet again.

Emma frowned. What was in them? His possessions? It would be a strange way of moving in this day and age, but she was the first to admit she didn't understand many things about the modern era. She had spent the last ten years in school—first catching up on the time she'd missed while learning practical things like how to read, how a stove works, and how to drive a car.

She'd come a long way in a short time—from an illiterate to a PhD. Or perhaps, more accurately, from a woman who was afraid of a shower to someone who occasionally was interviewed on A&E or the History Channel as an expert on the past.

Sometimes the person she had become amazed her. There would have been no way to explain this life to the girl who had been kissed into a magical coma. She would have seen this entire world as make-believe, or magical. And she never would have believed that she would be able to do all the things she did without magic.

But she had none, and she was relieved. She would become a mage one day but, for the time being, she was as normal as the next person. If, of course, the next person had been in a magical coma for one thousand years.

The men left the house again. The blond man glanced in her direction and she cringed behind the lilac bush, hoping he didn't see her. Men had terrible reactions when they saw her. They acted just like Darnell. They became enamored, entranced, attracted. And she hated it.

When she had complained to Aethelstan, he had laughed at her. *This culture's story of Sleeping Beauty is based on your life, my dear. Of course men are going to find you incredibly attractive. You are.*

She didn't see it. Her skin was too pale, her cheeks and lips too red, her eyes too blue. And her hair was a glossy black in a culture that seemed to worship blondes. Blondes with hair the color of that man across the street.

She peered over the lilac bush. He was still carrying boxes. The UPS man had paused to wipe the sweat off his face, even though it wasn't that hot. He didn't look her way once.

Darnell yowled again. She sighed. She got up and went to her front door, pulling open the screen. Darnell bolted for the great outdoors, but she blocked him with her foot, and then pushed him inside. He gave her an affronted look as she pulled the heavy oak door closed, locking him inside.

The screen door whapped her in the side. She moved away from it, and headed back to her lilac bush.

As she did, she heard the truck start up. The UPS man was driving away, and the door was shut on the blond man's house. She had missed him.

But they were neighbors. She would see him again. She couldn't get near him—that would be risking too much—but she could watch him from afar. There weren't many men in this modern age who were *wulfstrang*.

Perhaps he had an old soul.

She sighed and went back to her tulips. A big bouquet of the last of them would look beautiful in her entryway. A little bit of spring indoors.

Just the thing to pick up her mood—and make her forget the mysterious stranger who had moved in across the street.

~~~

He wasn't ready to be back. Five days ago, he'd been standing at Stonehenge—now fenced off, so that no one could deface the marvelous rocks—and now he was back on campus. Strange that it all looked the same.

Michael Found rubbed his eyes. The sky was a lovely shade of blue, but the ground was still brown from the harsh winter. A few blades of grass made Bascom Hill look as if it were a patchwork quilt—a patchwork quilt covered with student ants. The students all looked the same too, in their tattered jeans and carefully funky coats. Backpacks were back in style—ergonomically designed, of course (it was a new century after all)—but still packed to the brim.

The air was just warm enough to bring most of the vendors to the Library Mall. T-shirts hung from stalls, and he could smell falafels even though it was only 10:00 a.m. A juice bar was open and had a line; so did the new coffee vendor, who hadn't been in business when Michael left Madison last July.

It was May and he was back, the sabbatical over. He had to step into his new job as department chairman whether he was ready to or not. The previous department chair, Mort Collier, had chosen the end of spring term as his retirement date. Michael had just barely made it home in time for last night's private party. Mort had looked happy and younger than Michael had seen him look in years.

"It's a good job," Mort had said. "It just drains you. But you'll have the break to get your feet under you— and summer's an easy term. The hard stuff won't start until fall."

It felt like the hard stuff was starting now. His mind was still in England, thinking about the research he was doing for his current book, and instead, he was here, about to jump into the fray. Michael had been Mort's assistant and heir apparent for three years now. He knew the drill. He just wasn't ready to be the one responsible.

But he was. Mort made it clear that he would only help in cases of extreme emergency—and Michael had no idea what those cases would be, although he suspected they would all be political.

Michael was not looking forward to the political part of his new job.

Nor was he looking forward to the first thing on his morning's agenda. He was going to a lecture. Mort had urged him to see the history department's newest acquisition, a female medieval history professor who had somehow gotten a long-term contract in the space of a single semester.

At the party, all Mort could do was rave about this woman. Michael hadn't had the heart to tell Mort he'd already heard of her—and had read her so-called masterpiece.

Light on the Darkness was pop history at its worst, and her scholarship was abysmal. And her name didn't help matters. Emma Lost. He could only guess at the jokes the graduate students would make about that. Dubbing the history department the Lost and Found Department was only going to be the beginning. Michael had been around students long enough to know it was going to go downhill from there.

He jogged up the steps leading to the 1970s eyesore the university had deemed the Humanities building. Built after the Vietnam war protests (in which one group of misguided university students had bombed the UW's Army-Math research center), the Humanities building had thick concrete walls, steel doors, and pencil-thin windows in only a few of the offices. There was an interior courtyard—and there were windows facing that—but all they showed was a patch of grass and the rest of the building. Sometimes, when he'd been hunkered in this building for weeks, he felt as if he were in a 1950s underground bomb shelter, waiting for the end of the world.

He let himself inside. The interior smelled of blackboard chalk and processed air—he doubted this place had had a breeze inside it since it was built. What surprised him was that he had missed the smell. The musty, fusty buildings he'd been in while he was in England usually smelled of ancient dust and mold. For some reason, the processed air smell to him was the scent of cleanliness.

There were no students in the hallways—for obvious reasons, no one hung out in Humanities—and those who were here were already in class. He hurried to the lecture hall where Professor Lost was teaching her two hundred–level undergraduate survey on the Early Middle Ages, and sighed softly.

He wished he were hiking in Cornwall. He had planned to end his trip there, but he had run out of time. He was going to use his favorite bed-and-breakfast in Mousehole (pronounced Mozzle) as his home base, and he was going to go around to all the historic and magical sites—even to one of the many purported sites of Camelot. Jogging concrete stairs and hallways in the Humanities building was a poor substitute.

The door to the lecture hall was open, and he slid into the back. It was a huge room, with stairs descending to what the faculty unaffectionately called "the pit"—a small floor with a large blackboard behind it, screens that could come down for film viewing, and a movable podium up front.

Michael had once told Mort that it felt as if he were a Christian in the Roman coliseum, waiting to face the lions. Mort had laughed and said that it was his job to capture the students, not to let them capture him.

Michael had never quite found the trick to that. He was better at research and scholarship than actual lectures. He actually liked the organization his administrative duties required of him, and if he never taught another class, he doubted anyone—including him—would miss it.

Obviously Emma Lost's students didn't feel that way.

Michael had never seen a two hundred–level Middle Ages class so full. And more surprisingly, most of the students were male—and, if he didn't miss his guess, several of them were the school's top athletes. He'd never heard of nonmajors taking a medieval history course as an elective—the nonmajors flocked to American history, and then to famous events, like the Civil War or World War II. And the jocks avoided the history department ever since Mort had canceled all of the History for Dummies classes (as they were affectionately called) ten years ago.

So what were the jocks doing here?

Michael gazed down at the stage and didn't see a professor at all. The teaching assistant had her back to him. She was gathering a pile of papers and placing them on the table that doubled for a desk.

Then she turned around, and his breath caught in his throat.

She was slender yet curvy in all the right places. She wore her long black hair loose, and it flowed past her knees. It caught the light, shiny and reflective like hair in a shampoo commercial. But her hair wasn't her most stunning feature.

Her face was. She had a true peaches-and-cream complexion, the kind he hadn't seen outside of Ireland, and never on a brunette before. Her eyes were almond shaped, her cheekbones high, and her mouth a perfect bow.

He sank into one of the ugly orange plastic chairs, his legs no longer able to hold him, and it took him a long time to remember to close his mouth.

No wonder this lecture hall was filled with men. No wonder they all stared like—well, like he was. She was the most beautiful woman he had ever seen in his life.

She walked over to the podium and grabbed the cordless microphone. It thumped once, making him start.

"Sorry about that," she said. "I just had to make sure you all had the revised assignments list."

She had a throaty alto with a bit of an accent, an accent he couldn't quite place. It was almost Scandinavian, but not in the broad comical tones he usually heard all over the upper Midwest, the accent that had been so aptly lampooned in the movie *Fargo*. No, this was more like a hint of an accent, as if English were not her native language. She clipped the ends of words the way a German would who had long been acclimatized to the United States.

"All right," she said, leaning against the podium but not stepping behind it. "Since you all seem to be having so much trouble believing that the people who lived a thousand years ago were the same as the rest of us, with the same problems, similar cares and worries, and similar feelings, let's try to bring their world a little closer, shall we?"

Even though she was chastising the group, she didn't seem at all angry. In fact, Michael felt himself being drawn closer to her.

"We still practice a lot of rituals that began in the Middle Ages," she said and then she smiled. It seemed as if the entire room had been lit by its own sun. "And frankly, the rituals made a lot more sense back then than they do now."

Michael's hands were shaking. He had never been drawn to a woman by her beauty before, but he couldn't help himself. She was absolutely, positively mesmerizing.

"For example," she said, that smile still playing around her lips, "one of the Suebic tribes worshipped the Mother of the Gods. They wore an emblem to honor that rite—it was the image of wild boars."

Half the class tittered nervously. The sound brought

Michael back to himself for just a moment. He caught his breath, but couldn't make himself look away from her.

She didn't even seem to notice their reaction. "To them, the boar guaranteed that the worshipper of that goddess would be without fear even if he was surrounded by his enemies. At Yuletide, the warriors made their vows for the coming year on a sacrificial boar. You all continue that practice. You make New Year's resolutions."

A young man in the front of the room said, "You don't know that the events are tied. You can't just say—"

"Justin," she said in a weary tone. "What did I tell you about comments in class?"

"Geez, Professor Lost, I…"

Michael stiffened. He frowned at the woman, still engaged in conversation with the young man in the front of the room. She looked as young as her students. There was no way that this could be Emma Lost.

He had expected a middle-aged woman with a narrow mouth that never smiled, and small beady eyes that constantly moved back and forth searching for people who saw through her terrible scholarship. He should have realized that she was tiny and telegenic. After all, he'd been hearing that she made the lecture rounds before she came to the UW, and she was still being called by interviewers as an expert on all things historical.

"My favorite senseless thing that's still practiced in this century," she was saying, "occurs in the spring. Now remember, that medieval people understood the world based only on what they could see."

Michael gripped the plastic top of the chair in front of him. She looked so relaxed down there, one ankle crossed behind the other, the microphone held easily in one hand. He was always behind the podium, struggling with notes.

"There is a bird in England called a lapwing which, for those of you who don't know, is a plover—"

The hand of the boy in the front row rose again.

"—which," she continued with a grin, "for those of you who don't know is a wading bird—"

The boy's hand went down.

"—and it builds a nest, which looks remarkable similar to the scratch of a hare, which for those of you who don't know, is a rabbit. Because of the similarity in nests, many of the early English believed that rabbits—"

She paused, waiting for the class to come up with the answer on its own.

"Laid eggs," Michael whispered.

"Laid eggs," she said, her eyes twinkling. "And that's why the Easter bunny lays Easter eggs."

Another hand went up. This one belonged to a studious girl who sat in the middle. "Our books mentioned that the word 'Easter' came from the pagan goddess 'Eostre.'"

The grin faded from Professor Lost's face and she was watching the girl intently. Michael felt his back straighten.

"We haven't discussed the pagans much—"

"We've discussed the Christian church's influence and various beliefs." Professor Lost sounded almost defensive.

"A little. But the book mentions that it's impossible to know what pagan beliefs really were because the early Christians did what they could to destroy any history of paganism."

Professor Lost's magnificent eyes seemed to have grown larger. Michael wondered what it was about this topic that made her uncomfortable. It was well known that the Christian church did its best to convert all it contacted to Christianity. Had she run into trouble in the past by teaching pagan history? He doubted that. She didn't look old enough to have been teaching long.

"What's your question?" Professor Lost asked.

Apparently the girl heard annoyance in the professor's tone and flushed. "Well, in, like, fiction books, they say the pagans practiced magic. Did they?"

Professor Lost's face shut down completely. All the personality left it. Michael leaned back wondering how she would handle this. Magic was his special area of historical expertise—and the subject of his next book. He knew the answer. He wondered if she did.

"We don't discuss magic in this class," she snapped. "Now, if there are no more questions, let's return to our discussion of Alfred the Great. He was about twenty-three years old when he was crowned in 871..."

Michael stood. He knew more about Alfred the Great than he wanted to. Even though medieval history hadn't been Michael's area before, he'd had to study it as his history of magic project grew.

"...was an outstanding leader both in war and in peace, and is the only English king—"

There was a small break in her voice. Michael looked over at her and found her staring directly at him. He felt her gaze as if it were a touch. Her eyes were wide, her mouth parted, and all he wanted to do was run down those stairs and kiss her. For a long, long time.

He shook himself. *That* would have shocked the students. The new chairman of the history department going from class to class and kissing the professors. That would really shock old Professor Emeritus Rosenthal who was giving a lecture on British Naval History in the next room.

The thought of kissing Professor Rosenthal broke the spell, at least for Michael. But Professor Lost was still staring at him as if he were the answer to all her prayers.

She would soon discover that he wasn't. He hadn't been all that impressed with her famous lecturing skills.

"I wouldn't call Alfred the Great a king of England," he said, his voice carrying in the cavernous room.

She blinked as if catching herself, and then said into the microphone in a very cold voice, "And who might you be?"

"I'm Michael Found."

"Michael *Found*?"

Several students tittered. She glared at them and they all leaned back. Michael felt like he wanted to as well.

"I don't appreciate jokes, Michael *Found*, and I know your name is not on my student roster, so if you would kindly—"

"I'm the new chairman of the history department."

To his surprise, she blushed. She turned a lovely shade of rose that accented her dark hair and her spectacular eyes. "Oh, well, then, I guess you can interrupt at any time."

They stared at each other for a moment. The students seemed to be getting tennis neck turning their heads back and forth, trying to see what was going on.

She cleared her throat. "What would you call Alfred the Great if not a king of England."

"England was divided into tribal areas at that period. Alfred was king of the West Saxons in southwestern England, but he didn't—"

"He conquered London in 886," she said. "All the English people who weren't subject to the Danes recognized him as their ruler. By my book, that makes him a king of England."

"By your book, yes," Michael said, "I suppose it does."

She frowned, obviously not understanding the comment. She would later.

"I didn't mean to interrupt your class," he said. "You're the only tenured professor I haven't met yet, and I wanted to hear you work." He glanced at the students. "You can all go back to learning about Danelaw."

That blush rose again on her skin, and he felt that same attraction. He dodged it by turning and going out the door. As he did, he heard her say, "Well, you never know what's going to happen on a pretty May morning. Let's talk about Alfred, though. He was the youngest son of…"

Michael hurried down the hall. His heart was pounding. He hadn't challenged a professor in front of a class since he was a student himself. And as a professor, he hated being challenged by a colleague. He had no idea what had provoked him to do that.

But as he reached the stairwell, he realized he did know. It had been his reaction to her beauty. He knew that her work was poor and that she had gotten fame, fortune, and an undeserved tenure for her rotten scholarship. She had looked bright enough, but she clearly didn't understand that history was about facts, not fiction.

He had always been attracted to smart, capable women. Men who were interested in women solely because of their beauty were contemptible. He had always prided himself on seeing a woman's intelligence before he noted her physical attractiveness.

Except this time. He had gone in knowing that she was going to be an embarrassment to the university, hoping that she would prove him wrong, and then all he had done was stare at her like a lovesick puppy—which was exactly the way all the undergraduate men, including half the football team, were staring at her.

So he had challenged her, and she had actually answered him with something resembling an argument.

Still, he was unimpressed with her analysis and her so-called lecturing skills. Discussing Easter eggs and boar's heads might be fun over beers, but such things had no place in a two hundred–level history course. Those courses were difficult in the first place because the instructor had to cram as much information as possible into a very short semester. To waste time with frivolities like New Year's Resolutions and the Easter bunny was the sign of an undisciplined mind.

He climbed the stairs to his office two at a time, but the movement didn't drive the feeling from his stomach. She was beautiful and he wanted to go back down there and stare at her. He half envied those kids who got to see her every Monday, Wednesday, and Friday.

She was precisely the kind of woman a man could worship from afar.

Emma's hands were shaking as she picked up her books. The gorgeous man from her block had been in her 9:00 a.m. lecture, and she hadn't even noticed him until he stood to leave.

Michael Found. What a horrible, awful coincidence. She would bet that he was born with his name. In her day, very few people had last names—and usually they were descriptive, just like hers was. She had chosen the name Lost a few days after she had woken up in the Computer Age. She had felt it described her then. It didn't describe her nearly as well now, but it was what she was known as, well known, surprisingly enough.

She turned to see a handful of students hovering near the stairs. She suppressed a sigh. Usually she hurried out—she knew that half the boys had crushes on her—but she had forgotten this time. Michael Found—her new boss—had a lot to answer for.

She talked to the students—that was her job after all—reminding them about the readings, refusing offers of coffee, and telling inane anecdotes, all the while walking up the stairs. She had to hurry to get to the sanctity of her office. She didn't have office hours on Monday, and she might get some personal time.

Heaven knew she needed it.

She managed to escape quicker than she expected, and then took the stairs to the cubicle the university let her call home. She unlocked her office, and stepped inside. Her office was small and rectangular. She had decorated it herself with her own furniture—the book had paid for a lot of extras—which meant that she had a Danish modern desk, a thick leather chair, and a comfortable seat for students who needed help.

On the wall behind her desk, she put a Danish modern bookshelf covered with the books she'd assigned for class, as well as extra copies of her own book. On the wall across from her was a large photograph of Portland, Oregon, the city where she had "come to herself" as Aethelstan so euphemistically put it. She used

that photo to ground herself and remind her where she
had come from.

Her other decorations were her degrees—no one
except her Oregon friends knew what a victory those
degrees were—and literacy posters. She volunteered for
two different literacy organizations and she tutored students who needed extra help. She figured it was the least
she could do, considering all the tutoring and special
help she had.

She pushed the door closed, flicked on the green desk
lamp, and sank into her comfortable leather chair. Then
she closed her eyes. When she did, she saw Michael
Found. He was even more gorgeous up close—those
blue eyes so startling that they seemed to blaze across a
room. His voice was deep, rich, and musical, and he had
a lovely subtle Midwestern accent.

She wondered if he had seen her reaction to the magic
question. He probably had, and he probably thought her
a cross and unhelpful teacher.

Unfortunately, that was a question she had no idea
how to answer.

Scholars had the magic issue all wrong. First, they
started from the premise that magic did not exist. Then
they drew their conclusions from there. They believed
that all medieval people who believed in magic were
pagans—and that was not true—and that all pagans
were the same. Actually, it was so much more complicated than she could ever explain. If she had trouble getting her students to believe that New Year's
Resolutions were originally a medieval custom brought
to the Computer Age, she had no idea how they would
take the fact that half the mythical people they studied

and a good eighth of the real people were mages just like Aethelstan.

And, if she were honest, like she would be someday. She hadn't come into her magic yet. She had twenty more years before that happened, and she wished it were longer. Men got their magic at the age of twenty-one, but women didn't get theirs until fifty or so. All magic arrived full-blown, so a mage had to learn how to control her magic before it arrived.

Emma had spent so much time studying that she didn't want to apprentice herself to anyone, at least not yet. And besides, the last time she had done that, it had gone badly as well.

Besides, there was plenty of time to deal with the magic before it came. Aethelstan would probably teach her, with Nora acting as referee. But Emma wanted to enjoy life as a normal—there was that word again! Well, as normal as she could be—American in the New Millennium.

She deserved that much.

Maybe the next time a student asked the magic question, she'd tell them what the other scholars believed. Who cared that it was wrong? Only she knew.

But she was such a perfectionist that knowing made all the difference.

A knock at her door made her jump. She sighed. If it was that football player again, she'd complain to his adviser. She got up and pulled the door open. The department secretary, Helen Knoedler, stood outside, hands clasped in front of her.

Helen had been with the department longer than anyone. She was a tiny elderly woman who seemed grandmotherly until she opened her mouth. Then she spoke with a voice so deep and powerful, it should have come from a man who wielded an ax instead of a woman who reminded Emma of a sparrow.

"I don't know what you did," Helen said dryly, "but Michael wants to see you first thing tomorrow."

Emma felt that blush return. He was probably going to take her to task for being so harsh on the students. Or maybe he was going to talk to her about staring at him. Or maybe he realized she was the person who had been spying on him when UPS delivered his boxes the day before.

Helen watched her reaction then raised her eyebrows. "You know him?

"I just met him this morning. Sort of."

"Well, you made an impression."

So did he. "What's first thing?"

"He gets in about nine, or so he tells me. Can you come?"

"Sure," Emma said. "My first class isn't until eleven tomorrow. Do you know what it's about?"

"Not a clue," Helen said. "And I don't want to know. I'm still handling the paperwork the changeover has caused."

"I saw Mort yesterday," Emma said. "I can't believe he's leaving."

Helen frowned at her. "He's not leaving. He's just not going to chair the department anymore. He'll be back in his office, harassing all of us next semester."

Emma smiled. She was glad of that. She hadn't realized that Mort would continue teaching. That was good. He needed to.

Then her smile faded. "I hadn't met the new chairman before. Was he brought in from somewhere else?"

"Michael?" Helen laughed. She had a deep-throated chuckle. "He's one of those rare lucky ones. He went to school here, then managed to get a job here. That almost never happens. Most graduates who stay in town—"

"Drive a cab." Emma recited the litany. "I know."

"He's been around forever. He was just on sabbatical in England."

"England? What was he doing there?"

"Walking everywhere. The man is a health fanatic. And he was studying something. I never did pay attention."

Emma felt a chill run down her back. She hoped it wasn't the Middle Ages. She definitely didn't agree with his comments on Alfred the Great. She had no idea how he would react to some of her "speculations," which weren't speculation at all.

They were actually memories.

"Why would he want to see me? I mean, we met this morning?"

"Michael is a different animal from Mort. Now Mort would take you out for a beer and ask you about yourself."

Emma smiled. "I remember."

"But Michael believes in doing things by the book." Helen shook her head. "Which means I'll have to redo my desk, believe me. So what he wants with you is beyond me."

Then she grinned.

"Except the word is—and my ancient eyes tell me it's true—you are the most beautiful professor to grace the history department in some time. Michael's single."

Emma felt her blush grow. She wanted to put hands to her cheeks and stop it, but she couldn't. She had never learned how to control that response. "Wouldn't it be illegal for him to date me? I mean, technically, he's my boss."

"Technically, sweetie, the university is your boss. He's just the head of the department. And while this campus frowns on teacher-student relationships, you're at least two degrees and one bestselling book away from that distinction."

Emma swallowed hard. She didn't want to fend off her boss for the rest of her tenure.

"Don't look so solemn," Helen said. "Michael was voted one of Madison's most eligible bachelors a few years back. He's what we called in my day a good catch."

"I'm not trying to catch anything," Emma said.

"Looks to me, honey, like you're afraid you will catch something."

That was more accurate than Helen knew. Emma shrugged. "I like my life."

"You and that cat."

Emma frowned. "How did you know I had a cat?"

Helen reached over and plucked a black hair off Emma's sweater. "I know the signs," she said and held out an arm. She had short gray and orange hairs on hers. "But a cat isn't a substitute for a man."

"I don't need a man," Emma said.

"I never took you for a feminist," Helen said.

Emma grinned. "Oh, Helen," she said. "I'm the original feminist. That part of my history simply got lost in the translation."

─~~~─

By the time Emma got home, the beautiful spring sunshine had given way to showers. The rain was cold, too, and reminded her of one of the worst days of an Oregon winter.

She lit a fire, ordered a pizza, and peered out the dining room picture window at the matching house down the block. The lights were off, so Professor Found wasn't home yet. She wondered what he was doing—having dinner with old friends? Seeing a movie with a woman? Catching up on his new work in the office?

Then she caught herself. Mooning. The worst thing she could do. The man was too handsome by half, and she didn't need to be thinking about him.

Thinking about him was almost as bad as looking at him, and looking at him made her forget all her vows.

Which would someday come back to haunt her.

She closed the blinds all through the house and put on some Brahms. She had fallen in love with her CD player, and the way music was available at the touch of a button. That was, in her personal and quite private opinion, the absolutely best thing about this brave new world she had woken up in.

If someone asked her, of course, she would lie and talk about indoor plumbing (which used to terrify her) or refrigerators (on her first day, she had asked Nora how they captured winter) or the amazing availability of food (even though she missed growing it by hand). But in reality, it was the luxuries that caught her. Shoes that actually kept the feet dry. Lights at the touch of a finger. And music whenever she wanted it.

Not to mention books and movies and audio books. Stories, like her father used to tell her, only more complex. When she had been a young woman, education was beyond her means—there was no such thing as

education for all—and there was no way to mass produce books. No one had even dreamed of movies, and
theater as people understood it now hadn't really been
invented yet either. And the idea of television, well, it
still boggled her. She had a few favorite shows, but she
watched them in private, because she still stared at the
box gape-mouthed, unable to fathom how other people
took it so completely for granted.

Darnell was asleep in front of the fire, his long black
body stretched out so that his stomach absorbed most of
the heat. She had asked the person who took her order
at Pizza Pit to make sure the delivery guy knocked this
time. The last time, when he'd rung the doorbell, had
been a disaster.

As if in answer to her thoughts, the doorbell rang.
Darnell leapt out of his sleep onto all fours like a lion
defending his turf. He growled softly in the back of
his throat.

"Stay here," she said, knowing it would do no good.

She walked to the front door, grabbed the cash she had
placed on the table beside the entry, and peered through
the peephole. Sure enough, it was the pizza guy, looking
very damp, the pizza steaming in its thermal pouch.

Maybe she would have to add pizza as one of this
age's greater achievements. She certainly ate enough
of it.

She pulled the door open and put out a foot to hold
Darnell back even though Darnell was nowhere in sight.

The pizza guy was young—a student, obviously, and
just as obviously, he hated the job. He mumbled the
price and as she opened the screen to hand him the cash,
Darnell came at a flying run from the fireplace.

She figured her foot would be enough, but it wasn't. Darnell was prepared for it. He leapt over it as if it were a fence and he were a horse, and he wrapped his paws around the delivery guy's leg, biting and growling and clawing as he did so.

The poor pizza guy screamed and dropped the pizza. The thermal container slid down the brick steps, but didn't open.

Emma bent over and pulled Darnell off the boy's leg, but the damage was done. The delivery guy's jeans were torn and his skin was scratched and bleeding.

She tossed Darnell inside, and slammed the screen door shut. "I'm sorry," she said. "But—"

"Jeez, lady your cat's nuts. I've never seen an insane cat before. Has it got rabies?"

Actually, it took her a moment to understand the delivery guy. He actually said, "Jeezladyyercatsnutsive neverseenaninsanecatbeforehasitgotrabies?"

"No, he doesn't have rabies." She was amazed she could sound so affronted. She'd never seen a cat act like Darnell either—at least, not a domesticated house cat. She'd seen nature videos of lions back when she was in her learning phase, and the leader often attacked anything that threatened the pride. Apparently, she was Darnell's pride.

The delivery boy was wiping at his legs.

"Look," she said, handing him the cash. "I'm sorry. There's an extra tip in here—"

"They warned me you had a nuts cat, but I didn't believe them. I mean, what can a nuts house cat do? Hiss at you? Now I'm going to have to get shots."

"He's vaccinated."

"Yeah, but I'm not." The delivery boy stomped to his car.

Emma looked up, and saw that Professor Found's front door was open. He was standing on the stoop, staring at her. He'd probably come out when the delivery boy had screamed.

She blushed again—three times in one day had to be some kind of record—and hurried back inside the house. Darnell was sitting in front of the fire, cleaning his face, looking quite proud of himself.

"You're not a lion. I don't care what you think of yourself. If you ever met a real one, you wouldn't know what to do." Then she squinted at him. "You don't even look like a lion."

Darnell stopped washing and glared at her. Apparently she had affronted his sense of self.

She shook her head and reached for the pizza. Then she realized she hadn't brought it inside.

She sighed and went back to the door. Sure enough, the pizza was still in its thermal container at the bottom of the stairs. She glanced at Professor Found's house. He was still on the stoop. When he saw her, he raised an imaginary glass to her.

Her face grew even warmer, but she wasn't going to count that as a fourth blush. The other one hadn't ended yet. She scurried down the stairs, grabbed the pizza, thermal container and all, and hurried inside her house.

How embarrassing. He'd seen her at her worst teaching, and then this. She had no idea how she would face him in the morning.

Maybe having Michael Found for a neighbor wasn't

the good thing it had originally seemed like. Maybe he had arrived just to make her life a living hell.

Well, the only thing she could do was be on her best behavior in the morning. And maybe then, they'd get off to a better start.

Not that she wanted anything closer than a cordial working relationship.

Even if he was the best-looking man she'd ever seen.

Chapter 2

EMMA DREAMED SHE WAS SINKING. IT WAS A PLEASANT feeling. She was on a soft surface, wrapped in a warm comforter, her feet nice and toasty. But everything was moving down, as if a hole had opened up beside her, and if she wasn't careful, she would roll into it.

Then she heard a muffled snore and felt hot breath on her neck. That feeling did not come from her dream.

She scrambled awake so fast she nearly did tumble into the hole.

She was on her back, staring at the white ceiling. Sunlight poured into the room, illuminating the quilts she had hung on the wall to give the place color. She still had that feeling of lying at the edge of a precipice.

And then she heard a whistled exhale. She turned her head to the right, and saw a huge black lion asleep on the bed beside her.

She screamed and tried to get out of bed, but the lion was lying on the comforter, and she was wrapped up in it as if it were a cocoon. She cursed as she tried to pull herself out, then finally scrambled backwards, hitting her head on the oak headboard.

The lion opened its eyes. They were golden, sleepy, and confused. It yawned and stretched, its hind feet sliding off the foot of the bed, and its front paws touching the tip of the headboard.

Then it yowled. If an animal could look terrified, the

lion did. It raised its head to her, overbalanced itself, and fell off the bed with the loudest thump Emma had ever heard.

Just like Darnell would do if he were surprised.

She put a hand over her heart and peered over the edge of the bed. The lion was lying on its back, its head raised like a sea otter's, and was peering down at its body as if it had never seen it before.

"Darnell?" she whispered.

The lion made a plaintive mew, which, if the sound had been made by a house cat would have been small and sad, but since it was made by a lion, shook the entire room.

"Oh, my," she said, putting a hand to her mouth. Poor Darnell. "Oh, my, Darnell, who did this to you? Why would someone do this to you?"

She peered around the room to see if there were signs of any magical person invading her bedroom. She no longer had any enemies, at least that she knew of. Aethelstan would never do anything like this, and neither would his sidekick, Merlin. Nora hadn't come into her abilities yet.

Emma froze. *Come into her abilities yet.* She closed her eyes. Even if someone wanted to hurt her—and if they did, why had they gone after poor Darnell? (Unless that pizza delivery guy was actually a mage... but he was too young, and she would have known. At least, she thought she would have known. Oh, dear. Maybe all the pizza people...) Her eyes flew open.

Darnell was struggling, his gigantic paws in the air. There wasn't enough room on the floor for him to roll over.

She was the only one who had thought of him as a

ferocious lion, and she hadn't mentioned that to anyone else. She wouldn't mention it to anyone else.

"Oh, Darnell, I'm so sorry."

And scared. Her mouth was dry. She was twenty years too young for powers. She was only thirty.

At least, she was only thirty in years that she was awake. If she counted the years she had been in that magical coma, she was one thousand and forty.

Magic wouldn't work that way. It wouldn't count all those nonyears—would it?

"That's not fair," she said.

Darnell mewed and waved his paws weakly. They were so big—bigger than her hand. She flopped across the bed and scratched his large stomach. His mane spread out on the floor like a nimbus of hair around his familiar—if much larger—face.

"We have to think this through, Darnell," she said, continuing to scratch. He squirmed a little—tummy scratching was one of his favorite things—and then he started to purr.

She could feel the rumble all the way from the floor to the bed.

If it was her magic that had caused this, then she was in serious trouble. She hadn't studied. She didn't know how to control it. All she had were a few words and phrases that Aethelstan had taught her for emergencies.

She clenched one fist as she had seen Aethelstan do. "Change back," she whispered to Darnell. "Be my house kitty again. Change back."

His hind paw kicked the air in rhythm to her scratching. She had hit a good spot. But he was still huge, he still had a mane, and his tail had a tuft at the end of it that hadn't been there when they both went to sleep the night before.

"Change," she whispered. "Reverse. Go back."

Nothing happened. No light, no sound, not even a different feeling.

Her breathing was coming hard now. She couldn't leave him alone, not oversized like this. He would be able to break out of the house—heck, he would break the house and everything in it, and he wouldn't even realize he was doing anything wrong.

Then the authorities would come for him and do whatever they did to loose lions. Loose black lions. Loose black lions of a type that didn't occur in nature. He would be a freak and he would get all sorts of media attention and she would have trouble busting him out of wherever they held him and—

Oh, she had to clamp a hold on her vivid imagination. She had to focus.

And then she remembered a single word, one of the emergency words, that Aethelstan had given her. In the old language. He had said it meant "reverse."

She sat up and waved her arm as she had seen him do, and uttered the word at the top of her lungs.

There was a bright white light, a crackle and sizzle, and then a small explosion. It felt as if something had left her and danced in the air before dissipating.

She sat for a moment, not wanting to look at the floor.

What if she had turned him into something else? What if he hadn't changed at all?

What if she had killed him?

A small black house cat with lovely gold eyes jumped onto the bed, and butted his head against her arm.

"Darnell," she said and scooped him close. "Oh, Darnell. I think we have a problem."

Darnell whined, then squirmed. His interpretation of the problem was obviously different from hers. His was that he wanted breakfast, and wanted it now.

If only she could recover that quickly.

She let him go and he ran to the bedroom door, then looked over his shoulder as if asking her what she was waiting for. She brought her knees up to her chest. It had been so long since she had had any real instruction in magic. She could barely remember what she knew about the arrival of powers.

Full blown. Out of control. Those were the phrases she had always heard. But she wasn't sure if getting magic was like going through puberty—did the changes happen in spurts? Or was she one day magic-less and the next day magical?

She didn't know.

Darnell yowled. She looked at the clock. It was too early to call Aethelstan in Oregon. Neither he nor Nora would appreciate a call at 5:00 a.m.

She wiped her hands on her nightgown. She had to handle this on her own, at least for a few hours.

And during those few hours, she had to meet with the new chairman of her department.

She hoped he would let her cancel.

Of course, no one answered the phone in his office, and Helen said he would arrive just a few minutes before nine. Helen had told her that Professor Found was a stickler for detail, and missing this first meeting wouldn't sit well with him. So Emma decided to go through with the meeting. After all, it would only take a few minutes, and she would use the rest of the time to call Aethelstan and see if she could find a short-term solution to the problem.

Besides, she had gotten through the rest of her morning routine without a hitch. Darnell seemed no worse for the wear. Her breakfast tasted fine. She had to put on a dress because all of her jeans and sweaters were dirty— and when she cursed her lack of housekeeping skills, the clothes didn't automatically get clean on their own.

Even when she encountered a morning traffic jam on University, the cars didn't miraculously disappear.

If her powers had arrived full blown and out of control, something else would have happened by now.

She stopped only briefly in her office before going to Michael Found's. And during that time, she got annoyed at herself for adjusting her skirt, and brushing loose strands of hair into place. It felt like she wanted to impress him, and not because he was the new chairman of the department. Maybe she'd be able to forget how handsome he was, and concentrate instead on letting him know that she wasn't as flaky as she seemed.

Her high heels clicked on the concrete stairs as she made her way to Professor Found's office. When she reached the top, she felt calmer.

Helen sat at a large desk in a vast open area that in any other profession would have been known as reception. But she wasn't a receptionist. She guarded the copy machine, the fax, and all the other equipment, and let a graduate assistant handle the phones.

She waved a hand in greeting as Emma passed.

Emma started toward Mort's office, but Helen pointed her in the opposite direction.

Emma walked down the narrow corridor, reading the names beneath the numbers on the steel doors. Ultimately, she didn't need to: Professor Found's door was open, and he was waiting for her inside.

His office was a surprise. It was bigger than hers—which she expected. All offices in the administrative section of the building were large—but it seemed warm and friendly. Bookshelves covered the walls, and plants hung off every available surface.

The furniture was ergonomically designed—she recognized the styles from the ads—except for the reading chair in the corner. It was upholstered with thick heavy cushions that bore the imprint of Michael Found's body. A footstool sat in front of it, and books spilled off the table beside it onto the floor. She couldn't see the titles from the door, but not all of them seemed like scholarly tomes.

He was standing behind his desk. He wore jeans and a red and black checked flannel shirt that accented his flat torso and his blond hair. Up close, his eyes seemed even bluer than they had in the lecture hall—the bright blue of a summer sky.

"Professor Lost," he said.

"Professor Found."

She suppressed the urge to giggle. No wonder the students had started cracking jokes.

"I've read your book."

Her breath caught in her throat. She had been planning to ask him to reschedule the meeting, but she wanted to hear what he thought of her work first. "I hope you enjoyed it."

His fingers formed little tents on the desktop. His gaze hadn't left her face, but it felt as if his expression had gotten even more remote. "Close the door, please."

She stepped inside and pushed the door shut with her foot. A compliment usually didn't take a closed door. She braced herself. This wouldn't be the first time a man had tried to take advantage of her small stature behind a closed door, although until that moment, she hadn't thought Michael Found the type.

"Your book," he said slowly, "is the biggest pile of bunk I had ever read."

She wasn't sure she had heard him correctly. He wanted her to close the door so that he could trash her book? No one had trashed her book. It was a critical and popular success. It had gotten her offers from some of the best universities in the nation. It had gotten her this job.

"Bunk?" she said softly.

"Bunk," he repeated. "The research is shoddy, the conclusions poor and the study of paganism has absolutely no basis in fact."

No wonder he had looked so interested in her comment about magic the day before. He had read her book. She had discussed some of the systems in Chapter Fifteen.

"All of my work is based in fact," she said.

"Not according to your footnotes. I'm familiar with those sources. Many of them contradict what you've written."

"Maybe you should have cross-checked them," she snapped. "They support my argument."

"Your argument is that no one knows what happened in the early Middle Ages except you."

"I'm not the first scholar to say that what remains from that period is open to interpretation."

"But you are the first to say that an entire system of apprenticeship existed in the non-Christian religions."

"I didn't call them a religion!"

"Which is another flaw!"

They had both raised their voices. She took a step closer to him. What an arrogant idiot he was. She had read his credentials in the course guide over pizza the night before. His specialty was world history from 1600 to the present day. He had no right to criticize her.

She took a deep breath. All of her friends had warned her at various points in her life that her temper flared too quickly. She didn't need to lose it in front of her department chairman, not during their first meeting.

"It was the Christian Church that labeled a lot of those practices as religion," she said as calmly as she could. "The church was working on converting people who had never heard of it. The record is biased toward that conversion."

"History is always written by the winners."

"Do you always speak in cliches or is this something you're just doing for my benefit?"

His blue eyes flashed. "I'm not planning to do anything that will benefit you, Professor Lost."

She straightened her shoulders. She was dangerously close to losing her temper. That last sarcastic sentence was the first sign that she was about to lose control. She had to hold onto it. If she got mad, he would never forget it. People who were on the receiving end of her wrath never did.

"I'm not asking you to do anything to benefit me," she said softly.

He flattened his hands on his desk. "I'm in charge of

the hirings and firings here, and frankly, I'm not pleased with anything about you."

She crossed her arms. "You're not in charge of hiring or firing. The university has committees for that."

"Committees that take the recommendation of the department heads very seriously." He leaned toward her. "You're a fraud, *Professor* Lost. You make up your research and then go on the History Channel pretending to be a real historian."

"I am the most real historian you'll ever have in this department," she snapped. "I know more about primary research than all of your colleagues put together."

"Do you?" he asked, his voice even softer. Somehow it sounded more menacing that way.

She swallowed, wishing she could take back the words. Of course she had done more primary research than the rest of them. She had lived in that time period. She *knew* what she had written was fact. The rest of them were guessing.

"Yes," she said, "I do."

"Then why don't you cite more primary sources in your book?"

"I've cited enough for every other scholar in the world, Professor Found. England in the early Middle Ages is not your time period. Why don't you trust the people who specialize in the area?"

He smiled then, and the beauty of the expression caught her even though she wanted to slap him. "I do specialize in the area, Professor Lost."

"Not according to your write up in all the college guidelines," she said, then flushed. She hadn't wanted him to know that she was checking up on him.

He raised his eyebrows as if the comment amused him. "Those were written when I was hired. For the last five years, I've changed specialties. I just came from England. I've been studying the Dark Ages."

"Oh," she said. "So you want to get rid of me because I've got more credentials in the field you aspire to. I'm teaching the classes you want to teach."

"No, Professor," he said. "I'm telling you this so that you know that I know what you think you know."

She blinked. She wasn't sure what he had just said. "Excuse me?"

"You've made everything up." He picked her book off his desk. "This entire volume is a work of fiction. It's well written, it's interesting. It's easy to see why the literati embraced the whole thing, and it's pretty with all those color photographs. It's a very nice coffee table book. But just because the book critic in the *New Yorker* says you can write doesn't mean you can produce a good work of historical scholarship."

"You're jealous," she said.

"No." He slapped the book on his desk. "I don't want a fraud in my department."

"I'm not a fraud," she said.

"Ms. Lost—"

"Professor Lost," she snarled.

"—You are the worst kind of fraud. You are attractive, articulate, and intelligent. You tell a coherent and plausible story. But you are lazy and inept and ultimately you will embarrass this department. I want you out of here before you do that."

"You can't fire me," she said. "I was hired with Mort's highest recommendation. I'll tell the academic review board that you're jealous and you want to clear me out of here because I teach the very subjects you believe you should teach."

"And I'll show them how poor your documentation is." His eyes narrowed. "When I get through with you, you won't be able to get a job at any reputable campus anywhere."

A surge of panic rose inside her and she fought to keep it from showing on her face. She wasn't suited to anything else. She was awful at all the other jobs she had tried. Teaching was her calling, and writing books about her past was the best thing she could do.

This good-looking pompous ass was threatening more than he knew. He was threatening her very survival. Her very future.

She clenched her fists, struggling to control herself. The office felt hot and stuffy. The furniture was closing in on her. If only she had room to breathe—

This time she felt the little puff of energy leave her before she saw the bright light. There was a thunderous clap that echoed around her, and she saw stars for a moment. When her vision cleared, she was standing in an empty room—with Michael Found.

He staggered forward as if he had been leaning his weight on something and it was now gone. His face was pale.

"What was that?"

She opened her mouth, but nothing came out. She blinked, unable to think of a response. Except that she needed to reverse the spell.

She was full blown and out of control and she had to get out of here very, very fast.

The door opened and Helen looked in. Her face was pale. "Um, Michael," she said, "how did all your furniture get into my office?"

He looked at Emma, whose mouth was still open. At least she wasn't blushing. Her heart was pounding and she had to mutter the reverse order, but she didn't want to do it in front of them. Then they'd know she caused all of this.

"Michael?" Helen asked. "What's happening?"

"I have no idea." His voice sounded calm, but his right hand shook. He clenched his fist. "I was telling Professor Lost—"

"Stop!" she said before she thought the better of it. She didn't want Helen to hear about that humiliating conversation. She didn't want Helen to hear anything.

Michael Found made a choking noise and for a brief, terrifying moment, Emma thought she had taken his voice away. Then he cleared his throat, and took a step toward the door.

"Helen?"

Emma looked at Helen, ever so slowly. Helen was no longer moving. She was frozen in position, and her skin was gray. Well, not exactly gray. It looked like it was made of stone.

She had become a statue.

"Oh, no," Emma muttered softly.

Professor Found approached the department secretary as if he thought what she had was catching. When he reached her, he touched her arm.

"She's cold," he said.

His back was to Emma. She whispered the "reverse" word ever so softly and twirled her hand.

The stone around Helen cracked and fell to the floor, then vanished.

"Michael?" Helen said. "You didn't answer me." She leaned back slightly. "And don't sneak up on me like that."

"I didn't sneak up," he said. "You turned to—ah, hell."

He looked at Emma, who shrugged.

"To what?" Helen asked.

"Don't you remember?" he asked.

"I remember asking you a question you have yet to answer. What's going on?"

"I wish I knew." He frowned at Emma. She didn't have to work at looking panicked. She was barely breathing, afraid of doing anything, thinking anything. She had to get out of here and get some help.

"One minute I was having a discussion with Professor Lost, the next thing I know, my furniture is gone."

He turned back to Helen who peered into the room. Emma understood her confusion. There weren't even any dust bunnies in here—and considering how many books had lined the floor, there should have been.

Helen's gaze met Emma's and then she looked away. Emma used that moment to try the reverse spell again, but it didn't work.

"Do you know what's happening, Professor Lost?" Michael asked.

Emma clenched her fists and pushed past him. "I'm sorry. I have to leave."

"But we're not done…"

"Oh, yes, we are. You're having a weird furniture problem. We can resume this discussion some other time." Emma slid past Helen. "Sorry," she said softly.

Helen didn't seem to have a response. Emma almost

ran down the hall, her heels preventing her from moving too fast. When she reached Helen's office, she had to slow down to make her way past the piles of furniture.

It was a neat spell, more or less. The furniture had actually arranged itself in its proper positions—the bookshelves against the wall, the reading chair in a corner with its footstool in the proper place—but there wasn't enough room for everything, and so the space was crammed.

Emma was lucky that the spell had worked as it had, otherwise Helen could have been crushed under a load of ergonomically designed furniture.

The thought made Emma shudder. It could have been so much worse.

Although it was bad enough. It would take a lot of work to get the furniture moved back to Michael Found's office. She wished she could spell it there, but she knew now that wasn't possible.

She pushed open the stairway door, paused because she felt light-headed, and went down to her office, hoping she wouldn't see anyone else. The last thing she needed was another magical accident.

Things were bad enough.

Michael still stood in the middle of his office. With a clap of thunder, the furniture had magically reappeared, almost as if someone had commanded it to do so. Everything was in its place. Even the plants draped as they had before. The same books were on top of his reading stack, and Emma Lost's disgraceful tome was in the spot where he had slammed it on his desk.

Helen had taken one look at the restored furniture,

shaken her head, and hurried away from him, as if he had caused it.

He wasn't sure what had caused it. Or if anything had really happened. He was still vaguely jet-lagged, and he had been very angry at Emma Lost. The woman was as infuriating as she was beautiful.

And she seemed to firmly believe that she hadn't done anything wrong.

He walked back to his desk and touched its wood surface. It felt the same. He frowned, trying to remember the exact sequence of events. Had he walked through the space where the desk should have been? Or had he walked around it as though it were still there?

Had someone played a trick on him, knowing that he was writing a book on magic? It wouldn't surprise him. Students were endlessly creative. And if David Copperfield could make the Empire State Building disappear then a talented student could make Michael believe that his office furniture had vanished.

There had been that flash of light, and it had affected his eyesight for a moment. Was that some sort of special effect that made it seem as if his furniture was gone?

That would certainly explain why Helen had come into his office. The students had probably projected the images of his furniture in her office, making it seem as if the furniture had transferred.

Brilliant. He would have to search for the source of it in a moment.

Even though that didn't explain why Helen's skin had been so cold, why she had looked as if she had been made out of stone.

He had never really touched her before. Maybe her

skin was naturally cold. Maybe he had only thought she had looked frozen in stone.

Maybe she was in on it.

He shook his head. Helen wasn't really one for practical jokes. Neither, it seemed, was Emma Lost. She had bolted from his office like a frightened child.

He ran a hand through his hair. He supposed he owed her an apology—for the weirdness, not for saying she was incompetent. He would have to be clear about that. Which, of course, would continue the argument.

But he had to let her know where he stood. This was his department now, and her presence was tainting it. It would be unethical for him to keep her on board, knowing how bad her research was. It would be like the *Washington Post* keeping on that woman who had made up the newspaper articles that had won her the Pulitzer Prize. Yes, the work *seemed* credible, but it wasn't. And if Emma Lost got caught, it would reflect badly on the school, the department, and him.

He put a hand on his desk just to make sure it was there. It was. It felt smooth and warm to the touch, just as it always had. Now that magic trick had seemed amazingly real. Just like Emma Lost's research. For most people, all she needed was to be convincing, but Michael was a man who liked proof. A man who understood reason, and who believed in accuracy above all else.

She may have thought she found a sinecure here at the University of Wisconsin, but she was about to learn that she was wrong.

—∿—

Emma opened the door to her office and slipped inside. She put a hand to her forehead. Could this day get any worse? Darnell turning into a lion, being told that her boss was out to get her, and then making his furniture disappear while turning his secretary to stone.

This problem had to be solved, and it had to be solved now. Emma couldn't walk through campus like this. Her magic might spontaneously erupt and then what would happen? The statue of Lincoln might come alive. Or the famous photo of the pink flamingos on Bascom Hill might become a reality—with real flamingos instead of the plastic lawn variety.

Or something worse might happen, something like— turning Michael Found into a toad.

Then Emma shuddered. *She'd* been changed into a toad once and it hadn't been a very pleasant experience. It certainly wasn't something she wished on anyone, not even anyone as irritating as Michael Found.

She stopped in front of the photograph she had put up of Portland, Oregon. The majestic bridges crisscrossed the Columbia River, a beautiful skyscape that she would never have seen in her youth.

Aethelstan was there, with his restaurant, and all his knowledge. If she had control over her magic, she could pop herself there right now.

But she didn't. And that was the problem. She was half afraid to move or even open her mouth. She didn't know what would happen next.

Then her shoulders relaxed. Aethelstan had given her a few other emergency words and the most important, he had said, was the one that took her to the Fates.

The Fates were the women who governed the rules of

magic for Emma's people. The Fates settled all disputes, and governed as a ruling tribunal, holding legislative and judicial powers in their beautiful hands. Emma hadn't given them much thought, since she didn't plan to come into her magic for another twenty years. But the Fates would be the best ones for her to see. They would understand that something had gone wrong—that Emma's coma had interfered with the natural flow of things—and they would repair this damage.

They would also be able to put off her magic for another twenty years. They would yell at her for not training, of course, and she would have to promise to train, but that couldn't be so bad. It wouldn't be bad. She wouldn't let it.

She clenched a fist and mumbled the small incantation that Aethelstan had given her.

There was a small crackle, and then a bang. For a moment, she thought the incantation hadn't worked, and then she realized she was hot. Very hot. And the air was so humid that she could feel it like a presence against her skin. Her dress clung to her and her hair had immediately become damp. A trickle of sweat ran down her cheek, and settled at the base of her jaw.

She was in a grotto. The sun was out—a blazing summer sun—but she was under weeping trees of a type she didn't recognize. The pool before her glistened greenly in the shade.

Emma swallowed. She must have done something really wrong. She was alone here, in a place she didn't even recognize. Her stomach clenched and she flashed back to waking up from her thousand year coma in that VW microbus, in a world made of steel and asphalt, facing a woman who spoke a completely different language.

Emma still had nightmares about that moment—and the first car ride, moving at speeds impossible to her tenth-century brain.

Had she just switched venues again? Had she hurt herself another time? She clasped her hands together and made herself take a deep breath. The worst thing she could do was panic. Especially with her magic bouncing loose like this. If she panicked—

A woman's head broke the water's surface. She pulled herself onto a nearby rock like a seal, her long blond hair covering her nakedness like a shroud.

"Oh, dear," she said when she saw Emma. "I hadn't expected visitors."

"Forgive me," Emma said, "but I'm looking for the Fates."

"Well, why else would you be here?" The woman leaned into the water until it covered her nose and mouth. She spoke, and Emma heard the words as if she were underwater: *Atropos, Lachesis. We have a guest.*

Emma felt her back stiffen. She had heard of the Fates, but never really met them. Of course, she had read all that the mortals had written about them. The Greeks were the mortals most familiar with the Fates. They had actually gotten close enough to understand some of what the three women did.

Atropos held "the abhorréd shears," which cut the thread of life, and Clotho—the blond whom Emma had been speaking to—spun the thread of life. Lachesis was the one who determined how long that life would be. Some called Lachesis's duty to determine a person's destiny, but in truth all three of the Fates did that.

Two other heads broke the surface. One belonged to a

redhead whose hair was a beautiful, curly auburn—even while wet. The other to a brunette. They each swam to different rocks and climbed on. They remained naked.

Emma shifted uncomfortably. She was too used to the mortal world. People did not have conversations while naked. At least, not four people. Maybe two. And certainly not her.

"So, child," Clotho said. "Why did you disturb our daily swim?"

Emma glanced at all three of them. They looked like mermaids—beautiful, slender, and powerful all at the same time.

"Are you uncomfortable, my dear?" the redhead asked. "You could join us."

She waved a hand and another rock appeared.

Emma's dress felt like a wet blanket, and she had never been so hot in her life. But she had no swimming suit, and she couldn't imagine getting in that water, naked or otherwise. She threaded her hands in front of herself, swallowed, and tried to sound calm.

"I came into my magic," she said.

"Well, it's about time." The brunette leaned forward, held out her hand, and a pair of scissors grew out of the air. She used the scissors to trim a strand of her hair, and then the scissors disappeared.

The brunette, then, was Atropos.

Emma took a deep breath. "No," she said. "I've still got twenty years."

"Twenty years of what?" Lachesis, the redhead, frowned at her.

"Freedom," Emma said. "I don't know if you know who I am."

Clotho rolled her eyes. "My child, you have been the topic of debate in the august body for a thousand years. Believe me, we were more relieved than you were when Aethelstan finally found a solution to his problem."

"And understood what we told him all along."

Emma had no idea what they were talking about. "What did you tell him?"

"That you would *lead* him to his one true love. For some reason, he thought you were his one true love."

"Until he met her, of course."

"And then that certainly confused him."

The Fates laughed.

Emma didn't think this amusing at all. That misunderstanding had cost her a thousand years of her life. And, if the truth be told, that first kiss with Aethelstan— the one that sent her into the magical coma—was nice, but it wasn't great. No hearts and flowers and bells and whistles and fireworks like she saw in all the movies. Just a pressing of the lips and then a weird feeling in the pit of her stomach before everything went black.

"Please," she said. "I'm here about the magic."

"Oh, yes." Lachesis waved a hand over her hair. It dried instantly into a flowing, waving black cap, shorter than it had been a moment before. "You said something about freedom."

"You are quite free," Clotho said. "No one has interfered in your life in ten years."

"I know," Emma said quietly. "But I would like you to."

The Fates were silent for a moment, and then Atropos sighed. "We cannot adjudicate like this."

"Why not?" Lachesis said. "We have done so before."

"It makes the girl uncomfortable," Clotho said. "She has adopted her new century, society, and culture beautifully."

"Well, not beautifully enough," Atropos said. "There are places where nudity—"

"Please," Emma said. "Can we talk about my magic?"

Lachesis snapped her fingers, and the grotto disappeared. It became a courtroom made of mahogany. The air was cool, and Emma's wet dress gave her a chill. She shivered.

The Fates sat behind a large judge's bench, their names before them. Instead of holding a gavel, they each held small symbols of their duties: Clotho a spool of thread, Atropos a pair of scissors, and Lachesis a ruler. They wore long black robes and all three had their hair piled on top of their heads. Lachesis wore a pair of glasses at the edge of her nose, making her look both beautiful and wise.

"All right," Atropos said. "This is better."

"No," Clotho said. "The child is freezing. You cannot come to court looking as if you've been swimming with your clothes on."

She snapped her fingers and Emma found herself wearing a silk suit. It was a shade of purple she never wore at home, but she had to admit that it set off her hair. Even her shoes were purple. Her hair was up just like the Fates' and a briefcase sat at her feet.

"There," Lachesis said. "Much better."

"We were discussing your magic," Atropos said. "And your freedom, although I do not see how the two are tied."

Emma took a step forward and nearly tripped over the briefcase. She resisted the urge to kick it aside. Her head was spinning. Too much had happened since that morning—which was precisely why she was here.

"I'm just getting used to having lost a thousand years of my life," she said. "I wasn't ready to learn magic."

"That's not our concern," Clotho said.

"It seems that you've adapted quite well to your new life," Lachesis said.

"You've all that your culture says you should have," Atropos said.

"Life," Clotho said.

"Liberty," Lachesis said.

"And the ability to pursue happiness," Atropos said.

"That's not how it goes," Clotho whispered.

"That's what that delightful redhead told me," Atropos whispered back.

"What redhead?" Lachesis said.

"The one who claimed he wrote those words. Very tall. Knows a lot for a mortal, especially a dead mortal."

"Excuse me," Emma said. "We're not discussing Thomas Jefferson."

"We are," Atropos said.

"It seems appropriate in a place like this," Clotho said.

"I suppose we could be discussing that other one," Lachesis said.

"Madison?" Atropos asked.

"No."

"Hamilton?"

"No."

"Washington?"

"He was only a president. All the major decisions were made during the Continental Congress. I remember because Benjamin Franklin was about to let his true abilities slip that night he got drunk with John Adams and we had to—"

"Hey!" Emma shouted.

The Fates all stared at her. Emma swallowed. Her temper was flaring. She took several deep breaths, trying yet again to control it.

"I am only thirty years old," Emma said. "I'm not supposed to come into my magic yet."

"My dear," Clotho said softly. "I know this is a delicate subject for a woman, but you are in truth one thousand and forty years old."

"You should have come into your magic nine hundred and ninety years ago," Atropos said.

"But you were in a coma," Lachesis said.

"A magical one," Clotho said.

"And even we do not entirely understand magical comas. Perhaps the Powers that Be—"

And with that all three Fates bowed their heads and spread out their hands in a reflexive movement, the way a Catholic might cross himself.

"—determined that no mage could come into her powers while unconscious," Atropos finished.

"That certainly would be unfair," Clotho said.

"Imagine if she dreamed in her coma," Lachesis said. "Why the very air around that glass coffin would have been—"

"Excuse me," Emma said again, trying very hard not to yell. "I would like to stay on topic here."

"I thought we were on topic," Atropos said.

"For someone who has come to us, you are very rude," Clotho said.

Emma closed her eyes. She was making a mess of this too.

"Rudeness is a part of her new culture," Lachesis

said. "I understand that no one knows which fork to use anymore."

"I had heard that multiple forks aren't the issue," Atropos said. "That even on the most elegant tables, the silverware has been reduced down to a single fork, a single knife, and a single spoon."

"No soup spoon?" Clotho asked.

Emma was going insane, there was just no doubt about it. She clenched her fists, unclenched them, and then decided she already had nothing to lose.

"I'm sorry I'm rude," she said, opening her eyes, "but my very life is at stake here."

"Oh, not anymore," Lachesis said. "That was ten years ago. Now you must simply change the way you look at things."

"Change the way I look at things?" Emma asked, aware that her voice was rising with her blood pressure. "I turned my cat into a lion this morning. I nearly killed the department secretary by dropping furniture all over her office. My magic is out of control."

"Yes, it is, and you must learn how to control it," Atropos said.

"That is a failure on your part, my dear," Clotho said. "You should have been training."

"I thought I had twenty more years!"

"We don't understand why," Lachesis said. "You are, after all, one thousand and forty years old."

"I am still in my childbearing years," Emma snapped.

Atropos frowned. "You're certain?"

Emma felt a blush warm her face. "Of course I'm certain."

"Well, that is an interesting turn of events. Physically,

she is thirty, then. I guess that means that the nature of magic is tied less to the body than we thought." Clotho set down her thread and frowned.

"Perhaps the conventions of millennia simply got codified into a particular way of looking at things," Lachesis said.

"We should go through the ancient records from the original Fates and see if they made a ruling on this," Atropos said.

"I'll bet they did," Clotho said. "I'll wager if we look, we'll find incidences of magic that went out of whack during the hormonal excesses of pregnancy and as a deterrent—"

"Look!" Emma said, coming as close to the bench as she dared. "You can debate the legal stuff later. Right now, I want my magic-free existence back."

"Oh, child, you don't know what you're asking," Lachesis said.

"Yes, I do," Emma said. "I want my twenty years of no magic. I want to train. I want a normal life—"

"You will never have a normal life, my dear," Atropos said. "No one who has experienced two different millennia without living every day of the thousand years in between. You're the first of our kind to effectively time travel, although I have heard of accidental hallucinatory trips into memory that may or may not have been actual time travel—"

"Please," Emma said, "stay on the point."

"The point is," Clotho said, "that if we take away your powers now, the effect will be permanent."

"Why?" Emma asked. "I haven't done anything wrong."

"Whether you have done anything isn't the issue

here," Lachesis said. "Our powers are limited as well. We may be the ruling body of our people, but we follow rules set down by the Powers That Be. If we didn't, there would be—"

"Chaos," Atropos said. "It would be terrifying."

"We think," Clotho said. "I'm quite curious about the historical record now. You know we never delve back into the mists of time. We only work from the last six thousand years."

"Convention," Lachesis said.

"Laziness," Atropos said.

"Whatever," Emma said. "Maybe you could look in those old rules and see if you can temporarily take away my powers. I am a special case. You just said so."

"Yes, and while we empathize," Clotho said, "we don't want to set any terrible precedents."

"If we allow you to lose your powers while you train, it would give lazy young people permission to put off their training until it suits them," Lachesis said.

"Magic isn't about *your* convenience," Atropos said. "It's about learning how to accept your own personal power."

"Why, some mages could deny their own power for centuries," Clotho said.

"And then it might explode out of them in damaging ways," Lachesis said.

"Rather like it's doing to you," Atropos said.

"Hmmm," they all said in unison and then turned toward each other.

"But," Emma said, afraid that they were going to start another sideways conversation, "you said I was a special case."

"Your problems are a special case," Clotho said.

"A very special case," Lachesis said.

"But I'm still having problems," Emma said.

"Of course," Atropos said. "This is, apparently, the life that you were meant to have."

Emma shook her head. "That's not possible."

"Why not?" Clotho asked.

"There would be no reason for me to have gone through all of this," Emma said.

The Fates looked at each other. Lachesis's glasses slid farther down her nose. "What is the prophecy for this one?"

Atropos frowned. A book appeared before her. She spoke in an ancient tongue. Emma didn't understand any of this.

"What prophecy?" Emma asked.

"We are all assigned one. You know that, child. It was why Aethelstan guarded you," Clotho said.

"Of course, he misunderstood his," Lachesis said.

"So what's mine?" Emma asked.

"Comforting, I would think," Atropos said.

"Loosely translated," Clotho said, "you will find the answer you seek."

"Answer?" Emma asked.

"We do not interpret," Lachesis said. "Merely report."

"But the question you did ask us is what purpose your thousand year sleep served," Atropos said.

"Well," Emma said, "it got Aethelstan his one true love."

"Perhaps that's it," Clotho said, sounding tired.

"Here," Lachesis said, handing Emma a slip of paper. "This is your prophecy. I forget which language this is, actually."

"Well, it's not any I read," Emma said, staring at it.

"It's yours to do with what you will," Atropos said. "Now, we must get to our luncheon. I haven't gone this long after swimming without food and a nap since—oh, what was that?"

"The séances," Clotho said.

"Those mediums. Amazing they could tap into things when they had no real powers," Lachesis said.

"They weren't tapping," Atropos said. "It was Pandora, making a mess of things. We let her go and once again, she opens the wrong box—"

"Oh, yes," Clotho said. "It's been a hundred years or so. My memory plays tricks on me."

"Anyway," Lachesis said. "Luncheon."

She lifted her arms, and belatedly, Emma realized they were going to leave her.

"No!" she shouted.

"No?" the Fates asked in unison. Lachesis still had her arms raised.

"See?" Clotho said. "She's rude."

"I'm desperate," Emma said. "If you can't take my powers away temporarily, what will I do now? I can't live like this."

"You certainly can't," Lachesis said, lowering her arms. Her eyes flashed with irritation. Emma wondered what happened to people who repeatedly irritated the Fates.

"You must be trained before you do some harm," Atropos said.

Emma nodded. She knew that. "Can you train me?"

Clotho gave her a gentle smile. "No, child," she said, and Emma thought she heard some sympathy in Clotho's voice. "We do not train. We govern."

Emma folded her hands together. The longer she waited to start her training, the more damage she would do. "Then can you send me to Aethelstan?"

"No," Lachesis said. "That's interference and we are not allowed to interfere in that way."

"Then what do I do?"

"Follow the rules of the apprentice, child," Atropos said.

She wouldn't need Michael Found to fire her. She would have to quit all on her own. Being an apprentice was a twenty-four-hour-a-day task. "I can't! I have a job."

"A mortal job," Atropos said.

"Can't we bend the rules a little?" Emma asked. "Can't Aethelstan come to me?"

Clotho shook her head. "No, child. The rules exist for a reason. You must travel to him. You cannot take lessons from him until you arrive. And then you must do as he teaches you."

Emma suppressed a sigh. The last time she and Aethelstan spent any time alone, she had ended up throwing dishes at him. His wife Nora had mellowed him, but not enough for Emma's tastes.

"Because your powers are out of control," Lachesis said, "you should have a traveling companion. It will be safer."

Emma blinked. A traveling companion? All of her friends had jobs. And all of them were mortal, with no idea that magic existed. The only true companion she had was her cat.

"I'll have Darnell," she said.

"Your cat will not be able to utter the words of the emergency incantations that Aethelstan gave you," Atropos said.

"Can't we spell that? Can't we give him a voice?" Emma asked.

"You could," Clotho said. "We would be able to tell you that spell."

Emma felt her shoulders slump in relief.

"But we should warn you," Lachesis said, "we have tried this before."

"Cats do not follow instructions," Atropos said.

"They have a wicked sense of humor," Clotho said.

"They enjoy torture," Lachesis said.

"In the past, they have withheld the words just to see what would happen next," Atropos said.

"And," Clotho added, "have you ever had a conversation with a cat? It's quite limiting. They're mostly interested in food."

"And birds," Lachesis said.

"That's food," Atropos said.

"Not in their original form," Clotho said.

"All right," Emma said, hoping she wasn't being too rude again. "So I spell Darnell. Will that work?"

Lachesis shook her head. "Ultimately, we believe you will need a human companion."

"Who?" Emma asked. "All of my magical friends are in Oregon and you won't make them appear in Madison."

"Then take a nonmagical one," Atropos said.

"My nonmagical friends would never understand this. Besides, they have jobs too."

Clotho sighed. "Not only are they rude," she said softly to the others, "but their priorities are strange. I would think friendship would be more important than work."

"I think survival comes first," Emma said.

Lachesis shook her head. "I will never understand mortals."

Emma wasn't sure she would understand the Fates. "Please," she said, "I came to you for help. Can one of you accompany me to Aethelstan?"

They looked at each other.

"Be in the mortal world?" Atropos said.

"Could you imagine?" Clotho said.

"We've discussed it," Lachesis said.

"Oh, it would be interesting," Atropos said.

"I could wear my nose ring," Clotho said.

"And my tattoos," Lachesis said.

"The only drawback would be—"

"Mortals!" they said in unison and then they shuddered, also in unison.

"It was tempting," Clotho said, "but it is not possible."

"Besides," Lachesis said, "we don't intervene. We govern."

"Sometimes governing means helping your subjects," Emma said.

Atropos smiled. "We have helped you, dear. What you must do is really quite simple."

"Travel to Aethelstan," said Clotho.

"With a companion who will be able to help you should the need for emergency incantations arise," said Lachesis.

"And train until you can control your magic," said Atropos.

"We know you can do this," Clotho said. "You've already done things twenty times more difficult."

"Because I had no choice," Emma said.

The Fates smiled in unison.

"And you have no choice now," Lachesis said.

"Change your attitude," Atropos said.

"This could be an adventure," Clotho said.

Then Lachesis raised her arms and looked at her companions. "Lunch?"

"Oh, please," Atropos said as all three of them vanished.

For a moment, Emma stood alone in the empty courtroom. An adventure? No, it was going to be a nightmare. Just like getting back to her office would be.

Whoever she invited would find out that magic was real. That person would have to be strong and courageous—and able to deal with Emma.

She knew no one like that. No one at all.

Then she looked around the courtroom. "Hey!" she yelled. "Sorry to be rude, but I have no training and no idea how to get out of here!"

"Ooops," a voice said from the air. It sounded like whoever was speaking had her mouth full. "That we can fix."

And then Emma was back in her office, staring at the Portland poster. She heard a small sound behind her. She turned—and found herself face to face with Michael Found.

Chapter 3

MICHAEL FOUND LOOKED EXTREMELY CONFUSED. HE glanced over his shoulder at the door behind him, then frowned at her. "Weren't you wearing a dress a minute ago?"

Emma looked down. She was still wearing the purple silk power suit that the Fates had given her. Even the briefcase had arrived—landing at her feet beside her.

Professor Found glanced at the door again. She knew what he was thinking. He had obviously been in here before her, and he hadn't seen her—which he should have, since this office was so small.

She wondered if he would ask the question. Did he have enough guts to say that he had seen a woman appear out of thin air? Or was he going to focus on her clothing?

"Um," he said softly and ran a hand through his thick blond hair. It fell back into place messily, making him seem young and vulnerable. "I—didn't realize you were in here."

She swallowed. What could she say? That she had been visiting the Fates? That her magic was out of control? Or should she lie and tell him that she had been here the entire time?

She opted for a third choice. "It's my office," she said, managing to sound slightly offended.

"Yes, it is." He glanced at the door again. "I must be very jet-lagged. You were wearing a dress earlier, right?"

"Yes," she said.

"And you were standing there the entire time?"

"The entire time what?"

"The entire time that I have been in your office?"

"Frankly, Professor," she said, "I have no idea how long you've been here. I've been trying to deal with my future."

He brought his head back as if he'd been slapped.

"I suppose that's why you came down here," she said. "To make it clear that I won't be put up for tenure any time soon?"

"Actually," he said, and then looked over his shoulder again. It was almost as if he didn't believe the door was behind him. "I came to apologize for the weirdness in my office. But now I—"

"You wanted to apologize?" She wasn't sure she heard him correctly. What would he have to apologize for? She was the one who had caused the "weirdness" as he so delicately put it.

He nodded. "I'm pretty convinced that my students did something while I was away. You see, I was in England doing research on my next book, which is a history of magic, and I—"

"You are writing about magic?" she asked, amazed that she was able to keep the contempt from her voice.

"Yes. That's why I've been studying your historical period. So many of our current beliefs about magic—at least of the Western kind—seemed to come from that time period. Of course there are others—"

"Of course," Emma said. That same calm tone was in her voice, but she felt as if she had dropped into another time period. One similar from the one she left, but just different enough to confuse her.

"—voodoo, for example, which—"

"I'm familiar with the history of magic, Professor," she said. "What do you think that has to do with me?"

"It doesn't." He sighed and shrugged. Then he glanced over his shoulder yet again. "I mean, I think the students set up an elaborate practical joke and you just seemed to walk in on it."

"Oh," she said. Her legs could barely hold her. She walked to her desk and sank into her comfortable leather chair. Aethelstan had warned her about this. He had said that mortals would always find a way to rationalize what they had seen. They now believed they were too sophisticated to believe in magic, so when magic happened before them, they made up elaborate stories to deny what their eyes had told them.

"So," Professor Found said. "I wanted to apologize for that. I would like to continue our discussion at some point."

"I don't think it was a discussion," she said. "You've decided that I'm incompetent and I doubt anything I do would convince you otherwise."

"Well," he said, "it's not like we can return to the Middle Ages to see which scholar has a direct line on the truth. We must use the evidence that they left us, and it seems to me that you haven't used any of it."

She sighed. "I used more of it than you gave me credit for. If we could go back to the Middle Ages, you would see that I am right. In fact I'm so right—"

A clap of thunder sounded and the entire room shook. Lightning flared and Emma felt the words die in her throat. The energy didn't leave her this time. Instead, it picked her up and moved her as if she were a bit of cloth.

She was in a white whirling light, and somehow Michael Found was in it with her. His mouth was open, his hair streaming back, and his eyes were wild.

They landed in a filthy street and Emma winced at the nearly forgotten stench of pigs, manure, and good old fresh English mud. A goose flapped its wings near her and honked. Several carts rode past, and ahead, she heard merchants hawking their wares.

She looked forward, knowing what she would see. Sure enough, she was at the old market. Tradesman were calling for custom in her native tongue, a group of dogs were fighting near the entry to an alley, and four half-naked children played in the fetid water near the meat stall.

"Oh, no," she whispered in English.

Michael Found looked stunned. He took a step forward, then touched the faded wood wall beside him. An elderly woman slapped his hand as he went by.

"That'd be off-limits to the likes of you," she said in what Emma had learned to call Old English. It probably sounded like Danish to Michael.

He snatched his hand back, clutching it to his chest. Then he looked at Emma, who said to the old woman, "He's new here. He doesn't understand."

"Well, teach him fast. And get on proper clothes. You cannot go to the market looking like that."

"Yes, mistress. Thank you," Emma said, nodding her head.

The old woman smiled, revealing a mouth half full of blackened teeth, and then moved on. Emma looked down. Her new shoes were buried in the mud—only from the smell she had a hunch there was more than mud surrounding her.

She had lived like this, and she hadn't known any better. All that she had learned in the past ten years of germs and bacteria and infections had made her squeamish. She wanted, more than anything, to take a shower.

"Where are we?" Michael Found asked.

"You don't want to know," Emma said.

He shook his head and took a step toward the market. "This looks like—"

"Be ye outsiders, then?" a man asked, speaking in Old English, from behind Emma.

"No," Emma said in the same language, knowing that some villages hated outsiders. "We are here to see our family."

"Tell me who that be and I'll find them for ye."

"What is this?" Michael Found asked in modern English.

"Shut up," she said under her breath. This was getting more complicated all the time. If he weren't quiet, they might have to go before the village elders and pay a poll tax or worse. Be judged part of an enemy tribe and then be tortured into giving up secrets.

If only they could go back to her office. She had thought time travel impossible—

Thunder clapped and light flashed around them. She staggered forward, realizing she was in the office again. The stench of the village clung to her nose—and her feet. The new shoes were completely ruined, and her single step had left a large muddy manure print on her tile floor.

"What just happened?" Michael Found asked, cradling the hand that had been slapped. Then he held it out and stared at it. It was still red.

"You don't want to know," she said.

He lifted one of his mud-caked feet and sniffed, then made a terrible face. "It really happened, didn't it? All those things, this morning. They had nothing to do with me. You're doing it."

"Please," she said. "You wouldn't understand."

"Try me."

She shook her head.

"This was no trick, was it? There was no way, even with practical jokes and a special effects budget the size of David Copperfield's that you could make an entire medieval village appear and then disappear. We were actually there, weren't we?"

"It looks like our feet still are," she said lamely and wished she could laugh. Then she remembered that it was the wishing that changed things. She didn't dare wish anything.

She couldn't stay here.

Michael Found frowned. "Your research is based on that, isn't it? Trips like that. Did you invent a time machine?"

She let out a small, desperate chuckle. "No."

"Then what? I know that this was real somehow. I've studied enough magic to know there are things that can't be easily rationalized or explained."

She closed her eyes and leaned on her desk. The office stank of mud and cow dung, and she probably did too. Imagine how she must have smelled for the first twenty years of her life.

She shuddered. Amazing how the last ten years had changed her.

"Professor Lost?" he said.

"So well named," she murmured.

"What?"

She opened her eyes. His beautiful face wasn't far from hers. He had long blond lashes that accented those marvelous blue eyes. "You may as well call me Emma," she said wearily. "I don't really like the reminder that I'm lost at the moment."

His frown grew deeper. "What?"

She sighed. "Professor Found."

"Michael."

Was that kindness she heard in his voice? She didn't deserve kindness at the moment.

"Michael," she said. "You already think I'm a fraud and a cheat and a terrible professor. And I've botched this meeting horribly, and I can't stay anyway, thanks to the Fates, so I guess there's not much more I can do."

"About what?"

"I mean, if I tell you the truth, it won't make things worse." She almost made that last statement into a question. It just might make things worse. But the job was going to go away anyway. Her dreams of a normal life were over.

He was watching her, his expression wary. But his arms were no longer crossed. If anything, he was a little too close to her. And, strangely, she didn't mind.

"What truth?" he said gently.

"I'm a witch," she said. "A young witch. Well, maybe not that young." And then she snorted. "Purple! You don't think they knew the poem, do you?"

"What poem?" He looked at her as if she were still speaking Old English.

"Nora's mother quotes it all the time. Something about old women wearing purple because it's their right to wear purple and to act eccentrically." She shook her head. "Were they telling me that I'm old? Or was this the royal purple? Or was it simply a color they liked?"

"Who?" Michael asked.

"The Fates."

"What?"

She shook her head. "Never mind. It's not important."

"Emma, I'm not following any of this."

"I know," she said. "It's my fault."

She stood and brushed off the purple skirt. In her brief moments in the past, she seemed to have acquired bits of hay on the front of it. She straightened her shoulders, looked Michael in the face, and pretended at dignity.

"I'm a witch," she said again. "A young witch who just came into her powers. Unfortunately, I never bothered to learn how to control them. So everything that happened, everything you saw, I did. And I didn't mean any of it. I just don't know how to stop this from happening."

He stared at her for a long moment. His frown had become a look of concentration, his blue eyes seeming to peer right through her own.

"I'd make some kind of sarcastic response," he said, "but I'm half convinced. Maybe it's the mud on the shoes."

"Or the fact that you lost all your furniture."

He smiled. "I got it back."

"You did?"

"You didn't know?"

She shook her head. "If it happened, it happened by accident. All of it. Including that little foray back in time."

"You've done that before."

"Not really," she said.

"But your Old English is fluent."

She was tired. "That's another story."

"Emma—"

She held up a hand to silence him. "I'm sorry, Michael. For all of it. I'm even sorry for your suspicions. I'll buy you a new pair of shoes too, once I get all of this under control. But I just came into my powers this morning, and I'm afraid what will happen if I go to my classes today. Can you find someone to take my class? I'm in no condition to teach anyone anything."

"I'll take it," he said softly.

That didn't surprise her. Of course he would. That was what he had wanted all along.

"And not because I feel I should be teaching it," he said quickly, as if he had heard her thought. (He hadn't, had he? Oh, that would be embarrassing!) "But because you need the assistance."

Then he peered at her. Before she could stop him, he put a hand on her forehead. His touch sent a tingle through her. His palm was warm and smooth and dry. And comforting. "You don't look well."

She blinked hard. She wasn't fighting tears, was she? She never cried. She hadn't even cried when she found out she had lost a thousand years of her life.

She wouldn't cry now just because she had found a life she loved and was going to lose that too.

She moved her head away from his hand.

"I'll be all right," she said and left.

―∿∿―

Wounded dignity. He'd never completely understood that phrase before.

Michael Found stood in front of Emma's desk, his hand still tingling from touching her skin. It had been so smooth and soft, and she had looked so sad.

It was her sadness that startled him the most.

From his encounter with her the day before—from the times he'd seen her interviewed—and even from her book, he had thought her a capable, no nonsense woman who never allowed anything to upset her. He had thought that she had chosen a time period that allowed itself a lot of interpretation and then had written her pretty little piece of fiction—all as a rational, calculated way of setting herself up in some major university somewhere, a place where she could be a celebrity with minimal effort and summers off.

The sadness she had displayed a moment ago, the wounded dignity that allowed her to grab her purse, and slosh quietly out of the room, leaving muddy footprints behind her, had changed his mind about that.

He hadn't lied to her. He was inclined to believe her. And that bothered him more than he wanted to say.

The entire morning had bothered him. The loss of the furniture, the way Helen had turned to stone, and then that visit to the medieval village. He hadn't lied to Emma. He could think of no way she—or anyone else—could have faked that.

Which left him with several other theories, each as kooky as his time travel question, and none of them rational.

Except, strangely, her explanation of being a witch.

He slumped in the chair she had placed across her desk for students. He knew he should leave her office, but he wasn't willing to, not yet. He wanted to stay close to her. If he had known her better, he would have taken her home and made sure she was all right. She seemed so lost suddenly.

Then he smiled. So that was what she had meant when she had said *so well named*. He had just used her last name. She was feeling lost.

Well, he wasn't feeling found. He was feeling a bit lost himself.

His study of magic, indeed, what he had told his colleagues when he took on the project was the idea that various forms of beliefs in magic had shown up in all primitive cultures. Yet the beliefs also showed up in cultures that considered themselves modern, from the spiritualist craze among the Victorians (leading to odd séances) to the New Age crap that was happening now.

He was going to try to do a comprehensive history of magic in several volumes, and he planned to cover the entire world eventually. He had had to start somewhere, though, and he had decided to start where he was most familiar—in the West. Magic explained everything from the arrival of spring to the ferocity of winter winds. The Celts were the most creative of all, explaining ground fog as banshees—the ghosts of women who had died in childbirth—and carrying on superstitions that still held today.

But what if magic were real? What if all the scholarship was founded on the wrong premise? What if there was more to life than what a man could see or feel?

He shuddered. He had certainly felt his arrival in that medieval village. He had smelled it, too. And heard a language that he had never heard spoken in his life, although he had seen parts of it written. He didn't understand it, although Emma Lost seemed to.

And if she did, then didn't that mean at least some of her scholarship was accurate?

He shook his head. Everything he believed in had been turned upside down today. What would happen if he wrote a book claiming magic was real?

If he wrote it as history, he'd be the one whose work would be dismissed as bunk.

If he wrote it as a New Age tome, he'd probably get rich.

He smiled vaguely. He had no interest in getting rich. He had, as he had told her, an interest in learning the truth. And the truth was that she was one very upset woman—a woman who had fled his office after his furniture disappeared, a woman who left her own office without locking it after taking him to a place that had looked like England in the tenth century.

He glanced at his watch. It was quarter to. He had promised Emma he would take her class. He barely had enough time to look up its location and title. He certainly didn't have enough time to prepare a lecture. He was glad he had been boning up on his medieval history, because he was going to let the students query him about everything.

But he wished he hadn't made her that promise. He wished there was enough time to find someone else to take the class. He wanted to talk with Emma Lost some more.

He told himself that he wanted to find out what she knew about magic. But what had him the most intrigued was the way her skin had felt beneath his palm, the way her luxurious hair caught the light. That fantastic face and those stunning eyes that seemed gray sometimes, green sometimes, and blue at others.

He was attracted to her, and either she was crazy as a loon, or he was. Or he was dreaming, and he would wake up to find himself in his own bed, feeling foolish.

Part of him, though, wanted it to be real. Part of him wanted to believe her.

And that was the part of himself that made him most wary. He wasn't sure whether he was reacting to the events of the morning, or to Emma Lost's beauty.

He had an uncomfortable feeling that if he looked deep enough into his own soul, he wouldn't like the answer.

Chapter 4

THE DRIVE HOME WAS UNEVENTFUL. EMMA TOOK OFF her shoes and stockings outside, and then tossed them into the nearest garbage can so that Darnell wouldn't have anything to roll in. She hoped he was still house-cat sized. She didn't want to face the lion again, not after the events of the morning.

She still couldn't get the stench of the village out of her nostrils. It had looked like her village, the one she had grown up in, where she had met Aethelstan, and that had saddened her. She had forgotten how poor it was, how ignorant everyone was.

For a brief moment, she had thought she would have to live back there again, and she wasn't sure she could do it. That brief foray into the past made her realize how much she had grown, how much she had changed, and how hard it would be to ever go back.

She took a shower, using a lot of lavender-scented soap. Steam rose around her, and she scrubbed until she felt marginally clean.

Darnell watched, as he always did, from the back of the toilet. He hadn't reverted to lion form, and he was no worse for his experience of the morning. He seemed to have forgotten it, or deemed it unimportant, or perhaps deemed it his due. She could never tell with Darnell. He was quite egotistical, even for a cat.

After she dressed, she went into her study to call

Aethelstan. Darnell did not follow her, which relieved her. She wanted privacy right now. Or maybe she was just being protective. Whenever people were close to her, they might feel the effects of her wayward magic.

Before she dialed, she checked the time. A little after ten a.m. on the West Coast. Aethelstan would be in his restaurant, getting ready for the lunch crowd. So far as most people were concerned, Aethelstan was the famous chef Alex Blackstone—so popular that he always got hired to cater Hollywood parties. Famous people flew to Portland just to dine in his restaurant. He had been approached to open others, but he didn't want a franchise.

Only Emma, Nora, and a few other people knew that Aethelstan didn't need the money. Everyone else seemed to think he was a crazy artist who wanted to protect his creation. Actually, Aethelstan wanted to enjoy his marriage. Building an empire—even a food empire—was not his style.

The phone rang for a long time. As it did, Emma carried the receiver to her favorite overstuffed chair. She had placed it near the window, which had a spectacular view of the backyard. Spring became the garden. The greenery and the budding trees made this place seem like home.

The thought made her blink hard. She would have to leave here. Studying in Portland would take years. She wasn't even sure she would be able to come back here to visit.

Thanks to her writing income, she could afford to keep the house, but she wouldn't be able to enjoy it for ten, maybe twenty years. And right now, that felt waaaay too long.

Finally someone picked up the phone. She could hear dishes clanging in the background and the sound of water running in a sink. "Quixotic."

"I need to speak to Mr. Blackstone," she said.

"I'm sorry. He's in a meeting—"

"Tell him it's Emma."

"Ma'am—"

"It's miss," she snapped. "I'm an old friend and it's an emergency."

"Yes, ma'am—miss—yes. I'll get him."

The anonymous voice put her on hold. The piped-in music was soft jazz, sophisticated and quiet. No obnoxious recording telling her the week's specials or the restaurant's hours. Just pretty music, already setting an atmosphere.

Aethelstan was good at things like that.

Then there was a clunk and the music was gone.

"Emma." Aethelstan's deep warm voice filled the phone. He had managed to keep just a bit of his British accent, even though he had lived in the States for more than a century. "Are you all right? Pedro said there was an emergency."

"I came into my powers, Aethelstan," she said.

She heard him exhale. Then he said, "Hang on while I transfer phones. Better yet, let me call you."

"All right." She listened as he hung up. Then she carefully hung up as well.

The early afternoon light was filling the room. She had decorated it in white and gold. The furniture was all upholstered in the same material, a light floral pattern that didn't overwhelm. The carpet was gold, the walls white, and the pictures she had hung on the walls were all flowers. Thanks to the modified Wright design, the study looked like it was part of the garden. This had always been one of her favorite rooms in the house.

Today, though, it failed to comfort her.

When the phone rang, she started even though she had been expecting it. She was more tense than she had realized.

"I thought you weren't going to come into your powers for another twenty years," Aethelstan said without preamble.

"Me, too," she said. "But the Fates said it all makes sense."

"You already spoke to the Fates?"

"I asked them to reverse it, but they wouldn't."

"No," he said, "they wouldn't. They say that—"

"They don't interfere. They govern."

Aethelstan chuckled. "They used that one on you too, huh?"

"Yes," she said, feeling more discouraged than she had a moment before.

"I think it's their way of staying aloof from our affairs." His voice had become gentle now. She could almost see him in the room, his tall form leaning against the doorjamb, his dark hair combed back from his hawkish face. He had aged in the thousand years—only the equivalent of fifteen human years, but that made him seem impossibly old to her, even now.

Certainly not the young man she had thought the most handsome in their little village.

"I'm in a terrible bind, Aethelstan," she said. "I turned Darnell into a lion this morning—"

"Did you use the reverse spell?"

"Yes. And it worked, just like the one you gave me to

go to the Fates." She paused. "You knew this was going to happen, didn't you?"

"Let's just say I plan for all contingencies," he said. "I certainly didn't know, but I was afraid it might."

He was silent for a moment. She sighed, knowing what he was thinking. "I meant to get training," she said.

"It was overwhelming, being awakened a thousand years into the future. It's my fault, really. I should have insisted—"

"Someday," she said, "you'll have to stop blaming yourself for those lost years of mine. I have."

"No, Emma," he said softly. "You haven't. Not entirely. And you shouldn't. It was unconscionable."

"Well, you owe me, then," she said. "I need someone to train me."

It was his turn to sigh. He knew how difficult teaching her would be. The person who sparked her terrible temper the most was Aethelstan. Probably because she was still angry at him on some level, although she would never admit it to him.

"I will train you," he said. "I promised to do that a long time ago. But you're going to have to take some sort of leave from your job. I can't come to you."

"I know," she said. "The Fates reminded me. But you could pick me up, couldn't you? Or maybe just zap me to Oregon? Me and Darnell?"

"You know I can't," he said.

"You've broken rules in the past."

"Always to bad result."

The door to her study pushed open. Darnell sauntered in as if she were in his work space.

"This rule makes no sense," she said.

"Oh, it probably does to the Fates," Aethelstan said. "They usually institute things like this because someone did it, and caused harm to others."

"I might cause harm to others," she said. "My magic is really out of control. I almost dropped a roomful of furniture on a secretary, and I sent the uptight new department head back to our little village."

"You made someone time travel? I didn't think that was possible."

"Maybe it's not for people whose magic is under control," she said.

"Were you able to get him back?"

"Oh, yeah," she said. "He's back. I'll probably have to deal with him tomorrow. If you don't come get me."

"We've been through that, Emma," Aethelstan said with a thread of irritation in his voice. And she hadn't even meant to be irritating. Training with him would be very difficult.

"I was just testing," she said. "You never know until you ask."

"You've asked two times too many, Em."

She leaned her head back. Shadows from the birch trees played across her white ceiling. No one was going to rescue her. No one was going to help her.

She shook her head slightly. She'd read the fairy tales that had been based on her past. Most fairy tales were based on the mages in one way or another. Some were based on life in the Kingdoms, which she had never visited. Some were based on old legends from various historical time periods. Sleeping Beauty was the story closest to hers. At the end of that story, a handsome prince had kissed her and brought her out of her sleep. Then they had ridden off into the sunset.

Rescued. Taken care of. It sounded so easy and nice.

Instead of Prince Charming, she had gotten a female lawyer reciting an incantation in the back of a VW microbus. Instead of being rescued with a kiss, she had been put to sleep with one. And instead of living happily ever after, she had had to learn new skills and develop a life of her own.

"Emma?" Aethelstan asked.

"I'll fly out tomorrow," she said wearily. "I'll call the airline when I hang up."

"Um, Emma?" He was using that tone again, the one he always used when he was afraid she would yell at him.

She raised her head. It felt very heavy. Her whole body felt heavy, tired, and ill used. She wondered if that was because of her mood or if the magic use had taken something out of her. "What now, Aethelstan?"

"You probably shouldn't use public transportation." He spoke the words quickly, as if he were afraid she would interrupt. "No planes, buses, or trains."

He had a point. What if she sent the plane's crew back to her village? Just the crew, and not the passengers. Her magic wouldn't be able to save any of them, and the crash would be horrible. And how would the poor FAA explain the absence of a crew in the cockpit?

"Emma?" Aethelstan asked warily.

"I guess you're right," she said. "I'll drive then. I can do that, can't I? I don't relish the idea of walking from Wisconsin to Oregon."

"I think it would be best for all concerned if you got here as quickly as you could," Aethelstan said. "I think driving is the least hazardous way you could travel."

"Thanks for that vote of no-confidence."

"Emma, out-of-control magic is very dangerous."

"I know that," she said. "I was trying to convince the Fates of the very same thing."

"They know. They just can't act before something happens. Only after."

She frowned. "You mean if I accidentally commit a crime because of my magic, they can punish me?"

"I'm sure they'll be lenient." He was trying to sound reassuring. "And it would have to be a magical crime."

"Well, that makes me feel so much better." She put a hand to her forehead. A headache was threatening. "I'm all on my own with this, aren't I, Aethelstan?"

"Only with getting here, my friend. Once you're here, we'll get you up to speed as fast as possible."

"Great. And if I turn my car into a pumpkin in the Rockies, and I'm trapped inside without a phone, I get to die inside a giant piece of rotting fruit?"

"I'm sure it won't come to that," Aethelstan said, not sounding sure at all. "Tell you what. I'll give you a list of mages who live along the way. If things get truly out of hand, they'll be able to help you."

"How many are there?"

"I don't know. We don't have a census. But I haven't heard of any deaths for a long time, and very few are imprisoned, and we get more and more with each passing century, so—I don't know. A million or so worldwide."

"No," she said, trying to sound calm. "Between here and there."

"Oh, about twenty I think. And ten are friendly enough to be of some use to a newly hatched witch."

"I like that phrase about as much as I like hot pins poked under my fingernails," she said.

He grunted. She recognized that sound. He was getting really impatient now. "This isn't going to work if you criticize everything I say."

"I promise I'll be good, Aethelstan." She crossed her fingers. When she got there, he'd have to take her as she was. Temper and all.

"I'd suggest you bring someone with you on the drive. Someone with common sense enough to poke his fist through that imaginary pumpkin of yours if need be."

"I would have thought of that," she said.

"Before or after the fruit rotted around you?" Aethelstan asked.

She sat up even straighter. "I have lived on my own for more than six years now—in a brand new culture in a brand new millennium. If anyone can survive on her own, Aethelstan, it's me. I'm the ultimate survivor."

Her words seemed to echo down the phone lines. After a moment, Aethelstan said, "I know you are. I'm only suggesting you have a companion in case the magic goes really haywire."

That was where their problem was. Their communication was terrible, even though both of them meant well. "The Fates have already ordered me to bring a traveling companion," she said. "They claim Darnell isn't enough, even if I do give him the power of speech."

"I think mortals would be rather startled if a cat tried to play Lassie," Aethelstan said.

"What?" Emma asked.

"*Lassie*. The TV show?" He sighed. "It's not repeated much, except on Animal Planet. I guess you can't catch up with all the cultural references in ten years."

"I've done pretty good."

"Better than I would have expected," he said.

"Would it be against the rules to have Nora fly out here and drive back with me?" Emma asked.

"No," Aethelstan said. "But she's in court for the next two months. It's a very big case, and she's the head counsel on it."

"What about Amanda and Jeffrey?" Amanda was Nora's mother and Jeffrey was her husband. They had taken care of Emma after she found she couldn't tolerate Aethelstan. And Jeffrey, a history professor, had helped Emma understand the world she was in now, and had inspired her to share his profession.

"They're in the Caribbean. On a cruise. It's a second honeymoon and it just started. They're supposed to be gone until August."

Emma sighed. She opened her mouth just as Aethelstan said, "And don't ask about Merlin. Even if he wanted to come, I suspect he'd be held under the same restrictions I was."

Merlin was Aethelstan's best friend. He was another mage. His real name wasn't Merlin, of course. That was simply the name he'd had when Emma had met him, over a thousand years ago. He was the Merlin of yore, although he didn't like to admit it. Nora called him Sancho, and Emma had never heard Aethelstan use any name other than those two. Some day, maybe, Merlin would trust Emma enough to tell her his real name.

"Surely there's someone you trust enough to bring along," Aethelstan said.

"Not among my mortal friends," Emma said, "at least not here."

"Well," Aethelstan said, "what about that boss of yours?"

Emma winced. "What about him?"

"You said you already sent him to the past. He has to know something is going on."

"Oh, he knows," she said. Darnell sat up straighter at the mention of another man. "I told him."

"Well, then," Aethelstan said.

"He thinks I'm insane. Or that he is. And I don't think he likes me much."

"Emma, you have to find someone."

She nodded, knowing he couldn't see her and not really caring. "Maybe I'll put an ad in the *Isthmus*."

"In the what?"

"The local weekly."

"Emma—"

"Email the list of contacts, Aethelstan. I'll let you know when I leave, and keep you apprised of the journey."

"Do that," he said gently. "I'll be worrying about you."

"Thanks," she said and hung up.

She cradled the phone for a moment. He would worry. For all their differences, for all of their prickliness, he really cared about her. After all, he had guarded her for a thousand years. He still felt a little protective.

It was probably bothering him greatly that he couldn't come out here and take care of her.

Then she shuddered. Maybe it was good she would be on her own. And Aethelstan was right. Michael Found might be the perfect person to travel with her. He already didn't like her or trust her, and he had experienced the magic.

She certainly couldn't make their relationship any worse.

Darnell was watching her from the floor. The poor cat. He hated traveling—and had complained on the entire long drive out here from Oregon. Now he had to go back. If she trusted modern conveniences more, she'd put him on an airplane and have Nora pick him up on the other end.

But with her luck, Darnell would chew his way through the kitty carrier and bite every attendant within walking distance, forcing some draconian airline official to put him to death.

Then she frowned. She wasn't really sure if they could legally put Darnell to death. Law figured a lot more into daily life in this century than the one she was born in.

In any case, she'd have to bring Darnell with her. And that was almost as ugly as the idea of traveling with Michael Found.

Except that she found her heart leaping at the very thought of him and those spectacular blue eyes of his. And that marvelous blond hair. Those shoulders. And those lips.

She would have to stay away from those lips.

Even if she didn't want to.

The idea didn't seem quite as good the following morning. Especially as she walked up the stairs to his office. This time, she was wearing jeans and tennis shoes, and a heavy silk sweater. She didn't have a class, and she had put a note on her door canceling office hours.

So far, today nothing had happened. She had kept her thoughts under rigid control and she had forced Darnell to sleep in the basement, much to his dismay. That way, she hadn't been able to hear him yowling his displeasure and subconsciously wish him to some desert island or something, and she didn't have to worry about having one of her dreams attack him.

Darnell had come out of the basement looking so angry that she kept away from him. And the basement door would never be the same.

But so far she was accident-free and hoping to remain so. It would require her to get through this meeting with Michael Found. She would make it as short as possible.

Even if she didn't ask him to go with her to Oregon, she still had to see him. She needed an emergency leave of absence and he was the only one who could grant it for her.

Even though there were still two weeks left in the semester, her students would be all right. The last week of lectures was mostly overview, and then there was finals week, in which no classes were held at all. She would have her exams done and ready before she left. A graduate student could handle them and she could grade from Oregon.

The biggest problem she had was keeping the length of her training a secret. She didn't want Michael to know she might have to be gone for years.

Helen was not at her desk, and Emma felt vaguely relieved. If anything went wrong this morning, at least Helen wouldn't be an accidental victim.

The other office doors were closed as well. It seemed most of the history department administration didn't show up until 9:00 a.m. Fortunately, it was only 8:30.

Michael's door was open, as she knew it would be. He was sitting in the reading chair, his legs stretched out before him, and as she knocked he set aside his book.

Her book.

Her stomach lurched. She didn't like how this was starting.

When he saw her, he smiled and stood. "Emma," he said, his voice warm.

She loved the flat vowels of his. After talking with Aethelstan yesterday, Michael's Wisconsin accent sounded reassuringly normal.

"Thanks for seeing me again after the—weirdness—yesterday."

"I'm happy to. I'm just glad I got your email in time."

She nodded. He extended a hand toward the empty chair in front of his desk. She walked to it, feeling more like a supplicant than a professor. Amazing how much had changed in twenty-four hours.

Michael sat behind his desk. He folded his hands in front of him and rested them on the blotter.

She sat, careful not to clutch her purse before her. Nora had always warned her that was a sign of nervousness, and Emma didn't want him to know how nervous she actually was.

"I hope the class went all right," she said. "I'm sorry that I stuck you with it."

"It went fine. You have some inquisitive minds in there."

She smiled, but she knew it didn't reach her eyes.

"You didn't come to talk about the class, did you?"

She shook her head. This was going to be harder than she thought. She really didn't want to leave this place. It had become her home in a short ten months. And now everything was going to change.

Again.

"I'm afraid I need an emergency leave of absence," she said.

"I expected as much."

"I have to leave Madison," she said. "The rest of the semester is pretty easy to take care of. I can write up my exams and the lectures—"

"I've already thought of that," he said. "Your graduate assistant seems more than capable."

Emma nodded. "I can grade by mail."

"If you leave an answer sheet—"

"No," she said. "There are a few students who don't test well and who know the material. It wouldn't be fair to them."

He studied her for a moment. Her heart sank. She knew what he was going to say before he said it.

"You're not going to let a student who doesn't complete the requirements pass the course, are you?"

Of course she wasn't. She clasped her hands tight. She was bristling and trying to control it. Her right thumb actually dug into the knuckles of her left hand. She concentrated on the pain so no wayward thoughts would do any damage.

"It's just that there are a few students who would probably get a B on a standardized test, and after their work this semester, they deserve an A."

"I looked over your course papers," Michael said. "You have written quite explicitly that grades would be based twenty-five percent on the midterm and seventy-five percent on the final. You can't bend the rules just because you've changed your mind."

"I've learned," she said, "and my grades should reflect that."

"Your grades," he said, "should follow the guidelines that you set up. Rules give us structure."

She stared at him for a long moment. "They also suffocate us."

He let out a small sigh. "You know, you almost had me convinced that the strange things in your book came from your experiences. I see now that you're just not willing to follow the strictures of scholarship."

"No," she said, her thumb digging in so hard that she would probably bruise. "You are simply using rules as a way to close your mind."

He paled ever so slightly. Had someone accused him of that before? She didn't know and she certainly was never going to find out. This would probably be her last interview with Michael Found. It was clear that he had made up his mind about her and nothing—not even the events of yesterday—would change that.

"You'll make out an answer sheet. Your graduate assistant will grade the exams and use them and the midterms to determine the final grades. That way, when you leave, you can concentrate on your own—problems."

She bowed her head. Her arms were rigid and she was breathing harder than she wanted to. Reigning in her temper was proving to be the most difficult thing she had ever done.

"Don't worry about us here," he said. "We'll take care of everything."

She was sure he would. And, she was sure, the Fates would as well. If Emma got control of her magic and used it to convince Michael to give her the job back, the Fates would intervene because of improper usage. Not to mention that it would make her feel terrible.

Although she was still tempted to try it.

She made herself stand before her thoughts got

completely out of control. "I'm planning to leave in the morning," she said. "Unless you feel I need to stay longer."

He shook his head. "I'll tell everyone that you had a personal emergency, which is true, isn't it?"

She nodded.

"Everything will be just fine here. When you leave tomorrow, you'll be able to concentrate on yourself."

She suppressed a sigh. She didn't want to concentrate on herself. She had had to for the past ten years just so that she could adapt to this culture. She had finally achieved her goal, and now she was being forced to give it up.

Was her entire life going to be about losing everything she grew to care about?

"Thanks, Professor Found," she said, and walked to the door.

"Michael," he corrected. "Remember? We resolved that yesterday."

She put her hand on the doorknob and turned to him. "I think it would probably be better for both of us if we forgot all about yesterday." She made herself smile. "Thank you for letting me go."

He opened his mouth and for a moment, she thought he was going to say, *My pleasure*. Instead, he said, "Take care of yourself, Emma."

The gentleness in the words touched her, even though she didn't want it to.

"I will," she said. "I have no other choice."

―∾―

He tried to work his way through the day. He had budgets to oversee and course plans to examine, and a lot of catching up to do. But all he kept seeing was the look on Emma's beautiful face when she said that rules were suffocating. She looked like a woman who was drowning and had no idea how to come up for air.

Immediately after she left, he tried to tell himself that whatever was happening with her was none of his business. He graduated from that to contemplation of things he didn't understand, and then found himself daydreaming about her, wondering what she would look like naked.

That thought jarred him enough that he pushed his chair back, and stood. He had to clear his head. Emma Lost was a lovely, troubled woman who did not believe in the same things he did. Even if her tale of magic were true—and he was having more trouble with that than he wanted to admit—there was still the issue of her inability to follow even the simplest of guidelines.

Letting students skate by because they were articulate in class was just the tip of the iceberg. There was still her poorly documented book. There was not a category in any history book's bibliography for magical time travel. The "I saw it therefore it must be true" defense barely worked in journalism anymore let alone history of the Middle Ages.

He shook his head hard enough to strain his neck. He put his hand on the sore spot and grimaced. The Emma Lost problem was taken care of, at least for now. She was on leave for the rest of the semester. He would write a report about her during the break and when he came back, he would see the faculty review board. They would find a way to dismiss her quietly, to save everyone embarrassment, particularly Mort who had championed her.

Somehow that whole idea made him uncomfortable. But it was probably because it was getting close to noon and he hadn't had much breakfast. Although he didn't admit it to Emma, he had had to hurry to get to his office that morning. He'd gotten her email at eight, when he logged on shortly before his shower. It had taken all he could do to make it to the office and look comfortable before she arrived.

He sighed. She made him as giddy as a schoolboy. It would be a big relief for him to have her out of his department, away from his university, and off his block.

Out of his town.

He grabbed his leather bomber jacket off the coat rack behind the door. The jacket was his favorite—all soft and broken in by time and use. He had worn it for years and even though it didn't fit with his professorial image, he was loathe to let it go. It symbolized a younger part of himself, the part that had loved wrestling and motorcycles and hockey. The part that he had to let go the higher up in academia he went.

He left Humanities and crossed the Library Mall. His stomach rumbled at the smell of roasted peppers and fresh falafels, but he knew better than to order anything off the vendors' carts. Let the students worry about indigestion all afternoon. The food on the carts wasn't good enough to taste repeatedly throughout the day.

The day was beautiful but still a bit chilly. Spring weather that reminded him summer was around the corner. Despite the chill, students studied on blankets in the grass. All the benches were taken, and a large number of students sat on the steps leading up to the Historical Society. They were eating their lunches, engaged in what seemed to them to be life and death conversations about intellectual matters.

That was probably the thing he loved the most about the university atmosphere, the way that ideas got bandied about, discussed, considered, and reconsidered. Most people outside academia seemed more concerned with their 401(k)s than the continued relevance of Machiavelli in the modern world. Heck, half of them probably thought Machiavelli was some Internet start-up company.

He crossed Langdon Street and went past the rows of bike racks to get to the Memorial Union. The Union was a large stone building that was, in all important ways, the emotional center of the UW campus. Alumni who had graduated decades before still made pilgrimages to the Union to eat Babcock ice cream and sit for a half an hour on the Terrace.

There were some students—he called them the lifers, the ones who had paid tuition for more than eight years and still hadn't gotten a single degree—whom he swore lived in the Union. Every time he appeared, they were there, sitting at a table in the Rathskeller, discussing music or buying theater tickets at the box office, or reading a book in the quiet room on the second floor. Michael didn't know these students by name, but he had seen them so many times that he had a nodding acquaintance with them—they'd nod happily when they saw him as if he were an old friend and he, polite Midwesterner that he was, would nod back.

Because the day was sunny, the line at the ice cream counter went all the way around the Union's entry and trailed off down a corridor. Michael dodged it and went deeper into the building to the Rathskeller.

The Rathskellar was the grill that served folks who usually ended up in the Stift, which was licensed to serve beer and wine. Because the University had under-age students, the beer and wine section couldn't be near the food.

The delineation between the Stift and the Rath was unclear to all but Union employees and the food and beverage inspectors. Both areas were done in a nineteenth-century German design, like the beer halls that they were clearly made to emulate. There were even paintings on the walls of a war between two different kind of dwarflike bearded Germanic men, one group pushing kegs of beer at the others like cannon, the other attacking with bottles of wine.

The place always smelled of frying hamburgers, pop-corn, and fresh beer. After his experiences of the last two days, he wanted a lager, but he knew he couldn't have one. He was still working. So he bought himself a Coke, then he went out into the sunshine-filled Terrace, and ordered a bratwurst at the Bunker Brat Stand. He loaded the brat with sauerkraut, German mustard, onions, and pickles, aware that the meal he was eating made the in-digestion he had faced on the Library Mall seem tame.

But brats, even without beer, were comfort food and he was feeling greatly in need of comfort.

The cast iron tables and chairs were scattered all over the upper concrete layer. The roar of conversation filled the air. Students, faculty, and townspeople sat in tight groups. The tables were full all the way to Lake Mendota.

The lake sparkled in the bright sunlight. This was the place that made him—and every other graduate of the UW—feel truly at peace. When he was a student, he'd never been able to study out here—study his course-work, that was. He'd study the women—especially during summer school when the temperatures hovered around ninety, and they wore as few clothes as they could get away with. He'd also study the other students, just because he loved people watching.

People watching would relax him and made him focus on something other than Emma Lost.

A group of students sat at the edge of the lake, dangling their feet into the water—a dangerous proposition, considering that the ducks that floated below had a tendency to think anything that came from above was food. Those ducks were the only wildlife he'd ever known that obsessed about popcorn. Huge signs covered the area leading to the lake, begging students not to feed the ducks. And of course, the students ignored it.

The grease from his brat was beginning to seep through the paper plate, and condensation had formed on the side of his paper Coke cup. He had to find a table, or he would have to carve a spot for himself on one of the stairs. He went down a level, closer to the lake, scanning tables for available chairs and not seeing any.

Finally, he saw one, and he hurried toward it before anyone else could snatch it. He barely managed to beat a scrawny freshman who took one look at Michael and backed away nervously.

Michael grabbed the chair and swung it toward the nearest table.

"Hi," he said to the woman who sat alone. "Do you mind if—?"

And then he stopped himself. The woman was Emma Lost.

She looked even more lost than she had the day before. He wasn't sure he had ever seen such sadness in someone's eyes.

He froze, one hand on the back of the chair, the other precariously balancing brat and Coke. "I'll, um, just sit over here."

"No," she said softly. "It's okay. There's room. And if you're not careful, you'll spill everything on that poor psych major."

He glanced down. A girl was lying on the concrete with her back to him. She wore shorts despite the chill, and her toned legs were crossed at the ankles. A stack of psychology books spilled out of her backpack, and she seemed completely absorbed in the tome she was reading. Every few seconds, she'd highlight a passage with a yellow marker.

She hadn't even seemed to notice that he had nearly set the chair down on her bare thighs. He hadn't noticed either, until Emma had pointed her out.

He set the brat and Coke down, then moved the chair around the girl, and sat. The chair groaned under his weight. Emma looked at his meal as if she couldn't imagine how anyone could eat that stuff.

It was not the kind of food a man should eat in front of a woman he found attractive. But he couldn't think of a way to beat a hasty retreat.

"I didn't mean to intrude," he said.

"I know." Her voice was gentle. He could barely hear it over the din around him. "I've been here long enough. I'll vacate the table soon."

But she made no move to leave, and he suddenly understood what she was doing.

She was saying good-bye. Did she know that he was going to make sure she wouldn't come back? Probably. It was becoming clearer and clearer that whatever her problem with rules and regulations and honesty, she was a very intelligent woman.

"This is one of the most beautiful places on Earth, don't you think?" he asked and then inwardly winced. How lame was that?

But she didn't seem to notice. Instead she seemed to be pondering his words.

"It shouldn't be," she said. "That great stone building behind us, the ground covered in concrete. Why, you even have to strain to get your feet into the lake from here. You're better off going down the bike path a ways."

He picked up the brat, and some of the kraut fell out. He had forgotten a fork.

"But there's something about the people having a good time around you, and the view of the lake, and the smell of beer that makes this seem—I don't know—comforting, maybe." She sighed and leaned her head back. "I'm going to miss it."

"Everyone does," he said. "People who have left Madison always make pilgrimages to the Terrace."

She laughed without humor. "The modern Madisonian's Holy Land, huh? If it were taken over by nonintellectuals, would there be a crusade to save it?"

He hadn't expected the whimsy, especially since the sadness was still in her eyes. Part of him wanted to make that sadness leave. "Where do you think Richard the Lionheart lives? California?"

"California's certainly far enough away," she said.

"But England is a small nation that thought it was more important than it was. And it was cold and perpetually damp. I would think that if we were to find the modern Richard, he'd be in Washington State or Oregon—"

She stopped abruptly and the wistful look was gone. The sadness, banished for just a moment, was back.

He set his brat down. "Is that where you're going? The Pacific Northwest?"

"Oregon," she said softly. "It was my home until I came here."

"That's why you have the poster in your office."

She nodded.

"I suppose you missed it."

"Oregon?" She seemed surprised. "Maybe a little. In the winter. I hadn't been around snow much before this. But Madison's the first home I've ever made for myself."

Her voice trailed off again. She seemed inordinately sad. There had to be more to this than she was telling him.

"You'll be coming back, won't you?" he asked, and then mentally kicked himself. He didn't want her to be back at the university. He had just spent the entire morning thinking about that, about how he didn't want her in the department.

About how she would look naked.

The thought made him glance at her face. She was staring at the lake, fortunately. He wondered if she had seen desire flicker across his own face, and hoped not. No matter how attracted to her he was, he didn't want to be involved with her. He wanted nothing to do with her and her vanishing furniture and instant time travel.

Still, she had the clearest, freshest skin he'd ever seen. It was a creamy color and the slight wind had brought out the natural rose of her cheeks. She was the only person he had ever met who had no blood vessels in the whites of her eyes. That made her pupils seem even brighter than they were, fresher, as if they had more life in them than any other woman's eyes he had ever seen.

"Michael," she said, turning toward him, and then she stopped. He felt the beginnings of a blush warm his face. He hadn't blushed since he was eighteen and Sally Marquardt, who was the advanced age of twenty-five, had whispered a sexual suggestion in his ear that had so shocked him that he had no other response.

"Are you all right?" Emma asked.

He swallowed, picked up his brat again, and bit it even though he wasn't hungry anymore. The sandwich was cold. There was nothing worse than cold sauerkraut. "Fine," he managed around the food.

Then he washed the offending bite down with a slug of Coke.

Emma was still looking at him contemplatively. "Michael, aren't you even curious about my magic?"

"Hmmm?" he asked, surprised. He hadn't expected the conversation to go in this direction.

"I mean, that's your area, right? Magic?"

He nodded. "The history of it."

She glanced over her shoulders as if she were afraid of being overheard. Were there magic police who arrested anyone who revealed the secret? He took another sip of Coke so that a nervous laugh wouldn't escape him.

"But you just discovered that magic really does exist. Doesn't that change what you're writing?"

He froze. That was the thought he'd been trying not

to have ever since yesterday morning. The short analysis he'd done then had been more than enough to terrify him.

"Emma," he said. "If I write a historical text that claims magic exists, I'll lose any credibility I've ever had with my colleagues."

"I suppose." She leaned back. A delicate frown creased her forehead. "But you could talk about practices none of them even know about, and you don't have to sanction it, just say that some people believe it exists."

"How would I do that?" he asked. "There isn't much primary material on real magic, is there?"

"Of course there is," she said. "You just have to know how to read it. I'll help you."

His fingers gripped his Coke cup so hard that it crumpled inward. Coke spilled over his hand, and down the table, onto the psychology major still studying at his feet.

"Hey!" she said. "What're you doing?"

He grabbed a handful of napkins, apologizing as he did so. The psych major scooted away from him—too close to a table full of beer drinkers and glared. He thrust the napkins at her and she snatched them away.

"You're awful careless," she said.

"I wasn't the one studying on the ground."

"Yeah, well, you know, you should always pay attention to your surroundings. It's not like I wasn't there, you know?"

He didn't quite follow that, but then it wasn't really worth his time to try. He turned back to Emma. She had mopped the rest of the Coke off the table, and had just tossed the wad of paper at a nearby garbage can.

"Why did it make you so nervous when I said I'd help you?" she asked.

He wasn't entirely sure. Maybe it was the thought of working beside her in a library, the fragrance from her dark hair wafting toward him, or maybe it was the way her soft voice had haunted his dreams.

Or maybe it was the fear of having her inept scholarship taint his own.

"I thought you had to go to Oregon," he said.

She bit her lower lip. On most women that gesture would have looked young and calculated at the same time. On Emma, it looked delightful.

She took a deep breath, as if she were stealing herself. "I thought maybe—we could help each other."

His shoulders slumped. She did know that he was going to get rid of her. She was bargaining for her job. She should have realized that he was a man with principles, a man who actually took his work extremely seriously.

"Look, Emma," he said. "We don't agree on methodology. Even after our experience yesterday, I don't think that what you've written would hold up to rigorous scholarly standards. You've skated by on your looks and your charm. But I'm not that kind of person. I make certain each and every detail…"

He let his sentence trail away when he realized that all the color had left her cheeks. She looked ethereal, suddenly, and very fragile.

She shook her head. "Obviously, I misjudged you."

She stood, her hands fumbling on the back of her chair for her purse. The purse fell, and she cursed, bending over to retrieve it, her hair covering her face like a fine shawl.

He hadn't meant to make her angry. He was just trying to explain. He didn't want her to leave like this.

He stood too, scooting his chair back, and slamming the legs into something hard.

"Hey!"

He turned. The psychology major shoved his chair back at him. It hit him in the back of the knees, and he sat down, abruptly.

"You're an ass, you know that?" she said.

"Well," he said, "you're the first person I know who lays down in the middle of a bunch of tables to study."

"I've never had any problem until now."

He glanced toward Emma, but she was pushing her way through the crowd, her head down. He slid out of the chair sideways so that he wouldn't hurt the psychology major again and hurried after Emma, banging his shins on metal chairs as he went.

She disappeared inside the Stiftskellar and as he stepped inside, he couldn't see. His eyes refused to adjust to the sudden darkness. He blinked a few times and had the horrible, irrational fear that she had vanished. Literally vanished.

And then he realized that fear wasn't really irrational.

She was making her way past the scarred wooden tables, filled with relaxing students. A few watched her as she went by—all of them male, all of them looking curious as to why such a beautiful woman would seem so upset. When they saw Michael hurrying after her, they seemed to understand.

He finally caught up with her near the exit. He grabbed her arm. She turned around so ferociously that he let go immediately and held his hands up like a robbery victim.

"I wanted to apologize," he said quickly. "I can be

a real pain sometimes. I didn't let you finish and I assumed and I answered the point I thought you were making instead of the point you made and—"

She put a finger up, a silent order for him to halt. To his own surprise, he followed it. She still looked fierce. He had a sudden real sense that he never wanted to see her angry—all-control-gone, so-furious-that-anything-went angry. The very idea took his breath away.

"Leave me alone," she said, her voice husky, her accent pronounced.

"I—"

"Our encounters haven't been pleasant, Professor Found. It would be better if we just ended things here."

He took a breath, half wondering why he even bothered. But he felt compelled. If this was going to be the last time he saw her, then he didn't want her to think him a total jerk.

"I was just curious," he said as softly as he could. "How do you think we can help each other?"

Her eyes got big. She clearly hadn't expected him to say that. Then she shook her head. "Never mind. It was a stupid idea."

"Let me be the judge of that."

"You?" She raised her thin, delicate, perfectly formed eyebrows. "You think everything I do is stupid. Or dangerous."

"Not everything," he said. "And I have no idea if that quick trip we took was dangerous, but I suspect the furniture, if it had fallen wrong, might have hurt someone. And that doesn't take into account turning Helen—"

"Enough!" Emma said. "Let's just pretend this conversation never happened, shall we?"

He shook his head. "Tell me."

Her shoulders slumped. "You're not going to leave me alone until I do, are you?"

"No," he said, even though he wasn't sure if that were true.

She took him by the elbow and led him into the well lit hallway. There she stopped. It took him a moment to realize that she felt the hallway, with its ebb and flow of students, high ceiling, and constant conversation, was more private than the dark wooden booths in the Stift.

Emma took a deep breath. She looked nervous. "I just thought that I could help you find out the true history of magic."

"And how would I help you?" he asked. His heart was pounding hard. He didn't want her to tell him that she wanted tenure or some guarantee that she'd have a job when she returned.

"I'd like you to drive me to Oregon."

"Excuse me?" Whatever he had expected her to say, that wasn't it.

"I need someone to drive me to Oregon. With my powers so out of control, I can't fly. I mean, what happened if I sent the entire plane to the Bermuda Triangle? Or just the passengers, without the plane itself? And I figure trains and buses are the same way—"

"So you'd like to risk my life by having me travel with you?"

She shook her head. "It's a little more complicated than that. You see, I need training, only part of the rules are that my teacher can't come to me. I have to go there. And with everything out of control, I need someone who can utter a few counter-spells or find help in an emergency."

"Don't you have any witchy friends who can do this?"

People continued to flow around them. No one seemed to notice or care about this weird conversation. One of the benefits of university life, he guessed. Any topic was fair game.

"Technically," she said, "they can't come to me because they could train me. And I don't know anyone in Madison who has this power. Besides, none of my real friends here know about this, and I don't have time to convince them."

"But you've already convinced me," he said dryly.

"Haven't I?"

He sighed. "A bit unwillingly. I'm still willing to think I'm crazy—or you're delusional—or that jet lag is the most powerful force in the universe."

She was staring at him. Her wide blue eyes held something different from the sorrow he'd seen earlier. Regret? Embarrassment? He couldn't tell. But he didn't want her to run away again.

"I'm not sure I entirely understand," he said. "Why can't you just wiggle your nose and transport yourself to Oregon?"

"I don't have that kind of control."

He'd seen enough evidence of that. "Then why can't your teacher just zap you there? Surely that's not the same as coming here."

"I have to get there on my own. It's the rules."

"Who makes these rules?"

"The Fates," she said. "I saw them yesterday. They won't bend the rules for me."

"Why would you expect them to?" he asked.

She opened her mouth as if to answer him, and then closed it. "It doesn't matter."

"Yes, it does." Although he wasn't sure why.

"You ever read *Sleeping Beauty*?"

"Sure," he said slowly.

She froze like a deer in headlights, as if she had just heard what she had said. "Never mind. It's too complicated. Really. I was just hoping you could help me out here. Otherwise it's me and Darnell on our own for two thousand miles."

"Darnell?"

"My cat," she said.

He paused. He was actually tempted. A week alone with this woman would be an adventure. There was a mutual attraction, and she was the most beautiful woman he had ever seen and—

She had a tendency to make things disappear. Literally. And his life hadn't been sane since he'd first laid eyes on her.

"When would you want to leave?"

"I told you. I have to go as soon as possible. That's why I'm leaving tomorrow."

The fantasy burst. There would be no adventure. He had a book to write, a new job to learn, and a lot to catch up on. "I'm sorry. Even if I wanted to go, I couldn't get the time away. I just came back from a long sabbatical, and—"

"It's all right." Her smile was rueful. "It was a silly idea, like I said. I was just feeling a little desperate, that's all. I shouldn't have dumped on you."

"Emma, really, if I could go, I would."

She nodded, but he could tell she didn't believe him. She touched his arm softly, and then turned around and walked away. Her head was down again and her movements lacked the fluid grace he had seen in them before. She was obviously disappointed. She had hoped he would go along.

He stifled the urge to follow her again. Instead he watched her go. Maybe he wasn't really attracted to her at all. Maybe her magic had drawn him to her, like a love potion or a charm spell. He wasn't entirely himself when he was with her. And if he believed she had the power to send him back to the tenth century, he certainly believed she could make him think he loved her when he really didn't.

Time and distance would ease the attraction, if it wasn't real.

Although it sure felt real.

He shook himself. He'd been attracted to women before and had gotten over it. He'd been in love before, and survived the breakup.

He could handle never seeing Emma Lost again.

Couldn't he?

Chapter 5

EMMA HUNG UP THE PHONE AND PUT HER HEAD DOWN on her desk. Darnell sat in the window, watching her over his shoulder. He was worried—not so worried that he couldn't occasionally yip at the neighbor's cat prowling the yard—but keeping an eye on her just the same.

She was worried too. She had just spoken to her last friend in town—an acquaintance, really, a woman she had met at a faculty fund-raiser just a month ago. The woman had been polite—everyone had been polite—but no one was willing to travel with Emma to Oregon, not even if she waited a week or two.

And she hadn't told any of them about the magic problem or the supervision. She hadn't said a word. All of her friends were simply too busy to take a week or two away from their lives. That is, a week away that hadn't been scheduled months in advance.

Darnell rose to his hind legs and plastered his front paws on the window. He was growling. Apparently the interloper cat had come too close.

At least Emma hadn't turned Darnell into a lion again. That would really scare the outdoor cat. Fortunately for the invader, all Darnell could do was give him the evil eye.

She couldn't quite smile at her own attempt at humor. She was in trouble, and she knew it. She had even thumbed through the *Isthmus* personals, hoping to find someone looking for an odd job. She'd checked the ride board at both the Memorial Union and at Union South, but no one was heading to Oregon. The closest companion she could find were a handful of students going to Seattle or to San Francisco.

She'd called them, but none of them wanted to go out of their way to drop her in Portland.

And then there was Michael Found. Her cheeks warmed just at the memory of him. He had pursued her at the Union, sitting with her, talking with her. At one point she had even thought he was flirting with her. But when she finally asked him, he had said no.

Not just any no, either. But one that started with, *even if I wanted to go*. Like her offer had offended him.

It probably had. She offended him. He made that clear too, in his discussion of her "poor" work. And still she had asked him.

She had told him she was desperate, and she really, really was.

Maybe if she waited until the end of the semester, she would find more rides. Maybe.

That feeling of energy leaving her—a feeling that was becoming familiar—struck again. She sat up to see red lights flare out of Darnell's eyes. The lights burned into the yard, and she heard a cat scream with terror.

Emma ran to the window in time to see the neighbor cat slide under the fence, fluffy white tail between its fat little legs. The red lights pouring out of Darnell's eyes followed the invader like laser beams in a bad science fiction movie.

Thank heavens he was a cat and didn't have an

immediate understanding of what those powers could do. But she did, and as he turned toward her, she ducked, repeating the reverse spell over and over.

The lights dimmed, and then faded out, but not before they left a smoky trail on her hardwood floor. She glanced at the wall opposite Darnell and saw two little holes, still smoking, that went all the way through to outside.

Little fires were burning on her lawn as well.

Darnell mewed at her piteously. Apparently the entire thing had frightened him as well.

She went to the window, picked up her strong elderly cat, and held him close. "I'm so sorry, Darnell."

She wasn't even sure this time how the spell had happened, but she knew it had to do with some stray thought of hers. Maybe she should leave Darnell here, with someone. But Darnell was old and he was her familiar. She'd heard horrible tales about what happened to mages who lost their familiars. She was having enough trouble already.

"I'll keep you as safe as I can, Darnell," she whispered. "But this proves it. We can't wait until the end of the semester. We have to leave tomorrow."

Darnell squirmed in protest. She was holding him too tight. He jumped out of her arms, careful to avoid the charred floor, and ran to the door. There he stopped and licked his body as if her touch had offended him.

Great. A long trip with out of control magic and an oversensitive familiar.

Life certainly wasn't getting any easier.

—⁓—

Michael woke up, his entire body tense. Something was wrong; he could feel it.

His bedroom was dark, but not pitch black. Light flowed in the west window from the streetlight on the corner, covering the room in familiar pale blocks. He could see the hardwood floor and the corner of the black comforter that had slipped off his bed. The shadows from the ancient spider plant some long forgotten girlfriend had given him crisscrossed the bed, making it seem as if the light were coming through a forest.

He glanced over his shoulder at the clock on the nightstand. He couldn't read the illuminated digits—a stack of books he'd been picking his way through blocked the readout. He leaned back and squinted. Two forty-five a.m. Strange. He didn't feel as if he'd been awakened out of a deep sleep.

But he still had the sense that something was wrong. Then he heard the clock chime in the living room. *Bong. Bong. Bong.*

He frowned. Something was wrong with that too.

Bong. Bong. Bong.

He reached for his robe and slipped it on.

Bong. Bong. Bong.

Then he put on his slippers—*bong*—as he realized—*bong*—that he didn't have a chiming clock in the living room—*bong*—or anywhere else in the house.

A shiver ran through him, even though the room was warm. His front door opened and then closed. He reached for the phone beside his bed, knocked down more books, and winced. Now, at least, the intruder would know where to find him.

Michael grabbed the phone and listened for the dial

tone. There was none. Then he realized he was hearing Christmas music—"God Rest Ye Merry Gentlemen," to be exact—and over it, the sound of a window opening.

Boy! Patrick Stewart said—or was that George C. Scott? Or Alastair Sim—*What day is it?*

Michael looked at the phone as if it had bit him. Then he jiggled the disconnect button several times. When he put the phone back to his ear, he heard Patrick Stewart, or George C. Scott, or Alastair Sim say, *Then it all happened in one night! The spirits visited me in one night!* And he laughed maniacally.

Michael hung up the phone and hurried to his window. He tried to yank it open, but it was stuck shut, almost as if it were painted shut. Now how could that be? He'd had it open just the night before.

Footsteps echoed in the living room. Michael cast about wildly, wondering what he would do. He tiptoed to the closet and found his baseball bat. It was the only weapon he had.

He waited near the door, breathing shallowly, listening. The footsteps got closer. His heart was pounding. Who was doing this? What did they want? It didn't even sound as if they were searching for anything.

Then his bedroom door opened and the room flooded with light as if someone had aimed a spotlight through the door. A long, robed shadow covered the floor.

Michael raised the bat—

…and felt his arms freeze into place.

"Really," a harsh, nasal voice said. "Is that any way to greet the Ghost of Christmas Present?"

Michael felt his jaw drop. Lights came on all around him. Not his lights—but candles, all of them under glass chimneys, just like something out of Dickens. His head itched. He moved it slightly, and the balled end of a stocking cap hit him in the face. He looked down and realized he was wearing a nightshirt—not the robe he had put on moments before.

"Put down the bat," the voice said, "and we'll have a discussion."

"I can't move my arms," Michael said.

"Ooops," the voice said. "Forgot."

Michael's arms were suddenly under his own power. They collapsed around him, and it took all of his control to keep the bat from clunking him on the head. He set the bat behind him, close enough to pick it up again if he needed it.

But he wasn't sure how he would need it. This was the strangest nocturnal visit—in fact, the only nocturnal visit—he had ever had.

The lights came up even farther revealing the figure in the center of the room. The spotlight went out and Michael realized that the man facing him was the size of a small child. Only he didn't look like a child.

He was perfectly proportioned, square with a pugnacious face. His chin curved outward, and his nose curved inward—or it once had. But it looked as if it had been broken several times. He had a long white beard that flowed to the ground, and he wore a wreath of holly around his head. His robe was green with fur trim.

"I thought the Ghost of Christmas Present was tall," Michael said.

"Damn that Dickens," the intruder said. "That was funny at first, but after one hundred fifty years, it's beginning to annoy me."

"And," Michael said as if the intruder hadn't spoken, "it's not Christmas Eve."

"So?"

"It's May."

"So?"

"And"—this was the part that really offended him—"I'm not Scrooge."

The little man raised his eyebrows, making him look like Puck out of *A Midsummer Night's Dream*. Puck dressed as Oberon.

Michael shook his head. He'd been to American Player's Theater one too many times.

"Really?" the little man said. "Not Scrooge?"

"No," Michael said. "Sorry to disappoint you."

The little man shrugged. "I'm not disappointed. And I'm not confused. You share quite a few traits with him, you know."

"I'm not cheap. I give money to all kinds of charities and I believe in helping—"

"Professors who are in dire need? Women who need a hero? People whose research doesn't meet your exacting standards?"

Michael took a step forward. He should have known that Emma was involved in this. "Who are you?"

"Let's just call me Ghost, shall we?"

"No," Michael said. "What's your name?"

"You mortals and your insistence on names. I don't know you well enough to give you my name, and from what I've seen of you, I don't think you're trustworthy enough to know it. It's Ghost to you," the little man said.

"I'll be damned if I call anyone Ghost," Michael said.

"Be careful before you curse yourself." The little man

crossed his arms. "But since you don't believe in literary characters—even if I was Dickens's inspiration—I see no more point in being uncomfortable."

He bobbed his head forward and there was a puff of smoke around him. When it cleared, he was wearing jeans with cuffs, tennis shoes that predated Nike, and a T-shirt with a pack of cigarettes rolled in the right sleeve. His beard had vanished too—making him look almost normal.

"Okay," he said. "So you won't call me Ghost. How about Casper?"

"That's your name?" Michael asked, still feeling as if he were one step behind.

"I didn't say that." The little man hadn't moved.

"Then why should I call you Casper?"

"Well, I'm friendly…" the little man said.

Michael rolled his eyes. "It's the same as calling you Ghost."

"Not quite. Casper, at least, is a real name. In fact, some Biblical accounts say it was the name of one of the Three Wise Men."

"You're not going to try to convince me that you're one of the Three Wise Men?"

"Heavens no," the little man said. "I was conning the Norse at the time."

Michael shook his head. He felt as if the conversation had moved fifteen steps away from him without his permission. "What do you want?"

"What does the Ghost of Christmas Present always want?" Casper said. "To show you what will be."

"I thought that's the Ghost of Christmas Future."

"Yeah, well, I didn't feel like hiding my face and wearing that smelly robe and sticking out a skeletal hand. Ever since they did that sequence in a Mr. Magoo cartoon, it hasn't felt right."

Michael stifled a grin. He couldn't imagine the little man in front of him being scary at all in a black-robed costume with only red eyes where the face would be. He would have looked more like a Jawa from *Star Wars* than the Ghost of Christmas Future.

"You have a point," Michael said, careful to keep all trace of the smile out of his voice. "So, how're you going to get me to change my miserly ways?"

"You know," the little man said, "I don't see what you have against her."

"Against Emma?"

Casper—Michael had mentally given in and allowed the little man his made-up name—shook his head. "See? You knew who I meant without me having to say a word."

"Actually you said quite a few words, and I knew who you meant because she's the only woman who has ever turned my world upside down."

"Ever?"

Michael let out a sigh of exasperation. "In this way."

"Really?"

"Really," Michael said with a little too much force. "She's the only one who used a spell to send me back to the tenth century."

"I'm sure others wanted to," Casper said.

Michael glared at him. Casper held his hands out, as if wordlessly protesting his innocence. "You have already proven a trial to me."

"I have?" Michael asked. "You're the one who invaded my house, put a recording of Dickens on my phone, and glued my windows shut."

"I didn't use glue," Casper said. "I've never used glue in my life. I would never stoop to glue."

"'Stoop to glue'?"

"Yes, stoop. Glue is something mortals use because they lack the talent to bind things themselves. It's primitive, pernicious, and slightly gross, actually."

Michael shook his head. He couldn't believe this conversation. "I'm going to get myself a beer. You want one?"

"I can't drink on the job, and you shouldn't either," Casper said.

"I'm not working." Michael started for the kitchen, but as he stepped forward, the bedroom door slammed shut.

"Can't let you do that," Casper said. "You might blame all of this on alcohol."

"What am I supposed to blame it on, a bit of bad beef?"

"You know," Casper said, "for a history professor, you know your literature."

"It's kind of hard to miss considering some big-voiced, middle-aged actor has to play Scrooge in some TV movie every Christmas."

"You have something against Scrooge?"

"No, but you'd think—"

"See? I knew you had a lot in common."

Michael caught his breath. "I wasn't saying that."

"You said you have nothing against Scrooge. Anyone sane has something against Scrooge."

"I *meant A Christmas Carol*. I have nothing against *A Christmas Carol*, but just once I'd like to see *Great Expectations* revived every summer, or *Oliver Twist* whenever there's a cold snap or how about a *Tale of Two Cities*?"

"What, you couldn't find a weather connection for that one?" Casper asked.

Michael walked back to bed and sat down. Maybe if he put his head on the pillows and closed his eyes, this whole nightmare would go away.

"And you know," the little man said, "they redid *Great Expectations* a few years ago. Modernized it, with Anne Bancroft and Gwyneth Paltrow. Stunk. And I'm sure that the musical *Oliver!* is being revived somewhere as we speak—"

"All right!" Michael said. "If a man can drown in words, I'm going down fast. What is it that you want?"

"Actually," the little man said, sitting down next to him, "I wanted to meet you."

"Why?" Michael asked.

"Because you resisted Emma. You know, you're one of the few men on the planet who could. The other one's married, rather happily, and had always been slightly miscast as Prince Charming."

"What?"

"Never mind," Casper said.

"I thought you were going to show me the future."

"Only a small portion of it." Casper lay back on the bed and tucked his hands under his head. He kicked the bed frame with his sneakers. The rhythm was irregular, and even more irritating because of it. "The part you created when you said no to Emma today."

"I said no to Emma today because I have a job, and besides, she's really not—"

"You said no to Emma because you're scared." The little man propped himself up on one elbow.

"I am not."

"Yes, you are. Beautiful women scare you. You wonder if you can even see their personalities or figure out if they have minds. That's why you've dated dogs all these years."

"I haven't dated a single dog."

"All right," the little man said. "Mice."

"They're not mousy. They were all brilliant, funny women—"

"Who never really interested you. Stimulated you, yes. You loved talking to them, but bedding them was a real chore, wasn't it?"

Michael pushed himself off the bed. "Who the hell are you and what are you doing in my house?"

"Well, you didn't like Casper and you didn't like the Ghost of Christmas Present, so how about I say that I'm your guardian angel."

"You don't look like an angel."

"I'm not, really. I'm more of a yenta."

"You don't look like a yenta either."

"I don't look like the Ghost of Christmas Present, I don't look like an angel, I don't look like a yenta." The little man put his hands on his hips. "Who, then, do I look like?"

Michael swallowed. "Well," he said, wishing he hadn't been asked this question, "you look a little like Grumpy."

"Grumpy. Grumpy? Who's Grumpy?"

"Me, actually. I would like some sleep."

"No, you compared me to someone named Grumpy…" The little man's voice trailed off. "You mean from the Disney cartoon. That awful *Snow White*? 'Whistle While You Work' and all that?"

"Yes," Michael said.

"I don't look like Grumpy."

"Well, you certainly don't look like Sneezy."

"Thank heaven for small miracles," the little man said.

"So, you better get on with this haunting before I say you look like Dopey."

"You'd be lying."

Michael shrugged. "If that's what it takes to get you out of my bedroom, yes, I'd be lying."

Casper shot him a nasty glare, then clapped his hands together.

Suddenly the air got unbearably hot and dry. Michael felt sweat break out all over his body. Sunlight so brilliant that it hurt his eyes reflected off sand and desert plants that he couldn't identify. There were heat devils dancing off the pavement around him. Something wailed in the distance.

"What the—?"

Casper put a finger over Michael's mouth, silencing him. Then, with his other hand, Casper pointed.

Michael let his gaze follow the point. Down the road, he saw a silver BMW, its tires flat, its hood open. The windows were open as well, and a black cat leaned its head out of the driver's side. The cat was yowling at the top of its lungs, a mournful, horrible sound.

Michael took a step closer. The tires weren't flat. They had melted. Bits of rubber stuck to the pavement. Tires didn't melt—at least, not at regular temperatures, and as hot as this desert was, the temperature was regular for the desert. There was a faint acrid odor of burnt rubber.

Smoke wisped out of the open hood. The cat's yowls seemed to get louder. Casper put his hand on Michael's arm and pointed again.

Michael looked down. He saw feet sticking out into the middle of the road. Small feet wearing delicate female shoes. He held his breath and approached the car.

The cat saw him and began to scream at him in cat-language, as if he were somehow responsible. He'd never heard such fury from an animal before. As he passed in front of the creature, it actually hissed at him, and that made him think twice about rescuing it.

Then he forgot all about it as he reached the front of the car.

Emma lay on her back, her eyes closed, her skin so sunburned it looked as if she had been tossed in an oven and crisped. Her palms were facing skyward, her mouth open, her lips cracked.

He knelt beside her. "Emma?" he said, reaching for her.

Casper yanked him back. "Don't touch."

"But she needs help."

"She's beyond help."

Michael looked up at the little man. "She's dead?"

"She will be soon," he said.

"Then we should do something."

"You forget," the little man said. "This is your future. Her future."

The cat yowled.

"And his future."

"He'll die here, too."

"Of course he will," Casper said. "No one will come along for hours. By then it'll be too late. For both of them."

Michael's hands hovered over her. "What happened?"

"Obviously, she worried about the heat. And that

triggered the wrong kind of magic in her mind. It either made things even hotter, or melted her tires, or hurt her in some way. All that really matters is that there was no one else here to help her."

The cat spit and growled.

"At least," Casper said, "not in any meaningful way."

The cat's growl got lower.

"If you can speak," Casper said, pointed at the cat, "then you made a serious mistake."

The cat disappeared into the car.

Casper shook his head. "She shouldn't have trusted a cat. Cats generally don't consider all the consequences before taking action. Or failing to take action, as the case may be."

"It's not my fault," said a small deep voice.

The hair rose on the back of Michael's neck. That wasn't the cat was it? "Come on," he said to Casper. "You can help her. Wave your hands or something. Bring her back."

"I am helping her, you idiot." Casper shook his head. "Do I have to write it in smoke? If you'd been traveling with her like she asked, she'd be fine now."

"So you travel with her."

"I can't. No one magical can."

"That's a stupid rule," Michael said.

"Well, so are blue laws, but a number of your communities still have those."

"So break the law," Michael said. "Challenge it, just like we would do with a blue law."

"You think that's so easy. Here you'd get fined or arrested. In my world, loss of magical powers, banishment, imprisonment for centuries. Doing stupid little tasks for other people so that you can learn a lesson. It's not worth the hassle, believe me."

"Even at the cost of Emma's life?"

The little man's face was getting red. Sweat dripped down one cheek. "I'm not costing Emma's life. I'm trying to save it."

"You want me to travel with her?"

"The light dawns," Casper said sarcastically.

"Why can't one of her other friends?"

"They have jobs," Casper said.

"That's not any different from my excuse."

"Excuse?" Casper asked.

Michael grimaced. He was feeling hot too. "You know what I mean."

"No, I don't," Casper said. "She came to you, and you turned her down."

"It sounds like a lot of other people did too."

"But you weren't supposed to!"

Michael froze. "Says who?"

Casper hit his forehead with the heel of one hand. "Forget I mentioned it."

"No," Michael said. "Who says I wasn't supposed to say no?"

"The prophecies," Casper muttered.

"Prophecies?"

"That's all you're getting out of me," Casper said.

"What prophecies?"

"We all have prophecies," Casper said. "At least us magical beings."

"I see. And what are they about?"

"You know," Casper said. "The important stuff."

"Life, liberty, and the pursuit of happiness?"

"Not really."

"Then what?"

The little man looked at Michael as if he were crazy. "If I have to tell you, you're even denser than I thought."

"Consider me dense."

"Love, you mortal moron." He yanked Michael upwards. "Now come on, we have to get out of here before I ruin this T-shirt."

"What about me?" a small voice asked. The cat peeked his head out of the car. "Take me with you?"

"Sorry, Darnell. Against the rules."

"I'll die," he said plaintively.

"Should have thought of that when you decided not to say the reverse spell."

"How was I supposed to know how bad it would get?"

"How indeed," Casper said.

"How about a little common sense," Michael said.

The cat glared at him. "You I don't need, pal."

"I don't think you're in a position to be choosy," Michael said.

"I coulda said the reverse spell," the cat said. "In fact, I did say the reverse spell. It didn't work."

"You have to say it within the first five minutes," Casper said.

The cat raised its chin. "I was testing to see if that was correct."

"Well, now you know," Casper said.

"What good is knowledge if there's no tuna, no milk, no way out of this place?"

"Your only way out," Casper said, "is to be nice to this man."

"Him?" the cat said. "He's too interested in my Emma."

"I think the problem is that he's not interested at all."

The cat's golden eyes narrowed. "Then you don't see real well, do you, old friend."

"We were never friends, Darnell."

"Still."

Casper tugged Michael away from the car. "Let's go before I kill that cat myself," he said in a loud whisper.

"I heard that!" the cat said.

Casper raised his arms.

"Hey!" the cat said. "You can't leave me here!"

"You're not really here," Casper said. "At least, not yet."

Then he brought his arms down, and Michael found himself back in his bedroom, Casper beside him. The room smelled of candle wax, and was infinitely cooler than that desert had been. The candlelight looked dark in comparison to the bright desert sunlight.

Michael sank onto his bed. "Now I'm really confused."

"No, you're not." Then Casper peered into Michael's face. "Oh, don't tell me. You are confused."

"That's what I said." Michael pulled off the nightcap. It was made of flannel. No wonder he had gotten hot. Who ever heard of wearing a nightcap in a desert? Whoever heard of wearing a nightcap, period?

"How can you be confused? You said you watch *A Christmas Carol* every year."

"Yeah."

"So you think Scrooge died broken and alone on the same night as he saw the spirits? I mean, really. The man was redeemed."

Michael's head was starting to ache. "I'm getting that beer."

"I told you," Casper said. "No beer. You gotta trust this."

"I haven't had a beer, and I still don't trust it," Michael said. "Maybe we should try it my way."

"Listen," Casper said. "I let Marley get a beer. We all know how that ended up."

"I'm *thirsty*," Michael snapped.

A tall glass of water appeared in his hand. "There, you whiner," Casper said. "I have no idea what Emma sees in you."

"She sees something in me?"

Casper rolled his eyes. "She asked you to go with her, didn't she?"

"Yes, but—"

"She showed you her magic, didn't she?"

"Yes, but—"

"She flirted with you, didn't she?"

"I think so, but—"

"You *think* so? The woman's terrified of being kissed, and still she flirts with you. You should be flattered by that."

"Terrified of being kissed?"

"You didn't know?"

"How should I know that? Who's afraid of being kissed, anyway?"

"Sleeping Beauty," Casper said.

"That's not how the fairy tale ends."

"Do you believe everything you read?" Casper said.

"I distinctly remember a happily ever after in that fairy tale," Michael said. "Happily ever after would include kissing."

Casper raised his hands to the ceiling. "*I'm tired of dealing with mortals!*" he shouted, as if he expected someone else to be listening.

Michael looked up and saw nothing, only the flickering candlelight on the expensive wood ceiling planks. "You know, you and that cat aren't that different."

"I don't lie," Casper said.

"The cat lies?"

"All cats lie."

Somehow Michael believed that.

"Look," Casper said. "I've come as close as I can to breaking all the rules—and believe me, that's not something I ever want to do again, so you know I'm real serious about this."

"About what?"

"Rethink saying no to Emma. She needs you."

"She needs someone," he said. "I'll help her find a traveling companion."

"You really are a nincompoop."

"Should the Ghost of Christmas Present talk that way?" Michael said.

"It's the twenty-first century, not the nineteenth. If someone had told Scrooge that years earlier, maybe the man wouldn't have been such a stuffed shirt."

"I'm not a stuffed shirt," Michael said, but he was speaking to the air. Casper—and the candles—were gone. The only thing that remained was the glass of water.

Michael took a sip. The water was the crispest, cleanest, clearest water he had ever tasted. It was so good that it made him forget all about having a beer. It quenched his thirst almost immediately—

And then the glass vanished too.

"Hey," Michael shouted at the ceiling, just as Casper had done a moment earlier. "I was enjoying that!"

But he got no answer. And, after a moment, he

stretched out on his bed, to think about all he had seen. He closed his eyes, and within seconds, he fell asleep.

———⟡———

Michael woke up, his entire body tense. Something was wrong; he could feel it. His stomach twisted. It was happening again.

He opened his eyes to find sunlight across his bed. His body was tense because he had fallen asleep with his back on the bed and his feet on the floor. He wasn't wearing a nightshirt—and there was no flannel nightcap on the blanket beside him. His feet were bare. The robe was where he had left it when he went to bed, and his slippers were tucked near the bed on the clean hardwood floor.

A dream. It had all been a dream. A very realistic dream, but a dream nonetheless.

Still, he scooted up on the bed, moved a pile of books and picked up the phone's receiver. No more English thespians reciting Dickens. Instead, he heard the blessedly familiar sound of a dial tone. He never thought that noise would fill him with such joy.

He snatched his robe off the nearby chair, and then went to the window. It opened with no effort at all. It hadn't been glued shut—or painted shut—or magicked shut. It worked just like it always had.

A young boy zoomed by on his skateboard and Michael resisted the urge to call out to him.

Boy! What day is this!

Michael grinned. He wondered if the British accent he always picked up when he was in England would have returned this morning. But the boy rolled on by, and Michael missed his chance to test it.

He wasn't Scrooge, after all, and this wasn't Christmas morning, and he hadn't seen a large goose in the window of a shop down the street.

Fortunately. He would have to wonder about his sanity if he did.

He felt an odd, unfamiliar kind of euphoria. Emma was still alive—no death in the desert for her—and that talking cat (amazing how such things made sense in dreams!) was just a figment of his overwrought imagination. Everything was fine. He was in Madison, it was May, and he'd had the strangest nightmare of his life.

And it was over now. The nightmare, not his life. Odd how some dreams were so very vivid and others faded away the moment a man woke up.

He turned around, still feeling giddy, and froze in place, staring at his baseball bat. It wasn't in his closet. It was leaning against the wall, just behind the door, exactly where he had set it when the little man had entered his bedroom.

"Sleepwalking," he murmured. That was the only explanation. Or at least, the only explanation he'd accept.

Because if he believed he had a nocturnal visitor, he'd have to believe that somehow Emma Lost would be—well, lost—without him. And he couldn't believe that. He wouldn't believe that. Any more than he would believe that Grumpy was really named Casper, and was the Ghost of Christmas Future masquerading as the Ghost of Christmas Present.

It was too ridiculous. And Michael Found wasn't a man who tolerated the ridiculous in any way.

Chapter 6

FOR THE FIFTH TIME, SHE HELD UP HER FAVORITE shawl, and for the fifth time, she set it back on the bed. Emma stared at it, the white lace too ethereal for a chilly Oregon day, but perfect for a cool Midwestern evening. She had bought the shawl to wear in Madison, and she had done so. She couldn't imagine wearing it in Portland.

She sighed. If she needed it, she supposed, she could probably spell it to Portland. Or have Aethelstan do so. The rules didn't prevent him from bringing her stuff to him. Just her.

Darnell perched on the pillow, watching her through slit eyes. He was too disturbed to even pretend he was asleep. He had been through this before—the trip out to Madison had been a nightmare, and she had promised him he would never have to endure a long car trip again.

Now she was breaking that promise.

She picked up the lid of her largest cloth suitcase, and tried to close it over everything she had packed. It looked impossible. She glanced at Darnell, wondering if he would weigh it down for her, but he closed his eyes completely.

Whoever said that cats didn't have opinions had never really watched one.

She sat on top of the suitcase and worked the zipper closed. Then she tugged the suitcase off the bed, and let it thump onto the floor. Thank whatever technological god there was that someone had put wheels on suitcases. She had no idea how people would have survived without that particular invention.

Then she brushed off her hands and stared at her bedroom. It looked as if someone had raided it. Pictures were missing, and so was her jewelry case. A few drawers on her dresser still stood open, revealing only bits of thread and sachets inside. A hanger still swung back and forth in her empty closet, and an abandoned pair of shoes tumbled against each other like unwanted children.

She was leaving all her furniture here, and bundling the house up tight. She had given her key to one of her closer friends, and had received a promise that the friend would check the house once a week in good weather— and every day in stormy. That was the best she could do.

She wheeled the suitcase to the front door, next to the rest of the luggage set, Darnell's cat bed—which he hated and never used, but always insisted on having with him—several of her favorite blankets, her pillow, and a cooler full of food. Her cell phone sat on top of the pile, along with its cord and recharger. Her computer was back in its box, her disks in another box. Her research for her next book was in a third box, and the novels she had planned to read this summer—before the magic struck—were in yet another box.

Fortunately her car was pretty large. She had no idea how she would have gotten this stuff into something small.

She went into the kitchen and pulled out the cans of Darnell's food, along with his water dish and bowl. On impulse, she took her favorite coffee mug out of the cabinet. Then she stared out the kitchen window at her garden.

She wouldn't get to see how spring eased into summer. She had watched the other seasons turn, but she would miss this one, and it was the most important. She wouldn't see which of her strange Midwestern plants blossomed into flowers, and which had only green leaves. She wouldn't see how the yard looked in the height of its color.

She leaned her head against the glass. It felt cool against her skin—little comfort for what she was feeling. The pit of her stomach churned. The Fates had told her to bring someone with her, not to trust Darnell alone, and she was defying them. Not on purpose, but because she had no other choice.

Emma hoped they would forgive her.

From the counter, she grabbed a box of tuna-flavored cat treats. She was going to try her first intentional spell. Darnell had to speak, and he had to understand the countermanding words she was going to teach him.

She hoped this would work. Because if it didn't, she had no idea what she was going to do.

He couldn't help himself. Michael grabbed an apple for breakfast and left his house through the kitchen door. He was lying to himself, and he knew it. He swore he was walking toward Emma Lost's because it was a beautiful spring morning and he needed the exercise. But what he was really doing was reassuring himself that she was going to be all right.

The neighborhood was quiet. Most people were still inside, preparing for their day. He could hear the traffic on University Avenue a few blocks away, but no cars turned down their quiet street.

He had moved to this part of the city because the thick trees and twisty streets had appealed to him. The center of campus was more than two miles away, which he felt was perfect. He could walk there on warm days, and on cold or rainy days, drive without the least bit of guilt.

Guilt, which was what he was experiencing now. And he hadn't even done anything.

Emma Lost's house was the twin to his, a coincidence that had bothered him when he first figured it out. He had always imagined that a couple with no sense of history would buy that house. After all, the previous owners had gutted the interior in the 1960s, long after Frank Lloyd Wright had designed the place. They had removed the stone fireplace and put in a modern one. They had taken out the sloping patio wall, and the built-in furniture, and they had changed the kitchen. He had seen that house first, and felt like it was a masterpiece that had been defaced. He couldn't imagine living inside it.

Yet, Emma Lost had. That was enough to prove to him that she had no real respect for history, for all that people had lost throughout the years. She was young, impulsive, and difficult, and he couldn't imagine rearranging his life to take her to Oregon just because he had had a bad dream.

As he approached the house, he saw a car in her driveway. The car's trunk was open and suitcases filled it. The car was silver—the same silver he'd seen in the dream.

The hair on the back of his neck rose. Coincidence, he told himself. He had seen her car before. It had registered in his subconscious, but not his conscious, and he had brought it forth in that silly dream.

As he got closer, he realized that the car was a BMW—one of the larger, newer models. She had probably purchased it with the money from her bestselling book.

The thought made him pause. *Was* he jealous of her as she had insisted? He'd never had a bestselling book, and he'd put more work into his. His history was accurate. Hers was based on—well, magic at best, imagination at worst.

Imagination. She was certainly affecting his. The next thing he'd probably see would be a talking black house cat, sitting in the front seat, waiting for his mistress to drive him on his next adventure.

Michael reached the stone wall that divided Emma's property from her neighbor's. The car's trunk was nearly full, and the back was stuffed as well. He saw a catbed in its own place on the seat, with an untipable travel water dish and a small container of cat food in the window. A cat box was on the floor.

Goose bumps rose on his arms.

More coincidences. He knew she was leaving, he had seen the cat before, and it was logical that she'd take him with her.

He stepped around the car, peering in the side. Blankets, a cooler, and a pillow. That would help. The car seemed like it was in good shape—

The front door banged, and Michael whirled, feeling guilty for peering into Emma's car. But the guilt left immediately, replaced by a something that felt closer to terror.

A big, black lion bounded out the door, its golden eyes frantic. It saw Michael, growled, and ran across the street. Emma hurried to the door, yelling, "Darnell! Darnell, stop!"

But the lion continued, plowing through the neighbor's roses and roaring in pain.

Emma started across the street. Michael peeled himself off the side of the car, and blinked, wondering if he should call animal control.

Emma reached the roses and stopped. "Darnell!" she said, and there were tears in her voice. "I'm sorry, really. I didn't mean to do this. I was trying to—"

"I know what you were trying to do!" A deep, male voice rumbled from the lilacs beside the neighbor's house. "It didn't work!"

"I'm sorry—"

"Sorry isn't good enough," the voice said. Michael was holding his breath. He knew that voice. He'd heard it in his dream the night before. It was the cat's voice.

The cat she had called Darnell.

Casper had called him Darnell, too.

That was one coincidence too many. Michael started across the street.

"Darnell, please. I can't leave you here, and if you stay like that, then something will happen to you. Remember that Katharine Hepburn movie we saw? *Bringing Up Baby*. The one with the lion?"

"It wasn't a lion. It was a leopard." Darnell sounded as contrary in real life as he did in dreams.

"It doesn't matter," Emma said. "They had some people come after the cat and tie it up and take it to a circus."

"There aren't many circuses anymore," Michael said as he stopped beside her.

Emma jumped so high that he wondered if she'd ever tried out for women's basketball. When she landed, she glanced up at him. He smiled, showing a calmness he didn't exactly feel.

"What she's trying to tell you, Darnell, is that if anyone sees a lion in this neighborhood, they're going to call animal control. If they discover that you're a black lion—which, I believe, has never occurred before in nature—they're going to study you and dissect you and—"

"I'll be famous. I've watched enough television. They'll make me a celebrity." He actually sounded pleased by this.

Michael frowned. A cat was a cat was a cat. Wasn't that the point of the dream last night? That the cat had behaved according to its feline nature, not common sense?

"They'll force you to go on tour, parade you in front of people when you want a nap—"

"Pet me, worship me, feed me anything I want."

"No," Michael said. "That would be if you were still a house cat. But you're a lion. People are afraid of lions. They'll cage you, subdue you with a chair."

"And a whip," Emma said a little too eagerly.

"I thought you said there were no more circuses." Darnell's voice held suspicion.

"I said there aren't that many. But that means there are a few. Why, just an hour from here, in Baraboo, is the Barnum and Bailey Circus Museum, a tribute to the most famous circus of all."

"We saw that driving here last fall, Darnell, remember?" Emma said. "I pointed it out to you."

The cat cursed. The words were filled with invective, and had something to do with mice butts, bird beaks, and teeny tiny brains. Then he came out of the bushes.

Lilac petals covered his large back, making him look as if he had gained purple and white spots. He padded forward on his big paws, looking very uncomfortable. The mane changed the look of his face, but the gold eyes were the same ones Michael had seen the night before.

Darnell walked up to Michael, then sat. "I don't like you, pal. You were going to leave me last night."

"Last night?" Emma asked.

Michael sighed. The final confirmation, not that he needed it. Damn Casper. Damn Emma. Damn them all. This wasn't his business. "Casper told me to."

"*Casper* is an idiot," Darnell said.

"Casper?" Emma asked.

"Don't ask," Michael said.

"Look," Darnell said. "I can handle it from here. I got the message of the damn dream. I'll say the words on time and in the right order—"

"You didn't say them in the right order?" Michael asked.

"They don't make a lot of sense," the lion said. "I'm fluent in English because I have to listen to it all the time, but I draw the line at Norse or whatever the hell that is."

"What is?" Emma asked. "What's going on? Why are you talking to my cat?"

"Because he's talking to me," Michael said.

"We don't need you," Darnell said. "She and I will be just fine."

"That's not what Casper said."

"*Casper* lies," Darnell said.

"That's what he says about you."

The lion snorted. "Then why didn't he tell you his real name?"

"He didn't want to," Michael said.

"What *is* this?" Emma asked.

"This idiot thinks he's your hero," Darnell said.

"No." The word came out of Michael's mouth quickly, although he wasn't sure if that was because he objected to being called a hero or being called an idiot by a lion who used to be a house cat.

"I don't understand," Emma said.

"It doesn't matter," Michael said.

"It does to me!" Darnell growled the words. "You left me to die."

"I've never met you before."

"Yes, you did. Last night."

"And Casper told you that wasn't real."

"Casper who?" Emma asked.

Michael ran a hand through his hair. This wasn't going at all like he had planned. "I thought you needed help getting to Oregon."

Emma straightened her spine. "I have help."

"Darnell? He won't fit in your car."

"He will in a minute."

"That's what she said fifteen minutes ago," Darnell said. "I hate being this big. I don't fit into my bed."

"You have never liked that bed," Emma said.

"But it's mine," Darnell said.

She shook her head. "I'll fix it."

"That's what you've been saying—"

"Stop!" Michael raised his hands. How did one woman create so much chaos? Everything else in his life seemed orderly compared with her. "Do you have any human help?"

"Oh, so now he's a bigot," Darnell said.

Michael felt his face grow warm. Maybe he would strangle that cat... when Emma got him back to the proper size.

"What business is it of yours?" Emma asked.

"None," Michael said. "Except that—"

"Tell her," Darnell said. "Tell her you had to be convinced by a magical dwarf to help her. Tell her—"

She turned toward Darnell. "Merlin was here?"

"Merlin?" Michael asked. "That was *the* Merlin?"

"Yes, but he's pretty different from the one in the Arthurian myth," Emma said.

"Casper is Merlin?"

"Don't let it twist your tail," Darnell said. "We have other problems."

"If Merlin was here," Emma said, "why didn't he see me?"

Darnell sighed as only a cat could. Then he laid down and put his large head on his paws. "All yours, pal."

"I don't know. I didn't believe he was here until this morning when I saw—" Michael sighed too. He didn't know how to go on with this. "Well, what matters is that he said you had no help."

"I. Have. Darnell." Emma's eyes were flashing. Michael had no idea why she was getting so angry.

"Human help," he said.

"I don't see what business it is of yours."

"You made it my business," Michael said.

"Oh?"

"When you asked me. Apparently that set some sort of cosmic prophecy in motion."

"A prophecy?"

"He wasn't supposed to say no," Darnell said from

the ground. "Are we ever going to work on changing me back to normal?"

"In a minute, Darnell," Emma said. "I want to know about this prophecy."

"I don't know much about it," Michael said. "Except that I'm suppose to go with you. Do you still want my company?"

His stomach twisted as he asked the question, but he wasn't sure if that was because he wanted to go or he wanted her to say no.

She studied him for a moment. He couldn't read what was in her blue-gray eyes.

"Decide this, dammit," Darnell said. "I'm getting hungry. And this mane itches."

Emma put her hands on her hips. Michael had the strangest sensation that she was about to say no. What would he do then? Force her to take him with her? On the strength of a dream and a talking cat?

"Look," Darnell said. "If I have to be this size to talk, you aren't going to fit me in the car."

"He doesn't normally talk?" Michael asked.

"Not in English," Emma said.

"Well then, change him back."

Her eyes flashed again. "That's so easy for you to say. As if I can snap my fingers and change him back. As if a simple little twitch of the nose makes things all better. You watch too much TV, Michael. If I could just fix this, you'd think I would have done it already, wouldn't you?"

"No," Darnell said.

Michael looked at the lion in surprise. "She hasn't?"

"Of course not. She's up there moaning that it went

all wrong and she says that stupid reverse spell, which only seems to work capriciously and then—"

"Shut up!" Emma said and clapped her hands together. The clap turned into a clap of thunder and light ricocheted off everything. And when it was over, Michael found himself staring at a pudgy black house cat, lying regally on the lawn.

"Meeeeoow," Darnell said, and Michael could have sworn that the cat grinned. Then he ran across the street—without looking both ways—and up the stairs to Emma's house.

"It's not usually that easy," she said, glancing at Michael. Then she ran across the street after Darnell. She opened the door to the house and they both went inside, leaving Michael standing in the neighbor's lawn, next to the ruined rose bushes.

He shook his head. Had she turned him down? Or ignored him? And then he realized that he had really offered to go with her. Oh, that would make his life easier. He'd just come back from England for a new job. How would he explain this?

And how would he live with himself if he backed out again? He'd have to be dumb not to accept all the confirmation he was receiving that magic was real.

He sighed and started across the street after Emma and her obnoxious cat. He'd make this work. Somehow.

~~~

Emma closed the door and leaned on it. The house already felt abandoned—and she hadn't hardly taken anything out of it. Darnell had gone to his rug in front of the fireplace. There was no fire burning, but that didn't seem to bother him. He began cleaning himself, picking the lilac petals off as if they were contaminating him. She could tell from the methodical way that he worked his fur that he was very distressed.

Well, she wasn't that happy either. She had resigned herself to traveling alone, and then Michael Found agreed to go with her. Because of Merlin.

She crossed her arms. It would be best if he went along. He was, as Aethelstan had pointed out, the best choice. But the illogical, irrational, angry part of her wanted nothing to do with him. She had a hunch he wasn't going because he wanted to, but because he felt obligated to.

At that moment, he knocked on the door behind her. She could feel the strength of the knock through the wood.

Emma sighed. She needed his help, and she couldn't afford to be proud about it. Somehow she would have to maintain her dignity through all of this—what was left of her dignity. After all, the man had seen her at her most out of control.

She pulled the door open.

"What?" she asked, knowing she was being ungracious and difficult and not really caring. It had taken a visit from a friend—and something so severe that Darnell had thought he was dying—to get Michael to help her.

"I would like to come with you to Oregon," he said. "That is, if you'll have me."

He actually looked nervous. She couldn't tell if that was because he felt forced to go and was afraid she'd say yes or if he wanted to go and was afraid she'd say no.

"All right," she said. "You can come."

He looked surprised. His mouth opened and closed and opened again.

Behind her, Darnell growled. She blocked the door with her body so there'd be no repeat Pizza Guy attack. The last thing she needed was for Michael to change his mind again.

Chapter 7

THEY LEFT A LOT LATER THAN EMMA HAD PLANNED. One whole day later.

It turned out that the offer to accompany her was a spur-of-the-moment thing for Michael. He had to ask for an emergency leave of absence (which, he was told, was only possible because it was the end of the Spring Semester, and none of the administration wanted to spend any time in the office during the break), then he had to pack, and then they had to fight over whose car to take.

Emma won the fight simply by refusing to remove her possessions from her car. In the end, he acquiesced—on the condition that she bring an extra set of car keys. She didn't have any, and so she had to get some made.

She had a hunch this trip was going to be a lot uglier than she had originally thought.

Darnell was relegated to the already crowded back-seat. He actually sat on his cat bed because he refused to be inside his cat carrier, which would be safer. Even though Darnell had lost his ability to speak English, he still had the ability to communicate. A cross-country trip in a cat carrier, his eyes and posture said, would be the equivalent of six days in hell.

Emma was beginning to think she had volunteered for six days in hell too. Michael had wanted to drive. He had asked her how many years of driving experience she had—and she hadn't told him the truth. That would have made him insist on driving. Instead, he had compared their driving experience and had deemed himself the most competent.

She had to haul out the old, tired, and perfectly un-reasonable argument to keep her position in the driver's seat. It was her car. She had the right to drive it any-where she wanted.

And she really wanted to drive it nowhere.

They pulled out of Madison at seven a.m. The ghastly early hour had been Michael's idea, to make up for the time he had cost her the day before. He had stayed up late, pouring over maps, trying to find the shortest route from Wisconsin to Oregon, and he had finally decided on what he called "the Northern route," taking I-90 through Minnesota, South Dakota, Wyoming, and Montana on the way to Oregon.

She had wanted to take I-80, which was flatter and easier, except for crossing the Rocky Mountains in Wyoming. She had never been to Utah or Nebraska, and she wanted to see both places.

Michael had told her that neither were worth her time.

That had angered her even more—who was he to determine what was worth her time?—and then he con-fessed that he had an irrational fear of deserts.

She looked at the map and said there were no deserts between Oregon and Wisconsin, and he'd said she only thought that because she hadn't driven the I-80 route. The last part, whether she went through Idaho or through Nevada, included desert.

She couldn't argue with an irrational fear of deserts any more than he could argue that she could drive be-cause it was her car. She decided they had reached a stalemate, which was about as good as she could hope for at the beginning of the trip.

What she really hoped was that the stalemate would last through the rest of the trip.

Michael slept through the first two hours of the trip. He tilted his head back on the leather seat, closed his eyes, and almost snored. Darnell fell asleep rather quickly too, and there was no almost to his snoring. The cat was a regular brass band, complete with tuba, when it came to the noises he made.

So Emma leaned back in her seat, turned on WORT softly, and listened to the alternate music voice of her home for the last time in a while. The early morning sunlight made the interior of her car look white and she wished that the tension in her shoulders would fade so that she could just enjoy the drive.

The rolling hills and farmland, the developers' signs, the trucks and cars all around her, seemed very distant from her. She was trying to memorize them.

At least this time when she had to leave her chosen home, she knew it. The first time, she'd fallen into a coma and awakened so far away from her home that she could never, ever go back.

Except for a flash a few days ago.

She glanced over her shoulder at the sleeping Michael. He looked younger in his sleep than he did when he was awake. The worry lines left his face, smoothing his skin and making him seem as young as the students he taught. He was a very, very handsome man, more hand-some than she had realized.

And he was sacrificing a lot to come with her.

She hadn't asked him what Merlin had said, but it must

have been convincing. Not even Darnell complained a lot that Michael was coming along. And Darnell, by rights, should have been hissing, biting, scratching, and yowling—especially after accusing Michael of having no regard for his—Darnell's—welfare.

She lost the radio station as she turned toward LaCrosse, and had to pick up Wisconsin Public Radio. The music she'd been listening to had become *Morning Edition*—lots of news and chat that really didn't concern her. But at that moment, the driving got hairy— apparently Michael's wonderful plan to leave early meant that they would hit LaCrosse at the end of morning rush hour, so Emma had to swerve and use the brake and stop and start a lot more than she had planned—so she couldn't fiddle with the radio.

All that driving made Michael snort, but didn't wake him up. Darnell on the other hand was awake and sitting up. Emma could see him in the rearview mirror.

"Not a word from you," she said, and was a bit surprised when Darnell laid back down and sighed. She had toyed with trying to spell him again for speech, just as a backup, but Darnell had run from her when she mentioned it.

She had taken that as a resounding no.

Michael made her write all the instructions down and he had taken the piece of paper home with him the night before. She hadn't seen it at all this morning.

Big green signs told her she was approaching the Mississippi River. There was a view wayside ahead and, after the rush-hour traffic, she was ready for a break.

She had learned on her first cross-country drive that the best thing to do was take the drive in short bursts.

She pulled off the road under the shade of several trees. There were some Winnebagos on the truck and trailer side of the wayside, but no other cars. As she stopped the car, Michael sat up.

"Where're we?" he asked blearily.

"The Mississippi." She unbuckled her seat belt and opened the car door. A rush of cool morning air came inside. It smelled of river water and flowers.

He rubbed a fist over his eyes like a little boy. "Is everything all right?"

"Yep." She got out, and then opened Darnell's door, snapping his leash on his collar with a movement so co-ordinated she even surprised herself. Darnell looked up at her with complete fury at the indignity, but he clearly re-membered the routine from the last trip. All of them would rather have him use the great outdoors than the catbox she'd managed to squeeze onto the floor in the backseat.

"Why don't you get some water and the morning buns on top of the cooler?" she asked Michael. Morning buns were her weakness. They were the specialty of a restaurant on the near westside named the Ovens of Brittany. At least once a week, she'd stopped there and picked up morning buns for her breakfast at home.

She'd miss that too.

"I still don't get why we stopped," he muttered as he fumbled with the seat belt.

Emma frowned at him. He'd be second-guessing her for the entire trip. She slipped her keys into the pocket of her jeans and closed the car door.

Darnell had to sniff each blade of grass before mov-ing to the next little patch. It was going to take forever to reach the railing with the view of the river below. So she picked up her cat and tucked him under her arm as she walked to the view site.

This time, Darnell hissed and spit and yowled. He kicked his chubby little legs and growled at her.

"I'm not impressed," she said. She almost made a comparison, then caught herself. The last thing she needed was a repeat of yesterday morning's incident.

She glanced over her shoulder. Michael was still struggling with his seat belt. She grinned. So much for male superiority over technological gadgets. And she hadn't even been born in this millennium. Her grin widened.

Darnell dug a claw into the soft skin of her belly and made her wince. She set him down, keeping a firm grip on his leash. He began sniffing anew, looking up with irritation at all the grass he'd missed.

She'd have to keep an eye on him. She knew from experience that he liked to chomp grass and vomit in the car just to annoy her.

The river sang beneath her. The Mississippi was wide and flat here, carving through bluffs that looked relatively untouched. She knew they weren't, though. The view that she was standing on proved that.

She wondered what the river had looked like when she was born. A trickle? A mighty overgrown torrent? There was no way for her to know, and no way historians like Michael would know either. History on this continent wasn't kept as well as it had been in England.

Finally, she heard footsteps behind her. Darnell looked up from his little grass feast and started to growl.

"Poor cat," Michael said with more compassion than Darnell deserved. "Looks like he gets carsick."

"What?" Emma said, turning around.

"Cats eat grass when their stomach is upset. You want some water, big guy?"

Darnell had been watching Michael warily. When Michael crouched and offered him some water, Darnell turned away, apparently embarrassed that his secret was out.

"You mean he doesn't do that to annoy me?" Emma asked.

"He might, knowing how contrary he can be, but it isn't likely. Did he travel with you before?"

She nodded.

"And threw up a lot?"

"A lot wouldn't describe it."

"I bet he didn't eat much either."

"Not until we got to our hotel for the night."

Michael nodded. "I'll get him a bowl."

He handed her the bottles of water and the bag with the morning buns and headed back to the car. Darnell had stopped eating grass and growling. Instead he was looking up at Emma with the most shocked expression she had ever seen on a cat's face.

She shrugged. "I had no idea he specialized in cats."

Darnell gave a soggy burp and sat down, watching Michael as if he were a lifesaver. She wasn't sure how she felt about that. She rather enjoyed Darnell's hostility toward Michael. It helped her keep her distance.

Michael got Darnell's water bowl, poured out the water in it, and brought it over. Then he poured in some bottled water and set it in front of Darnell.

"Drink," he said. "You'll feel better. And we'll keep the window open just a little too. It'll get that new car smell out and you'll be surprised how much better you feel."

Emma's eyes narrowed. "Why are you doing this?"

Michael grinned up at her. "I used to get carsick when I was a kid. It's not a pleasant way to travel."

Darnell was staring at him in wonder. After a moment, he bent his shiny black head and began to drink.

Michael stood up. He came over to the rail and drank out of his bottle. "Haven't you ever been carsick?"

She thought back to her very first ride in a car, before she even knew what a car was. Car terrified, but never carsick. "No."

"Ah, one of the lucky ones, then. My dad smoked, and we always had one of those pine air fresheners up front. The combined smell was bad enough to turn my stomach on a short trip. On a long one…" He shook his head.

"On a long one what?" She wedged her bottle against her stomach and tried to twist off the top with one hand. Darnell's leash was making the work difficult.

"Well, what I remember most about long trips was lying in the backseat, listening to baseball games, and staring at the clouds of smoke surrounding my father's head. If I try real hard, I can even recall the queasy feeling."

She frowned at him. He painted a vivid image—one that was so alien to her that she couldn't imagine growing up like that. Of course, she had never thought about the way modern adults had been as children. No one had ever discussed it with her.

"What?" he said. "What did I say?"

"Nothing." Apparently her expression hadn't been what he expected. "I hadn't realized you were an only child."

He shrugged. "Well, now you do."

Darnell walked over her foot and put his head

between the iron bars of the railing, staring at the water below. Emma tightened her grip on the leash. The last thing she wanted to do was lose Darnell because he got too curious.

But her tightened hold on the leash made opening the bottle impossible. After a moment, Michael took the bottle from her, twisted off the cap, and handed the bottle back.

"Thanks," she said.

"I couldn't stand watching it anymore."

She flushed. What was it about this man that made her feel chronically embarrassed?

Darnell's tail flicked back and forth as if something below had caught his attention. Emma wrapped the leash around her wrist.

Michael reached into the sack and took out a morning bun. He offered it to her, saw she had no available hand, and said, "I guess this one's mine because I'm not going to feed you."

She took another drink of water, not wanting to answer that. He munched beside her, and they both stared at the river. The silence was even more awkward than Emma had imagined a silence could be.

Darnell crouched, his tail still flicking.

Emma picked him up, and he thrashed, trying to see what was below. "I guess we're going to back to the car," she said.

"No," Michael said. "We're not."

He led her to a picnic table, and then took Darnell from her. The leash was still wrapped around her wrist, and she was tugged in the same direction as the cat.

Michael set Darnell down, and Darnell immediately

lunged toward the railing again. "You need to teach him some discipline."

"He's a cat," Emma said.

"That's no excuse," Michael said. "Why do people always assume that cats are not intelligent enough to learn discipline?"

"We don't," Emma said. "They are too intelligent to listen to anyone else's instructions."

"Even when it saves lives?"

Darnell looked up at him and growled.

"Hey, pal. I'm not the one who has poor impulse control." Michael pulled off a bit of morning bun and handed it to Darnell. Darnell forgot all about the iron railing and whatever lurked below, and swallowed the piece whole.

"I try not to feed him people food," Emma said.

"Yeah," Michael said sarcastically. "I can tell."

She sighed and grabbed a bun for herself. It was a cross between a cinnamon roll and a sugared donut, only with a light and fluffy French pastry feel. She took a bite and relished the taste, knowing she wouldn't find it anywhere else.

"You know," Michael said after he had eaten the last bite of his, "I hope you're not planning to eat all our meals at waysides. We really should stop at restaurants and sample some local cuisine."

"What about Darnell?" Emma asked.

"What about him?"

"We can't very well bring him inside a restaurant."

"No, but many places have take out or they let you eat outside." Michael grinned. "At worst, we could tell them he's a seeing eye cat. That leash might convince them."

She wouldn't smile. She didn't want him to think he was amusing. "There are stores along the way. I'm sure we can make do."

"I don't want to make do," he snapped.

"Well, I can't imagine the local cuisine would vary much from Wisconsin to Oregon."

He frowned at her. "You mean you don't know?"

She raised her chin, trying to ignore the funny panic in her stomach. For some reason she felt as if another embarrassing moment were on the way, and she didn't know why.

"That's right," she said. "I don't know."

"Didn't you drive that lovely car out here? Or did you buy it in Madison?"

"I drove," she said. "I had to. I had Darnell."

"People fly with cats."

"Not Darnell."

Darnell had wrapped his leash around her legs and had fallen asleep between her feet. For the first time in her memory, he didn't spend all of their rest stop eating grass.

"You drove all the way out and you never ate at a restaurant?"

She shrugged. "It wasn't practical."

"Well, we're changing that."

She straightened. "No, we're not."

"Emma, I'm not going clear across country and eating from 7-11s all the way."

"It'll change to Circle K's long about Montana."

"Whatever," he said. "I'm not."

She took a deep breath. "But what if my magic goes off in a restaurant? What'll we do then?"

"Make it better," he said. "Isn't that why I'm here?"

"It doesn't always go back the way it was," she said.

He grinned. "Then we'll beat a hasty retreat."

She glanced at the river. He was changing everything. Didn't he know that routine made trips easier? Didn't he understand that the less change the better?

"If you're so worried about that," he said, "why are we staying in hotels along the way? Where's the tent?"

"I don't own a tent," she said between her clenched teeth.

"One of those women too good to own a tent?"

She glared at him. "I've stayed in very primitive conditions, thank you."

"What? A place with no blow-dryers?"

She let out a small sigh. She wasn't about to tell him everything. "Something like that."

"Then what's wrong with a tent?"

"I like beds," she said. "And showers, believe it or not."

"Why should that be hard for me to believe?" he said. "I hadn't noticed that you had a problem bathing."

Her flush grew deeper. In every conversation she said the wrong thing. He didn't know that she used to be afraid of running water, that plumbing was nearly her undoing on the day she had awakened from her magic coma.

"Was I supposed to notice?" he asked with a little too much amusement.

She grabbed the morning bun bag and tucked her water bottle under her arm. "Get Darnell's stuff," she said. "I'll meet you in the car."

"Emma—"

"I don't need you hassling me," she snapped and started forward. Only then did she remember that Darnell's leash was wrapped around her legs. She tripped, caught herself, and dropped the bottle. Water splashed all over Darnell, whom she had apparently dragged along behind her.

He woke up, hissing and spitting, slapping the water bottle with both paws, and only succeeding to make himself wetter. He looked like a cat stuck in a ferocious battle with a vicious squirting hose.

Water alternately splashed and poured out of the bottle, depending on how hard Darnell whacked it, and Emma was getting drenched. Michael was making strange choking sounds that were too much like laughter for her tastes.

Finally she snatched the bottle out of the way, only to lose her grip on its slippery sides again, and watch it bounce toward Darnell. The cat hissed and backed up, wrapping the leash tighter around her legs. This time, she lost her balance and fell backwards into the soaking wet grass.

Michael stared at her for a moment, then offered her his hand. His expression was carefully neutral, the choking sounds he had been making a moment before gone.

Her eyes narrowed. The last thing she wanted to do was accept his help. Again.

Darnell shook himself off, spraying water all over Emma. Then he looked at her as if he were proud of himself, as if this had been all her fault.

The water was soaking through the seat of her jeans, and the leash was cutting off circulation in her left leg.

She looked at Michael's hand, then leaned over and snatched Darnell off the grass. Darnell's eyes widened in horror—and for a moment, she realized that he was afraid she was going to spell him. She had held him just like that the last time. Instead, she held his damp, squirmy body with one hand while untangling the leash with the other.

Michael continued to watch, his mouth twitching suspiciously. His hand was at his side, waiting, it seemed, for her to need its services again.

"Don't laugh at me," she snapped.

"I'm not laughing at you," he said, but it was clearly a lie.

"You are laughing at me," she said. "I don't like it."

"It was funny," he said.

"It was not," she said. "And you're being a jerk."

His eyes widened. "*I* am?"

"You are."

"Really," he said.

"Really. You're one oversized jerk."

His cheeks flushed. "That's what you think I'm doing," he said. "Being a jerk."

"Yes." She slapped the leash into Michael's hand. He looked at it like it hurt. It probably did.

She didn't care. She carefully set Darnell down, and stalked away from them both, trying to look dignified. She got a change of clothes from the car, and headed to the ladies room. She didn't look at either Michael or Darnell, but she knew they knew how mad she was.

As Aethelstan once said to her, her anger was hard to miss.

But she didn't care. Michael would just have to get used to her anger, like everybody else.

————⁓————

Michael managed to pull Darnell to the car where he dried both of them off with one of the towels Emma had so thoughtfully put in the back.

The cat didn't seem to mind his ministrations. In fact, the cat seemed as confused as he felt. He had actually felt close to Emma Lost for a moment, but clearly she hadn't felt close to him.

She came out of the ladies room wearing a pair of shorts that showed more leg than he had imagined she had. At that moment, a breeze came up, chilling him as much as a cold shower would have.

Thank heavens. He didn't want to ogle when he was mad at her.

She had actually accused him of being a jerk. When he had dropped everything to join her, a woman he barely knew.

"What was that about?" he asked as she approached the car.

"What?" she asked, her eyebrows raised, all innocence.

"That anger."

She shrugged and looked away. "I should have warned you. I have a terrible temper."

"No kidding," he said.

"It flares out of control and I can't—"

"Everything about you seems to be out of control, Emma." Michael stopped in front of her. "Your magic, your temper, your research."

He added that last because he knew it would piss her off. And, not surprisingly, it did.

"You shouldn't bring my research into this!" she said.

"No," he said, "I shouldn't. I'm sorry."

Her mouth was open as if she were going to continue berating him, but she stopped, narrowed her eyes and looked at him sideways, as if that would make her see him clearer.

"You shouldn't?" she asked as if she didn't trust him.

"I shouldn't. But someone let you get away with that temper much too often."

Her beautiful eyes narrowed.

"You act like a spoiled child."

"I do not."

"Do too.

"Do not."

"See? I haven't had that argument since grade school." Michael crossed his arms. "If you want me to continue on this trip—"

And as he said that Darnell's head popped out of the towel, his expression panicked. Apparently the cat wanted him to continue on this trip.

"—you're going to have to learn some control."

Emma crossed her arms over Darnell, trapping him against her. "Men always say that to me. Are you afraid of a woman with a temper?"

"Only a woman with an out-of-control temper and out-of-control magic," Michael said. "Somehow I have a hunch that's a bad combination."

He might have been wrong, but it looked to him as if the cat were nodding.

"You can't not go with me," Emma said.

"What?" Michael asked. "Why can't I?"

"Because you promised you'd help."

"I have helped. You're going a different route."

"You think that's enough?"

"Yes."

"And what if it isn't?"

He stared at her for a long time. "Maybe that's your problem."

"But you already said you'd stay."

"I did not."

"You said if I want you to continue on this trip. Sounds like that's my decision."

"Sounds like." Michael kept his voice deliberately flat.

Darnell was watching them both, his head whipping back and forth as if he were a referee in a tennis match.

"I want you to stay," she said.

"Then it's up to you. That temper stays under control."

"I'll lose my temper if I want to," Emma said.

"Fine," Michael said. "You'll do it alone."

Darnell raised his head, his eyes imploring.

"And I'll take the cat," Michael said. "Then you won't have anyone to inflict that temper on."

He reached for Darnell who crawled toward him like a whipped dog. The cat was a bad actor, but effective. Emma clutched at him as if her life depended on it.

"You can't take him. He's my familiar!"

"Why would it matter?" Michael asked. "Your magic is out of control. What difference would a familiar make?"

"He'd keep it from harming anyone."

Michael looked at Darnell. "Do you believe that?"

Darnell shook his head and pawed at Michael's arm.

"You can't take my cat!" Emma said, sounding panicked.

"I can and I will," Michael said. "He doesn't deserve this any more than I do. In fact, I think after that lion stunt, he's suffered enough."

Darnell was still pawing at his arm. Emma clung to the cat.

"You're going to make me beg, aren't you?" she said, and it seemed as if her temper was about to flare again.

"No," Michael said. "I'm just asking you to show the same kind of self-restraint most grown-ups use."

"I'm not a child," she hissed. "I'm older than you."

"I doubt it," he said.

"I am," she said. "Much older. That's why I'm having this problem."

"Of an out-of-control temper? That's a child's problem, not an adult's."

"No!" And then she tilted her head back as if she had said something she shouldn't have. "Please, Michael. Don't take Darnell. Stay."

She was begging, and it clearly embarrassed her. But he was angrier than he had thought he would be.

"All I'm asking, Emma, is that you control your temper." He made himself speak calmly.

"The thing is," she said softly, "I don't know if I can."

Michael looked at her. "You've never learned how to control your temper?"

She shook her head.

"You mean your parents let you run amok?"

"My parents..." She sighed. "Believe me, you wouldn't understand."

"Try me."

She reached across the distance between them and petted Darnell's head. The cat buried his face in the crook of Michael's arm.

"How about I say that I'll do my best to control my temper?"

"Not good enough," Michael said. "I didn't do anything except agree to accompany you across country. I'm doing you a favor. It would be polite if you remembered that."

He said that last with more force than he intended.

She looked up, her eyes wide with wonder. "You're mad."

"I guess so."

"Why can you lose your temper and I can't?" she asked.

"I haven't lost mine." *Yet*, Michael thought.

"Even though you're angry."

"Yes," he said. "Even though I'm angry."

"And you want me to be as bloodless as you."

That stopped him. Darnell tensed in his arms. Apparently she had meant that shot to see if he could control himself.

He made himself smile. "Even more bloodless. For the next few days, Emma, endeavor to be in a good mood."

Her eyes narrowed even farther. "You're just like Aethelstan."

"Who?"

"Aeth—the man I was promised to."

"Was?"

"Never mind," she said.

"What did he do?"

"Tried to take over my life!" she snapped.

"And that's why you ended the relationship?"

"Yes," she said.

Michael leaned as close to her as he could without dropping Darnell. "I don't want to take over your life. I want to get out of your life as quickly as possible. I want to get you to Oregon like I promised, with a minimum of fuss, and a minimum of grief."

Emma rolled her eyes. "Would it help to say I'm sorry?"

"No," he said.

She glared at him.

"Your choice, Emma," he said. "Do I stay or do I leave?"

She lowered her head and mumbled something.

"What?" he asked.

She frowned. "Stay."

"On my terms," he said.

"On your terms," she said.

Somehow her acquiescence didn't make him feel as good as he thought it would. He had an odd sense that he had just made the situation worse.

"Well, then," he said. "Let's get on the road. Is it my turn to drive?"

"It may never be your turn to drive," she muttered.

Michael grinned. For some reason, he was relieved that she hadn't called his bluff. Deep down, he hadn't wanted to leave.

And he wasn't sure why.

Chapter 8

EMMA CLOSED THE HOTEL ROOM DOOR AND LEANED ON it, the emergency exit instructions stabbing her in the middle of her spine. Darnell was in the center of the room, sniffing the floor as if he were memorizing it. Ahead of her, there was a queen-sized bed with an ugly green and blue spread, a dresser with a TV on top of it, and a table with two chairs. Her suitcase sat on the holder in the closet, and Darnell's litter box in the bathroom. His food and water dishes were under the table, and his oh-so-precious bed was beside the only upholstered chair in the room.

Finally. Privacy. She'd been thinking about it all day. How she needed time alone so that she could scream and kick and let out all that frustration from the argument that morning.

But now that she was here—in Sioux Falls, South Dakota, of all places—she was too tired to kick anything. She had no idea that reigning in her temper took so much energy. Her hands were sore from gripping the steering wheel hard. She had teeth marks on the inside of her cheeks from biting back comments—especially when the good professor changed the radio station away from the Brewers game to find *All Things Considered*— and her shoulders hurt from general tension.

The next few days were going to be the hardest of her life.

At least no magic had erupted today. So far.

She went into the bathroom and washed her face. When she had left the front desk, triumphantly holding her own key, Michael was still talking to the clerk about restaurants. His obsession with food would drive her insane. They had driven all over some small Minnesota town to find an authentic Norwegian restaurant for lunch, and the place smelled faintly of lutefisk, and had a buffet that looked as if it hadn't changed in decades.

Most of the foods were covered in gravies so thick she could hear her arteries clogging, and the only thing that passed for vegetables—at least that she recognized—was the relish tray the waitress had left on the table when she took the order.

That was not what Emma had had in mind when she agreed to Michael's food terms. But he had seemed like he was enjoying himself.

He had enjoyed himself since they crossed the Mississippi.

She used the thin terry-cloth washrag to wipe her face, pushing so hard that her skin was red. She hated being in the position of needing him more than he needed her.

Magic did that to her. Magic had done it to her before. When she had awakened from her coma, she had been at the mercy of Nora, Aethelstan, and all the other people who wanted to help her. She had needed their help, because she had no idea how to survive in this century.

Now she did know—information gained at great effort and cost—and she had to give up all her hard-won independence because her magic had come twenty years early.

She did owe Darnell an apology. She had never

treated him as badly as she had today. As she drove, listening to the damn news instead of the baseball game, she had wondered what really had gotten into her.

And what she kept coming back to was the warmth in Michael's gaze after she had slipped. He had been laughing—not at her, but fondly, the way a person did when he thought the joke was being shared with a friend.

She couldn't afford to be his friend. He was too good-looking for that. And she didn't like the way she felt around him.

So she got angry. It was easier than letting him get close.

She hung the washcloth on the shower bar, and dried off her face. No man could get close to her. She'd resigned herself to that long ago. So, if she were being honest with herself (and she saw no reason not to be) then she had to admit she had tried to anger Michael to keep him away from her. Far away from her.

She walked out of the bathroom to find Darnell sitting in front of the door connecting her room and Michael's. Darnell was staring at the door as if he could open it just with the power of his mind.

He had never pined for anyone like that before—except her.

"He's not coming in here," Emma said.

Darnell's ears twitched but he didn't move.

"We're going to have some privacy."

Darnell's ears went flat.

"I believe that you and I could use some time alone."

A shiver ran down Darnell's back. An elegant, on-purpose shiver.

She crouched. The damn cat was going to get her to apologize again. He was manipulating her worse than he usually did.

At that moment, someone knocked. At first she looked at the main door, the door to the hallway, but Darnell hadn't moved.

The knock came again. From the connecting door.

She sighed, and stood, her knees cracking as she did so. The man wasn't going to leave them alone.

"What?" she asked, hoping her tone would turn him away.

"I found us a really great restaurant. It's not far from here."

"I'm having room service," she said. "With Darnell."

"Good luck," Michael said. "The hotel's kitchen is closed for renovation."

Great. Well, if she had control of her powers, she'd sweep her arm over the place, finish the renovations, and fill the place with the best chefs possible.

If she had control over her powers. Which she decidedly did not.

She sighed. She was starving. The lunch buffet had annoyed her rather than fill her up.

"You know," Michael said, "it would be easier to talk through an open door."

"This thing is locked," Emma said sweetly. "You need a special key."

As she finished her sentence, she heard a key turn in the lock. Darnell's ears perked up and his tail twitched. Traitor. Had Nora felt like this when Darnell had switched his alliance from her to Emma?

Michael pushed the door open. He had put on a

different shirt—a blue one, which suited his blue eyes and blond hair. He smiled. Darnell walked up to him and rubbed on his leg.

Michael looked at her, eyebrows raised. "What did I do to deserve this?"

"It's probably what you didn't do," she said.

"True enough," Michael said. "Look, I'm hungry, and I'd like dinner, and I'd love it if you come along."

Darnell was winding his way around Michael's legs and purring so hard that no one—not even the desk clerk two buildings down—could miss his joy.

Little manipulator.

"What about Darnell?" she asked.

"What about him?"

"We can't just leave him here."

"Why not?"

"Because it's a strange place."

"A strange place with windows that don't open and a door that locks."

"That other people have a key to."

Michael stared at her for a moment. "You think someone will open this door and steal Darnell while we're at dinner."

She flushed again. Damn him. He twisted everything. "No," she said. "I think someone will open this door to do some maidly thing and Darnell will run through it, escaping into a strange world he's never seen before."

Amusement flickered across Michael's face—the same kind of amusement that had so angered her that morning. He was laughing at her again. He thought she was ridiculous.

Well, maybe she was, but Darnell—for all his quirks

and manipulations—had been her closest friend for ten years. Her best friend.

This time, though, Emma didn't say anything. And after a moment, Michael nodded.

"Here's what we'll do," he said. "You put a Do Not Disturb sign on the door, push the privacy button, and put on the chain lock, and then we'll leave through my room."

She was about to protest—after all the hotel had a key to the connecting door—when she realized she was just being silly. Yes, they had a key, but they had no reason to use it. Darnell would be safe.

"He howls when he's alone," she said.

"Leave the TV on. Someone'll think you're watching a bad movie."

She grinned. She couldn't help it. She had never had help with Darnell before.

"All right," she said.

Darnell sat down, ears back, glaring at her as if she had betrayed him yet again.

"Be good," she said to him, "and I'll bring you back something tasty."

He turned his head away. Finicky to the last.

"Ready?" Michael asked.

"Let me get my purse," she said.

Michael picked up Darnell, who didn't struggle, but who didn't look at him either. Emma put out the Do Not Disturb, double-locked the door, and turned on the television to some smash-'em-up cable movie with lots of explosions and car chases. That would drown out Darnell—at least for part of the evening.

Emma went through the connecting door. Michael

gently tossed Darnell inside her room, put his foot out to guard in case Darnell tried to escape, and closed the door.

They had done it.

On cue, a loud wail started behind the door.

"He always does that?" Michael said.

Emma nodded.

"Do me a favor," Michael said. "When we get back, stay in your room tonight. I don't want to break a cat's heart more than once a day."

She smiled back, and let herself out of Michael's room. Darnell's howls seemed softer in the hallway. Almost inaudible. Now, if there wasn't anyone in the room on the other side of her, she'd be just fine.

They walked to the car, and Michael got in the driver's side. She didn't protest. He was, after all, the one who had heard of the restaurant. Besides, she was more tired than she wanted to admit. Even though they hadn't gone as far as she had wanted to, they had still driven a pretty full day. Michael had felt it would be easier to find a hotel that took a cat in a city the size of Sioux Falls rather than in some place like Murdo or Pukwana. Emma knew from experience that he was right.

Now that they were off the highway, Emma was pleased to discover that Sioux Falls was a pretty city. Spring gave everything a nice green touch. Flowers, planted around every house and near every important building, added a riot of color.

Michael drove them past a number of Victorian homes, many of them painted bright colors. This was a city that would be lovely even in the winter. The Big Sioux River was as much a presence here as the lakes were in Madison. In fact, the mixture of colleges, universities, and growing private industry reminded Emma of her adopted home town. The side streets that Michael turned the car onto reminded her of State Street, with funky shops that catered to students, bookstores on every corner, and restaurants crammed together like strands in a loom.

She felt more at home here than she had thought possible.

Michael found a small parking place and somehow got the car to fit into it. Emma fished in her pocket for money to feed the parking meter, but Michael stopped her. Everything shut down here after six, apparently. Even the parking was free.

People rode by on bicycles and couples strolled down the sidewalk. A group of students sat on the sidewalk in front of a nearby café, drinking lattes and playing backgammon. A woman bent over another part of the sidewalk, long skirts trailing behind her as she made a chalk drawing on the concrete. Her hands were stained and her face was lined with chalk dust.

Michael went around the drawing instead of stepping over it like all the other pedestrians had. Emma was touched by his considerateness—considerateness that seemed to be something he did without any thought at all.

The restaurant he led her into wasn't as funky as the others. It called itself a brasserie, and it was done in rich woods. The tables were covered with linen cloths and, although there were students in the bar, the people farther inside seemed to be older—professors and business-people. Emma scanned the price list, and suddenly understood why.

Michael gave the maître d' his name, and they were immediately led to a table near the window. Through the lace curtains, Emma could see the street—with all its quirks. The maître d' gave them leather-bound menus, and then left so quickly that for a moment, Emma thought she had made him vanish.

"I didn't expect anything like this," she said.

"See why we couldn't bring Darnell?" Michael asked with a grin.

"Oh," she said, "put a bow-tie on him and he'd fit right in."

Michael grinned at her, then picked up the wine list that the maître d' had left behind. "Mind if I do the ordering?"

Emma looked at the list. Even though Aethelstan and Nora had tried to teach her about the finer points of wine, Emma felt that spirits were spirits were spirits. She had learned how to read, write, and do higher math; she had learned everything from world history to running a computer. She did not feel that she needed to know the difference between one company's cabernet and another's blush.

"Go ahead," she said.

Michael hadn't even noticed her hesitation. He bowed his head over the wine list, and contemplated it as if it held the secret to life.

Emma scanned the menu, found something that looked interesting, and then set the menu down. A waiter brought full water glasses made of crystal. Another waiter brought a basket of warm bread and a container filled with olive oil. A third waiter brought a small candle and made a ceremony of lighting it in front of her.

If Michael hadn't been studying the menu so intently—and if the other tables hadn't had the same details—Emma would have thought he had planned this, like a date.

She shook herself. How paranoid was she? It had taken some sort of dream—induced by Merlin—that Michael wouldn't explain to get him to accompany her. He had nearly threatened to leave that morning, and now she was thinking he liked her enough to date her?

It would never happen.

A fourth waiter came by—this one a woman, who wore a tuxedo that looked one size too small. She took Michael's wine order and vanished before Emma could order her meal.

Michael looked at her with amusement. Again. Was she entertainment for him? She hated that. And when she realized that it was his fond, amused look that brought up her ire, she clenched her fist again. She'd have fingernail holes in her palm before the evening was over.

"You know, we're not in any hurry," he said. "Darnell can handle an evening alone."

"I'm just not used to places like this," Emma lied. In truth, she used to eat in a restaurant like this one quite often. Aethelstan owned a place that was, in her opinion, much nicer than this one.

"Well," Michael said, leaning back in his chair. "I figure what's the point of traveling if you don't get to enjoy things?"

"The point of this trip is to get me to Oregon as quickly as possible."

"I suppose," he said. "But if we were really going to do that, we'd drive nonstop from here to there."

"Nonstop?" she said.

He nodded. "But I figure you're having enough

control problems as it is. I don't know anything about the magic you're dealing with, but if it's like anything else, it's harder to control when you're tired."

That was very astute of him. One of the first lessons she'd had as a girl—one of the only lessons she'd had—was on the importance of rest.

"It seems like we're doing all right so far," he said.

She held up her hand, too late to stop him from finishing the thought. "Don't jinx it."

"Yeah," he said. "I suppose the day's not over yet."

"The trip's only just begun. If we make it all the way with nothing happening, then I know someone's looking out for us."

His eyes brightened. "Do you think someone is?"

She shook her head. "It's not anyone's job."

"You mean like a guardian angel?"

She smiled. He was a mixture of sensibility and complete impracticality. "No. We don't have guardian angels. Not really. It would be against the rules."

"But your friend, Merlin? He said I could call him a guardian angel."

She sighed. "Yours maybe. You're mortal. But I think he was just saying that to make sure you wouldn't ask any more questions."

"Probably right," Michael said.

The waiter approached, a linen napkin over one arm, a bottle with a corkscrew in the other hand. Another waiter followed with a silver wine bucket, filled with ice.

Michael said nothing as the waiter went through the inexplicable ceremony concerning the wine. First the examination of the label, then the examination of the cork (Michael, Emma noted, was so sophisticated that he knew better than to sniff the silly thing), then the tasting of a small bit of wine. Emma had never known anyone to send wine back after that tasting, but she supposed it was possible. Then, with so much gravity that it seemed as if he were a judge approving a life sentence instead of a man approving a bottle of wine, Michael nodded.

The waiter poured two glasses, put the bottle in the bucket, and slipped off, not quite as discretely as the maître d', but close. Perhaps one didn't become a maître d' in a restaurant like this until he could vanish with appropriate discretion.

Michael was studying Emma. Her gaze met his, and she was startled at his intensity.

"What did I do?" she asked quietly.

A small smile touched his mouth. It wasn't that amused look, which annoyed her, but something else, something almost embarrassed.

"What's it like?" he asked softly.

"What's what like?"

"Growing up, knowing you'll come into all this power one day."

She swallowed. He believed that she had grown up in the same world he had. She had to be careful how she discussed this.

"I don't know," she said. "It's—it's a curse."

He raised his eyebrows. "A curse?"

"Yeah." She picked up her wine glass. Until this moment, she hadn't realized he'd ordered a white. It was an amber color that actually looked appealing.

"Most of us"—he used his hand to indicate the rest of the room—"fantasize what we'd do if we suddenly had magical powers."

"Fantasize," she said. "Meaning you'd want this."

"Yeah." He sounded wistful.

She sipped the wine. It was sweet and fruity, and not nearly as tart as she had thought it would be. She set the glass down before she drank too much too fast.

"When I was a little girl," she said carefully, "it became clear to my parents that I would have powers one day."

"Clear how?"

"I don't know," she said. "I never got the chance to ask them."

"They're dead?" His question was gentle.

"Long dead," she said.

"I'm sorry," he said.

She almost told him not to be, that she had gotten over her parents so long ago that she had almost forgotten them, but that would raise questions she didn't want to answer. So she said the only thing she could. "Thanks."

"What happened when your parents figured out you would have powers?"

"They apprenticed me to a woman in another village."

"Village?"

She cursed herself silently. "Yes. I was born in—England."

"Really?" He leaned forward, looking fascinated. "I would have guessed Sweden or Norway. Your accent doesn't sound English at all."

She hid her smile by taking another sip of wine. "It's my heritage."

"The magic?"

"You could say that."

She set the glass down and played with the stem.

"Apprenticed," he said. "It sounds like something we would teach."

"Doesn't it though?" She knew she sounded formal, but she couldn't help herself.

"Weren't you angry? I mean, being sent off like that?"

"I didn't have time to be angry," she said. "My— mentor—put me to work almost immediately."

"Training you?"

"No. Doing menial tasks she didn't want to do."

"You sound as if you didn't like her."

"Well," Emma said softly, "you could say she was the model for every evil stepmother you'd ever read about."

He whistled softly between his teeth. "You're kidding. She was that bad?"

"Worse, actually."

"And your parents didn't care?"

"My parents didn't know."

"Why didn't you call them? Tell them?"

She looked at him, trying to keep her expression flat. "That just wasn't possible."

"Why didn't you run away?"

"And go where?"

"Home."

"My parents would have sent me right back."

"Even though the woman was horrible?"

"I was a girl," she said. "They would have thought I didn't like her because I didn't like the training."

"Oh." He frowned. "How did you get out of it?"

"It's a long story."

"We have the evening."

She shook her head. "I don't want to tell it."

Then she looked at him. He seemed—hurt was too strong a word—slightly wounded, maybe, that she wouldn't open up to him.

"No offense," she said. "It was, without a doubt, the most unpleasant event of my life."

"I'm sorry," he said. "I didn't mean to bring something like that up."

"You didn't know." She took the bread from the center of the table, and pulled out a piece. She didn't want it, but she needed something to do with her hands.

"It's just something, you know, that's the stuff of fairy tales," he said.

"Oh, I know," she said, this time a bit too dryly.

His gaze got intense again. "You don't like fairy tales."

"I think they sugarcoat everything. I mean, who believes in happily ever after?"

He stared at her for a long time, so long that she squirmed.

"Don't tell me you do," she said.

"I think if a man finds the right woman—"

"Excuse me." A completely different waiter appeared this time. Emma hated the way people snuck up on her in this place. "Are you ready to order?"

"Not yet," Michael said.

"Yes," Emma said at the same time.

"Well?" the waiter asked.

Michael shrugged.

"I'm hungry," Emma said.

"All right." He sounded a little disappointed, as if she had thrown off the rhythm of his dinner. "Let's order."

So they did, and with the litany of choices, it took longer than usual. Long enough, Emma hoped, for Michael to forget the topic of conversation.

But her hope was in vain. After the waiter left, Michael said, "I believe in happily ever after."

Emma sighed.

"You have to believe in something," he said. "What's wrong with believing that some people get happiness for the rest of their lives?"

"I don't think it's that easy," Emma said.

"Nothing that's worthwhile is easy." Michael spoke softly.

She poured olive oil onto her bread plate. His words resonated in her. She wasn't sure she agreed with him, but she wasn't sure she disagreed either. She wanted to think about that comment.

"That's what you didn't like about my book, isn't it?" she asked. "You think it was too easy. Especially after you found out about the magic."

"I guess I deserved that." He was silent for a moment. "Hell, it might even be true. I like to think that I'm more open-minded than that."

"You seem to hate my work with a passion that suggests more than the average intellectual disagreement." She moved the topic to the work so that she wouldn't have to discuss magic any more. She had never before talked about magic with someone who didn't have any, and she was afraid she'd let something slip.

"You haven't disagreed with many intellectuals, then, have you?" he asked.

"What?"

He smiled. "It's a joke."

"Oh."

The waiter brought their salads. Hers was a mixture of greens with some nuts and blue cheese underneath her dressing. She would have preferred some tomatoes or shredded carrots, something a little less fancy and a bit more tasty.

"Jokes," Michael said after the waiter left, "deflect."

Emma lifted her gaze to his. He didn't seem as amused anymore. The lightness had left his face.

"What do you mean?" she asked.

"I mean, you may have a point. Your book was too easy, for me, anyway."

She nodded.

"I guess that's why I'm asking so many questions. I'm trying to understand what your magic really is."

She stabbed the greens and hit a nut. It shot off her plate and onto the linen tablecloth. She picked up the nut with her fingers and, forsaking all attempts at dignity, ate it.

"Is this for your book?" she asked.

He shook his head.

"My magic," she said slowly, "is something I don't entirely understand."

"But you were apprenticed to someone who had magic. Surely you have some kind of understanding of it. When you learn to control it, can you do anything you want?"

"Could I turn you into a toad?" she asked. "Send the restaurant and all its patrons to France? Divert the river down I-90?"

"Yes," he said. "Can you do those things?"

"I suppose."

"So there are no limits, then."

"Oh," she said. "There're limits. A lot of them. And rules, too. We are more highly governed than mortals are."

"Mortals. You've used that word a lot. Does that mean you're immortal?"

She closed her eyes. That was the question she had been trying to avoid. "Not really."

"But sort of?" he sounded almost eager.

"I can die," she said.

"Which makes you mortal."

"Yes," she said.

"Then why refer to people without magic as mortals if you're one?"

"Convention?" she said, not too convincingly.

"Emma, please."

She bowed her head and concentrated on the salad. It wasn't that good. The dressing was too sweet, the nuts too salty, and the greens too bitter.

"Am I making you uncomfortable?"

She set her fork down. "I'm not supposed to discuss this stuff with the nonmagical."

"It seems to late for that," he said. "I mean, I already know that you have a lot of powers. And you need my help on this."

She sighed. He was right. It just felt odd. Part of her wanted to tell him that she couldn't trust him. But that wasn't right either. She could trust him. She had to trust him. That was one of the reasons he was here, in this strange restaurant, in this strange town.

"My life is longer than yours," she said. "Especially if I'm careful."

He hadn't touched his salad. He was holding his fork as if he had thought about trying the food, but the conversation had distracted him.

"You see," she said. "Magic takes energy. If I use

too much energy on my magic, I lose years of my life. I'll age."

"How old are you?" he whispered.

Her stomach turned. At any point in this revelations, he could just leave her. But he had asked, and she wasn't going to lie to him.

"Technically?" she asked, hoping that would side-track him.

"Technically?" he repeated. "What does that mean?"

"You mean since my birth or how long I've actually been—functional."

"Now I'm intrigued." He set his fork down and leaned forward. "How long have you been—functional?"

"Thirty years," she said with finality. There. It was done. She had told him how old she was—how old she felt.

"And how many years ago were you born?"

"I thought in this culture a woman's real age was sacred," she said, knowing that this wouldn't work at all.

His blue eyes were sparkling. "It wasn't thirty years ago, was it?"

She shook her head.

"How long?"

"One thousand forty years ago," she whispered.

"What?" He sounded stunned. "That's not possible!"

She closed her eyes, and listened, expecting his chair to scoot away from the table, his footsteps to stalk off.

"Emma," he said. "How is that possible?"

"I'm really only thirty," she whispered.

"You lied?"

She shook her head.

"What, do you all live in cocoons or something?"

She shook her head again.

"Then what do you mean? How could you be thirty and be born 1040 years ago?"

"I was spelled," she said.

"What?" His voice had gotten louder. She opened her eyes. He looked like a man who had discovered that aliens were real. And maybe, in his mind, he just had.

"Please," she said, "keep your voice down."

"Sorry." He said that softer than he had said anything else. "Please explain this."

Emma pushed away her salad plate. She wasn't even going to try to eat at the moment, not while her stomach was churning. "Remember I told you about my mentor?"

"Yes."

"Well, she cast a spell on me that lasted for centuries. I don't remember anything from that time."

His face held his concern. "How long was that?"

"A thousand years," she whispered.

"A thousand years," he repeated. "I would think you're yanking my chain, but you haven't done that. And my life has been so strange since I met you, that I'm beginning to believe anything you say. You're telling me the truth, aren't you?"

She nodded.

"How old were you when that happened?"

"Twenty," she said.

"Twenty." He ran a hand through his hair, tousling it. It made him look younger, more vulnerable. "My God. You wrote your book from memory, didn't you?"

"And found the sources who had found corroboration in your time," she said.

"My time." He picked up his wine glass and drained it. "My time. No wonder your book read like a novel. It was biography and memory."

"Yes."

"And I said you had made everything up."

"And I told you that everything was based in fact."

"And it was." He sighed. "I'm a fool."

She shook her head. "You're just a man who needs a lot of proof."

He smiled. "Still, you think?"

She shrugged. "You had quite a few rationalizations for the furniture. And I seem to recall a mention of David Copperfield and student pranks."

He sighed. "I did have some rationalizations, didn't I?"

It was her turn to smile. "Yes."

"That seems like a long time ago. I'm amazed at how much I've learned since then. It's as if I'm not in the same world anymore."

"You're not. You're in my world now." *And I was wishing I could stay in yours*, she thought, but did not say. She had lost the twenty years she had been hoping for, and no amount of wishing would get them back.

"It can't be such a bad place," he said.

"Imprisoned for a thousand years," she said softly, "turned into a toad, sent into a world I knew nothing about, and now all this. I don't think it's a wonderful place."

"I didn't hear about the toad. You were a toad for a thousand years?"

"Only a few hours," she said. "That was long enough."

"I don't understand."

"Of course not." She dipped her bread in the olive oil. "It's a long, confusing story."

He was silent for a moment, as if he were thinking. "This acquiring of magic, it's like puberty, isn't it?"

She dropped her bread in the oil. "What?"

"I mean, we all want to grow up, but we have to go through puberty first. Boys have incredible growth spurts, and our voices change—always at the wrong time—and we have embarrassing emissions."

She smiled at that.

"And girls—well, everything changes for you, too, doesn't it?"

"I guess it does. I didn't think about it much."

He studied her, as if he were trying to comprehend all of this. "You went through puberty over a thousand years ago."

She nodded.

"At a time when there was no concept like 'teenager.'"

"No," she said, "either you were a child or you were old enough to have your own children."

Her voice was flat. There were a lot of memories of that time, memories she didn't care to explore.

"And girls got married at thirteen, were parents by the time they were fourteen."

"Or dead in childbirth," she said.

His intrigued look faded. He leaned forward slightly. His hand moved on the tablecloth as if he wanted to touch her, then thought better of it. "So when you were put in your magic sleep, you lost more than parents. You lost a husband and children too."

"No." Her voice was soft. "I was an old maid."

He frowned. "I have no idea how someone as beautiful as you could be an old maid."

She flushed. Why did this man always make her blush?

He saw the color rise in her cheeks. "You know you're probably one of the most beautiful women in the world. Don't you?"

She felt her flush deepen. Her skin was so hot she wanted to pour water on it. "How am I supposed to answer that? If I say yes, I'm vain, and if I say no, I'm fishing for more compliments."

"I'm serious, Emma," he said softly. "I don't think our idea of beauty has changed that much in a thousand years."

"Oh, I don't know," she said. "When I was a girl, a fat woman was the envy of all."

"Because she was rich," he said.

She nodded. "Plump women were beautiful. Full-figured girls were desirable because they could have babies. These skinny models would have been considered horribly ugly."

"But Emma," he said, "I wasn't talking about your figure—which, I think, would have been acceptable in either culture. I was talking about your face."

"The face that launched a thousand ships?"

"Yes," he said.

She leaned back. "I told you that you weren't ready to teach my classes. That was Helen of Troy. I'm not that old."

To her surprise, he laughed. "I like your sense of humor."

"It comes in handy," she said. "Although it's not as effective as my temper."

"It is less annoying."

"I suppose." She picked up her bread, then dropped it. It was soaked in oil—the bread actually looked green. She picked it up and dumped it in her salad.

"No one wanted to marry you?" Michael asked.

She wondered why he was focusing on that point. "Well, someone thought he did."

"Thought?"

Her smile was small. "It's part of the long story."

"We have days."

She nodded.

"And you don't want to talk about it."

"Michael—"

The waiter stopped in front of them, a tray balanced carefully on his left hand. He lowered it, and removed their dinners. Michael was having some sort of chicken. Emma had ordered beef tenderloin marinated in a wine and mushroom sauce. The meal set before her was an artistic concoction of beef, mushrooms, and sauce piled on mashed potatoes, with some steamed asparagus on the side.

It smelled good.

The waiter told them to enjoy their meals, and left swiftly. Michael watched him go. "Do you think they're told to escape the tables quickly or do we just frighten him?"

"I think we frighten him," Emma said, picking up her fork.

He picked up his silverware and pushed at the chicken. It was covered with some sort of peach-colored glaze. "A thousand years," he said softly.

"Michael, I don't—"

"Want to talk about it, I know," he said. "But I have only two more questions."

And she had an entire plateful of food. She was going to be with him at least a half an hour. She had to be civil. "All right, two. Then we change the subject."

He nodded, and cut into his chicken. As he did, some rice skittered across his plate. His meal looked a lot less appealing than hers did.

"You said that you were in a magical coma for over a thousand years, that you were twenty when it happened, and you were born a thousand and forty years ago, and you're thirty now. So that means you were asleep for a thousand and ten years, and you've been out of it for ten years, right?"

"Right." She took a bite of the steak. It was juicy and rich, just like she expected. There were a lot of perks to this modern world, and good food was just one of them.

"So did you wake up with a complete knowledge of everything that had changed?"

She remembered that moment in the glass coffin when her eyes opened. The air was stale and old. Apparently she hadn't been breathing in her magic state. She had taken a thick mouthful of air, touched the coffin's walls, and panicked. Somehow she had managed to push it off. She sat up—

And there was the strangest looking woman, petite with blond hair, helping her, a woman who spoke a foreign language, and had Emma trapped in a metal cave, which Emma later learned was a VW minibus. Everything had been so different. And terrifying. That first afternoon, the car ride, the entry into Nora's loft apartment. Discovering sinks and refrigerators and tea that seemed to make itself.

All in the space of maybe an hour.

"No," she whispered. "I didn't wake up knowing anything had changed."

He stared at her so long that she was afraid he could

see right through her. He was probably imagining how ignorant she had been, how she had to learn elementary and personal things. He would probably be appalled to know that she had cried through her first shower, and had been terrified of the noise a toilet made. How she had believed that people actually lived in the television set, and that the only thing that really soothed her in those dark early days was the quiet rumble of Darnell's purr.

"My God," he said finally. "I was trying to imagine it. I can't. Not really. It must have been awful for you."

Her gaze met his. His eyes were a soft blue, and this time, he did take her hand. She was trembling. She wanted to pull away, but he held her tightly for a moment. Then he squeezed and released her fingers.

She slid her hand back. "You saw the world I came from."

"That was your home?"

She nodded.

"You went from living in that village to being a history professor—a famous history professor, with a bestselling book—in ten years?"

She eased her fingers into a protective fist. She knew what was coming next, and she didn't want to hear him say it. So she asked the question before he could. "And you want to know how much magic that took?"

He glanced at her fingers. His hadn't moved. "You told me you didn't have any magic until two days ago."

"But my friends do." She kept her voice flat, and emotion off her face.

"You said there are rules," he said. "I bet there are rules for this."

She shook her head. "There are no rules for this. We're in completely new territory."

"I wasn't thinking about the magic." His voice was gentle. "I was thinking how remarkable you are. Here I was worried that everything was too easy for you, and you've lived through something that would have driven most people mad."

Her breath caught in her throat, and she blinked hard. Then she looked down at her plate. No one had ever said anything like that to her before.

When she had woken up, she had panicked Nora. Nora was out of her depth. She had gotten help for Emma, but it took some time. Aethelstan was no help at all. He had problems of his own then.

So when she had come out of that spell, she had been a problem for everyone around her. They had all tried to help her, but none of them had really thought about what it was like for her, all alone in a world she couldn't understand. It was as if she had been born anew, with all her faculties in place, and expected to function like an adult when she was still a child.

"Emma?" Michael asked. "Did I say something wrong?"

She shook her head. She had to be alone, for just a moment. She had to have some air.

"I'll be right back," she managed, and hurried away before she could see the expression on his face.

———

Michael sighed and watched her disappear in the direction of the ladies room. He wasn't quite sure what her reaction to his words had been. Her eyes had teared, then she blinked and the tears receded, but the sad expression remained.

Then she had left him.

He shouldn't have pushed her. She asked that he leave the subject alone, and he pressed for two more questions to satisfy his curiosity. He hadn't been thinking of her at all.

But a thousand years. He'd heard of people coming out of comas after ten years, and having trouble adjusting to their lives. She had been born into a world where England was composed of warring tribes. The Roman wall wasn't buried under mounds of earth, and London was a filthy, dirty city barely one square mile in size.

If she had been raised in any way traditionally, she wouldn't have been able to read or write. She hadn't even been out of her village for her entire life, and now she had driven in one day what would have taken her weeks to do by foot.

She was remarkable. And beautiful. And stronger than he had given her credit for. He had never met anyone who had survived the things she had—or who could have.

He valued intelligence, and she had used hers to carve a world in a place that was more alien to her than Mars was to him.

And now she was being surprised by a magic that she didn't want. She hadn't agreed with his puberty analogy, but he was beginning to think it was more and more apt. Or at least it put things in terms he could understand.

He knew how it felt to have his body disobey him, to lose powers he had had—the power of innocence, the powers of childhood—and suddenly be trapped in a growing, out-of-control body that didn't always obey his commands. Multiply that feeling by a thousand and he might get close to the way Emma felt now.

He pushed at the chicken cooling on his plate. He had treated her horribly these last few days, and she had been in a hell he was only beginning to understand.

What she needed was compassion. What she needed was a friend. And no one else had been there for her. He had come along under duress.

No wonder she was overprotective of that silly cat. The cat was the only true friend she had.

Michael would get her to Oregon. And then he would make sure these people she was running to would really assist her. If they didn't, he would help her find someone who could.

Magic or not, he would do whatever he could to make sure the next thousand years of her life would be a lot better than the first.

Chapter 9

SHE COULDN'T HIDE IN THE BATHROOM FOREVER. Emma sat on the red velvet stool in front of the lighted mirror in the ladies lounge and rested her elbow on the marble counter. The face that looked back at her—with its sad eyes, pale cheeks, and thin lips wasn't a face that launched a thousand ships. It was a face that lost a thousand years.

Yes, she knew she was a world-class beauty—celebrated in story and song, she thought with a lot of irony—but that was part of the problem. And it was an even bigger problem now that he had noticed.

Because she liked him. He was kind, and worse, he understood—or tried to. What he had said—his compassion—had choked her up, left her feeling restless and unworthy and terrified.

What if he tried to kiss her? What if she let him?

She had kissed Aethelstan once—just after he had rescued her from her evil stepmother. It had been ten years ago, and nothing had happened. But Aethelstan, who was a lot more experienced now than he had been as a boy, could have blocked the spell.

Michael had no magic at all. And Emma's was useless.

Like puberty. She smiled faintly at that. He had been trying to understand—and for a mortal, that was pretty close. But not quite it.

A woman came out of one of the stalls and sat three

stools away. She reapplied her lipstick, then used a Kleenex to blot it. She kept stealing glances at Emma.

Finally, she said, "Hey, are you famous or something?"

Emma's stomach clenched. This had happened to her a few times. It usually happened the day after a TV appearance.

"No," she said.

The woman frowned. "You look really familiar."

Emma shrugged. "I have one of those faces."

"I'm sure I've seen you before," the woman said.

"Probably around town." Emma stood. The woman had forced Emma's hand. She had to leave now. But she wasn't sure how she would face Michael's sympathetic eyes.

"Weren't you on, like, some documentary?"

Too close for comfort. Emma slipped out of the restroom, pretending she didn't hear the last question.

Michael was still sitting at the table. His chicken looked untouched. His hand rested near the wine glass, but it didn't look as if he had touched that either. He was staring out the window, his features pensive.

His blond hair caught the light, showing all the different highlights. His features were clean, the bones in his face strong. He would have been considered handsome in the world of her birth, just like he was considered handsome now.

He was wrong. Some looks never went out of style.

She squared her shoulders and walked back to the table. As she slipped into her chair, she said, "Sorry."

He turned toward her. His features were masked. "I didn't mean to pry."

She shook her head. "I'm just not used to talking about myself."

"How about I make it up to you? Ask me any embarrassing question you want."

She thought for a moment, feeling tempted. Then she said, "How about no more embarrassing questions for the entire evening?"

For a brief moment, he looked disappointed, and then he covered it with a smile. "Fair enough. Light and frivolous conversation it is."

And it was. They talked baseball (a sport which Emma had fallen in love with), theater (which Emma knew little about), and news (which seemed to interest both of them).

The rest of the meal went quickly. Emma managed to finish her beef, and even enjoy some dessert. Michael was a witty and engaging dinner companion, who even insisted on paying for the meal. She tried to argue with him over that, but she lost.

"I was the one who chose an expensive restaurant," he said. "When it's my choice, I buy."

They drove back to the hotel in companionable silence that lasted until they reached their rooms. From Emma's, the blaring television didn't manage to cover Darnell's wailing howls.

"He doesn't do that the whole time you're gone, does he?" Michael asked.

"I don't know," Emma said. "I'm gone."

Michael rolled his eyes and opened his door. Emma followed him into the room. Before she had been too stressed to notice it much. It was the mirror image of her room, down to the colors. The stripes on her bedspread were the same color as the solids on his.

His suitcase was open on the suitcase rack, and she could see his clothes, neatly folded. It made her feel as if she had seen something personal.

She reached for the connecting door.

Michael glanced at her hand. "May I offer you a nightcap?"

"You travel with liquor?"

"No," he said. "But there are tiny bottles in my refrigerator."

"Tiny expensive bottles."

"And a pop machine down the hall. A bit of ice, a can of Coke—what more could you want on a nice spring evening?"

The two of them sitting on the bed, laughing and talking. He'd reach toward her and she'd lean in—

"I can't," she said.

"Can't?" He looked at her in surprise.

"Darnell—"

"Can come in here."

"Michael." She put a hand on his arm. His skin was warm, muscled. A little shiver of pleasure ran through her. His breath caught and their eyes met and for a moment, she thought he might kiss her right there.

She let go of his arm.

"I can't," she said again. "Really."

"What are you so afraid of, Emma?"

She swallowed. She had already told him too much truth tonight. She couldn't tell him any more, not and save her self-respect.

"Nothing," she said. "I just want a good night's sleep."

He hadn't moved. His eyes were intense. She was so close to him she could feel his warmth and she knew that if she made one wrong move, he would take her in his arms, and she would never leave.

"Thank you for dinner," she said, and let herself into her room.

Darnell stopped howling. He looked at her as if she had been gone for weeks. She scooped him into her arms and clung to him until he squawked.

"Oh, Darnell," she whispered. "This trip is going to be a lot harder than I thought."

That night, her dreams were a tangled mixture of memories and fears. The whole experience of her arrival into this new century, Nora's frightened face, Aethelstan's older one—so familiar and yet unfamiliar—and Emma's own strangled terror when she realized she could never, ever go back to the world that she was most familiar with, a world she hadn't loved, but a world she knew.

Finally, she woke up in the strange room, the unfamiliar darkness choking her, the air stale and a thousand years old. Her heart was pounding and she knew she was trapped inside, forever trapped. The panic held her until she felt Darnell's familiar warmth scoot closer to her back.

She put a hand on his side, like she used to do when she was first at Nora's. He grunted and rolled on his back so that he could get his stomach rubbed. The softness of his fur did relax her, and so did the clean sheets against her bare skin, the uncomfortable bedspread, and the hotel pillows.

All of those were part of now, and now was better than then. All of the thens. Even a now filled with magic.

She had to remember that. And remember too what Michael had told her at dinner—that most people dreamed of receiving the gift that she didn't want. Most people wished they had magic when they never could.

Michael. She would carry that image of him, sitting alone in a restaurant that he had chosen for its atmosphere, for the rest of her life. He had softened toward her, and she had liked it. Maybe she should have stayed for that nightcap.

Maybe she should have gone on this trip alone.

"Maybe," she whispered to Darnell, "I should stop thinking and go back to sleep."

Darnell's answer was a not-so-muffled cat snore. She smiled at him, and then, despite herself, peered at the crack beneath the connecting door. Michael's light was out. She grinned at herself. What would she have done if it wasn't? Knock, plead nightmares, and let him comfort her?

He probably would have talked to her, found her some warm milk and sent her back to bed. She had probably imagined that moment in the room. She wasn't used to touching anyone except Darnell. She wouldn't know what a normal touch felt like. Maybe whenever she touched a man, she would feel that spark.

Although she had never felt it with Aethelstan.

She sighed and groped on the nightstand for the remote. Nora once told her that she had officially become a modern woman when she used the television to fall asleep. Well, someone should circle a calendar. Tonight was the night.

Emma flicked on the TV, found that the hotel had only fifteen channels, and felt extremely disappointed.

She surfed, finding nothing to hold her interest except an infomercial for an online cooking school. Maybe that was what she should have done. She should have taken lessons from Aethelstan and opened her own restaurant.

How ironic. She had once thrown a plate—actually an entire pile of plates—at him when he had suggested that.

But it would have been a lot easier than taking this leave of absence from her current job. History professors didn't just vanish for a year or two, especially ones who got interviewed occasionally on the History Channel. Restaurateurs closed shop all the time.

The television did lull her to sleep, and she dreamed of cooking school and vanishing maître d's, of beautifully designed restaurants and food so scrumptious that it won every award ever given for dining. Somewhere in the mix was Michael, saying that such meals made trips worthwhile, and Darnell, who was sitting at a table, like those cats in the Fancy Feast commercials, delicately eating salmon out of a small crystal bowl.

And when she woke up, light was streaming in her window. Darnell was sitting on the round table, chittering at birds that he could see through the net curtains. He had adapted to this room a lot quicker than she had expected him to.

She stretched, feeling remarkably refreshed and hungrier than she should have been, given her dinner the night before. She got up, took a short hot shower, and was just getting dressed when she heard a hard, firm knock on the connecting door.

"Just a minute!" She struggled with the last leg of her jeans, and walked barefoot across the room. Her hair was still damp, and curled on the shoulders of her blouse. She hadn't buttoned her sleeves yet, and they flopped uncomfortably against her wrists.

The knocking came again, harder this time, and more urgent. "Emma!"

"I'm coming." She unlocked the door and pulled it open.

Michael was dressed immaculately, his hair combed and dried, his shirt pressed. Even his jeans looked tailored. "What did you do?"

His voice was not calm. Nor was it as deliberate as his clothing. His words were clipped and seemed to have an edge of panic in them.

"What did I do?" Emma asked. "I slept, got dressed—"

"No," he said. "To the hotel."

"Nothing."

"It's not nothing." He came inside and grabbed her shoulders, leading her to the dresser.

"Michael, this room's the same as it was last night."

"No," he said. "It's not."

He opened the dresser drawer and pulled out the fake leather book that gave all the pertinent information about the hotel. He flipped it open to the room service section.

The selections went on for pages, with everything from duck à l'orange to the chef's special perch with asparagus and lemongrass. Desserts ranged from simple cookies to award-winning petit fours.

"I don't understand," Emma said.

Michael flipped back to the front of the menu. Under the heading "About our restaurant," she saw the words "fifty of the world's greatest chefs vying to create the most unique dishes in the entire fifty states." And then there were reviews of the hotel restaurant from the *New York Times*, *Gourmet*, *Vanity Fair*, and a hundred other publications.

She felt cold. "I thought the restaurant was closed."

"Being remodeled," Michael said. "At least yesterday it was."

"Maybe this is what they're shooting for?" she asked, feeling her heart start to pound too hard.

"Fifty world-famous chefs? No restaurant has fifty chefs. Haven't you heard of too many cooks spoiling the infamous broth?"

"I didn't see broth on the menu," she said.

"You know what I mean!"

"That's actually an oversight, considering the extensiveness—"

"Emma!"

She stopped talking.

"What did you do?"

"I had a nightmare," she said in a small voice. "So I turned on the TV and watched an infomercial."

"And?"

"I had a dream about chefs."

"And?" His hands were still on her shoulders.

"That's all."

"All?"

She nodded.

"You had a dream, and suddenly *Esquire* is calling a restaurant attached to a chain motel the finest dining in all of North America, if not the world?"

"Maybe Sioux Falls needed a five-star restaurant. The place we were in last night—"

"Was just fine!" Michael's fingers were digging into her skin.

"No, actually it wasn't fine. The salad was bitter and the potatoes weren't mashed all that well."

"So now you're a food critic?"

"No." She slipped out of his grasp. "I'm just a little startled, that's all."

Darnell had wandered from his perch on the tabletop to the connecting doorway. Emma hurried toward him and pulled the door closed.

"Have you said a reverse spell?" she asked.

Michael nodded. "It's not going away."

"We have to say it in the first five minutes." She sighed. The good mood she had awakened with left her. "This could have happened hours ago."

"What do you plan to do?" Michael asked.

"I don't know," she said. Then she turned to him. "You remember what this place was like before?"

"Of course."

"But you're not supposed to."

He frowned. "What do you mean I'm not supposed to."

"You're mortal. You're supposed to change with the change. It always happens. I wonder if everyone else remembers."

She glanced out the window. She didn't seen any reporters or photographers or panicked people, but that didn't mean anything. It was still early.

"You're saying you did a spell by accident and you did it wrong?"

"Gee," she said, "what would be the chances of that?"

He looked at her sideways. "I don't think this is anything to joke about."

"What do you want me to do? Run around screaming? I did that with poor Darnell and see where it got us."

"It got him changed back."

"Not the screaming," she said.

Darnell was looking at her, his ears back. If anything, he seemed a little alarmed.

"I'm not going to even try to spell you ever again," she said.

He turned his head back toward the window, but his ears remained cocked. In fact, his entire body was tense. Apparently he had decided flight was the only way he could prevent another lion fiasco.

"Emma," Michael said, "we have to do something."

She rather liked the "we," but she didn't say so. "There may not be anything we can do."

"You'll leave all these chefs here, and the new restaurant?"

"Until I've learned how to fix it," she said. "I might have to."

He gave her a look of such utter horror that she had to turn away. Michael, who liked rules and order and everything in its place. She hadn't realized how much of a nightmare this trip might be for him.

"Come on," she said. "Let's go down there."

"And do what?" he said.

"Fifty world-famous chefs," she said. "Don't you think at least one of them can cook a good breakfast?"

But she wasn't really thinking of breakfast as she led Michael out of the room and down the hall. She was hoping that her subconscious had broken a rule and that she might survive on a technicality.

Aethelstan was one of the world's greatest chefs. He had marketed his own line of cookbooks and gourmet items under the name of his restaurant, Quixotic. If luck were running with her, then he would be in that kitchen—or at least in Sioux Falls—and he would probably be hopping mad.

She smiled at the thought. That wouldn't be so unusual with Aethelstan and her.

Then she sobered. Magic wasn't supposed to be used to get her together with her mentor. But she would argue with the Fates—or have Nora, who was a very good lawyer—do it. After all, if Aethelstan were here, he would have been summoned because he was a good *chef* not because of his magical abilities. And that, Emma had learned, was one of those technicalities that could wrap the Fates up for centuries.

"There are a lot of emotions running across your face." Michael sounded grumpy. Later she would have to warn him that he needed to be flexible to survive the rest of this trip.

"Just trying to figure out how to resolve this," she said.

He nodded and followed her the rest of the way.

The corridors looked the same as they had the day before, but the changes first became noticeable in the lobby. Large signs with elegant writing pointed the way to *Le Chef*. And all of the signs had that *Esquire* quote underneath.

"You have created a monster," Michael said, looking at the signs.

Emma's stomach tightened. She walked to the front desk. Michael followed.

"Excuse me," she said to the man behind the counter. He was fiftyish and looked tired. She couldn't tell if he was ready to go home to bed or if he had just gotten out of it.

When he looked up at her, the weariness seemed like

a warning: *this had better not be a problem*. Then his gaze rested on her face, and he smiled. The smile held too much warmth.

"May I help you, miss?" he asked, leaning toward her.

Michael came up beside her and put a hand on her shoulder. The desk clerk's smile lost a bit of its brilliance.

"Yes," she said. "We were wondering how long the restaurant's been open."

"It's open from six to midnight, miss." The desk clerk spoke slowly, forcing his voice deeper than it normally went just to impress her. Michael slipped his arm around her back. She stiffened, but didn't move away.

"No," she said, "I mean, how many years?"

"Oh." The clerk glared at Michael, who glared back. "Two."

"Two? Wow," Emma said. "I was under the impression that the place was being remodeled."

"No," the clerk said. "Why would we remodel it? Even the decor gets raves."

"Talented designer," Michael said.

"I wouldn't know." The clerk didn't even look at him.

"What would you recommend for breakfast?" Emma asked.

"Anything's good," the clerk said. "Best food I've ever tasted."

"That's a recommendation," Michael said.

The clerk's eyes narrowed, and Emma stifled the urge to smile. Insults, Midwestern style. Dry little comments that seemed so innocent to the rest of the world. She would miss that too, in Oregon.

"Thank you," she said, giving him her most charming smile. As she turned to walk away, Michael turned with her, keeping his arm around her back, pulling her even closer. His body felt good against hers. He was lean without an ounce of fat on his frame. She wanted to put her own arm around his back, feeling the muscles beneath his thin cotton shirt, but she didn't.

"What are you doing?" she whispered.

"I didn't like the way he looked at you."

"Get used to it," she said. "All men look at me like that."

Michael's eyebrows went up. "Did I?"

"Yes," she said. "But you had the grace to seem upset about it."

They left the lobby and entered a corridor that had been built to resemble the hall of a sixteenth-century castle. The walls were high, the ceiling even higher. The space was done in gold and antiques, with stained glass on the upper edges of the arched windows.

Michael's arm tightened around her. "My God. You did this?"

"Well, if I didn't, whoever did had a great peek into my dreams last night."

No wonder she felt odd. Dreams were supposed to be private, not be enlarged into a Disneyland-sized ride.

Two gilt doors stood open. A maître d' stood just inside, leaning on his podium as if he expected a rush of undesirables at seven in the morning. The closer Emma got, the more she realized that the area he was in was small and protected, like an anteroom. The real restaurant was behind him. She could only catch a glimpse of light and space mixed with greenery and plants before he spoke.

"Table for two?"

Michael looked at her.

"Yes," she said, trying to peer beyond the maître d'.

"Table for two," he said and that made her look at him, really look at him for the first time. In addition to his morning suit, he wore a microphone set like telephone solicitors did. After a moment, he nodded. "It will be just a moment. Step toward the front please."

"I'm half ready for them to close a metal bar in front of me and tell me to enjoy the ride," Michael said.

Emma nodded. She stepped forward and heard herself gasp.

The room before her was made mostly of glass with gold supports. Plants were everywhere, shielding tables, making dining private. The floor was a star-covered black that made all the morning sunlight somehow bearable. The ceiling had varied heights, which artificially created the sense of small alcoves in the large space.

The size of the place was what astonished her the most. It was at least as large as the hotel. Tables and plants and glass disappeared into the distance on both sides.

"You have a hell of an imagination," Michael said.

"You've told me that before," Emma murmured, still looking around.

"Yeah, well, I was speaking from limited knowledge then. Now I'm speaking with authority."

A slender blond woman wearing a black suit walked toward them. She too had a microphone set. "Table for two?" she said as if she knew the answer. "Come with me."

She led them down two steps into the main dining room. As they walked past the first set of plants, Emma realized that the dining room had been broken up into several special areas. One included a wood smoke oven and grill where a chef worked all alone—like a solo performer warming up an audience. Another had a buffet table. That area was full.

"Oh, jeez," Michael said. "This *is* you."

She followed his gaze. Off in a far corner was a section walled off in glass. A dozen cats sat on red cushions, gobbling food out of crystal cat bowls. One rather plump Burmese was pawing at the glass wall, and two toms were yowling at each other, fur standing straight up on their Halloween kitty backs.

She giggled. That image was straight out of the dream. "We should have brought Darnell."

"I promise not to tell him what he missed," Michael said with a straight face.

They had walked for what seemed like a mile before the woman stopped and indicated a glass table with a gold base. Emma pulled at her chair and grunted. The thing weighed more than she did.

"Allow me," the woman said and slid the chair back as if it weighed nothing. Emma sat on it, surprised at how comfortable it was, and realized she was too far from the table. She had no idea how she would scoot it forward.

To Emma's great satisfaction, Michael had needed help as well.

A waiter, in yet another morning suit, handed them both menus as thick as phonebooks. "Would you like to hear the specials?" he asked.

Emma started to say yes, but Michael interrupted her. "How many are there?"

"Fifty breakfast, sir. And perhaps twenty-five more that will run all day."

"This is not very efficient," Michael said to Emma.

She spread her hands, helplessly. "What do I know about restaurants?"

"How to make them pretty," Michael said.

"The specials, sir?"

"No, thanks." Michael hid behind his menu. The waiter hurried away.

The menu was divided by chef. Each section had different fonts and designs. Emma recognized a few of them as exact duplicates of famous restaurants that she'd been too. She didn't see anything from Quixotic, but she was thumbing through quickly.

Another waiter was approaching. Emma raised a finger as Aethelstan had taught her. "Excuse me."

The waiter stopped, looking vaguely annoyed.

"I was wondering if an old friend of mine is one of your chefs. His name is Blackstone."

"I don't know anything about the chefs except what's in the menus." The waiter hurried off.

"Blackstone?" Michael asked.

Emma nodded. "My mentor."

"You think he's here?"

"My subconscious made a cat food bar, didn't it? It may have brought Quixotic here."

"Your mentor owns Quixotic? Alex Blackstone?"

Alex wasn't his real name. No one magic used their real name. Besides, Aethelstan was so unusual, he would have had to explain it all the time. "Yes."

"You think he's here?"

"Well, half the chefs in here have their own television show or cookbook or item line."

"I saw that," Michael said. "I wonder how Oprah's fairing without her chef."

"At least Wolfgang Puck's restaurants can run without him."

"Yeah, but a few of these European chefs never leave their kitchens."

"They have now," Emma said.

Michael nodded. "Do you think that's changed cuisine worldwide?"

She froze. It had. It obviously had. She knew all of the names in here, and they all had going concerns in the world she had altered. Important concerns. "I better get to the kitchen."

"I don't think they'll let you in," Michael said. "Not in a place like this."

"Well, someone has to know if Aeth—Alex is here."

Michael raised his entire arm, and one of the maître d' clones came over. "I want to know about your chefs," he said.

"Anything sir," the maître d' said.

"We were hoping to taste some of Quixotic's food. Alex Blackstone. Does he work for you? I understand he's been rated—"

"Fifteenth," Emma whispered. She knew because Aethelstan was annoyed that he couldn't break into the top ten—at least, not without resorting to his magic, which in this instance, he called cheating.

"Fifteenth," Michael repeated.

"Ah, we get that request a lot," the maître d' said. "Unfortunately Mr. Blackstone was unwilling to come to our establishment. He claimed it was some sort of conflict of interest."

"How could that be, with fifty other chefs?"

"I have no idea, sir. But it does seem that nothing,

absolutely nothing, will get him to leave his own restaurant." The maître d' nodded formally and then left.

Emma sighed. "I had known that, too. But I was hoping."

"You knew that nothing would get Blackstone to leave?"

She nodded.

"Then why did you think he would be here? It was
your subconscious that did this, after all."

She shook her head. "I guess just once I want something to go right."

Michael gave her a strange and sad look, and then
turned his attention back to the menu. After a moment,
Emma did too. All of her favorite meals were here, of
course, and foods she had never heard of.

She and Michael ordered pastries and several different kinds of breakfasts—from waffles to kippers. They
also ordered several egg dishes—Thai frittatas, huevos
rancheros, and a traditional eggs Benedict.

Soon their table was covered with too much food to
eat—and all of it good. Michael was acting like a kid
in a candy store, trying everything, unable to decide
which he liked best. The pastries were dreamy—light
and fluffy and perfect. Emma had never had such a good
meal in her life.

They didn't finish most of the meats. She cut up some
of it—including the albacore tuna that was in one of the
omelets, mixed it with a remaining kipper and a bit of
steak—and took a to-go box for Darnell. He'd complain
about being left alone, but he wouldn't mind after he
saw the food.

Finally, Michael leaned back in his chair and
groaned. "I've gained fifteen pounds," he said. "And
it was worth it."

She smiled. "You don't look like a man who enjoys food."

"What a delicate way of saying 'the way you eat, you should weigh three hundred pounds.'" He closed his eyes. "I exercise."

"I haven't seen it."

"How do you think I knew about the restaurant?"

She frowned. She hadn't even thought about it. She had just assumed he was looking through the hotel guide. "What were you doing?"

"Running," he said. "After last night, I thought I'd log a few miles before we left. Now I'm really glad I did."

"I've never seen you jogging in the neighborhood."

"At home, I usually walk. The campus is big enough. And I run, not jog."

"What's the difference?"

He opened his eyes and grinned. "Jogging's for wimps."

"Oh," she said, not understanding at all.

The waiter left the bill, which was more than both of the hotel rooms combined. Emma stared at it for a moment. She could afford it, of course—the book had settled any money problems she might have had, and Nora had taught her how to invest the money— but she had never paid this much for food in her entire life.

"You'd think," Michael said with a lazy grin, "that you'd dream up a restaurant where the spectacular food is free."

She peered at him over the bill. "Some things are simply impossible to believe in."

He laughed. Then he looked around, and the

good humor left his face. "It's a shame for this place to disappear."

"It's a shame for it to stay. All these wonderful chefs have their own home restaurants. I wonder what's going on there?"

"All I know is that the Sioux Falls of your dreams is about three sizes bigger than the Sioux Falls we drove into last night. This place has had a significant impact on the city's economy."

"Why?"

He shrugged. "Probably to accommodate all the people who want to eat here. Or maybe it put Sioux Falls on the map."

"I thought it already was on the map," she said. "I remember seeing a sign that *Money Magazine* chose it as the best place to live in America."

"Over a decade ago," he said. "Madison's been chosen since then."

One simple, poorly done spell had had worldwide consequences. She had worried that Michael didn't understand the implications of her wayward powers. Maybe she didn't either.

"I have to change it back. As nice as this is, it's not right."

"I know," he said.

"Michael, if I can do this with one errant dream, maybe I should drive straight through to Oregon."

He considered for a moment. "Maybe. But you'll have to sleep even as we drive. And you'll sleep lighter, which means you'll dream more, not less. It's a couple of days from here."

She ran a hand over her face. How many disasters lay

ahead? Why did the Fates have this rule? As punishment for failing to get training?

Probably. It showed her just how important training was. When she got to Oregon, she'd be ready to listen to Aethelstan, no matter how angry he made her.

"I'm going to try the reverse spell again," she said quietly.

He nodded. "Should I stand up?"

"Why?"

"I mean, if everything disappears, won't I get hurt?"

She smiled. "It's not that far to the ground, Professor."

He smiled back, then braced himself. She spread her hands, touching her middle finger to her thumb as she had been taught, and repeated the words to the stronger of the two reverse spells she'd been taught.

Nothing happened. Conversation continued around her. A maître d' clone went by, leading a couple and two Schnauzers on leashes. Emma turned. She'd created a dog area too?

"Concentrate," Michael said.

"How many times did you try the spell?" Emma asked.

"Oh, maybe five. But I've never done it successfully."

She let out a big breath of air. "This one's too large. A reverse isn't going to work."

"I thought you weren't going to let the place stand." He glanced around, as if he were searching for an idea. "Will it hurt anything if it stays for a few days?"

"I don't know," she said. "Some of these things filter into the common memory."

"And become fairy tales?" he asked.

She didn't answer that. Fairy tales and myths and legends were a corruption of her own people's histories. "Urban myths. You know the one about the hook? It was a black magic spell. For days, this mage terrorized Kansas City and—"

"I don't want to know any more," he said. "The hook always scared me as a kid."

She looked at him in surprise. "I was beginning to think nothing scares you, Michael."

He grinned. "Nothing scares me now that I'm an adult. But back then…"

She half believed him. He'd survived all of her spells and strangeness so far. He was a good choice to be with her on this trip.

The Fates told her she needed someone in case a spell got out of hand. This one was out of hand. Maybe they weren't just talking about life and death issues. Maybe they were telling her, in their oblique way, that most spells needed two people to fix them.

But how would he help her fix this one?

And then she knew.

"Have you come up with something?" he asked.

She nodded. "Wake me up."

"What?"

"This restaurant comes from a dream. How do you make a dream go away?"

His eyes sparkled. "You wake up the dreamer. But you are awake. Aren't you?"

"I don't know," she said. "That's an existential question that I don't really think we have time for."

"But how do I wake up someone who looks awake to me?"

"Let's try this." She pushed the plates away, creating a space on the table before her. Then she folded her arms on the table and put her forehead on them. It felt good to close her eyes. She was very tired. Eating that much food always made her sleepy. If she didn't concentrate on it, she could fall asleep...

After a moment, she felt Michael's hand on her shoulder. "Not yet," she mumbled. "Let me sleep first."

"Emma," he said.

"Please." She rolled over. "A few more minutes."

She rolled over? She sat up, wide awake—only to find herself in her hotel room, in the bed. Michael was staring at her—or rather, staring at her breasts as if he'd never seen breasts before.

She grabbed the covers and pulled them up to her shoulders. Another blush started and traveled all the way down her neck.

"I guess it worked." She tried for a matter-of-fact tone, as if men were always waking her up and staring at her nakedness. With a look of desire so intense that she wanted to let the covers fall again.

She clung to them as if they were a lifeline.

"I—I guess it did." He was still looking at her, his gaze somewhere around her shoulders and her neck. Finally his eyes met hers and he seemed to realize where he was. This time, he flushed and she almost smiled.

It was nice to see the tables turn.

"I'll check," he said somewhat hastily and hurried to the dresser, pulling the top drawer open so hard that it came all the way out of its slot.

She scooted against her pillows and pulled the covers all the way to her chin. Darnell, who had been sleeping toward the foot of the bed, rolled off and landed with a squawk that almost sounded like an offended "hey!"

"Yeah," Michael said. "It worked."

"No more *Esquire* reviews?"

"No," he said. "A substitute page apologizing for the renovations."

Her stomach growled and she clapped a hand over it. She was hungry again. Which made sense, she supposed. Even the food, lovely as it was, was as substantial as a dream.

"So," she said, "did you fall?"

"Fall?" He was clutching the hotel guide like a lifeline.

"Out of your chair?"

"No." He sounded surprised. "It was strange. For a moment, I was two places—in the chair, and in my room, getting ready for the run."

She glanced at the clock. Fifteen minutes before the last time she woke up. Strange. Her powers shouldn't affect time this way. Or had something gone haywire inside her when she'd been in that magical coma?

She'd have to ask Aethelstan. Maybe this was a normal stage.

"Does this mean I'll have to run again?" he asked.

"No," she said. "But you didn't get the benefit from the run."

"I remember it."

"If the mind could burn calories from memory, don't you think we'd be doing that instead of exercise?"

"And I'm hungry," he said. "This isn't fair. I have to start all over."

"Well," she said, "we're certainly not going to get a meal like that again."

He smiled. "Wow. Puts a whole new twist on bingeing and purging. You could bottle this."

"Yeah," she said softly. "If I could control it."

He bent down, picked up Darnell—who had apparently been cleaning off the indignity of his fall—and put him back on the bed. "I'll let you get ready. I saw a bakery on my last run. I trust it'll still be there on this one."

"You don't have to run, you know," she said. "I mean, if you're trying to burn calories, think of all the ones you lost when the restaurant disappeared."

The desire had returned to his face. "No," he said softly. "I need some exercise."

And then he left through the connecting door, closing it gently behind him.

Emma let the covers drop, still feeling his desire as if he were in the room. Or was that warmth she felt hers?

This was going from bad to worse.

She got out of bed and headed toward her second shower of the day—and this one was going to be cold.

Chapter 10

MICHAEL REMEMBERED NOW WHY HE USED TO TAKE the northern route when he drove West. I-90 through South Dakota was one of the dullest stretches of highway in the Lower Forty-eight. It wasn't as bad as taking I-80 through Nebraska—that was miles and miles of grass and ditch—but it was close. The road was so straight here, and Emma's car was so sophisticated that he bet he could point the wheel, put on the cruise control, and fall asleep without leaving his lane.

He wasn't going to try it though.

Emma was reading the *New York Times* in the passenger seat beside him. She studied it with the concentration of a student who was going to be quizzed later on its contents. Michael bet that someone had once made her study the news to help her learn about the culture, and the custom had stuck. Whoever had taught her had done well, but Emma had done even better.

Until he found out about her past, he had thought she was a normal woman (well, not *normal*) who had been born thirty years before, and grown up, perhaps not in America, but in this ever shrinking worldwide culture.

He had been stunned to learn of her past.

He was still stunned. He'd been thinking of it all morning—or trying to. What he kept thinking about was the way her perfect skin trailed down her neck to her breasts and under the covers. He knew that she would be beautiful all over.

The thought made him even more uncomfortable than he had been before. He shifted in the driver's seat.

"You want me to drive?" Emma didn't even look at him over the paper. She had asked that same question every half hour.

"No," he said. "I need something to do and I can't read while we drive."

"Okay." The paper rattled as she turned the page. In the backseat, Darnell sighed.

Michael resisted the urge to sigh too. Emma had been reluctant to talk with him this morning. Of course, he wanted to talk about the big event of the day—the magical mystery restaurant—but she seemed embarrassed by that. Or maybe she was embarrassed by the way it ended.

He was so attracted to her. The way she had felt against him that morning at the front desk, when that silly hotel employee had been ogling her. Men always looked at her that way? No wonder she was skittish. But she had to know Michael was different. He hadn't done anything, even when provoked.

And God knew, he had been more provoked than usual when he had ended up in her bedroom, at her invitation this morning.

She had been so beautiful lying there, her black hair sprawled around her, her red lips parted, her dark lashes spread on her cream colored skin. Like the wonderful fantastical drawings he'd seen of Snow White—the amazing contrast between the darkness of her hair and the whiteness of her skin. Who was the fairest of the all? Emma, of course.

Only Snow White wouldn't be her legacy, would

it? She was more like Sleeping Beauty—lost for years, waiting for her handsome prince to wake her with a kiss.

He glanced at her, keeping one eye on the road. Her glossy black hair shone in the sunlight pouring in the car. He could see the nape of her neck and just a bit of skin disappearing under the color of her blue shirt.

"What are you looking at?" Emma asked, putting down the paper.

"Nothing," he said, turning his attention back to the road.

"You were staring at me. Why?"

"Trying to read the headline on the back page," he lied.

"Well, you can read if you want. I'll drive."

"No," he said. "Go on."

She raised the paper. He pushed the "seek" button on the radio, trying to find something other than oldies to listen to. Emma didn't seem to care, if there was no baseball available. She loved the sport with a passion he didn't quite understand.

Otherwise she listened to news or classical music. Which, he supposed, had been as new to her ten years ago as everything else.

He shook his head, still trying to comprehend it all. It would almost be like being a newborn, only with the ability to speak and understand, and with a memory of a previous life.

The radio control went through every number on the dial. Twice. "I'm going insane," he said. "You'll have to talk to me."

"I'm not here for your entertainment," Emma said.

"Too bad," he said. "You're succeeding."

She slammed the paper down and glared at him. He

laughed. "You're too easy, Emma. I'm beginning to learn which buttons to push."

"You angered me deliberately?"

"I told you. I need entertaining."

"What do you want me to do? Give you a row of dancing girls on the dashboard?"

As she said the words, a tiny puff of white smoke flared from her fingers toward the dashboard. A hundred tiny Rockettes kicked their marvelous miniature legs right in front of him.

"Oh, no," she whispered.

He could barely hear the music they were dancing to. And someone was controlling stage lights. The women didn't seem to notice that they were dancing in front of a giant who happened to be driving a car. Maybe they weren't Rockettes. Maybe they were the Ziegfeld Girls brought back from the dead.

"Michael!" Emma screamed and launched herself at the steering wheel. Michael pushed her away with one hand and swerved with the other.

A truck zoomed by, horn blaring.

He had been driving into the oncoming lane and he hadn't even seen it. He'd been watching the damn dancers.

"Um," he said as calmly as he could, "this was not what I meant by entertainment."

She was already muttering the reverse spell. The dancers disappeared as if they never were.

His heart was pounding. Darnell had climbed the back of the seat in his terror and was peering over it like a feline imitation of Kilroy. The idea of someone sketching a picture of Darnell, his face visible only from his nose upward, his two front paws framing his cheekbones like fists, with the sign *Darnell Was Here* beneath it was more than Michael could mentally take.

He snorted.

Emma whirled toward him, her expression panicked. Then he chuckled.

Her eyes widened. So did Darnell's. Only his claws were digging into the expensive leather seat back. He whimpered and slipped, landing behind Michael with a thud.

Michael laughed. He couldn't hold it back. The laugh had a bit of hysteria in it, but not that much, considering all he'd been through that day.

He pulled the car to the shoulder, then bent over the wheel, laughing so hard he could hardly breathe.

Emma put her hand on his back. "Are you all right?"

Finally he sat up, rubbed the tears from his eyes, and tried to catch his breath. "I'm sorry. It's just that they looked like some kind of children's toy, those legs rising up like a wave, and then sinking again. And then Darnell—"

Michael heard claws scraping up the back of the seat again, and thought the better of what he was going to say.

"Darnell?" Emma prompted.

"Looked as startled as you did," Michael said.

"I thought you were going to kill us."

"I thought you couldn't die," he said.

She shook her head. "If you'd hit that truck, we'd both be dead now. If I had had control of my magical abilities, I could have gotten us out of the way, but I didn't, so we would have died."

The laughter died in his throat. He turned to her, startled. Somehow he had gotten the impression, after last night, that only magic could kill her. "Well," he said, "never grab the wheel away from the driver. He'll fight you instead of the road."

"You didn't," she said.

"That's because it's happened to me before." The words left his mouth before he thought about them. He winced and turned away.

"Was everyone all right?"

"No one died," he said and got out of the car. He stretched and stared at the horizon. The sun was beginning to move toward the west.

He heard Emma's door open. She walked around the car to join him. "Are you all right?"

"That was a bit close, wasn't it?" he said. "I guess I hadn't realized."

"It was my fault." Her voice was soft.

"No," he said. "I came along to protect you. I should have been prepared for anything."

"Oh, really?" She leaned toward him. "They cover miniature dancing girls in the driver's training manuals?"

"No, but they do cover distractions."

"Michael, you can't blame yourself—"

"Actually, I can. You're supposed to be in complete control when you drive a car. I almost plowed us into a truck. Then I blamed you for grabbing at the wheel."

"I was the least of your problems." She leaned against the car and kicked some loose gravel.

A Datsun went by, much too fast. Another truck, going the opposite direction, and then a Subaru, with two women in the front seat.

"What memory did I invoke?" she asked.

"What do you mean?"

"When I asked about grabbing at the wheel?"

He felt his breath catch. "Nothing important."

She bent her head, then kicked a little more gravel. "All right. When you're ready, we can go again."

To his surprise, she walked to the passenger side and got in. He would have thought, after that little incident, that she would have insisted on driving.

He ran a hand through his hair. The breeze was cool even though the sun was out, reminding him that it was still spring. The air had an unfamiliar scent here, something a little spicier than he smelled in Wisconsin. Probably some plant he didn't recognize.

Another truck went by and then another. The interstate system, which kept America fed.

He sighed. He wasn't being fair. Emma had told him all her secrets, and he hadn't told her much at all about him. And only because he was embarrassed.

He slid back into the driver's side. Time to tell someone the story he'd buried long ago.

"Okay," he said. "I was sixteen. I had just gotten my license and I thought I knew everything."

She looked at him with surprise. Darnell sat up in the backseat as if he felt he should take feline notice. "You don't have to tell me. I mean, if it's personal—"

"No," he said. "You've been honest with me. It's the least I can do. And I mean it. It's the very least. It's not a life or death secret."

She turned toward him, folded the newspaper, and tucked it on the mat beside her feet.

"I was cruising with my friends in the car I'd bought and rebuilt from parts. I grew up in Northern Wisconsin and a mechanic's skills were prized. Most guys don't do that anymore, but then, those of us who could were like gods."

She smiled as if he'd told her a private joke.

"My girlfriend was in the front seat, my best friend in the back with his girlfriend, and they were having waaay too good a time. I was—shall we say, inexperienced?— but my friend wasn't and neither was his girlfriend. And I was sixteen. Did I say that?"

"Twice," Emma said.

"It was night. It was winter. We were driving along the main drag just inside town. That's what we did when we'd seen all the movies showing at the mall."

"Sounds like fun," Emma said.

Michael stopped and looked at her. She meant that. "No, Emma. It wasn't fun."

"Then why'd you do it?"

"It was a way to fill time."

She frowned. "You could have watched television. Or worked on your computer. Or played games. There's a lot to amuse people now."

"First off," he said, "we couldn't afford computers. That was in the days when only rich kids had them. There was no Internet, and staying home with the folks watching television Just Wasn't Done."

"Oh." Her cheeks colored a little. He liked the way she blushed. It made her face seem rosy.

"Anyway, I was doing okay with all the sounds coming out of the back."

"Sounds?" she asked.

"Moaning, kissing—actually, I think now, as an adult, I'd call it slobbering—"

"Ick!"

"But then, you know."

But she probably didn't. This was as far from her teen-age years as, well, Sweyn Forkbeard's six-month rule over England was from Queen Elizabeth the Second's.

"Anyway," Michael said to cover his discomfort, "I was getting a little too intrigued, if you know what I mean. And my girlfriend was hiding her embarrassment at the whole thing by huddling up against the door and staring at the road ahead of us.

"I really wanted to turn around and see exactly what they were doing—I used to tell myself that I want to tell them to knock it off—but I was a sixteen-year-old boy. I wanted to look."

She grinned. "Some things never change."

"And probably never will," Michael said. "We got to a bend in the road, and about that point, a bra came sailing over the backseat and wrapped itself around the rearview mirror."

Emma put a hand over her mouth.

"I—I—I—" He laughed suddenly. "I still get embarrassed thinking about this."

"Well you can't stop now," Emma said.

"Which is exactly what my friend's girlfriend said."

"You're kidding. I thought modern American girls were supposed to say no at that point."

"They were," Michael said. "She didn't."

"Oh."

"I was sixteen."

"We established that."

"So I turned around. I mean, it was more than I could take. I knew there were naked breasts back there, and I'd never seen any, not in person—" He felt a blush building.

He had seen some just that morning. Emma's gaze met his and he willed himself not to show the sudden embarrassment he was feeling. "—and I wasn't thinking or maybe I was using the wrong part of my anatomy.

"The next thing I know, my girlfriend is screaming, the car is sliding on ice, and I whip my head back toward the front of the car. We're going sideways down the road. My girlfriend is grabbing for the wheel and I'm trying to push her away, and we slide in circles all the way off the road and into a deep ditch."

"Was everyone all right?" Emma asked.

Michael nodded. "Bruised. But my car was totaled. It filled, almost instantly, with icy cold ditch water, which smelled pretty rancid. I have no idea what was in that ditch, and I don't want to know."

"Were you in trouble?"

"No," Michael said. "My dad said the loss of the car was punishment enough. I had put a lot of work into that car, and we'd only insured it for blue book at the price we'd paid."

"So you lost money?"

"And time."

Emma looked at him. "Why didn't you want to tell me?"

This time, he did flush. "I never told anyone this, not since I was sixteen. It was like my little secret."

"Because you were looking in the backseat?"

"I had no business doing that."

"And neither did they," Emma said. "Not in your car anyway."

He smiled. He hadn't told his father that part. He hadn't even spoken of it with his friend. Only Emma. And she, miraculously, had put it all in perspective.

"So," Emma said matter-of-factly, "did you get to see any?"

He frowned. "See any what?"

"Breasts."

Again his gaze met hers. In her eyes was a challenge, as if she wanted him to say something about the morning. "I think so."

"You *think* so?"

"It was dark—there were hands everywhere, and a lot of white skin. I'm hoping what I saw was breasts."

"I would have thought you'd have seen them after the accident," Emma said.

"Nope. Somehow she managed to get her shirt back on before the rest of us came to our senses."

"You sound disappointed."

"I got over it." Michael paused. "Thanks to this morning."

He was rewarded with her deepest blush yet. "I had forgotten that I sleep naked."

"No need to explain," he said. "It was my pleasure."

She looked down, and he felt her withdraw. A moment before, he had felt that intimacy again, the closeness that they seemed to flirt with, and now it was gone. Why? Was he doing something wrong?

"Emma—"

"We should probably get going again," she said in that prim little voice of hers. "Do you want me to drive?"

He sighed softly. The moment was gone. "No. I can do it. I promise to keep my eyes on the road."

———

Rapid City had tourist trap written all over it. From the time they'd entered the Badlands to the time they left

Wall Drug (which fascinated Emma to no end—Michael finally had to drag her out of there), Michael had the sense they were getting deeper into a world where no sane man would travel.

It all had a very 1950s feel—the signs, advertising attractions that would probably bore today's children within hours. Mount Rushmore had held a fascination for him as a child, probably because of *North by Northwest*, but today's kids would probably stare at it, proclaim it cool, and wonder where the high-tech roller coasters were.

A lot of the locals worked in the service industry, but he'd spent enough time here to know that the major employer was Ellsworth Air Force Base. Once you got past all the shops selling Black Hills Gold and attractions from the Crazy Horse Memorial to the Sioux Indian Museum, it became clear that the city had a military presence like few others he had ever encountered in the United States.

Emma seemed oblivious to it. But Michael, after having lived in liberal Madison, felt as if he were in an armed camp. Humvees and trucks and military vehicles drove side by side with the cars on the highway. Planes zoomed overhead, and in the parking lot at the Rushmore Mall, he saw young soldiers with their wives and children, heading for an evening out.

Michael had known finding a hotel room in Rapid wouldn't be hard this time of year, and he was right. Most of the hotels, which catered to tourists from all over the world, had no problem with cats. He and Emma got two rooms in an upscale chain—after he had made sure that there was a restaurant and it wasn't under construction—and they went their separate ways before dinner.

He had planned to do research into fine dining for the evening, but he didn't have the energy. The strange morning had worn him out, and after the breakfast he thought he had, but actually hadn't, he really didn't want a lot of rich food. So he decided that chain dining would be just fine.

He found that he couldn't stay in his room. He had already put in his run that morning—two, if his memory were to be believed—so he didn't want to overtax himself. But he could walk and stretch his legs.

The hotel was just off the interstate on rolling acres that had been shorn of trees. If he looked east, he could see the Rushmore Mall, and if he looked northwest, he could see the Black Hills. They disturbed him, just like the Badlands did. Perhaps it was because he knew the area's history—especially the last hundred years, filled with mindless slaughter of the Native Americans, which seemed to repeat over and over again. Or perhaps it was all the evidence of the strip mining that had polluted the land around Rapid and scarred the earth.

Or perhaps it was something more.

The Sioux believed that the Black Hills were the center of the world—that they had a mystical power. He had marked the Black Hills as a place to study when he got to magical beliefs in the Americas—and not just because of the Ghost Dancing and the events surrounding the original Wounded Knee massacre. There was a sense of age here, of things beyond his ken, and it was extremely strong.

For the first time, as he stood in the parking lot, he wondered if he shouldn't have taken Emma a different way. Would the power of the land enhance her abilities? Or was he being silly and superstitious?

He had no idea. But he was learning, with Emma, that it was better to plan for the worst because everything could change in the space of a heartbeat.

Darnell hated the hotel room. He paced its entire length, sniffing the floor, then stood by the door—demanding, in his own feline fashion, to be set free.

Emma pointed to his bed. "We're staying."

Darnell pawed at the door.

"We'd have to drive too far tonight. This is as good a place as any."

But Darnell didn't agree. He wanted out, and she would have to keep an eye on him to make certain that he didn't escape.

She sat on the edge of the queen-sized bed and patted the stiff paisley comforter. "Come here. Tell me what's bothering you."

His eyes narrowed, as if he feared she were going to put a spell on him. But she wasn't going to put a spell on anyone, not if she could help it.

"Okay, Darnell," she said. "You know how to nod and shake your head. I know you've learned that much and that you simply chose not to use it. But if you want your way, you have to talk to me."

He stared at her, ears flat.

"I'm not going to spell you, but I want to know what's bothering you." She smoothed the comforter. The room smelled slightly damp, as if the ancient air conditioner in the corner had been run too many times.

Darnell was watching her closely.

"Would you feel better if we moved to a different room?"

He shook his head once, then eyed her as if to say he wouldn't do anything more than that.

"How about a different hotel?"

Again, the head shake.

She sighed. "Is it the town?"

The cat hesitated for a moment, then shook his head again.

"The area?"

Darnell nodded. Once.

"How far do we have to go to make you feel better?"

He didn't move his head at all, but she could have sworn that his shoulders went up and down. Once. A shrug.

She sighed. "I wish you could tell me what you fear."

"Spirits," Darnell said, and butted his head against the door.

"I tell you he spoke to me," Emma said. She and Michael were sitting in a coffee shop. They had ordered, but none of the food had arrived yet. "He wants to leave. I promised him I'd tell you."

"He's not a lion again, is he?" Michael had his hand wrapped around his coffee mug as if he were holding onto it for security.

Emma smiled. "No. I didn't spell him to talk. I think I made a wish spell, and I think it was a simple one-time thing."

"A wish spell?"

"I said, 'I wish you could tell me what you fear' and

he said, 'Spirits,' and try as I might, I couldn't get him to speak again. He even opened his mouth a few times, but all that came out were some squeaky meows."

"Spirits." Michael gazed out the window, as if he could find answers in the parking lot. "I gotta say this area has me spooked too."

"Why?" Emma asked. And why wasn't she feeling anything different?

"All the history." Then Michael's gaze met hers. "Although to you, it wouldn't be history at all."

"Oh, no," she said. "That I feel. The land feels very old here, timeless, like it did near some of the Druid ruins when I was a girl."

Michael's gaze met hers in understanding. "Stonehenge."

She nodded. "Only here, the land feels damaged. Someone has poisoned the magic, and it's never going to be the same."

Michael sipped from his cup. "Maybe we should listen to Darnell. Maybe we should leave tonight and drive until he feels better."

"Oh, good," Emma said. "I thought part of the reason you were on this trip was so that I wouldn't have to take a cat's advice."

Michael smiled. "No. It was so that you wouldn't have to rely on his *judgment*."

"And there's a difference?"

Michael shrugged. "He's worried. I think we have to take that into account."

"Are you worried?" She slipped her hand around her mug. Its warmth soothed her.

"I'd be lying if I said I wasn't. I think we should take all warnings into consideration despite the source."

"Darnell has good survival instincts."

Michael nodded. "I figured."

"Would traveling until Darnell says stop make you feel better?" Emma wasn't sure how she felt about that. "I thought you were worried about me sleeping lightly and dreaming."

"I am worried about that," Michael said. "It feels as if we're in a damned if we do, damned if we don't situation."

Emma sighed. "Now you know how I've been feeling since the magic showed up."

Michael reached his hand out toward hers. Much as she wanted to take it, she didn't. She pretended she didn't even notice.

He left his hand outstretched, like an invitation.

"The problem is," he said slowly, "that if we start driving, we're committed. The roads start getting bleak from here on in. The only place I'd feel comfortable stopping in the middle of the night between here and Billings is Sheridan, and it's not the friendliest city I've ever been to."

"We could sleep in the car if we had to," Emma said.

"I don't want to," Michael said. "There's a whole lot of nothing between here and there, and sleeping in a car filled with stuff is an invitation to heaven knows what."

Emma sipped her own coffee. It was lukewarm. "If only I had control of my magic."

"If you had control of your magic, we wouldn't be on this trip."

She nodded. And if wishes were horses, beggars would ride. It was time that she accepted things the way they were.

"What did Darnell mean by spirits?" Michael asked. "Is there something I'm missing here?"

Emma frowned. "Spirits could mean several things. It could mean ghosts, memories of things that were—but they're not supposed to be harmful in any way. They are just images left on the land."

"What else?"

"Some kind of magic that I don't understand—magic that seems to have its own base. Places have their own magic, you know, and sometimes it seeps out and into the people who live on the land."

"If any place has that, the Black Hills do."

Emma nodded. She wasn't going to doubt how he and Darnell felt. "And then there is dark magic. Sometimes it sends its tendrils out like feelers. People often experience that like a cold draft on the back of the neck."

"Which do you think Darnell was feeling?"

"I don't know, and I'm not sure he can tell me. Cats experience the world differently than we do. He might have his own ideas—and I'm not going to spell him so that he can talk."

Michael grinned. "Rapid City doesn't need news of a black lion."

"If I do that to Darnell again, I have no idea what fate I'll suffer."

Finally Michael slipped his hand back. "What do you want to do, Emma? I'll go with your decision."

She finished her coffee and leaned back in her chair. Around her, people were shopping—young girls gazing at mall displays, families strolling through the center as if it were a park, an occasional harried businessman with shopping bags over his shoulder. It all looked so normal, so right. Yet she knew they all had cares and worries, things she couldn't fathom just from watching them.

Was Michael right? Did they all want magic?

Probably. But magic that they could control, a way of improving their lives, of having exactly what they wanted. Not something that peeked into their dreams and created fantastical things.

"What if we keep going tonight," she said, "and because I'm worried about spirits, I conjure my own? We won't know if I've done it or if they come from somewhere else. And we'll be on the most desolate stretch of highway, in the roughest part of the country—just the two of us."

Michael looked at her. It was clear he hadn't thought of this. "You could do it just as easily in your sleep."

"Maybe," she said softly, not looking at him, "we should keep the connecting door open tonight."

"Unlocked?" he asked.

She shook her head. The suggestion made her nervous. "Open, just a crack."

"So that the spirits that visit you will also visit me?"

Her gaze met his for a moment. He seemed more abrupt than she expected. She had no idea why that was. "I guess it wasn't a good idea."

His gaze still hadn't left hers. It looked like he was struggling with something. "The best way to protect you," he said softly, "is to be in the same room with you."

Her breath caught in her throat. She didn't want to be alone with him, did she?

Of course she did. And that was the problem.

"Michael, I can't."

"Why not?" he asked. "Are there some deep, dark secrets I don't know about you?"

She got up abruptly and put her coffee cup on the

counter. The waitress looked over her shoulder at Emma, who then asked for a glass of water. The waitress gave it to her and Emma walked back to the table.

"Should I take that to be a yes?" Michael asked.

"I could hurt you," she said. "In my dreams."

"You could do that from across the country," he said. "Someone'll put it right."

"You have a lot of faith in us."

"No," he said. "I'm gaining faith in you."

She smiled into her water, unable to look at him.

"Now," he said, "why don't you have some faith in me? We'll transfer to a room with double beds and I'll sleep in the one nearest the door. I won't try anything funny."

She felt a pang of disappointment then, but kept it from registering on her face.

"And," he said, "I'll guard you as best a mortal man can."

It was so tempting. But the problem wasn't really him. It was her. She wanted to be in his bed, beside him, touching him. And she didn't want to tell him. She didn't want him to get the wrong idea.

"I know you will," she said.

"Then what's the hesitation?"

She raised her head. He was watching her, his blue eyes so intense that she could barely breathe. "Did I ever tell you how I slipped into that magic coma?"

Michael frowned. "No."

She rested her face between her hands. Her fingers clutched at her hair. "Aethelstan kissed me."

"And then you fell asleep?" Michael's frown deepened. "Isn't it supposed to be the opposite? Aren't kisses supposed to break someone out of a magic spell?"

"Some spells."

"But not that one?"

"No," she said. "Not that one. At least, not so far as I know. And if a kiss was supposed to get me out of it, Aethelstan was the wrong man to try it."

"So," Michael said slowly, "you haven't kissed anyone for a thousand years?"

"Aethelstan, once," she said. "When he captured Ealhswith, my evil stepmother. I wanted to prove to myself that she was gone."

"And nothing happened?"

"I didn't slip into a magical coma, not then." Emma took a shaky breath. "But it wasn't a real kiss."

Michael hadn't moved. "What do you mean?"

"There was no passion," she whispered. "No real caring. It was a thank-you."

"On both your parts?" he asked.

She nodded. "Aethelstan was in love with Nora by then. I don't think he felt anything for me at all, except maybe friendship. And at that point, I'm not even sure he felt that."

Michael glanced around the mall as if he too were trying to find sanity in its normalcy. "What kind of spell did she put on you?"

"We think it was a kiss-and-tell spell, which is really potent and long-lasting, but we're not sure. She never did confess. And she stirred up the waters more than once. She told Aethelstan that it hadn't worn off, but he'd kissed a number of women in the meantime—"

"While you, his so-called beloved, were under a magic spell?"

Emma nodded. She had tried not to think about that. "It was a thousand years."

"My God, Emma, if it were my beloved, I don't care if it were a million years. I'd be doing everything I could to get her out of it, awake, and at my side."

"I think it was pretty clear to Aethelstan from the start that I wasn't his beloved." Her heart twisted. She hadn't spoken of this to anyone.

"Was it clear to you?"

She shook her head. That kiss—that first kiss—had been the center of her world. And then the end of it.

But when she had seen him after she had awakened, she had thought that he had been there for her in just the way Michael described. Then he had looked over her shoulder at Nora and Emma had known, right then, that he had never cared for her the way he cared for his future wife.

"It's all right," Emma said. "It worked out for the best."

"For him, maybe," Michael said. "But it sounds like you got nothing. Less than nothing. He stole a thousand years of your life and didn't even have the integrity to stand by you."

"It wasn't his fault."

"It sounds like some of it was."

"Michael, you don't understand—"

"I understand enough to know that this man treated you terribly. How can you defend him?"

Emma shrugged. "He's my friend."

"Some friend," Michael muttered.

She didn't know how to explain this to him. "Michael, I need him right now."

"Isn't there someone else you can train with? What about that list he gave you? Surely someone on there can train you."

"Not someone I trust."

"You trust him? After all that?"

She slid her hands out of her hair and folded them in front of her. Her heart was pounding hard. She hadn't expected Michael's strong reaction.

"Aethelstan stood by me. He didn't have to. He could have let Ealhswith have me. But he didn't, even though after a hundred years, he barely remembered me."

"He should have remembered you."

"No." Emma grabbed a napkin and tore a corner off it. "He remembered what had happened, but he couldn't remember what I looked like, or sounded like. You know how that is, how memories fade."

Michael put a hand over hers. Beneath them, the napkin was in shreds. "You wouldn't have faded in my mind."

She slipped her hand away from his. "You don't know me."

"I know you better than anyone else has," he said. "I'll wager you haven't told Aethelstan how much he hurt you."

She smiled. "I yelled at him a lot."

"It's not the same thing."

Michael was right. It wasn't.

"I don't blame him," she said. "I can't. He and Nora did all they could to make it up to me."

"But she married him."

Emma raised her head. "Because I didn't want him."

"What?" Michael leaned back as if she had surprised him.

"Aethelstan misinterpreted a prophecy. He thought we were soul mates. He was willing to be with me no matter what, no matter how wrong we were for each other." Emma smiled sadly. "I wasn't that strong."

"So what happened?"

"I threw plates at him."

"Plates?"

"In Quixotic. He wanted me to learn a trade. I still had a medieval perspective. I wasn't going to work. I was a lady."

Michael's lips twitched. "I see."

"And that was the end of it. We couldn't agree on anything. So I told Aethelstan I wanted nothing to do with him. And then he married Nora."

"Didn't that hurt you?"

Emma shook her head. "I was relieved. I was afraid I'd have to spend the rest of my life with him."

"Afraid?"

"Yeah," she said softly. "It would have been awful."

"Even though you loved him."

"I don't think I ever loved him," she said. She had thought about that for years. "I think we were caught up in all that excitement of attraction and first kisses. I don't think it was love, even back then."

Michael was holding himself rigidly, as if he were afraid a movement would betray him. Attraction and first kisses—where she and he were now.

"And then," Emma said, "we kissed, and I lost a thousand years. And when I woke up, everything was paved, and Aethelstan looked old enough to be my father."

"Wow," Michael said.

She nodded, then sighed. Her life, empty as it was, now open for him to see.

"So," he said. "What has all of this to do with sharing a room?"

She froze. She had forgotten how she had even gotten

on the subject. But she had been the one to bring it up. She pushed her chair away from the table, and slumped down. She didn't look at him—at least not directly.

"I like you, Michael."

"I like you, too, Emma."

"No," she whispered. "I really like you."

That smile was back on his face. She could see it out of the corner of her eye. "Does that mean you're worried about what'll happen if we share a room?"

"Yes," she said.

"What if I swear to protect your virtue?" There was no humor in his voice. She looked at him. The smile was gone now. He seemed very serious.

"I'm not worried about you," she said.

He took her hand. His touch was electric; she could feel it throughout her entire body. It was as if no one had ever really touched her before.

"I'd be lying if I said I wasn't attracted to you too," he said, "but I can promise that I won't kiss you."

He made it sound so easy. Maybe it was for him. She started to pull her hand away, but his grip tightened.

"Don't get me wrong," he said, his voice slightly husky. "I want to kiss you. Very much. But I understand your fear. I'm telling you that I respect it."

Her eyes burned and she had to look away. No one had been this tender with her, ever. Not even Darnell, who in his little catlike way, always had his own agenda.

"Now I understand why you're always pulling away." Michael's forefinger traced her knuckles. The movement was both gentle and erotic. A wave of desire ran through her. "I thought for a long time that you simply weren't attracted to me."

"It was better that way," she said, watching his finger move. She wanted to stop him, to make the feeling go away, but she also wanted him to keep touching her—forever.

"Not for me."

"Michael, we can't do anything. Nothing will come of this."

His hand covered hers again. "Emma, people can have long relationships without kissing. There's more to—"

She put her finger on his lips. "I know. I have cable."

He hadn't moved. It was as if he were holding himself back, as if his first inclination was to kiss the finger she pressed against him.

She dropped her hand. He tightened his grip on her other one—a squeeze, a reassurance.

"Michael," she said. "I have no idea how deep the spell goes."

"You said it was a kiss spell."

"I said she often lied about what kind of spell it was."

His face paled. "You mean that any kind of physical intimacy might trigger that coma again?"

"I don't know," she said.

"If something happened, couldn't someone appeal to the Fates? After all, it would be wrong. She's gone. The spell should have been removed. Right? Or wouldn't they see it that way?"

"They probably would." Emma clenched her free hand on her lap. More than anything she wanted to cover his hand with her own, feel the weight of both of their hands on top of hers. But she didn't.

She wouldn't.

"I don't understand the problem then," he said.

"Their sense of time is different from ours. They might reverse the spell, and I would still lose ten, twenty, forty years of my life. I'm not willing to do that again, Michael."

"I understand that," he said. "Oddly enough, it makes complete sense to me. But it sure makes for a lonely existence."

"I know," Emma said softly.

He studied her for a moment. The compassion on his face was almost more than she could bear. "At some point, Emma, you might want to find out if the spell still exists."

"You mean test it?"

He nodded.

"Why?" she asked. "Why would I do that?"

"Because right now you're operating on supposition. And you could live another thousand years—a lonely woman with a series of cats. What if, five hundred years from now, you find out that you were wrong, that the spell was gone?"

She let out a small shuddery sigh. She hadn't thought of that before.

"You see, even if you lose thirty years to a test, it will still prevent you from living alone for the next thousand."

"Assuming someone would want me," Emma said.

Michael placed his other hand over hers. The warmth and weight of his hands was comforting, and still arousing. "I would want you."

"You thought I faked all my research. You thought I was incompetent and a fraud."

"And I was attracted to you even then. God help me, Emma, even when I thought you were betraying everything I believed in, I still wanted to be with you."

She finally did put her hand on his. A hand pile, the most physical they would probably ever get. "That's why you said no to the trip."

"You were confusing me. I'd never felt like this about a woman before. My choices in the past were always very logical." Her gaze met his. He smiled ruefully. "And passionless. No wonder they didn't last."

"Anything between us would be passionless too, Michael," she said.

He laughed. "Emma, you and I have never lacked for passion. It's physical intimacy that's the problem."

"So the dream, that was just an excuse?"

"The dream had me worried," he said. "I didn't want to know that you had left the world because I was attracted to you."

"My beauty," she said sadly. "Just like everyone else."

He sighed. "I guess I deserved that. I even thought that for a while. But, Emma, it was more from the start."

"You'd like to believe that anyway," she said. Maybe when she got her magic, she would make her face plain, so that no one stared at her. She had so many things that other people wanted, and they were such empty, useless things.

"No, Emma," he said. "I know that it was more."

"You can't know that," she said.

"Oh, but I can."

"How?"

"I thought you were crazy. I'd seen beautiful crazy women before, and I've never ever been attracted to them."

She traced his knuckles with her finger. It was just as erotic in the reverse. She made herself stop.

"I used to wonder," she said, "if part of Ealhswith's spell wasn't to make me irresistible to men."

"You're saying my feelings for you are magic?" He pulled one of his hands out from under hers and caught hers. Now he was holding both her hands, gently but firmly. "How insecure are you, Emma?"

"I am about some things."

"How can you be? You're talented, smart, and beautiful."

"It's really quite simple." She slipped her hands away from his. "Darnell's the only person—if you want to call him that—who ever wanted to be with me more than he wanted to be with anyone else."

"Come now, Emma—"

"Think about it," she said as she stood up and walked away.

───※───

He did think about it. He sat alone in the mall restaurant, drinking coffee and waiting for his hormones to stop jumping.

No one had wanted Emma from the beginning. Her parents had given her away. The woman they had given her to was a hideous person, one that Michael didn't entirely understand. And then she had become infatuated with a boy, who had harmed her. After rediscovering him in a time of crisis, he turned away from her and married another woman.

For the last ten years, her best friend had been a cat. An elderly cat, who, for all his feistiness, didn't have many years left.

Why would Emma believe anyone would fight for her? Even Michael had shown her, by his actions, that he only wanted to be with her under duress.

Well, it was time to prove himself now. He would help her free herself from this curse. Even if she ultimately decided that she didn't want to be with him—and why would a beautiful magical creature want to be with a stodgy professor?—she would at least know that he had cared.

And she would be free to fall in love, sometime in her very long life.

Somehow the idea didn't comfort him. The best he could hope for was that when she really did fall in love, it would be long after he was gone.

Because, spell or not, she had stolen his heart—and only now had he realized it was missing.

Chapter 11

WHEN MICHAEL RETURNED TO THE HOTEL NEARLY AN hour later, Emma had already moved them to a new room with two queen-sized beds. Fortunately the desk clerk had caught Michael or he would have gone to the old room. He went up three flights of stairs, feeling slightly cranky and oddly uncomfortable that Emma had touched his things.

The new key card the desk clerk had given him worked like a charm, and Michael opened the door, only to find a growling Darnell. Even regular-cat-sized, Darnell looked ferocious, his incisors bared and his eyes flashing yellow.

"It's me, buddy," Michael said as he slipped inside.

Darnell's hackles fell. He backed away, and then walked to the window as if he had meant to growl at the man who had defended him two days before.

"At least we avoided a pizza moment," Emma said.

"A pizza moment?"

"He used to attack the pizza delivery guys."

"Charming cat you have there."

Emma shrugged. "I told you. He likes me. And that means he defends me, whether I need it or not."

Michael closed the door and stepped farther into the room. It was much bigger than the one he had left, and actually had a tiny view of the Black Hills in the distance.

Emma had all the lights on, even the bathroom lights.

The TV was tuned to CNN Headline News. She was sitting on the bed closest to the window wearing a thin blue-and-white striped robe and dark blue socks. Her hair was pulled away from her face, which had a fresh-scrubbed look. The room smelled faintly of bath oil, and Michael wondered what he had missed.

He didn't want to know. Or rather, he didn't want to think about it. He had promised, after all.

"You didn't tell me we'd move before I got back."

"I figured when your key didn't work, you'd go downstairs and found out where we were." She sounded matter of fact, but she hadn't looked at him. She was staring at the television. Her right hand was toying with the remote.

"What's Darnell think of this?"

To Michael's surprise, the cat yowled. Darnell was standing in the middle of the floor, legs spread, shaking his little feline head.

"Is he saying no?"

"I told you he could communicate without having to say the words."

"He really wants out of here."

"Well," Emma said. "I really want a good night's sleep."

She still hadn't looked at him. Apparently the conversation embarrassed her. Or maybe the situation did. Michael wondered if she had ever shared a room with anyone—at least after her coma—and he would wager that she hadn't.

"It's awfully early for lights out," Michael said, sitting on his bed.

"What do you want to do?" Emma asked. "Play a game of Parcheesi?"

Michael laughed. "Who taught you how to play Parcheesi?"

"Nora's mother. She adored the game."

Michael shook his head. "Parcheesi is not my idea of a good time."

Emma plucked at the thin bedspread. Her ears had turned red. Apparently she would take anything he said tonight in exactly the wrong way.

He sighed. He wasn't about to tell her that he didn't have pajamas or a robe. He got out of bed, and opened his suitcase, which Emma had thoughtfully placed on the suitcase holder in the closet. Then he removed a pair of running shorts and a T-shirt. It wouldn't be the most comfortable outfit to sleep in, but it would work.

For a moment, he hesitated. He'd shared hotel rooms before with other adults—adults he wasn't involved with—and usually they just turned aside as he changed clothes. But he doubted Emma would do that. He took his clothing into the bathroom, feeling like a virgin bride on the wedding night.

The scent of the bath oil was even stronger in here. The tub was still slick and water beaded on the porcelain. A damp towel hung on the hook behind the door. Had Emma expected him back sooner? Or had she known that he would be gone long enough for her to take a bath?

Or was her subconscious playing more tricks on them both, this time fallible, human tricks? Whatever it was, it was working. He finger combed his hair, and let himself out of the room, wishing he hadn't suggested this arrangement in the first place.

Darnell was still pacing. He looked like a tiny black

guard who was determined to keep his mistress safe. Michael picked him up. Darnell's body was rigid.

"We'll make sure everything goes okay tonight, big guy," he said. "You need some rest too."

Darnell squirmed out of his arms, and jumped onto Emma's bed. He laid at the foot and alternated between looking at the door and looking at the window. At least he wasn't pacing anymore.

CNN started its news cycle all over again. Michael sighed, pulled out his pillows, and settled on his bed.

It was going to be a very long night.

Even after she had turned out all the lights, Emma couldn't get to sleep. The room felt different than any other bedroom she'd ever been in. Michael's presence seemed stronger in the darkness—his even breathing, the rustling of his sheets, the occasional sigh. If she squinted, she could see his shape in the darkness, lying on his side, facing the wall.

He hadn't tried anything. He had promised and he had been able to keep that promise.

Part of her was very disappointed about that.

She fluffed her pillows for the six hundredth time and stared at the ceiling. She had wanted to get some sleep but now she wasn't sure it was possible, not with Michael so close. Everything had changed with their conversation. Now he knew that she wasn't avoiding him. Now he knew that she found him attractive. And, it seemed, he found her attractive too.

Michael's presence wasn't the only thing that kept her awake. She was afraid of her dreams. Michael knew to wake her up, but she wasn't sure if he'd remember in the heat of some strangeness.

Although there was a better chance of him remembering than Darnell would. Darnell, who hadn't left the foot of the bed, who continued to watch the window and door as if he expected one of them to suddenly open and something horrible to come through.

She pressed her fingers against her temple, trying to wipe out that thought. What she was most afraid of was that the something horrible would come from her very own mind.

It took nearly an hour, but she finally dozed. She had no idea how long she had been asleep when she awoke to the sound of voices. Whispering voices.

She couldn't make out the words, but the shush-shush sound of them made her hair stand on end. She was breathing shallowly, not sure if they would disappear now that she was awake.

Shapes surrounded her bed. Gray shapes that seemed to have no real substance. Over their whispers, she could hear Michael's soft breathing and Darnell's snores. They were asleep.

Or maybe she was dreaming.

She willed herself to wake up, but nothing happened. No changes, nothing. So she propped herself up on her elbows. The shapes moved like oil on water.

"What do you want?" she asked in her most menacing voice.

Darnell's snoring stopped. She had at least awakened the cat. Then she realized that Michael's breathing no longer held the even rhythm of sleep. He was awake too.

"I said what do you want?" She spoke even louder this

time. Michael shifted on his bed. She heard the creaking mattress, but she couldn't see him through the shapes.

The whispering had stopped when she had first spoken, but it started up again. This time it was louder.

Loose magic…

Loose magic…

Loose magic…

Darnell's fur was standing on end. He had risen to his feet and he was growling.

"What do you mean?" Emma asked.

So easy to take…

So easy…

"What the hell is this?" Michael asked. Just the sound of his voice reassured her. But it didn't reassure Darnell. He was still growling.

You don't want it…

Don't want it…

"What are you talking about?" Emma asked.

A simple gift…

A simple gift…

A simple gift—

Darnell yowled and launched himself at the shadows. He went right through them, although he was yelping as his fur met with their grayness. They shredded like fog in a breeze and then they vanished as if they never were.

Darnell landed on Michael, kicking and clawing. Michael grabbed Darnell and held him over his head. Darnell was fighting harder than Emma had ever seen him. He was frantic, yowling and hissing and clawing and biting.

"Emma!" Michael said.

She eased herself off the bed and crossed the small space between them. The air still had a slimy feel, as if the shadows had left something behind. She grabbed Darnell, got sliced for her efforts, and cradled him, trying to calm him.

He continued to growl, but he stopped clawing and trying to bite.

"I think we're awake, aren't we?" Michael asked.

"Your guess is as good as mine," Emma said.

"That felt real enough. But maybe I should try to wake you again."

She flicked on a light. "Nothing else has changed. Except that you're bleeding."

Michael's T-shirt was ripped, and blood seeped through the holes. She set Darnell down. The cat looked up at Michael as if he were apologizing.

"Take off your shirt," Emma said. "Let's see how bad that is."

Michael grabbed the bottom of the shirt and pulled it over his head. "I was fantasizing that you would ask me to undress, but not in these circumstances."

She had been fantasizing too, but her imagination wasn't up to the perfection of his muscled chest and lean torso. His shoulders were broader than she had thought.

The perfect male physique—in any century.

Except that this physique was bleeding from ten scratch marks, made by her cat.

Michael finished pulling off his shirt. She was still staring at him. She blushed.

"Um, let me wash this off."

"No," he said. "I can do it. Just keep that killer cat out of my way."

He didn't sound angry. In fact, his comment about Darnell sounded vaguely amused. He got off the bed and walked into the bathroom.

"Scarred for life!" he announced.

"Is it bad?" Emma asked.

"Nothing I can't fix."

She heard the sound of running water. She would have gone to help him, except for the memory of that chest—so very fine, even with Darnell's changes.

Darnell was still staring at the empty spot between the beds, his hackles up. He wasn't growling anymore, but he was braced, ready to attack if the things came back.

Emma gingerly reached out. The oily feel had left the air. It was as if the shapes had never been.

"What were they, do you think?" Michael asked. He had come out of the bathroom, a towel wrapped around his neck.

"I don't know," she said.

"This loose magic thing. Have you heard of it?"

She shook her head.

"Wow," Michael said. "Lack of education in your world is costly, isn't it?"

"I guess so." She let out a small sigh. "I suppose that's the point of all this."

"What is?"

"Making my life difficult so that I'll never disobey the rules again. Everyone says the rules are there for a reason. Only I didn't deliberately disobey them."

"Of course not," Michael said, sounding confused.

"I just thought I had another twenty years. I mean, I'm only thirty."

"Yeah—um." Michael frowned. "How do you figure?"

"I told you. Technically. I've only been awake thirty years. My body is only thirty."

"How do you know?"

"I can have babies," she snapped. "Do you know any thousand-year-old women who can have babies?"

"I-I guess I'd have to say that I do."

"What?"

"You're the first thousand-year-old woman I've ever met."

"I'm thirty!" Emma said.

Michael held out his hands like a man who was afraid of being shot. "Right. Right. You're thirty."

She nodded.

"And I'm Henry the Eighth. Reincarnated."

Anger rushed through her as quickly as desire had earlier. "How can you say that? It's not fair—"

"Life's not fair, Emma." He was speaking softly. "I grant it's been particularly unfair to you, in ways I could never comprehend. But you were born over a thousand years ago. I know that women like to fudge their ages, and you can pass for thirty—"

"Pass for thirty? *Pass* for thirty?"

"But by the way we mortals count ages, you're one thousand and forty, and no amount of fudging will change that."

"Except that I was in some kind of stasis. Except that I came into my magic before menopause. That never, ever, ever happens."

"That's something you'll have to take up with your own people."

"I have!" she said, getting off the bed. "And they're as stubborn about this as you are."

"I'm not stubborn on this."

"Well, it sounds like you are!"

"Emma," he said softly. "I'm not the one you're angry at."

"Really?" She put her hands on her hips. Darnell cringed. "You could have fooled me."

"Emma," he said in that same calm tone, "think about it. If you fight me, you'll be wasting energy. We have to find out what those shapes were."

She made herself take a deep breath. He was right, of course. She had survived the last ten years by fighting hard for herself and for what she believed in. But the end result was that she attacked before she got attacked. Her anger was her shield. She was beginning to learn that she didn't need her shield with Michael.

"I guess," she said, sitting on her own bed, "that they're Darnell's spirits."

Darnell looked at her, his golden eyes bright. It was as if he felt vindicated.

"We should find out what they're really about," Michael said.

She nodded. Then she sighed. "I'm sorry I got angry."

"It's all right," he said. "I'm getting used to it."

"Oh, that makes me feel better," she said with Midwestern irony.

He smiled. "You're beautiful when you're angry, Emma."

She turned away from him. He leaned across the space between them and took her hand. His touch was as electric as before.

She didn't have enough strength to pull away. "Michael…"

"Emma, listen. You're upset. It's been a stressful night. Let me hold you. Nothing else. Just two people comforting each other."

She shook her head quickly before she had a chance to change her mind.

"I promised not to kiss you," he said. "And I promise just a simple arm around your shoulder. Nothing else."

His hand felt so good holding hers. Just that touch made her calmer even as it stirred desire within her. "Michael…"

"I promise," he said.

She let him pull her back toward his bed. Then he moved over, giving her the spot warmed by his body. He fluffed the pillows behind them and put his arm around her.

Darnell growled.

"If you can hold her like this, pal, you're welcome to take my place," Michael said.

Darnell started up the bed.

"But holding *you* is no substitute. You have to put your paw around her."

Darnell sat down, then laid down, defeated.

Emma smiled, and leaned into Michael. He felt very, very good. She wanted to shift in his arms, to hold him in return, but she didn't.

It was too dangerous. Maybe when they got to Portland, where Aethelstan could help, then she could kiss Michael or respond in the way he wanted.

But not until then.

Michael rested his cheek on the top of her head. Being in his arms felt right. She had never felt like she belonged before.

She did now.

—∿∿—

Michael didn't sleep at all. He had the most beautiful woman in the world—one of the most beautiful women in all of history—in his arms, asleep. She might never let him touch her again. He didn't want to forget a moment of it.

Until tonight, he hadn't realized the depth of her panic—and the way that she defended herself when the panic took over. Her anger had probably kept her safe for a long time, but he suspected it wouldn't work against out-of-control magic and misty gray shapes that whispered in the night.

He had to get Emma to Oregon. If they continued at the pace they were on, they had two more stops after Rapid City—Billings and Spokane. The roads out West were increasingly desolate. He really didn't want to get stuck on one in the middle of the night. They wouldn't be able to walk for help—and the chances of someone passing by were much slimmer than they were almost anywhere else in the country. The West was a large region, filled with loners and empty spaces where only a few hardy folks could live.

The image of Emma in trouble, the image from his dream, had stuck with him. He didn't want any situation in which that scenario could come true.

So as dawn crept through the window, he gently shook her awake. Part of him had hoped that by doing so, they'd go back to the moment before the shadows entered the room. Part of him was glad when it hadn't happened. He had treasured holding her, treasured her warmth, her even breathing, the fresh scent of her hair.

She stirred and her hand eased up his chest, sending shivers of delight through him. She cupped his chin and for a long, heart-stopping moment, he thought she was going to kiss him. He wondered if he would have the strength to stop her.

He hoped so.

Then she smiled at him and slipped out of his arms. She disappeared into the bathroom, leaving him aroused, and touched, and wanting to defend her even more.

He wondered if she knew that she was his lady, and he her knight defender. If he were a medieval knight, he would ask for a token and keep it close to his heart. Instead, he would have to use the memory of her face as that token.

Then he sighed and eased himself off the bed. He had never understood courtly love before.

He wished he didn't understand it now.

Chapter 12

EMMA ARRIVED IN THE HOTEL COFFEE SHOP, FEELING shaken and uneasy. She had just gotten off the phone with Aethelstan, and she needed to tell Michael about the conversation.

Michael was sitting at a table by the window. It had a great view of the parking lot, still covered with winter gravel and sand despite the fact that it was May. A woman stood near the ditch, throwing day-old bread toward some birds that had gathered as if this were a daily ritual. This coffee shop was a far cry from the restaurant of Emma's dreams.

Michael seemed to feel that as well. He was stirring his plate of runny scrambled eggs as if he could create enough friction to finish cooking them. A large, soggy blueberry muffin stood beside his tiny glass of obviously canned orange juice, and some burnt toast was teetering precariously off the edge of the table.

Emma sat down. Michael had ordered her some orange juice and coffee. A menu still sat in front of her place. The waitress came over, pad in hand, and Emma ordered cereal and an English muffin, lightly cooked. After looking at Michael's eggs, she was afraid to order anything else.

"You don't look so good," Michael said after the waitress left.

"That's a terrible thing to say to a woman, especially

first thing in the morning." Emma sipped the orange juice. She was right. A mix, probably from a giant can of Tang, out of the back. She almost spat it back into the glass.

"You know what I mean."

"Unfortunately, I do." She hadn't been able to look at him since she woke up. She had been so comfortable in his arms. She had felt right there, and she knew if she let something like that happen again, she would forget herself.

Michael shoved his plate aside and picked at the blueberry muffin. He had been shy all morning too.

"Aethelstan was not encouraging," she said.

"He knew what the shadows were."

"No. But he said my guesses were good ones. And he had a few of his own."

Michael took a bite of the muffin and grimaced. He pushed that plate away as well.

"You have to eat something," Emma said.

"Who made up that rule?" he asked.

"Me. I have to ride with you."

He piled the toast on the eggs, then topped the whole mess with the muffin plate. "We'll stop at a 7-11 on the way out of town. Even Ding Dongs would be better than this."

"Ding Dongs?"

He smiled. "You have interesting gaps in your modern education."

"I'm sure you'll rectify that one," she said.

He nodded. "Aethelstan?"

She sighed. "He said that the shadows could have been feelers. There are several wizards in the area whose names he did not give me. Apparently this place draws a certain kind of practitioner."

"Not a good one, I take it."

The waitress set down a bowl with a box of Raisin Bran unopened in the center. Then she set down a single-serving size carton of milk, and an English muffin, toasted black.

"Yuck," Emma said, but by that time, the waitress had disappeared.

"This was the place you should have transformed," he said.

"And condemn fifty chefs to spending the rest of their lives here? Michael, you're crueler than I thought."

He picked up the milk and looked at the carton date. Then he opened it and sniffed it. "Passable, but I suggest Ding Dongs."

"I may take you up on it, but I need something to get me to there." Emma poured the Raisin Bran into her bowl, and covered the whole mess with sugar, then milk. The milk hadn't turned, but it was threatening to. "Aethelstan wouldn't say much about them, except that they were drawn here over a hundred years ago with the soldiers who fought in the Indian wars. This land has a lot of power and they were part of the changes we see now."

"So I was right," Michael said. "They're not good people. And they've sent out feelers?"

"Loose magic can be captured," she said.

"I'm still not sure what loose magic means," Michael said.

"It means magic that no one controls." Her voice shook. She had promised herself she wouldn't let him see how upset she was, and she was failing at that.

"I don't understand," he said. "If they could capture your magic, why didn't they do it last night?"

"Because I have to give it to them."

"You won't do that," he said.

"I might, if they manage to coax it out of me."

He shook his head. "Things just keep getting better and better."

"Aethelstan says they can't harm us once we get to Billings."

"Billings is most of a day's drive from here."

"I know." Emma ate for a moment. The cereal was passable—better, at least, than the burned muffin. "I talked to the desk clerk. He said that there's a shortcut between here and Billings."

"I've heard about Western shortcuts," Michael said. "They look shorter on the map, but they drive long because you're on single lane roads or going through mountains."

"He swears it's shorter," Emma said. "But he did warn me that it was desolate."

"Desolate, great," Michael said.

"Maybe we won't run into anyone there."

"And if we do, what, then? There'll be no phones or help."

"We're traveling in the day time. And if I remember right, it's not exactly populated on I-90. I looked at the map. It would cut off quite a few miles and we'd still end up in Billings."

"It sounds like a risk," Michael said.

"This whole trip is a risk, Michael," Emma said, "but the Fates promised me that it wasn't the hardest thing I've ever done."

Michael let out a small laugh. "Emma, you did the

impossible by learning how to survive in this culture. How could anything else compare?"

"That's their point, I guess." She ate one last bite of the cereal. Maybe these Ding Dongs, whatever they were, would be better.

"But I haven't done that," Michael said. "I spent most of my life wrapped up in books."

Emma smiled at him. "You'll be fine. You're *wulfstrang*."

"What?"

She hadn't meant to let that slip. "Maybe you need an adventure."

"I always thought my trips to England were adventure enough."

She leaned back in her chair. "Was your life at risk?"

"Only from bad driving."

"Did you save any damsels in distress?"

"Just an old woman who tripped going down the sidewalk. I caught her and she whacked me with her cane."

Emma chuckled. "At least my people haven't changed much."

"Your people," he said. "Your people didn't even speak English."

"Just its precursor. You could say that I'm proto-English."

"You could say that you're overeducated."

Her smile grew. "I'll take that as a compliment, Professor Found."

He nodded. "You should."

"And you should enjoy your adventure."

His gaze softened. "I enjoyed last night."

She felt a shiver run through her. "The shadows?"

"No." He smiled. "And, before you ask, I didn't enjoy

it when Darnell pushed his ample backside against my hip, either."

"I enjoyed it too," Emma said, picking up the check. "And I wasn't speaking of Darnell either."

"The poor cat. His ears are probably burning."

"I hope not," she said. "We'd pay for that, if that's the case."

"As if we're not going to pay for having breakfast without him."

Emma surveyed the table. "Something tells me that even Darnell wouldn't have enjoyed this meal."

Michael said, "Something tells me that you're right."

An hour later, they had finished packing the car and were on the road. Emma let Michael drive. He seemed tired that morning. She figured she'd give him the first shift, and then take over. It looked as if he hadn't slept as well as he said he had.

She didn't want to think about that.

Michael didn't stop at a 7-11. He stopped at a grocery store, bought a lot of bottled water and even more food, which he put into the cooler along with some ice packs. He didn't say much, but Emma could feel his concern about their route. At least he hadn't vetoed her decision to try the shortest way to get out of the Black Hills.

As they drove to the outskirts of town, a man rode by on a white horse. The man, who was wearing grimy army fatigues and a jacket too heavy for the weather, had a sleeping bag rolled up against the horse's flank. They seemed to be heading toward the center of town.

Emma watched them until they disappeared.

"So," Michael said, "want a Ding Dong?"

He had introduced her to an entire subcategory of food she had never seen before. Ding Dongs, Hostess Cupcakes, and packaged powdered donuts, all of which looked like they could have survived in her glass coffin for a thousand years. Michael swore that Americans learned to eat them on their mother's knee. Emma privately thought all mothers who taught kids to eat that stuff should be shot.

"No," she said.

"You have to try one. You're judging them by the package."

"The packages were older than that cereal I ate this morning."

Michael nodded. "But these were meant to last. Open one for me, would you?"

She did. The chocolate frosting had a plastic feel. She handed one to Michael. He took it.

"Try the second one," he said.

"Michael—"

"Emma, you have given me adventure on this trip. The least I can do is return the favor."

She laughed and bit into the Ding Dong. Beneath the frosting was chocolate cake and a creamy center. "What's in the middle?" she asked with her mouth full.

"I have no idea," he said. "Blissful ignorance. It's best when you buy prepackaged food."

She chewed for a moment, and then decided that this stuff wasn't so bad after all. Aethelstan would be having a fit if he knew what she was eating. He always swore that the best thing about long life was learning a culture's best foods and preserving them for the future.

She doubted he would want to preserve these. Not that it mattered. They probably preserved themselves.

"Good, huh?"

"I wouldn't say good." She took another bite. "Addicting, though."

"Yeah, they are that. When I was twelve I went through an entire case of them."

"Ew," she said.

He laughed. "I survived."

"I'm not sure I would." She finished the Ding Dong, and wiped her hand on a napkin that was in the bag. She had to admit that a Ding Dong was a better breakfast than the one she'd had in the coffee shop.

Michael turned north toward Sturgis. Emma sighed with relief that they were leaving Rapid City.

Aethelstan wouldn't tell her exactly where those other wizards lived—*You might confront them, Emma, and that wouldn't be a good idea*, he had said. To her credit, she hadn't shouted at him like she would have two days ago. He didn't respect her, he thought she was trouble, and there was nothing she could do about that. Besides, knowing where they lived wasn't critical information. It just would have eased her mind to know when she was out of their jurisdiction.

Aethelstan never worried about easing Emma's mind.

A group of white horses and riders rode single file on the road's shoulder. Emma frowned at them. Some people had tattered saddlebags, and most seemed to be wearing too many clothes. Many of them were older, with unwashed hair and dirty faces. Some mangy dogs ran at their side.

"What is this?" Michael asked. "I thought Harley enthusiasts went to Sturgis?"

"Huh?" Emma asked.

"Nothing. I have never seen so many people on horse-back. And where did they get such pure white horses?"

Emma hadn't noticed the horses' unnatural color until now. "Look at their hooves."

Michael glanced over, his fingers tight on the wheel. "Are those painted?"

Emma shook her head. "Paint doesn't shift color like that."

The hooves were a rainbow color that changed with the light, the way real rainbows did. The dominant color was reflected in the horses' manes and tails.

"You're saying you did this?" Michael sounded incredulous. "Is it another dream?"

"A slip of the brain more likely," Emma said.

"I'm not following you, Emma."

"Of course not." She sighed. "Last night, while we were at the mall, I decided not to keep wishing that things were different. I thought something Nora's mother used to say. If wishes were horses—"

"Beggars would ride." Michael shook his head. "So those are homeless people."

Emma nodded. "The modern equivalent of beggars."

"We have to change this," Michael said.

"I don't know," Emma said. "They're traveling easier than they usually do."

"Taking care of a horse is expensive. They can't afford food and vet bills and all the other stuff."

"But those are wishes, not horses," Emma said. "And if one of those homeless people realizes it, just one, they'll get whatever they want."

"You're kidding."

"No, I'm not. So what do you think about changing it back now?"

"Won't this spell interfere with the space/time continuum or something like that?"

"I don't think so," Emma said. "And if it's too bad, someone'll slap me and make me change it when I get to Portland."

Michael let out a slight chuckle. "You weren't kidding about adventure."

"You'll find," she said primly, "that I lack a sense of humor."

"Yeah," Michael said. "The horses prove that."

She smiled at him, and settled back in her seat. The morning sunlight made the shadows from the night before seem a lot less threatening. Or perhaps it was just the stark beauty of this part of South Dakota.

The spring greenery gave the area a magical quality. The Black Hills themselves were dark and a bit foreboding. But the light was clearer here than it was in Madison, and the sky bluer. Perhaps there was less pollution, or perhaps the air was drier. She didn't know. All she knew was that the morning was one of the finest she'd seen in months.

Michael turned on Highway 212 at Belle Fourche. The highway was exactly what Emma had feared it would be, a two-lane paved road with buckling concrete. Once they left Belle Fourche, there were no houses or cars or even beggars on horseback. They were the only ones on the road.

After they turned off, Darnell moved from the backseat to her lap. He seemed to want comfort, which was very out of character for him. He purred as she petted him, and stared out the passenger window, his muscles tense and alert.

He didn't like this area. She wondered if he would have behaved this way if they traveled I-90 through Wyoming instead.

Michael didn't like it either. He shut off the radio after fifteen minutes of static—apparently they were too far away from any town to get a signal.

The road stretched before them like a mythical road—disappearing into the distance. The only signs of civilization were the fences that ran along both sides of the road. They were on ranchland, but Emma saw no cattle, no equipment, nothing but miles and miles and miles of fence.

"I was afraid it would be like this," Michael said a half an hour into the ride.

Emma didn't answer. She didn't want to get into a fight about the choice. Instead she watched the road and tried to ease the tension out of Darnell.

Another half hour in, Michael made her dig out a map. "I thought there were supposed to be towns here."

Emma looked at it. They should have gone through Alzada before the first time Michael spoke up, and they should be about to enter Hammond.

"There were supposed to be towns," she said. "But I haven't seen anything."

He took the map from her and spread it on the steering wheel. "They're awfully small," he said. "Maybe they're ghost towns."

"Ghost towns?" Panic shot through her. "You mean we're heading directly for the spirits?"

Darnell dug his claws into her leg as if he could hold

onto her and remain safe. She had to pry them loose one paw at a time.

Michael laughed. "Ghost towns don't refer to spirits. It means towns that were once there and have since died. Sometimes the buildings remain, sometimes just the place names."

"Oh." Emma took a deep breath, trying to calm herself. The little things that she didn't know still amazed her sometimes. "Do you mean there may be nothing on this road from here to Billings?"

"Why do you think I bought all the food?"

"How did you know?"

"I didn't. I've just been on western back roads before. They're not easy."

And she would have traveled this by herself, with no food, no water, no preparation. Just like she might have gone through the desert herself. Maybe Michael's dream hadn't been that far-fetched after all. Part of her had wanted to believe that Merlin had made up the whole thing to get Michael to travel with her. She hated to think she would have made such elementary mistakes.

But she was the first to admit her knowledge of this world was lacking. She was better than she had been but, as Michael pointed out, there were still astonishing gaps in her knowledge. Knowing how to survive in places like this seemed to be one of them.

"If you know this would be so desolate," she said, "why did you agree to come?"

"Because your friend said we had to get out of the Black Hills fast, and this route cuts almost two hundred miles off our trip to Billings. If things go all right, we should be there in five hours instead of nine."

"If things go all right," Emma repeated, numbly.

"I won't lie to you, Emma. If we break down here, it could take a day or more to have someone find us. And then we'll have all the time it takes to get the car repaired. We'll probably have to go back to Belle Fourche or Sturgis to find someone who can order in the parts."

She slumped even farther, trying not to let that idea sink in. Because if it did, she would be afraid that she would cause the car to break down, and that would be a bad thing. A very bad thing indeed.

Darnell's claws were in her legs again. Thanks to Darnell, both she and Michael would be scarred for life from this trip.

At noon, Michael pulled over to the side of the road.

"Are we having car trouble then?" Emma asked.

"Nope," he said, getting out.

"What's going on?"

"Personal trouble." He walked to the back of the car. She watched him. He stood for a moment in the empty road, looked at the fences blocking both sides, the long flat treeless land that extended in either direction and shook his head.

"Would you mind looking away?" he said.

Suddenly she understood what he was about. She turned around, and waited, realizing that she would have to do the same thing.

She worked at prying Darnell off her. Then she closed Michael's door, set Darnell in the cat bed, and waited. When Michael returned, she got out and found a private place to get rid of the morning's beverages.

She hadn't used the outdoors like this in a long,

long, long time. She grinned. The entire experience made her think of her girlhood—of holes in the ground and wooden toilet seats (although they weren't called that) and the rags that an occasional kind soul left for someone's use.

Now she would shudder at the unsanitariness of it all, but when she first arrived at Nora's apartment, she had been frightened by the sterile chrome and porcelain, the clean smells. The bathrooms had truly told her that she was in a new time.

Who would have thought that the cool wind on her bare skin would be something that she had missed?

"You alive?" Michael shouted.

"Yep." She finished and came around the car. Michael was still standing outside, leaning against the side and staring at the grassland beyond.

"Can you imagine living here?" he asked. "There's nothing. You must really have to hate people."

"Or just be very private," she said.

"Would you like it here?" There seemed to be some worry in his voice, as if he were afraid she would say yes.

"I like Madison," she said.

"Me, too. Despite the weather."

She smiled. "Oh, the weather is part of what I like. You forget. I like adventure."

"I'm not forgetting," he said. "It's becoming clearer and clearer every day."

He opened the door to the backseat and caught Darnell as he tried to get out. Then he handed Darnell to Emma, who clutched him tightly. Darnell looked all around, seemed to decide that he disliked desolation, and sniffed the air. Michael opened the cooler, took out some sandwiches that he bought, and two bottles of water. He set them on the hood, took Darnell back from her, while she took out Darnell's leash. Emma clipped it onto Darnell as Michael closed the door.

She set Darnell on the road, and he turned his face into the wind. He still didn't seem happy—it was more like he was sniffing for a sign.

It only took a few minutes to eat sandwiches when you were leaning against a car. The food tasted good, though, better than it probably should have, given that the sandwiches were hours old.

Emma ate hers and stared at the land beyond the fence. Brown with patches of green. Dust whipped past her, getting into her mouth as she chewed. She had become a product of the twenty-first century. She was used to eating clean and fresh food inside. She liked the amenities, from the bathrooms to the hotel rooms to the cars. If someone had told her when she first woke up that she would rather stay in this century, covered as it was with concrete and steel buildings, she would have been appalled.

Now she was appalled at ever moving back to the tenth century.

"What's that?" Michael asked. He was pointing in the distance. Emma looked. For a moment, she saw a heat shimmer. Then she could see through it, to the village of her birth.

She muttered the reverse spell as fast as she could, her heart pounding. The last thing she needed to do was vanish from here, leaving Darnell alone and unprotected in the middle of nowhere.

The heat shimmer vanished.

"You did that?" Michael asked.

She nodded. "I was thinking about the past."

"Miss it?"

"No," she said. "I just realized how much I like it here."

He smiled at her. Then he brushed her hair back tenderly from her face. "I'm glad that you like it here."

She captured his hand with her own. "Michael—"

"Emma, I liked holding you last night."

Her fingers tightened over his. "We already had this discussion."

"And we didn't finish it. I say let's test it. If something goes wrong, I know how to contact your Fates. At worst, I can get your friend Aethelstan—"

"No." The word came out before she had a chance to think about it. She pulled away from him. "I'm not ready. Too much has gone wrong these last few days. It would be better if we didn't experiment until we were safe."

"Safe?" He let his hand drop at her side.

"Portland."

"That's a compromise, then?"

She took a deep breath. She hadn't realized she had come toward his position. But she had. She nodded.

He smiled. "Emma, you're more practical than I give you credit for. It's a marvelous idea. You won't change your mind?"

She already was. But his question made her defensive. "Of course not."

"Good." He opened the driver's door. "Let's get going. I have real incentive now to get to Oregon."

"Some would say a kiss isn't enough reward for what you're doing."

"It is if the kiss is a special one." He got inside the car.

"Great," Emma said to herself as she crossed toward her side of the car. "Not only do I have to worry about losing another thousand years of my life, but now I have to worry about whether or not that kiss'll be good enough."

Life had been a lot easier when she had been on her own. Less interesting, and not as much fun, but easier.

She wished she could convince herself that she missed being alone. But she found that, despite the pressure, she was looking forward to the end of the journey—and not just because the magic would be under control.

———⁓———

Emma lost all track of time on the empty windy road. She wondered if it would go on forever, if it was a curse sent by the same people who had sent those shadows the night before. She was actually glad she wasn't driving. The emptiness was hypnotic in its own way, lulling her into a kind of stupor that felt almost like sleep.

The car was pretty quiet. Michael had shut off the staticky radio and Emma hadn't brought any CDs. He wasn't talking either, and Darnell was asleep.

The sun wasn't as bright as it had been. Sometimes Emma thought she saw more shade on the land around her than there should have been, given the dearth of trees. And the air had gotten colder.

"Is it darker than it should be?" she asked Michael.

"I don't know," he said, "but I'm beginning to wonder if we've fallen through the Rabbit Hole."

"Which rabbit hole?"

He looked at her sideways. "You've never heard of Alice in Wonderland?"

"I'd heard, but I had no idea that it had something to do with rabbit holes."

Michael laughed, and proceeded to tell her the story of the hapless Alice who was at times too big, and at other times too small. Darnell woke up for the part of the Cheshire Cat, which, Emma thought, suited him perfectly.

Then the road turned and buildings appeared as if out of nowhere. Houses and a garage. The street widened. They had arrived in a town.

"Well, whaddya know?" Michael said. "Civilization."

As he spoke the words, a nearly grown calf ran down the middle of the street. Michael hit the brakes, narrowly missing the animal. It shied and skittered toward one of the buildings.

At that moment, a cowboy, complete with chaps, rode a horse toward the calf, swinging a rope over his head. He held the reins in one hand and then lassoed the calf easily. The creature bucked and started, but the cowboy held him fast.

"Another vision?" Michael asked Emma.

She hadn't been sure at first, but now she was. The horse was brown and healthy, the cowboy as real as Michael. The calf was bleating, a sound she knew she had never heard before and therefore couldn't conjure up.

"No. This is real."

"You've got to be kidding. That's harder to believe than a restaurant with fifty chefs."

"I'm not kidding," she said. "My horses are all white with rainbows. This one's just brown."

"Poor thing," Michael said sarcastically.

"And that cowboy doesn't look like a beggar to me."

Almost as if he'd heard her, the cowboy tipped his hat

at her, and then rode toward the center of town, pulling the calf behind him. Michael waited a full five minutes before starting to drive again.

"Why did that unnerve you?" Emma asked.

"I thought the Old West was long dead," he said.

"Apparently not in Wyoming."

"I don't think we're in Wyoming anymore," Michael said.

"I thought the quote was about Kansas."

"That too." Then he looked at her. "You know *The Wizard of Oz*?"

"Who doesn't?" she asked. "Even my parents had heard of the Wizard of Oz."

"I hope you're yanking me," he said.

"I told you," she said with a smile. "We can't do that."

He caught his breath and then looked at her. His eyes were twinkling. "At least until we get to Oregon."

She felt a wave of desire, then willed herself to suppress it—which was harder than it had been. The feeling didn't just go away because she wanted it to. Great, she thought. Just one more thing that was out of control.

The town they were in was small—she could see the end of it as they finished turning the corner—but it felt like heaven to her. She hadn't realized how unnerved she had been by the emptiness. There was a gas station with a convenience store at the far edge of town. Michael pulled in.

The cowboy was no longer anywhere to be seen.

Emma got out and stretched her legs. Darnell watched from the backseat. This time, he seemed to have no desire to get out of the car. Michael got out too, and proceeded to fill up the tank. Emma smiled. He had done that all along on the trip, just as if it were part of his job. Now she was beginning to understand why twenty-first-century women kept men around.

She went inside the store.

It smelled of wrapped plastic and cleaners, like most convenience stores did. Some dangerous looking burritos sat beside an ancient microwave, and beneath them were some cold corn dogs, along with a sign inviting her to heat them up and pay for them. She doubted that heat would make them any more palatable. She wandered the aisle, looking for something that could satisfy her sweet tooth, and finally settled on another package of Ding Dongs. Not only had Michael gotten her hooked, but she now understood the practicality of the things. If the stock in this store hadn't turned in fifty years, the Ding Dongs would still be edible.

"Lemme guess," a voice said behind her. "Shortcut."

She turned and saw a burly man behind the counter. He had a friendly face with a sunburn obviously left over from the year before. He wore a button-down shirt and jeans. His convenience store smock hung over a chair behind the cash register. Clearly he didn't worry much about being caught dressed improperly by the franchise owners.

"Was it that obvious?"

"Whenever I see a face I don't recognize, I know you succumbed to the temptation on the map."

"Did we make a mistake?" she asked.

"Oh, no," he said. "You're cutting some time off. It's just most people can't handle the deserted road. Most of them are raving for company by the time they get here."

"I have company," she said. "He's filling up the tank."

The man nodded. "Good thing. This ain't a woman-alone shortcut."

"Why?" she asked. "Is something wrong?"

"Just don't like it when people take chances. You break down here, nobody'll know for a day, maybe more. Sometimes cell phones don't even work in this country. Interference from the hills, I think."

"Like the radio."

"Yep."

"Don't you get lonely out here?" she asked.

"Gotta be a special kinda person to live here," he said. "Me, I'm considered the sociable man in town. That's why I'm workin' here. Most folks from the area go days without talking to anyone but family."

"Sounds like you do too."

"Naw. We get regulars in here. Just not shortcut takers."

"People don't repeat this trip?"

"I never seen one. And believe me, I would."

"You'd remember, too, I suppose."

"Oh, yeah, missy. I don't forget a face. Especially one as pretty as yours."

She blushed like she always did, and Michael took that moment to walk in the door.

"Everything all right?" he asked, and she liked the protective sound in his voice.

"I was just complimenting your lady. I think she's probably the prettiest woman I ever seen."

"She would be," Michael said as he wandered toward the refrigerator units. "She's the prototype for Sleeping Beauty."

"Michael!"

"Ain't he a rude one?" the man said. Emma wondered

if he'd heard Michael's comment as an insult, and if so, exactly what kind of insult. She couldn't even venture a guess.

"I think the strain of the road's getting to him."

"Well, if you don't want him, you're welcome to stay here."

She smiled. "What's the attraction?"

"Spaces so wide open even jackrabbits have to carry their own lunch." The man leaned against the counter and crossed his arms. "Sometimes a person just likes to be alone."

"That's true," Emma said. "But I've done that. I'm ready for company."

Michael looked at her over the row of snack-sized Doritos. She carefully did not meet his gaze.

"Well," the man said, "you'll see more traffic once you hit the reservations, but not a lot. You'll hook back up with ninety around the battlefield. You ever been to the battlefield?"

"I've never been to a battlefield in my life," she said, confused. "At least that I know of."

Michael, who was still watching her, flinched. Then he opened one of the cooler's doors and took out some more bottled water.

"The Custer Memorial Battlefield. Only they politically corrected the name. I think it's the Little Bighorn Battlefield now. Either way, it's one of the more interesting places to go in these parts. I don't think it looks all that different from a hundred-odd years ago. The past really lives there."

She opened her mouth to ask who Custer was, when Michael said, "So you recommend stopping?"

"If you got any interest in history, I sure do," the man

said. "All the land around here's filled with history. The Indian wars, white settlers, soldiers. Then there's all the stuff we don't know, from before the white man even showed up. That's the stuff I wonder about. I been thinking I should research it, but mostly I don't. I stay here, read the paper, and watch for occasional tourists."

"Do we count as tourists?" Michael asked, bringing the water to the counter.

"I don't know how you can be anything else. You're not from here."

Emma set her Ding Dongs beside Michael's water. He looked at her, amusement glinting in his eyes. Then he said to the man, "I thought tourists had to stay a while to count."

"Well," the man said, "you're staying about as long as most folks do here. So I gotta count you as something."

"Fair enough," Michael said, as he paid for their treats and the gas. "Thanks for your time."

"Don't mention it," the man said. "It's a rare treat to see a new face, especially one as pretty as yours."

"I don't think he meant me," Michael said when they got outside.

"Why did you tell him I was the prototype for Sleeping Beauty?" Emma asked. There was more of an edge to her voice than she had expected.

"What's he going to do, believe me?" Michael asked. "And even if he did, who would he tell? A jackrabbit?"

"We forgot to ask him what that cowboy was doing," Emma said.

"I think that's fairly obvious," Michael said.

"Not to me." She opened the passenger door and slid inside. Michael went to the driver's side. That was when she realized that it was her turn to drive. She was getting less possessive about it. He would probably think that a good thing.

"I forget," he said as he closed the door. "You're the person who has no idea who Custer is."

Darnell yowled and stretched, as if asking what they had brought him to eat. Emma reached over the seat and scratched his ears. That didn't seem to satisfy him.

"I think I've heard of this Custer," Emma said. "But I can't remember everything that's happened in every country in the last thousand years."

Michael chuckled. He pulled out of the parking lot and headed west. The empty road loomed. Emma glanced back at the town. She would actually miss it, brief as her stay was. She should have asked the clerk how long it would take to get to I-90.

Best laid plans.

"George Armstrong Custer," Michael said, "fought in the Civil War for the Union. Then he came out West to fight the 'Injuns.' He was not a talented officer, and he made a lot of mistakes during the war, most of them covered by his superiors. Only out here, as you can tell, there's no room for mistakes."

He rested one hand on the steering wheel, the other on the space between them.

"At Little Big Horn, he fought the Sioux, Cheyenne, and Arapaho, and lost. It was his arrogance that brought him here. He was outmatched, outmaneuvered, and outgeneraled by people he considered savages. The irony was that he didn't live to see what his actions had wrought. The sadness is that he brought down a lot of good people with him."

Emma settled back into her chair. She had underestimated Michael too. He was a good history professor. He knew the value of storytelling. His students probably loved to hear him talk about things in that professorly voice of his.

She knew she did.

"I sense there's a lot to this battle."

"Oh, only the whole history of the West, I think. It was the last big victory for Native Americans. It's got everything from greed to valor." Then he grinned at her. "I take it you want to hear about it?"

"You know I do."

So Michael told her the history of the land they were driving through, and surprisingly, the trip went rather quickly.

———※———

There was about an hour of daylight left when they reached the Little Big Horn Memorial Battlefield. The Visitor's Center was closed, and the parking lot was empty.

"We have sixty-five miles to Billings," Michael said, "and I doubt we'll be able to eat near here. Let's just go on."

"After all this?" Emma said. "Let's stop for just a few minutes."

Michael pulled into a parking space. Above him was a well-marked trail that led to a series of grass-covered hills. Some were covered with markers, and one had a monument on it. There were signs everywhere.

To the left, there was digging going on. Emma got out of the car, and walked toward it. A sign read that this was the beginning of the Indian Memorial.

"What's this?" she asked Michael as he approached.

"This is a U.S. historical site," he said, "even though it's on Crow reservation land. If it's like any of the others out here, it'll be slanted toward the white perspective."

"But the whites were wrong," Emma said.

He put his arm over her shoulder. "You clearly missed centuries of manifest destiny."

"Now that's a phrase I do remember."

"Well remember this. It was the British who tried to conquer the world for the white man—at least they tried it first."

She slipped her arm around his waist. "See why I don't want you to teach my medieval history classes? You forget the Vikings."

He let out a small sigh.

"I think there's an argument to be made that it was the Norse blood, running through English veins, that led them to try to conquer the world."

"Do me a favor," he said. "Don't write that as your next book."

"I promise," she said. "Maybe I'll just write *Memoirs of Sleeping Beauty*."

"Strangely enough," he said, "I think that'll sell."

"A book about sleeping? Don't hold your breath."

They walked up the paved trail toward the hills. The man from that town had been right; Emma could feel the history here. Although she wondered if it might be because she had just heard the entire tale from Michael. Or perhaps there were restless ghosts here, ghosts that were still fighting a battle from long ago.

"Do all battlefields feel like this?" she asked.

"Recent ones," he said. "The battlefields from the

World Wars have this feeling. But I went to the site of the Battle of Hastings where—"

"It's my specialty," Emma said. "Even the worst medieval history professor knows that battle. Without it, William wouldn't have Conquered."

"Just testing," Michael said with a grin. "Anyway, I didn't feel anything there. It was as if the ghosts had finally been laid to rest."

"You think it was just time? Or do you think that different battles did it?"

"Time," he said. "I've been to a lot of ancient battle sites in England, and they don't have the resonance of these more modern ones."

"Ancient battle sites," Emma said. "It's still hard for me to hear about something that happened nearly a lifetime after I was born being called 'ancient.'"

"Sorry," Michael said. "I never think of you that way."

"As ancient?" She turned to him, trying to look stern. "You want to try that again?"

"As someone born so long ago," he said.

"You mean someone old?"

"Emma…"

She laughed. "Oh, this could be fun."

"Hasn't anyone else ever teased you about your age?"

"The mortals who know about it know Aethelstan, and he's older than I am. Besides, my age was kind of a touchy topic around them."

Michael nodded. He opened the small gate that led to Custer Hill. A big monument stood to one side. Emma looked out over the surrounding countryside. Tall brown grass as far as the eye could see. There were some trees near the river, a touch of green on a brown ocean.

There was so little here. It was hard to understand why anyone would fight over this land, and yet they had. Fighting for land had been important throughout human history. She simply hadn't understood why until she owned her own house.

She hoped she would be able to go back to it someday.

"You seem down," Michael said.

"No," she said. "Just thinking of home."

He nodded. She had no idea if he understood what she meant, and she wasn't going to clarify, not at the moment.

Michael was right; the notices and the histories were written from a decidedly pro-white perspective. It seemed like some changes were tacked onto the bottom of signs, but everything felt uncomfortably skewed to her.

Instead she wandered over the path. A wind had come up, and clouds were blowing in. Toward the west, one of the clouds had become fuzzy. It was raining out there.

Here, the sun was going down, and its brilliant light was painting the clouds red and gold. The land wasn't much, but the sky was spectacular. The reds and golds against the vivid blue made her breath catch.

The first time she had crossed the country, she hadn't really looked at it. She was looking at the century instead, at the changes that happened in the world since she had been born. But those changes were becoming part of the background now, and that allowed her to see other things.

She didn't believe that the sky was this blue, this broad, this beautiful in Wisconsin. It certainly wasn't in Oregon. Something about the emptiness of this land accented the sky.

Michael came up beside her.

"I can't believe they fought over this place and then did nothing with it," she said.

He smiled. "Spoken like a true European."

"What does that mean?"

"It means that you believe land should be conquered. That's how you were raised. And strangely, a thousand years later, so was I."

She looked at him sideways. "You find it odd too?"

He shook his head. "Ultimately, the fight wasn't about land. It was about the way people should live. Rather like your fight now, Emma."

She sighed. "I have no choice about how I will live. My destiny has been chosen for me."

"That can't be true," Michael said.

"It is true." She folded her hands behind her back. The sun was getting lower. The sky had more red in it now than gold, and shadows were covering the hill around her.

"You're on a journey," Michael said. "If I under-stand my fairy tales, people with magic take journeys to discover their destinies, not because they already have them."

Emma felt her shoulders tense. "Your reading was probably wrong."

"Probably." Michael seemed unconcerned by her correction. Then he frowned. "How can there be tree shadows when there are no trees?"

Emma looked at the ground. He was right; the shad-ows looked like long trees. But there seemed to be no source for the shadows.

"Oh, no," she said. "We have to get out of here."

She ran down the path toward the car, Michael right

behind her. The shadows rose off the grass, no longer trying to masquerade themselves. They formed human-like shapes, so dark that she couldn't see through them, and they headed straight for her.

One of the things reached out its hand and touched her face. The fingers were cold and hard as rubber. She jerked herself away from it, and kept running.

She had nothing to hold them off. She had no idea how their magic worked, what it could do to her. What it could do to Michael, to Darnell? She felt like the Indians must have felt when they first saw guns. They had no idea how to defend themselves against something they didn't understand.

And yet somehow, they'd found a way to survive.

The shadows blocked the path. They formed a solid black line in front of her. She stopped, and Michael slammed into her, putting his arms around her as if he could protect her.

She turned, but the shadows were all around, fencing her and Michael in.

"Now what?" he asked.

"I wish I knew," she said.

Chapter 13

THE SHADOWS MOVED CLOSER. THEY LOOKED LIKE walls, closing in. Emma glanced up and saw that they were forming a roof that would soon hide the sky.

They would box in Emma and Michael. And after that, she had no idea what would happen.

Then she heard a faint howl. Darnell? Had they gotten to him?

"What's that?" Michael whispered.

"Darnell," she said.

"I don't think so," Michael said. "Listen."

She did. She heard a whoop and then another howl. Only it really wasn't a howl. It was a yelp, a human voice raised in a battle cry. It sent a shiver down her back.

The ground rumbled beneath her feet. "Earthquake?" Emma asked.

Michael's grasp on her waist tightened. The whoops and yelps grew louder—and there were more of them. Hundreds of voices, shouting with purpose.

"It's not an earthquake," Michael said. "That's horses. Hundreds of horses."

The shadows were shaking, unable to keep their cohesive wall. The roof they were building fell apart, revealing a dark blue sky. The yelps grew louder and louder, and so did the sound of hooves. It really did sound like thunder, but it felt as if the earth would never stop shaking.

Emma put her hands over Michael's and leaned on him. She was so glad he was here. He was keeping her calm. Being in the circle of his arms gave her the illusion of safety, in the middle of all this chaos.

Through the shadows, she could see ghostly figures—horses and warriors carrying feathered lances. But not warriors that she had grown up with. Native Americans, men, their long hair flying, their weapons in their hands.

"Sioux," Michael said faintly. So he could see it too. "Hunkpapa, Oglala. God. I think that's Crazy Horse, and Sitting Bull. Emma, do you see that?"

"Yes." Her fingers tightened on his. The Sioux began firing arrows into the shadows. Others rode past, using their lances like spears, shouting and yipping and crying with the fierceness of the fight.

They rode on and on, coming closer and closer, and each time a tip—whether it was from a lance or an arrow—hit a shadow, the shadow popped and vanished. The entire front wall of shadows was gone in an instant, and still the warriors kept coming.

The earth was shaking so hard that Emma could hardly keep her balance. In addition to the war whoops were the whinnies of horses and the continual pops of the shadows.

Arrows flew past her. A few came so close that she could have reached out and grabbed them—if she had been fast enough. But she could also see through them, just like she could see through the horses and their riders.

The popping continued all around. Michael whirled them both in time to see the wall to the east come down, then the wall to the west. He was pulling her so close that she couldn't have moved on her own if she had wanted to.

Then the final wall vanished. The riders came toward Emma and Michael, their fierce painted faces filled with the joy of a victory she wasn't sure she understood. The ground shook even more, and dust rose around them, ghostly dust that she could see but which didn't catch in her lungs. There was also the ghost of smells— horseflesh, sweat, maybe even blood—but so faint that she wasn't sure if she were imagining them or if they were real.

The riders stopped before her, and placed the tips of their lances down. Emma eased herself out of Michael's grasp. It was full dark now, and the ghosts seemed to glow against the black sky.

"Thank you," she said.

They nodded their heads in acknowledgment, then they rode around her and Michael the way that a stream flowed around a rock. They rode down the hill toward the river and vanished into the trees.

"Good Lord, Emma," Michael said, "I can't believe you did that."

"I didn't do it." Her voice was shaking. She was shaking, even though the earth was no longer.

"Who else could have?"

She shook her head. "No, Michael. It wasn't me. I thought those shadows had us."

"It was you," he said. "You have a lot more control than you think you do."

She looked at him. His face was closer to hers than she expected, his blue eyes sincere. He didn't look frightened—she doubted he ever was.

"If I had control, Darnell wouldn't have become a lion."

"He changed back."

"There wouldn't have been a restaurant."

"It changed back."

"Wishes wouldn't be horses."

Michael smiled. "You won't change that one."

"You know what I mean." She ran a hand through her hair. There was dirt in it. Maybe that dust hadn't been so ghostly after all. "This had to have been someone else."

"Who?" Michael asked. "Your friends are forbidden to help you. Would your Fates have done something like this?"

"No," Emma said softly.

"Then I submit that you saved us."

"I have to check on Darnell." She shoved her hands in her pockets, and walked down the path. There weren't even hoofprints in the grass. It looked as it had before— only without the shadows.

"Emma." Michael was keeping up with her. "Just humor me for a moment. Were you thinking about the battle?"

"Of course," she said. "I was trying to figure out a way to escape those shadows."

"No," he said. "Little Bighorn. Did it ever cross your mind while we were being attacked."

"Of course not." She slipped, then caught herself. The path was hard to walk in the dark.

She felt like the Indians must have felt when they first saw guns. They had no idea how to defend themselves against something they didn't understand.

And yet somehow, they'd found a way to survive.

"No way," she said.

"What?" Michael was still beside her. The man's least endearing trait was that he was hard to shake. "You remembered something."

"It was nothing."

"Emma, I'm on your side, remember?"

She stopped and looked at him. He seemed almost excited by this, like a historian who had discovered a handwritten history of England signed by King Arthur.

"I thought," she said, "that we didn't know how to defend ourselves, and neither did the Indians when they first saw guns."

Michael grinned. "The corollary being, of course, that they defended themselves pretty well here. Emma, you're brilliant."

"No," she said. "I'm inept. If I had control, I would have just banished those shadows."

"You did banish them," Michael said softly. "You just did it in a metaphorical way, which is how the subconscious works."

"So now you're a psychiatrist?"

"No," he said, "I was thinking of dreams. Dreams work in images and metaphors."

"Like restaurants with fifty chefs."

"And a special space for cats." He put his arm around her waist and headed down the path with her. She tried very hard not to lean on him.

As they got closer to the car, she could hear Darnell. It wasn't his panicked yowl. It was his Where-Is-Everyone?-I-Need-Dinner yowl.

"I'm sorry, Michael," she said as they reached the parking lot. "You signed on for adventure, but not this much. My whole life has been one bad situation after another."

"But you've survived all of them," Michael said, "and come out stronger."

"I guess that's one way to look at it."

He grinned at her. "It's the only way, Emma. You're a bona fide heroine of a fairy tale. Of course things are going to happen to you. But I'm not worried about them."

"You should be," she said.

He smoothed a strand of hair out of her face. His touch was gentle. "I believe in happily ever after, Emma, and since you're the heroine, you'll get out of this just fine."

"What about you?" she said.

"I'm betting I'm the hero."

She let out a small laugh. "And we ride off into the sunset? Isn't that how Westerns end?"

"No." He cupped her cheeks with his hands. "They usually end with a kiss."

She ducked back as if he had slapped her. "Michael, you promised."

He sighed. "I'm lousy at delayed gratification."

"It's a good thing you weren't around before the invention of birth control."

He laughed. It was a reluctant sound. "I was talking about a kiss, Emma, nothing else."

"And I was referring to your past."

"As a way of avoiding being kissed."

"Michael, please." She put the car between herself and him. Darnell launched himself at the window. He was mewing piteously—his If-I-Don't-Eat-Right-Now-I'll-Die mew.

"You know, I should really be offended," Michael said. "I have never had so much trouble kissing a woman in my life."

"It's not about you."

"I'm beginning to wonder."

"You know it's not about you. You've seen the magic."

"And what I've seen so far has been reversible."

"Michael, you have to believe me."

"I do, and I also know we're only a day or so from Oregon. What if I call your buddy Aethelstan, tell him that you've been kissed into a coma, and ask him to come here and help?"

"I don't think the Fates will like it," she said, leaning on the door.

"Oh, come on," Michael said. "You'd think they would expect it."

"I don't know what they think," Emma said.

"Take a risk, Emma," he said softly.

She stared at him across the car. He was hard to see in the dim light from the visitor center. "Would you?"

"I think so, yes. Since we have backup."

"Backup," she said sarcastically. "It sounds like you're trying to lead an assault on a building."

"Well," he said, "if the shoe fits—"

"Wrong fairy tale," she snapped.

At that moment, Darnell uttered his Feed-Me-Now-Or-Die-Horribly screech. Emma pulled the car door open, happy for the distraction. Darnell nearly tumbled onto the pavement. She caught him with one hand.

"You'd think a cat as smart as you would learn how to operate a ring-top." She reached into the food bag and removed Darnell's Fancy Feast. White Fish and Salmon—a touch of the Northwest. He returned to mewling piteously and paced the backseat of the car as if it were the kitchen floor.

"Great," Michael said, sounding more annoyed than he should have. "That stuff reeks. Couldn't you have waited until we got to Billings?"

"Did you want to listen to Darnell the whole way?"

"I don't know. It might have been better than smelling that stuff on an empty stomach."

Darnell shoved his face into the bowl. He looked nothing like the pretty white cat on the commercials. There was nothing dainty about him.

"He'll be done in a minute." Emma took the empty can to a nearby trash bin, and stared at the battlefield. She saw no more ghosts, no more shadows. Safe. For the moment, at least.

Then she came back to the car. Michael was in the driver's seat. She was about to tell him to move over, when she changed her mind.

Let him drive. It would give him something to concentrate on besides her. She let herself into the passenger's side, and slumped in the seat, crossing her arms over her chest and closing her eyes. She wasn't tired, but Michael didn't need to know that.

And he didn't need to know that the smell of Fancy Feast was making her empty stomach churn.

—∿∿—

It was nearly midnight when they reached Billings. They found a roadside motel with an all-night restaurant. They argued in the car for a few minutes about whether or not to get adjoining rooms, but the argument was half-hearted. They got a room with two doubles, and hoped that they were far apart.

Of course they weren't. The beds—the largest doubles

Emma had ever seen (an entire baseball team could sleep on one)—were so close together that she could barely see the space between them. The room wasn't billed as a suite, but it had a living room separated from the bed area by a tasteless, see-through wooden screen.

"They don't do anything small in Montana, do they?" Michael said as he brought in the suitcases. Emma waited until he closed the door before she set Darnell down. Darnell immediately ran for the beds and jumped on the one nearest the TV.

The cat developed a routine even on the road.

Emma used the remote to turn on the television and grabbed the room service menu. Michael stood in front of the TV and shut it off.

"No infomercial dreams tonight," he said.

"Okay," she said. "I'll read."

"Nope. We're sticking together until we get to Oregon." He didn't sound as pleased by that as he had a few hours earlier. She wasn't quite sure why he was so upset. "Dinner in the restaurant."

"What about Darnell?"

"Darnell's Fancy Feast is sticking with me. I'm sure he remembers it as well."

Darnell snuffled and managed to look forlorn.

Michael held out his hand. "Come on, before that cat makes you change your mind."

She got off the bed, but she didn't take his hand. She grabbed her key and followed him out the door. Darnell watched from the bed, his eyes accusing.

She closed the door, and her stomach rumbled. Dinner was a good idea.

Even after midnight, the restaurant was full—a good

sign. Most of the patrons looked like truckers, and most of them seemed like regulars, another good sign. So Emma ordered chicken-fried steak with lots of gravy, real mashed potatoes, and fresh corn. She wondered if Aethelstan knew of her gastronomic sins, and if he would make her pay for them later.

She and Michael didn't talk much. She wasn't sure what they had to say to each other. It almost felt as if they were fighting—but for the first time, she wasn't the one who initiated it. He was. And he didn't seem to use the shout-and-recover method. He seemed to like the sulk-and-stew method.

"You know," she said, "they say talking about it makes things easier."

"I have been talking about it," he said. "You're just stubborn."

"I'm just experienced."

"No," he said. "You're not."

She leaned back in the booth. "I don't know what I've done to make you so mad."

"I'm not mad," he said, stabbing his fork into a french fry as if it had offended him. "I'm worried."

"There's nothing to be worried about," she said. "We'll figure this out when we get to Oregon."

"Great," he muttered. "That makes me feel so much better. It's like high school, only worse."

"I never went to high school," Emma said, "so you want to explain that?"

"It feels like I'm a teenage boy who can only kiss his girl if her father's watching."

Emma felt a wave of anger run through her. She took a deep breath to suppress it. "One, I am not your girlfriend. Two, we are not in high school. Three, Aethelstan is not my father—"

"Worse, he's your ex-fiancé."

"Yeah, from a thousand years ago."

Michael picked up his burger. He had to squash it with his fingers just to get it to fit in front of his face. "You don't understand."

"Of course I do. You're a product of your generation. You want everything now. Well, Michael, not everything can happen now."

"This isn't about delayed gratification. Not really." He took a bite of the burger, chewed, and closed his eyes. "This is the best burger I've ever had."

"This is about a burger?" she asked.

"No." He leaned forward and lowered his voice. "I'm worried that once we get to Oregon, you'll come up with some other excuse."

"Excuse?" She set down her fork. "Suddenly this is about a physical relationship we don't and may never have?"

"The 'may never' is the key part."

"Yeah," she said. "Because you're pissing me off."

"As if that's hard." Michael picked up his burger and ate as if the conversation weren't bothering him at all.

"What did I do to you?" Emma asked. Her voice was rising. "I was honest with you. You know what the problem is."

He nodded. "And it has me worried."

"Because you can't go to bed with me?"

Heads turned toward them. The entire coffee shop heard that. Michael ignored them. "No. Because I have a hunch the problem goes deeper than a single kiss."

Emma gritted her teeth. She was not going to yell at him, not again. "What problem?"

Michael took a bite of his burger. The other patrons were still watching them. Michael didn't look at them, but Emma glared at each and every one of them until they turned away.

Finally her gaze met Michael's. He was watching her with complete patience. That irritated her as well. Why would he be patient while trying to make her angry?

"I think," he said slowly, softly, "you're afraid of someone getting close."

She snorted. The idea was preposterous. "Yeah, right."

"So tell me why none of your friends even knows about your history. Why none of them would drop everything to help you out."

"People don't work like that," she said.

"Really?" He ate a french fry. "I did."

"After you were visited by the Ghost of Christmas Present."

"That wasn't his name."

"I know," Emma said. "But that's not the point."

"What is the point?"

"You didn't want to come with me either. People don't like me."

"Maybe you don't give them a chance," Michael said.

Emma shoved her plate away. Her stomach was too upset to accept food. "So it's my fault that people don't like me."

"I didn't say they don't like you. I said they don't know you."

"And I'm supposed to tell them the truth?"

"Your closest friends, yes."

"I told you the truth."

"Because you had no choice," Michael said. "That's not real flattering when it comes down to it."

"I'm supposed to flatter you and then sleep with you, is that it?"

"No," Michael said evenly. He shoved his plate away too. "Your anger is your defense. It keeps people away, and it keeps you from hearing things you don't like."

Her cheeks flooded with warmth. That felt too close to her own thoughts from the last few days. She felt almost as if she were naked before this man.

"Okay," she said. "Make your point. I'll do my best to listen." Then she glared at the other patrons who had started staring again. "If you people mind your own business."

Everyone turned away, but she knew that they were listening just the same. She would have been listening, if she were them.

"Emma," Michael said softly, "you've been awake for ten years, and you've never dealt with this kissing problem before?"

"I've been busy," she whispered. "I've been learning about this culture."

"You're the most beautiful woman I've ever seen. Fairy tale beautiful. Movie star beautiful." Michael was leaning so close that he was nearly bent double. But he was whispering as well. No one could have heard this part of the conversation. "You can't tell me that there haven't been interested men."

"I can also tell you that a double negative is grammatically confusing."

Michael shook his head and leaned back. "No games,

Emma, please. You have had this problem before, haven't you? You chased every man who was interested away."

"There's never been an interested man," Emma said.

"You said every man flirts with you."

"That's not interest."

"Of course it's interest," Michael said. "You just haven't been interested in return. I think you're too scared."

"I'm not scared of anything."

"Except another magical coma."

She drew in a quick breath. "You said you'd respect my wishes. You said no kissing."

"And I'll keep that promise," he said. "But for the last day, I've been wondering if that's the only promise you'll have me make." He slid out his hand and extended it. She didn't move hers. "Emma, listen. I'm trying to say something very serious and making a mess of it."

She picked up her water glass, sipped, and waited, trying to keep herself calm.

"I'm worried and here's why." He scooted closer to her. Apparently he felt the other patrons were still listening. "Your parents gave you away. The woman who was supposed to raise you turned out to be some hellish creature out of Grimm. The man who claimed he loved you kept you in a box for a thousand years and then when you woke up, married someone else."

"It wasn't like that," Emma said softly.

"The only close friends you have live half a continent away—and they happen to be your ex-fiancé and his wife. You've told me the only person—your word—who ever accepted you for you was your cat."

He slipped his arm around her. She sat rigidly, not

wanting to lean into him at all, not wanting to let him know how good his touch felt.

"Emma," he said, "I'm going to kiss you. And if something goes wrong, I'll make it right. You have to trust me. I won't let you lose a single day, a single moment of your life. I promise."

Her heart was pounding hard. "Michael—"

But at that moment, he leaned into her and his lips caught hers. She started to pull away, but he tightened his hold on her shoulder. His lips teased hers, tasted hers, and she couldn't help herself. She tasted him as well.

He broke contact first. "See," he whispered. "We're safe."

"That's not a kiss," she said. "That's not the kind that—"

He kissed her again, this time taking her face in his hands. He caught her open mouth, held it, and they shared the same breath. He waited, almost as if he were asking a question, almost as if he were asking her permission.

She gave it by not moving. She didn't know what else to do. She hadn't been kissed, really kissed, for a thousand years.

He slipped his hands into her hair, pulled her so close that she couldn't tell where she ended and he began. The kiss grew deeper, and she moaned, sliding her hands around his back.

Applause echoed throughout the restaurant and the two of them pulled away from each other as if they'd been burned. All of the patrons at all of the tables were clapping, watching them, and smiling. Emma's cheeks flamed so deeply that she thought the heat would scorch her. Michael was blushing too. The blush ran from the roots of his hair all the way down his neck.

"I'm sorry, Emma," he whispered. "I forgot where we were."

She stared at the clapping patrons for a moment, too stunned to be angry. And then she realized that she was awake. There was no coma—and that was certainly the most passionate kiss of her entire life.

She turned to Michael and slipped her arms around his neck, kissing him again, not caring about the patrons, the restaurant, or anything else.

"Emma," he said against her mouth, but she didn't stop. She had never felt so alive, so free.

A slapping sound made her start. The waitress had slammed the check onto the table, then left her hand on top of it so that they would both turn to her. She was grinning.

"Sign this to your room and get out of here, you two," she said. "You'll have a lot more fun somewhere else."

Emma felt her cheeks flame even more. Michael laughed uncomfortably and slid the check toward him. His hands were shaking.

Everyone in the restaurant was still watching them. Emma wasn't angry at them for it—she was too happy. She was still here, everything was fine, and Michael wanted her. Michael wanted her as much as she wanted him.

He slid out of the booth and so did she. As they stood up, the restaurant patrons started clapping again. This time, Michael took her hand and held it up. Then he swept it down, pulling her into a bow. The crowd roared its appreciation, and the applause got louder.

Michael then tugged her from the restaurant, laughing as he went. "I've never received applause for kissing someone before."

"Me either," Emma said.

He stopped on the sidewalk, pulled her close, and kissed her again. This kiss was deeper than the last. She wrapped her arms around him and raised her left foot just like the women did in the movies. That threw her off balance, and Michael had to catch her to keep her from falling.

"Always wondered why they did that," he murmured. "Now I know."

He scooped her up in his arms and carried her toward the room. She started to protest, but he kissed her again—a quick, affectionate peck on the lips.

"How many men get to carry Sleeping Beauty?" he said.

"You're the first," she said, then she smiled. "That I know of."

He laughed, and then tried to balance her with one hand as he fumbled in his pocket for his key. He was teetering precariously. Emma put one hand against the wall.

"Let me," she said, and pulled her key from her pocket.

"I think you should probably open the door as well," he said.

"Might be better if you put me down."

"Don't want to be carried over the threshold?"

"I'm not wearing white," Emma said and slipped to the floor. Michael put his arms around her waist as she opened the door. She turned toward him, kissed him again, her hand lingering on his face.

She was free. A thousand years of curses and she was free for the very first time. The joy inside her was more than she could bear. And she was pleased that she was experiencing this with Michael. Her Michael.

His kiss froze, and he pulled away from her. Her stomach lurched. Had she done something wrong? Then she followed his gaze and turned around.

A man sat on the love seat. He was a large, muscular man with sun-leathered skin. He wore a denim shirt with snap buttons, jeans, cowboy boots, and a large black hat. The scent of Old Spice filled the room.

He was petting Darnell, an aggressive hard pet designed to hold a cat not to comfort him. And Darnell was struggling, but he wasn't meowing like he normally would have.

"I see I've come at a bad time," the man said.

"Who the hell are you?" Michael asked, shoving Emma behind him as if he were going to protect her.

"Tell the mortal he's dismissed," the man said.

"I'm not leaving," Michael said.

"Tell him if he insists on staying, he'll have to be voiceless. A statue, perhaps. I can strip him for you, see if he rivals Michelangelo's *David*."

Emma slipped around Michael. As she did, she whispered, "Don't say anything else."

"Wise advice," the man said. "Mortals should be seen, not heard."

"Let go of my cat," Emma said.

"Your familiar, such as he is," the man said. "If I control him, I control you."

"No one controls me," Emma said.

"That's fairly obvious." The man pulled Darnell closer. Darnell opened his mouth and moved it in an obvious meow, but made no sound.

"Give me my cat."

"If I give you the cat, I lose my advantage."

Emma remembered the language spell she had cast on Darnell. She repeated it now, and clapped her hands. Nothing happened.

"You lack control, my dear." The man had thin lips that nearly disappeared when he smiled.

Then Darnell swelled up, like a little kitty balloon, and became a black lion. The man let go. Darnell took a swipe at him, and the man placed his hands in front of him, creating a barrier. Darnell batted at it, but couldn't get through.

"Call him off," the man said.

"No," Emma said. "Not until you tell me what you want."

"I think that's obvious," the man said, keeping his gaze on Darnell. "Those were my shades you vanquished so indelicately on the plains. You know, you didn't have to destroy them. You could have just sent them back to me."

"I don't like being threatened," Emma said.

Michael's lips twitched as if he found that comment amusing. But he was being good and not saying anything at all.

"I wasn't trying to threaten you, my dear. I was just trying to find out who would squander such a marvelous resource." The man shrugged his shoulders forward. "Will you call off this beast?"

Emma almost called Darnell by name and then realized what the man was trying to get her to do. If he knew Darnell's name, he could control the cat.

Emma looked at Michael. "Would you calm him please?"

Michael went to Darnell and touched the back of his mane. Darnell roared so loud that the walls shook, but he sat down, giant tail twitching. He watched the stranger like a house cat staring at a mouse.

"Who are you?" Emma asked.

The man made a slight clicking sound with his tongue. "You know better than that, my dear. I'll tell you my name if you tell me yours."

"I'm Bonita Sueña," Emma said.

The man laughed. "Then I am El Vaquero Feo. You may call me El."

"Feo will do just fine," Emma said.

"And your companion?"

"Is just a mortal. Nothing to be concerned with."

Michael's eyes narrowed. Emma couldn't let him know that she was trying to protect him. She hoped he would forgive her later.

Feo shot a quick glance at Darnell. He clearly didn't trust the cat. Emma wondered how many times Darnell had bitten and scratched him while they were alone together. Darnell at larger than life sized had to be a bit terrifying to anyone who'd already felt the cat's sharp teeth.

"There's a lot of loose magic swirling around you, Bonita," Feo said. "I've never experienced anything like it before."

"What concern is it of yours?" Emma asked.

"It seems that you don't want it. Your ability to use it seems rather" — he looked at Darnell — "limited."

"So?"

Feo leaned back on the love seat. He was trying to look relaxed and casual, but it was clear that Darnell made him nervous. "I've met a few others like you. Newly minted and uncomfortable with their futures. See their magic as a burden. You seem to have the added discomfort of coming into yours quite early."

"Actually," Emma said, "I got mine a lot later than usual."

Darnell's tail was twitching faster and faster. Michael kept one hand on Darnell's mane.

"I'm prepared to relieve you of that burden," Feo said. "And you can name your own price."

"I can sell my magic to you?" Emma asked.

Feo opened his hands like a benevolent ruler. "It would make your life so much simpler, wouldn't it?"

"What would it do to yours?"

Feo shrugged. "I am but a humble man who had humble talents. Over the years I learned that I could augment them. It's not the same as being born with great abilities, but it is better than what I originally had."

So that was why Darnell made him nervous. Emma suppressed a smile. The man was a minor wizard whose spells were easily dissolved. No wonder he was angry that she had completely destroyed his shadows. They must have taken him weeks to build.

"And if I were to sell you my—talent," Emma said, "what would I get in return?"

"Em—um, Bonita," Michael said. "Don't."

She didn't even look at him. Neither did Feo. It was as if Michael didn't even exist.

"Name your price," Feo said.

"I could ask for all your magic in return, couldn't I?" Emma said. "Or your control?"

"That would be ridiculous," Feo said. "It would defeat the purpose of my visit. I'm trying to free you of this burden, not make it worse."

"Oh," Emma said. "So anything but your magic."

"I could extend the life of your toy there," Feo said. "Make him pretty as long as he lives."

"I could do that," Emma said.

"Then why haven't you?"

Emma smiled. "I haven't tried him out yet. No use wasting magic on something that's untried, don't you agree?"

Michael shot a glance at her.

"Yes," Feo said. "Besides, there are so many of them. Why keep just one?"

"Your price?" Emma said, reminding him of the discussion.

Feo shrugged. "Whatever you want."

"And if I say no?"

He stood, acting like a powerful man in control of a situation. Darnell yowled, the hair rising on his back. Feo glanced nervously at him. It ruined the effect.

"I'm afraid I'd just have to take that loose magic," he said. "And then you wouldn't get anything for it at all."

Darnell's yowl got higher pitched. Michael's hand on his mane seemed more and more ineffective.

Emma held out a hand. The command usually worked with Darnell—the smaller Darnell, anyway. She wondered if the larger one would listen.

"You can't take my magic," Emma said. "No one can. I have to give it away."

He tilted his head back, studying her. "You're more educated than I thought."

"I told you," Emma said, "I'm in control."

His smile was small. "If you were, your magic wouldn't be running loose on hillsides waiting for anyone to use it."

She started. The horse-wishes were here too? How far had that spell spread? "Unless I meant that to happen."

"Nonsense," he said. "No one willingly lets loose that kind of power."

"You seem to think someone would give it away," she said.

He snapped his fingers and both Michael and Darnell froze in place. They looked like a man and lion statue, gleaming under the lights. "I could kill them both if you don't give me that magic."

His spells were small, Emma had to remind herself. The last time she had summoned ghosts that had destroyed his magic using pointed things. All she needed was something pointed—a knife, a car key—and she'd get Michael and Darnell back.

"You could," Emma said, "but that wouldn't work in the eyes of the Fates. A gift coerced is not a true gift."

He cursed. "Who taught you?"

"Ealhswith," she said, and it was her turn to smile. She did it slowly, the nastiest smile she could muster. She tried, in her mind, to imitate her evil mentor's smile as best she could. "Are you sure you want to mess with me?"

The self-assurance left his face. "Is this some kind of trick? Are you working for the Fates?"

"I might be." Her smile got nastier. "Think of it. A multidimensional sting operation."

He looked up, then down, then back at her. "I'll know if you're lying."

"Sure you will," she said, sarcastically. "Your magic is just that strong."

"There are others in this area who know that your magic is loose. They'll know that I didn't get it. They'll come after you."

"My magic isn't loose," Emma said calmly. "I'm sure you'll tell them that."

"They don't listen to me."

"I'm beginning to understand why," Emma said. "Now, unfreeze my cat and my mortal."

"Are you sure you won't change your mind?" Feo asked.

"Feo, I'm within my legal rights to turn you into a toad. I believe I could get at least a century's worth of toadness out of you before the Fates even protested. Do you want me to do that?"

He was trembling visibly now. He snapped his fingers. Both Michael and Darnell stopped glistening. Darnell was growling again. His tail started twitching so fast that Emma knew he was going to pounce in a moment. She bet that Feo had forgotten to put his little force field back up.

"Okay," Feo said, his voice trembling as much as his hands. "I'm leaving. But you have to promise me that you won't mess with me again."

"I'm not promising anything," Emma said.

And then Darnell launched. Michael didn't even try to grab at him. Darnell was growling like a lion in a nature documentary. He soared at Feo who clapped his hands together, and vanished in a cloud of noxious smoke.

Darnell leapt through the smoke and landed, coughing, on the cheap coffee table. The table buckled, and then collapsed.

Darnell lay there for a moment, obviously trying to catch his breath. Then he sighed.

"I don't suppose I can convince you both that I did that on purpose," Darnell said.

"I know it was on purpose," Emma said. "You meant to hit Feo. He disappeared. It was his fault."

"Of course. Exactly." Darnell sat up and started licking himself. Then he stopped and glared at her. "If the prey is gone, can I revert to my normal size? Otherwise this bath will take forever."

"I'll see what I can do," Emma said.

"Don't try the reverse spell," Darnell said. "Tell me to shut up and clap your hands. That's how you did it the last time."

"I don't need you telling me how to do spells."

"Well, someone has to tell you. No matter how you bluffed that idiot. He must really be one weak-assed magician if he's stealing powers from others."

"If he's afraid of you," Emma said.

Darnell sat even straighter. "I'm extremely intimidating at this size."

"Naw," Emma said. "You're just a pussycat."

Darnell stood up. "Lady, I like you. You feed me. But don't push me."

"Why not?" she said. "If you attack me, Michael will call animal control and they'll capture you, cage you, and put you down."

"Not if I talk to them."

"Darnell has a point," Michael said.

"Who asked you?" Emma said, not turning to him.

"You're the one who mentioned his name," Darnell said.

"Shut up," Emma said.

"Okay."

"I thought you said that would work," Emma said to Darnell.

"You didn't clap your hands. Do I have to do all of this for you?"

"You haven't done anything so far."

"So far, I've been forced into the backseat of a car, I've had to listen to gooey love talk. I've had to share your attention with that guy—"

"Hey!" Michael said.

"—and I got cheated out of several meals. Then I get held prisoner by a piece of prey, who wore too much cologne, thank you very much, and I have to get it off my fur and—"

"Shut up!" Emma said and clapped her hands. The clap turned into thunder and then a lightning bolt sizzled through the room, illuminating everything, including the dirt on the furniture. Emma felt the energy leave her and go directly toward Darnell. The light surrounded him for a moment—he seemed to grin as if he knew he had manipulated her—and then he shrank down to normal size.

He didn't even try to thank her. He just returned to licking his shoulder as if that were the most important thing in life.

Which, to him, it probably was.

Michael let out a small sigh. He hadn't left his post near the love seat. "You think that man is gone?"

"Yeah," Emma said.

"Bonita Sueña? You know what that means?"

"I was trying for Sleeping Beauty."

"You weren't even close."

"I was close," Emma said.

"No, you got Beautiful Dreamer." Then he frowned. "Actually, that would be La Sueña Bonita."

"No," Emma said. "That's the beautiful dream."

"I thought you didn't speak Spanish."

"I didn't say that. I just don't think fast in it."

"Then why didn't you use your native tongue?"

"Because he already had enough clues about who I was," Emma said. "No need to give him any more."

"So that's why you chose to call him Feo."

She smiled. "The Ugly Cowboy didn't suit him, but Ugly sure did."

Michael smiled back at her. His eyes warmed. She went to him and he put his arms around her, holding her close. They rocked together. He felt very, very good.

After a moment, Michael said, "Is Feo right? Do you think there're others?"

She nodded against his shirt. That was probably what she had felt when she had been entering this region. The dark magic.

"Do you think they're more powerful?"

"Than me? I'm sure of it."

"Than him."

She considered for a moment. "Their powers don't matter that much since they have to get my permission to take my magic, and it can't be coerced."

"That could be a fine line, though." Michael rubbed his hand up and down her back. "You might not even know you're being coerced."

"Michael, I'd know."

He shook his head. "Magic can work on you, just like the rest of us."

"Any spell would be coercion."

"The person who spelled you would have to get caught." He put a finger under her chin and brought her face up to his. "Right?"

She looked away. "Right."

He turned her face back toward his and kissed her. A

long, slow, sweet kiss that had passion, but also had a sorrow to it. Then he leaned his forehead against hers. "I think," he said softly, "we should go."

"Go?"

"Drive to Oregon. Nonstop."

"But, Michael." She gestured toward the bed. "We were going to stay the night."

He kissed her again. This kiss was less sweet and a lot more passionate. She slid her hands under his shirt, feeling that firm, strong back of his. His hands were in her hair, easing her closer.

"Jeez, guys, get a room."

Emma and Michael pulled apart. They both looked at Darnell. His golden eyes twinkled.

"That is the phrase, isn't it?" he asked. "Get a room?"

"I thought you lost your voice," Michael said.

"Not this time. She got the size, not the voice. I was annoyed at first, but I think this is going to be useful. I can weigh in with my opinion without having to throw myself at windows. And I say, 'Get a room.'"

"We have a room," Emma said.

Darnell sighed. "You persist in that activity with that—man"—there was enough disgust in Darnell's voice to freeze all of Lake Mendota—"I will simply have to find a way to stop you."

"We could put you in the car," Michael said.

"I will scream repeatedly if you do that."

"Lock you in the bathroom," Emma said, beginning to like the idea.

"I'll do a play by play of your activity, based on sound effects alone."

"Oh for heaven's sake," Michael said, letting his

arms drop, "I don't think a bucket of ice water would have been this effective."

"Then my work here is done." Darnell lay back down on the smashed coffee table. ·

Emma looked at Michael. "We could still put him in the car."

Michael shook his head. "Much as I want you on that bed," he said, "I think we need to be safe first."

Darnell glared at them. "Oh, so now he's saying that logic controlled his lust."

"That's enough, Darnell," Emma said.

"Not really," Darnell said. "I've decided I like having a voice. I could tell you tales of my life all the way to Oregon. Imagine the perspectives I have. The miraculous things I've *smelled* would take half the night, not to mention—"

"That's enough!" Emma said.

"Try the reverse spell," Michael said.

"It's been longer than five minutes."

"Try it anyway."

"Voice or no voice, I'll yowl if you decide to continue that cheap Hollywood passion in front of me," Darnell said.

Emma started reciting the reverse spell.

"You can't quiet me forever. You may take the English away from me, but my brain is my own—meeooow."

"You did it!" Michael sounded as pleased as she felt. Apparently neither of them could stomach listening to Darnell for the rest of the trip.

"Now we can lock him in the bathroom," Emma said.

Darnell yowled in protest—or perhaps it was in threat. Emma smiled fondly at him, knowing that this was one case in which she didn't care if he screamed all night.

"I don't think we should," Michael said softly.

"Of course we should," Emma said. "I have a hunch he'll be a bigger pain if we leave him out here."

"No." Michael kissed her gently. "I want to do this right."

"I'm sure you will." She leaned against him. "In fact, I'm trusting that you will. I believe—"

"Emma." His voice was getting softer. She was beginning to realize that his quiet moments were warnings that she might want to heed. She didn't know what he had to warn her about, though.

He slid his hand in hers and moved his body away from her so that they could see each other's faces. His had a frown creasing his forehead.

She had a hunch she wouldn't like what he had to say.

"I want our first night to be the best night either one of us has ever had," he said.

"I do, too," she said. "We can do that here."

"No," he said. "We can't. Here we'll hurry, knowing that our time is limited. We'll both be worried that some other evil wizard will interrupt us. Let's get you to Oregon, and then we'll take time for us."

Her heart twisted. She hadn't realized how important this moment was to her until now. She stared at him for a long moment, trying to think up an argument. For a moment, she thought of pushing him onto the bed. After a few kisses, he might reconsider.

But he had a point. A good point.

"How long do you think it'll take us to get to Oregon?" she asked softly.

He shrugged. "Seventeen, eighteen hours, maybe less. Washington and Montana have pretty high speed limits."

"We're tired," she said.

"We could take turns sleeping in the car." He caressed her cheek. "If we wait until we get there, we have an incentive to get there faster."

She chuckled. "Yeah, and if we get picked up for speeding, we tell the police officer that we're trying to get to Oregon to consummate our relationship?"

"He'll understand."

"He'll wonder why we're not stopping under some tree—or at least the next hotel." Her smile faded. "Michael, I know you're being practical, but—"

"Practical is what we need right now, and you know it. Feo, the shadows, they're just a warning. If what you told me about your wicked stepmother is even half true—"

"She wasn't my stepmother."

"You know what I mean."

Emma nodded.

"Then there've got to be others with powers like hers. We can't assume they'll leave us alone. We need to take these warnings seriously. Let's get you safe, and then let's worry about us."

Emma sighed. "Magic is such a damn inconvenience."

"I suspect we'll change our minds once you know how to use it."

"We won't," Emma said. "As you pointed out, I'm a bona fide heroine. Trouble follows me."

"Trouble's your job."

"Then I'd like to quit."

"You'll change your mind," Michael said.

"Don't bet on it," Emma muttered, and went to look for Darnell's cat carrier.

Chapter 14

EMMA DROVE THE FIRST SHIFT FROM BILLINGS TO Missoula. She stopped for gas in Butte, and Michael woke briefly but he remembered little about it. He had been more tired from the earlier drive than he had thought.

His sleep was restless and fitful, filled with dreams about white horses, ugly cowboys, and shadows that ate cats. He was a bit surprised to find his dreamself frightened for Darnell, and feeling quite protective of the surly old cat. He hadn't realized that Darnell had wormed his way into Michael's affections.

The sun rose between Butte and Missoula. Michael woke up as they headed through the Rockies, the sunlight pouring into the back of the car as if someone were holding a lamp behind them, trying to show them the way.

Emma drove smoothly and surely. It was hard to believe that she hadn't even heard of a car ten years before.

He watched her surreptitiously, not letting her know that he was awake. She was so beautiful and her life was so strange. He had struggled hard to be the brave, sensible one. He had wanted nothing more than to make love to her on that bed in that huge hotel room. But he had meant every word that he had said. He wanted to take his time with her. He wanted their moments together to be the best in their lives.

They had breakfast in a roadside diner in Missoula. They didn't talk much. Emma was so exhausted that there were smoky rings under her eyes. She didn't even ask Michael to drive for her. When they went back to the car, he got in the driver's side, and she tucked herself onto the passenger seat, letting sleep take her immediately.

The drive over the Bitterroots was one of his favorites and he was glad he was awake for it. In the early morning sunshine, everything looked fresh and new. He cracked the window just a little and let the scent of pine flow in. The mountains had a smell all their own, a smell he loved almost as much as the scent of the sea.

In Wallace, Idaho—a small town that still bore its mining roots in its downtown—he saw four homeless people on horseback. They were stopped at the side of the road, talking to a fifth man who was swinging his arms wildly. At his feet were sacks filled with money.

Apparently he had gotten his wish. Had he just figured out then that his horse was a wish? Or did he think the money had dropped from the sky?

Michael almost thought of stopping to talk with him, and then changed his mind. Let them enjoy their own miracle. Every life deserved at least one.

Emma was his miracle. He wasn't sure how she managed to find him, but she had. She had found him, somehow, and her presence had opened him up.

He hadn't realized that there was magic in the world. His life had been structured, his goals simple ones. He hadn't experienced true chaos before, hadn't realized how flexible he could be, and how much fun it could sometimes be. The phantom meal he ate at Emma's restaurant was as solid a memory as the meals he had eaten in Paris—and as impossible to reconstruct. How delightful they had all been.

She had introduced him to other miracles too—the ghostly Sioux on the Little Bighorn Battlefield, Darnell the talking cat, and the little glimpse of medieval Europe. Suddenly the world seemed less restrictive than it had ever seemed before. Not only was there magic, but the magic enhanced his life.

He wasn't sure how he would write about that when it came time to do his book, but he knew he had to. He had always looked at magic backwards. He had thought that the belief that magic existed came because human beings couldn't explain their world so they needed something—magic, strange religions, mysticism—to help them comprehend the incomprehensible.

Instead, he would approach his history of magic study the way he would approach the history of religion. He would accept the beliefs—just as he would accept the beliefs of Buddhists or Jews or Catholics—and then he would write the history from there. It would be a crossover text—one that the New Age stores would buy, and one that historians would use as well. He would document everything—his research had to be solid—but his approach would be new for a scholarly text.

He smiled as he drove through Coeur d'Alene and looked at the spectacular lake, sparkling in the sun. The biggest problem would be writing things he now knew were true—such as the ability to turn a cat into a lion or the fact that magic users lived very long lives—as if they were something unverifiable, and therefore unproven.

As he thought about that, a little shiver ran down his back. He frowned, and glanced at Emma. She was still sound asleep, her dark hair flowing over her like a blanket. Darnell was awake and watching him as if he could hear Michael's thoughts.

Michael shivered again. He hoped that Emma's magic hadn't gone awry. The last thing he wanted was for that cat to read his mind.

But something Michael had thought of had disturbed him, and it had done so on a very deep level. He glanced at Emma again. He'd been thinking about magic. Magic and... long life.

His stomach twisted. Feo had mentioned that, using such derogatory terms. Emma had played along, even though Michael had seen the anger in her eyes. Feo had called Michael insignificant, had called him a toy.

Michael hadn't really focused on the man's words. His manner had been disturbing enough. But he had said something that had angered Michael—and he'd had to set it aside so that Emma could concentrate on Feo.

"I could extend the life of your toy there," Feo had said. "Make him pretty as long as he lives."

Extend the life... as long as he lives.

Michael would grow old and die, and Emma would look the same as she did now. He would be the first man in her life, true enough, and probably special for that. But he wouldn't be the last, and he probably wouldn't be the one she spent the bulk of her life with. That would be a man of her own kind, a man who would live forever—or however close to it that Emma lived.

She would be the most important thing in Michael's life, and he would only be a footnote in hers.

His hands gripped the wheel tightly. He glanced in the rearview mirror. Darnell had fallen asleep. Emma had stirred slightly, still sleeping as well.

Michael made himself take a deep breath. He had fallen in love with Emma, and she had told him that she cared for him—which was probably as close to an admission of love as he would get from her. She needed to learn how to be close. He was willing to teach her, even knowing the future imbalance in their relationship. Even knowing that she might not be interested in him as he aged and she didn't.

Somehow he had always thought, like everyone else, that magic would make life easier. He was continually surprised that it did not.

Emma drove down the familiar streets of Portland. When she had seen the bridges crossing the Willamette, her heart had leaped. She had missed this place more than she wanted to admit. The bridges were lit up against the black sky, their arching shapes familiar and comforting. The lights reflected in the river below, stretching them, blending them into colors that seemed planned, even though they weren't. The city itself was spectacular, and beyond it, despite the darkness, she could see the outlines of the mountains.

She had missed it all more than she had thought she would.

Darnell had climbed into the front seat for the first time on this trip. He was standing between Michael and Emma and had his front paws on the dash, his tail wagging slowly, as if he were hunting prey. But she knew he wasn't. He was wagging his tail happily, but doing it slowly so that no one would think he was practicing doglike behavior.

Michael had one hand on Darnell's belly, bracing him, and Darnell didn't seem to mind. But Michael wasn't watching the cat. He was looking at the city through the passenger side window, seemingly lost in thought.

Emma wondered what he made of Portland, how he felt now that they were so close to their destination. They hadn't said much during the day's meals—one or the other of them had been waking up from fitful naps—and ever since Spokane, Michael had seemed distant.

She wasn't sure if he really was distant or if she was perceiving everything through her exhaustion. Mixed with that exhaustion was a sense of relief. Her life would gain some semblance of order now that she was back in Oregon. Aethelstan would help her learn how to be the mage everyone seemed to think she was.

She took the downtown exit that led to Nora and Aethelstan's loft. The neighborhood was made up of shops and warehouses and lovely old office buildings, all made of brick and stone. The loft was high enough that it had a view of the city and the bridges, but there weren't enough trees or grass for Emma. There was no place in the neighborhood for a garden, and the exhaust fumes from a nearby busy street made most window box plants look sickly.

Darnell's tail went faster and faster as they turned onto the street where he used to live. Michael seemed to withdraw further into himself. She didn't blame him. He probably had no idea what would happen next. Neither did she.

She parked in her favorite on-the-street spot next to the only real tree on the entire block. The loft was several stories up. She hadn't called ahead; she wondered if they would be home. The restaurant kept late hours, and sometimes Aethelstan was there until long past closing, planning his next great dish.

Still, they would be expecting her sometime soon. They knew she was driving. They just didn't know when she would arrive.

She shut off the car, and glanced at Michael. He was still staring out the window as if they hadn't stopped moving. Darnell was in her lap, purring. Apparently, he was happy that the trip was over.

"Well," she said, "let's see if they're home."

"Are you sure you want me along?" Michael asked quietly. He hadn't turned to her. He was still staring out the window. She could see tension in his shoulders and back.

"Why wouldn't I want you to come along?" she asked. Darnell sat down and looked at Michael as if he were spoiling the fun.

"These are your old friends. You've come to them for help, and I'd just be in the way."

She let out a small breath. She hadn't realized that Michael was nervous about this. "You won't be in the way. You're the reason I made it here. You kept me sane and helped me survive. Remember that vision of yours? It could have come true."

"It was a dream. It might have been nothing more than that."

She slipped her hand over his. "Come with me, Michael," she said. "I want you to meet the other people who are important to me in this world."

He turned to her then. With his other hand, he caressed her face. His fingers were cool against her skin.

"Funny," he said softly, "I'm the one who made us drive this last part nonstop, and I'm the one who doesn't want the trip to end."

"I'm sorry the drive's over too." Then she smiled. "But we had incentive to get here, remember? And it had nothing to do with magic."

He smiled too. "Do you think your friends will take care of Darnell?"

"All we have to do is ask." She kissed his hand, then reached for the car door. "Ready?"

He nodded. "The official end of the road. A few days ago, I wondered if we'd make it."

"A week ago, you thought I was crazy for suggesting it."

"I've learned a lot since then," he said.

"Me too," she said, feeling surprised. "Me too."

—∾—

Michael carried Darnell inside the building, holding the cat in front of him like a shield. Emma led the way as if she had been here a thousand times—which she probably had. Darnell got squirmy once they were inside the elevator.

"You can put him down," she said. "He used to live here. He knows the way."

So Michael set down Darnell and felt strangely unprotected. He was tired, more tired than he cared to admit. He didn't want to meet these people wearing rumpled clothes and having brushed his teeth in restaurant bathrooms. They were important to Emma; he wanted to impress them.

Fat chance of that.

Darnell stood in front of the doors, waiting for the

elevator to stop. Emma leaned against the wall, watching the floor numbers tick by. Michael wanted to touch her, but he wasn't sure if he could any longer. Even though she had reassured him, his status was about to change, and he knew it.

The elevator doors opened, and Darnell was the first one out, trotting down the corridor as if he owned the place. And, being a cat (and an extremely self-possessed one at that) he probably thought he did.

Emma slipped her hand in Michael's. Then she smiled at him. "We're together," she said.

He nodded. He squeezed her hand in what he hoped felt like reassurance, and then he walked at her side to the big steel door at the end of the corridor. Emma knocked on it. Darnell stood in front of it, tail wagging.

Michael heard footsteps, a pause as someone looked through the peephole, and then bolts slid back and the door opened.

Casper, the Ghost of Christmas Present, stepped out. He looked different than he had in Michael's dream; he was wearing a white linen suit, spats, and a fedora. He looked a little like a pug dog attempting to imitate James Cagney.

"Merlin," Emma said and crouched so that she could hug him. He patted her back, looking vaguely embarrassed, then slipped out of her grasp.

"So you took my advice," he said to Michael.

"It seemed like the right decision at the time," Michael said.

"And now?"

"And now I know it was."

Emma stood and smiled at Michael.

"Well, I can't stay," Casper said. "Got some things to do at the restaurant. Hi ho!"

And then he walked to the elevator, whistling "Whistle While You Work."

"Hi ho?" Emma asked Michael.

"That first night, I insulted him. Guess this means he forgives me."

"What did you do?" A new voice asked. "Compare him to Sneezy?"

A pretty petite blond who looked like she had once been captain of her high school cheerleading squad was peering out the door.

"Grumpy, actually."

"I always thought he looked like Doc." Then she smiled. "You must be Michael."

He nodded but she missed it. She had wrapped her arms around Emma. Emma hugged her back. Darnell ran inside and Michael heard a long drawn-out hiss. It didn't sound like Darnell's.

"I missed you so much!" the woman said as she eased herself out of the hug, and extended a hand to Michael. "I'm Nora Barr. I can't tell you how grateful Alex and I are that you brought Emma to us."

"My pleasure," Michael said, shaking her hand. She stepped back and invited them into the loft.

It was breathtaking. The sunken living room was decorated in reds and silvers. A chrome staircase twisted its way to the upper story where a sleeping area hid behind a silver screen. But the most dominant part of the loft were the windows, which, even though it was night, were still open. Through them, he could see the lights of the entire city and the bridges over the river.

"Wow," he said. He would never have imagined Emma in a place like this.

"We like it," a male voice said.

Michael turned. A man stood in the entrance to the kitchen. He was tall, with dark hair that covered his collar. He had classic features and eyes that looked almost silver. So this was Aethelstan, the man Emma had once loved. No wonder. He looked like every woman's ideal—tall, dark, handsome, and mysterious.

Aethelstan seemed to be assessing Michael as well. "You made good time. I would have thought that this trip would have taken longer."

He almost made it sound as if Michael had hurried to get here so that he could be rid of Emma.

"We ran into some troubles along the way," Emma said.

"Darnell turn into a lion again?" Nora asked. Then she looked around. "Where is he? He was harassing Squidgy a minute ago."

"Squidgy?" Michael asked.

"She and Darnell were both my cats once. They lived together for ten years, something Squidgy hates to be reminded of." Nora smiled and in spite of himself, Michael found himself smiling back. He hadn't realized that he'd been prepared to hate these people. After all, Nora had taken Aethelstan away from Emma, but it suddenly didn't seem that clear-cut.

"He turned into a lion once or twice," Emma said, "but it was the loose magic thing that made us decide to get here as fast as we could."

A frown crossed Aethelstan's face. "You two look exhausted. Why don't you sit? Would you like something to eat? Some coffee, maybe?"

"No," Michael started, but Emma said, "That would be good."

Aethelstan disappeared into the kitchen. Emma led Michael to the couch. As he sat, he saw Darnell in the small hallway that led toward the back, his whiskers forward, batting at a roly-poly black cat who had its ears back and was hissing vehemently. Darnell seemed to be having the time of his life.

"Should I break them up?" Emma asked Nora.

"Squidgy can take care of herself," Nora said. "Can't you, love?"

Squidgy rose on her hind legs and swatted Darnell five times on the face before he could even swing a paw. He sat, dazed, as she made her way into the living room.

"I never thought anyone could take him on," Michael said.

"Well, Squidgy decided a few years back not to take any crap from him," Nora said. "I think living alone's been good for her."

Aethelstan came out of the kitchen carrying a silver serving tray. On it was a silver coffeepot, and several kinds of appetizers, all of them warm and smelling good.

Michael must have looked surprised.

"They're from the restaurant," Nora said. "He microwaved them."

Such a simple explanation, and an unnecessary one for most people. But apparently they had all realized that Michael thought they were magically produced.

"Sorry," he said, feeling stupid. "I haven't had a lot of sleep."

"You drove straight from where?" Aethelstan asked.

"Billings," Emma said, and then she told him about

Feo and the shadows. "Michael was the one who said we needed to get here fast."

Aethelstan's silver eyes studied him for a moment, as if reassessing him. "I think we owe you great thanks. Your friend Feo was the least of the wizards in that area. The others were probably planning something much more elaborate."

"Emma said they couldn't do anything without her permission, but I was worried nonetheless."

"Rightly so," Aethelstan said. "That group doesn't always respect the boundaries of our laws."

"I would have been all right," Emma said.

"No," Aethelstan said, "you wouldn't have."

Emma's face flushed. "You don't know what's all happened. I've improved."

"Probably," Aethelstan said. "But anything you think you've learned on this trip will have to be relearned."

"Relearned?" Emma said. "Why?"

"Because there are right ways of doing magic and there are wrong ways. The wrong ways lead to bad spells."

"Like the one you used to save me all those years ago?" Emma snapped.

"Yes," Aethelstan said.

Michael looked at him, surprised. He hadn't expected the man to admit a mistake so easily.

"And I don't want you to have any bad habits. I suspect you have a lot more power than most of us do, and a bad habit from you might make the spell even more dangerous."

"I can handle myself," Emma said.

"If that were true, you wouldn't be here."

"I'm here because I have no choice," Emma said. "You wouldn't come to me."

"I couldn't."

"Well, if those mages in Montana could ignore the rules, why couldn't you?"

"Emma, we've had this discussion."

"I've been thinking about this, Aethelstan, and I don't think this is a good idea. I don't think I can learn anything from you."

Aethelstan's cheeks grew red. Michael kept his hand entwined with Emma's feeling as if he were over his head. "I'm a good teacher, Emma."

"But you won't listen to me when I tell you something."

"I think that goes both ways," Aethelstan said. "You always misinterpret what I have to say."

"This type of discussion is not productive," Nora said.

"We'll handle it," Aethelstan said to her.

"Actually," Michael said, "Emma and I haven't really slept for two days. Give her a chance to get some rest and I'm sure—"

Aethelstan waved a hand, and all of Michael's exhaustion left him. He felt better than he had in years. Buoyant, almost giddy.

"Dammit, Aethelstan, you're supposed to ask before you do that." The shadows were gone from beneath Emma's eyes. She looked as fresh as she had the day Michael met her, and even more energetic, if that were possible.

"You liked being tired?" he asked.

"I *earned* it," Emma said. "I would rather have had a long night's sleep than a magical pick-me-up."

"The sooner we get started, the sooner we get back to our lives," Aethelstan said. "We have a lot of ground to cover."

"I'm not sure I want to cover it," Emma said. "Michael and I are getting a hotel room."

"It can wait," Aethelstan said.

"No," Michael said. "It can't."

"You're not tired anymore, and you've already spent days together. I would think you'd want some time to yourselves." Aethelstan was frowning. His wife was sitting beside him, trying and failing to suppress a smile.

"The opposite, actually," Michael said. "We're taking Darnell's advice and getting a room."

"Darnell?" Nora asked.

"Long story," Emma said. "But Michael's right. I'm not ready to start tonight, Aethelstan. I want some time to adjust to being here."

His eyes had grown darker. "You've had plenty of time to adjust, Emma. This is the problem. You keep putting off your training. You can't any longer. And we are going to get started."

He raised his arm again, but his wife caught it. "Don't," she said.

"Don't?" He looked at her. She seemed so small compared to him, but Michael was betting on her. She had a lot more power than appeared at first glance.

"This is Emma's life, and Emma's decision."

"Emma seems to be forgetting that she has to learn her craft."

"I'm not forgetting it," Emma said. "I'm just not sure I want it."

Michael felt his heart lurch. "Emma?"

She looked at him. Her eyes, a richer blue than Nora's, were filled with tears. "I want to go home, Michael."

"I thought Portland was your home."

"Madison," she said. "I want to go to Madison."

"Well, we can do that, I suppose," Aethelstan said. "Now that you're here, I can do whatever we need to get you on the right track."

"Alex," Nora said. "Just be quiet for a moment, would you?"

He looked chagrined. Michael frowned. Was Aethelstan blustering around Emma because she made him uncomfortable? It seemed that way, and not the discomfort a man felt when he was attracted to a woman, but the discomfort he had when he felt he had treated her poorly.

Emma was rubbing her index finger over Michael's knuckles. She was studying the appetizers no one had eaten. "What can you teach me, Aethelstan?"

"Control, Emma."

"And spells?"

"All the ones I know."

She nodded. Michael didn't entirely understand her mood shift. "This is going to take years, isn't it?" she asked. "You can't just put a spell on me and I'll have it all?"

"You can get the knowledge that way." Aethelstan spoke softly. He seemed to sense that he had overstepped as well. "But the practice is the important thing. And you need someone like me to help you correct your mistakes quickly and easily. Like those white horses. They're yours, aren't they?"

Emma nodded.

"That's dangerous magic to let float around," he said.

"They're just wishes."

"People can wish for anything, Emma." His voice

was gentle. "A million dollars or the death of someone they hate. Anything at all."

Michael felt his breath catch in his throat. He hadn't thought of that. And, he could tell from the look in Emma's eyes, that she hadn't either.

"You'll show me how to fix that?" she asked.

"And we'll make sure there's been no harm," Aethelstan said.

"All right." Emma was watching her fingers move over Michael's. He'd never heard her sound so docile. What had changed? Or was she always this way around Aethelstan?

Then Michael glanced up at Aethelstan and Nora. They were watching Emma with expressions of equal concern on their faces. They didn't like how this was going either.

Squidgy had made her way into the living room, her nose twitching at the smell of food. Darnell was sitting in the window, looking out at the city, as if this were his place and he had missed it.

Emma's finger was still tracing Michael's. Her beautiful face was downcast, her eyes shaded. He squeezed her hand. She sighed, and brought her head up. "I'm not ready to start tonight."

"Emma, every hour I leave you alone is another hour in which something can go wrong." Aethelstan's voice was harsh.

Emma's face flushed. She had obviously heard what he said as criticism. Michael was willing to bet that the man meant it as concern. "I need to be alone with Michael for a while."

"You just spent three days driving with him. It's not—"

"Alex." Nora put her hand on his knee. "If something goes wrong, you can fix it, right?"

"It's a waste of magic," he said, but he covered her hand with his own.

"And we can't afford to waste magic, can we?" Emma snapped.

"That's not what I meant," Aethelstan said. "You know the toll that magic takes. Why exact it if it's not necessary?"

"Maybe it is necessary," Nora said.

"Emma's just procrastinating. She hates this kind of work. She's had years to do it and—"

"I'm not procrastinating," Emma said. "I need some more time."

"That's what I'm trying to tell you," Aethelstan said. "You've used all your time and more. You're lucky you made it here. Michael, we owe you more than we can say for getting her here. I'm sure it wasn't easy—"

"Emma was the one who got us here," Michael said. Emma glanced at him in surprise. "I was just along for the ride. Added security, nothing more. I'm sure she could have done it on her own."

"That's not what Sancho said." Nora moved the silver tray. Squidgy was sitting beneath it.

"Sancho?"

"Merlin," Emma said. "You know, the Ghost of Christmas Present."

"He told you about the Dickens thing?" Aethelstan said.

"No, actually," Emma said. "Michael had a visitation."

"Sancho did that?" Nora looked at Aethelstan for confirmation. "I thought that wasn't allowed."

"It doesn't matter." Michael was getting annoyed himself. Who were these people to treat Emma like this? "I don't care what your friend said. Emma did just fine.

She saved us more than once. She's going to be one of the most capable magicians around."

Emma's finger had stopped moving over his. Her entire body was still, like a rabbit's scenting danger on the wind.

"She needs to start work immediately," Aethelstan said.

"She will. But let her get settled first. We had a long drive and we're—well, we were tired. Give her a few more hours, and I promise she'll be back here, ready to work."

Aethelstan studied Michael for a moment, clearly reassessing him again. Then he turned his gaze to Emma. "Will you be here?" he asked. "You won't spend days avoiding this? It's important, Emma. It really is."

"I know," she said in that same meek tone she'd been using.

Aethelstan sighed. "Look, you and I, we have our problems and I might not be the best teacher for you. I can get someone else. There are some good people in Europe right now."

"And there's Sancho," Nora said.

Emma nodded. "I know. I'll be all right."

"Emma, please." Aethelstan's voice lowered. "We're getting off on the wrong foot again, like we always do, but I owe you this. I'm the reason everything is so messed up for you. I'll help in anyway I can. If I can't teach you, then I'll find the best person to do the job. So don't delay this because of me."

"I'm not," Emma said. "Believe it or not, Aethelstan, this isn't about you."

Then she glanced at Michael. He couldn't read the expression on her face and he felt himself grow cold.

Was she going to send him home? Had she decided that her world was no place for a mortal?

Suddenly there was a loud crash. They all turned. The silver serving tray was on the floor, the coffee spilling out of the pot. Squidgy was standing on the tray so that the coffee wouldn't touch her delicate paws, and she was eating appetizers as if they had all been made for her.

Nora cursed and picked her up. Aethelstan grabbed the coffeepot and headed for the kitchen. Emma choked out a weak laugh. "Thank God for Squidgy," she said.

"That's why we went for silver," Nora said. "She's broken more dishes than any other cat on the planet."

Darnell hadn't even turned around. Michael bent down and began to clean up. Nora put a hand on his shoulder.

"Leave it," she said. "Go with Emma. You two clearly have something to settle."

Michael glanced at Emma. She was already standing. She wasn't looking at him, but at Nora. "Can you take care of Darnell for a while?"

Nora nodded. "He won't like being away from you."

Emma's smile was small. "After this week, he just might."

She headed for the door, and let herself out. Michael stood and started to follow her. Nora caught his arm.

"My husband isn't really unreasonable. He loves Emma. It's just that for a thousand years, she was helpless and he was her protector. He can't seem to get beyond that."

"Emma doesn't need protection anymore."

Nora smiled. "Once she woke up, she never did. She's a strong woman."

"Yes, she is," Michael said.

"You're in love with her, aren't you?"

He glanced at the door. It was ajar, but he couldn't see Emma. She was probably waiting in the hall. "How do you do it?" he asked. "How do you live with someone who was born before William the Conqueror?"

"It creates problems," Nora said. "But we work them out. You will too."

He shook his head. "My life is so short compared to hers. I'm a mayfly and she's damn near immortal."

"I don't think I'm the one you should be talking to about this."

"Emma assures me that it's not a problem."

"Then maybe you should trust her," Nora said. "She loves you too."

"How can you tell?" he asked.

"I've known her for a long time. She's never leaned on anyone before."

"She hasn't leaned on me either."

Nora's expression softened. "Then you haven't been paying attention."

Chapter 15

EMMA HAD NEVER CHECKED INTO A HOTEL IN THE morning before. She wasn't used to the hustle and bustle of the front desk, dealing with people in a hurry to leave, while she waited alone in the check-in line.

Michael stood near the suitcases. He looked pensive. The energy that Aethelstan had given both of them still had them bouncing, but it hadn't erased the circles from Michael's eyes.

Ever since his short conversation with Nora—which he wouldn't share with Emma—he seemed worried. Maybe Emma hadn't explained things well enough to him. Or maybe he was finally facing the reality of what she was.

Emma sighed deeply and found herself wishing that Darnell was with them. Darnell was her security, and she wasn't used to being without him. He was a constant, and she needed him more than she had realized.

The hotel was a modern upscale chain right in the heart of downtown Portland. The lobby was done in blacks and marbles, the ceilings were high, but the attitude was refreshingly friendly. Oregonians didn't seem to understand the word "snooty." Even the desk clerk, who was astonished that someone would check in at the strange hour of 7:00 a.m. was polite about it. He even managed to find them a newly vacated, newly cleaned room.

When Emma got the key she beckoned Michael. He dragged their luggage cart to the elevator and said nothing as they got on. Her heart was pounding.

"There's a lot of homeless near the river," Michael said.

"Hmm?" Emma glanced at him. He was staring at the door, almost as if they were strangers.

"All the white horses. Didn't you see them?"

She had. The river was only a few blocks from here. They had driven by it after they left the loft. There had been a lot of horses, and a lot of homeless, although not nearly as many as ten years ago. Portland was working on helping its poor, unlike other cities.

"I saw them," she said. "Aethelstan didn't approve of them."

"He didn't seem to be in the mood to approve of anything."

"I know," Emma said quietly. A lot of that was her fault. Aethelstan had never been able to figure her out, even though he tried. Sometimes she thought it was because she didn't know her own mind, either.

Although he wasn't that far off about her training. She was postponing it, and not just for some time alone with Michael. The whole idea of using her magic made her stomach twist. She had liked her world small, liked the house with its garden, her teaching position, her modern education.

What she had realized on this trip was that it would all vanish one day, no matter what she did. No matter how hard she worked. Aethelstan had been awake for that thousand years she slept. He opened a restaurant because a lot of the meals he loved weren't available anymore. Recipes, he once told her, survived centuries. Little else did.

The elevator doors opened, and Emma took the luggage cart. Michael grabbed an end, as if he still had to be useful. They pushed the cart to the room, which was on the far end of the floor. Emma used her keycard to let them inside.

The room still smelled of lemon polish. It was smaller than their Montana hotel room, but it had as lovely a view of the city as the loft did. Emma pushed the cart to the walk-in closet, unloaded the bags, then shoved the cart into the hallway and closed the door.

Michael leaned against the wall, arms crossed, watching her. "It seems that the mood is gone," he said. "I guess driving for two days'll do that to you."

Emma walked to the windows. Sunlight fell across her, warm and comforting. The river sparkled, a dazzling blue. Mount Hood looked cool and regal in the distance.

"What are your plans?" she asked.

He was silent for a moment. "We—um—had a date. I thought."

"I know," she said.

"And then I thought, I don't know, that we'd spend some time together."

She nodded. Originally he had planned to go home right away. He had done her a great favor.

"But it seems that your friends have a different agenda." Michael sounded calm. Emma worried when Michael sounded so calm. "They think it's dangerous to let your magic remain out of control much longer."

"They're right."

"So why come here, Emma? I won't hold you to that obligation. It was the heat of the moment." His voice grew wry. "And I've never found sex enjoyable when one of the parties looked on it as a duty."

"Is that how you see it?" The words came out of her before she could stop them.

"No," he said. "I thought that's how you did."

She shook her head. She wanted to go to him, but she couldn't. She was too confused inside. The training loomed ahead of her—the new life, which she couldn't change.

"Michael, if I ask you a question, promise me you'll be honest."

"All right."

She turned. He was still leaning against the wall, arms crossed. But he was frowning now, as if he couldn't figure out what she was going to do.

"Do you think I could have been a good teacher?"

He blinked as if that weren't what he expected, and then he smiled. "You already are. Those students loved to hear what you had to say. That's ninety percent of the battle."

His response was unexpected. She sat on the bed and patted the spot next to her. He crossed and sat, pulling the mattress down. He didn't touch her.

She took his hands. They were strong hands, good hands. Comforting hands. "You've never been involved with anyone either, have you?" she asked.

"I've had relationships."

"But you never married."

"No."

"Never lived with anyone?"

"That's right."

"Why not?"

He shrugged. "Always waiting for the right woman, I guess."

"And what would you do when you found her?"

His thumb covered hers. "Hope she felt the same way I did."

"What if she did?"

"I'd make a life with her, if she wanted me."

"I want you, Michael," Emma said softly. "I love you."

He didn't move. She had thought he would kiss her, hold her, maybe lean her down on the bed as he had done before. Instead, his eyes were empty.

"I'll live a fraction of your life, Emma," he said. "You'll just be getting used to your magic when I'll look old enough to be your father. Then I'll look like your grandfather. And then I'll die. You'll still be a new mage."

"I know." Her voice trembled.

"Feo, he said that there are spells to make me look the same age as you."

Emma nodded, feeling sad. "But not ways to lengthen your life, Michael."

He bowed his head.

"And," she said, "our life together would always be like this drive. You'd never know what sort of magical thing would come our way."

"I always need more adventure," he said.

She put her finger under his chin and raised his head. It was an intimate movement she had never performed with anyone before. His movement. "You sound hesitant."

"I'm worried," he said. "I can't help you any more. It's you and Aethelstan now, or whoever your tutor will be. You'll have to focus on moving forward, Emma, on realizing all that magical potential that everyone talks about. It's going to take years, and I can't stay here while you do that. I have to return to Madison, to my job if they'll still have me."

"I know," she said.

"Five years, right?" he asked.

"Minimum," she said, hating the thought of it. Magic every day, every moment. Always thinking about it, always concentrating on it.

"That's just a blink to you," he said. "But for me, that's five years I'll never get again."

Her heart twisted. "And you're not willing to do that? To wait?"

"Oh, God, Emma, of course I am." He put his hands on her face, brought her close as he had done so many times before. His touch felt so good. "I'll take you anyway I can have you. I love you. I'm just afraid you won't be satisfied. You have so much and all I am is a mildly successful professor who was happy to get tenure. I—"

She kissed him. She had to. She couldn't wait. He said he loved her, and she hadn't been sure. No one had said that to her in a thousand years. Not Aethelstan, not her parents. No one.

He kissed her back, slid his hands down her neck and onto her shoulders. Then his arms were around her, and she wrapped her arms around him.

So close, so perfect—but not yet. She moved her mouth away from his. Someday soon, she hoped, they'd get to go further than a kiss.

"I'll be right back," she said. "Wait here."

He looked confused. She kissed him again quickly and quickly uttered the spell that sent her to the Fates.

The air crackled, and as it snapped, she saw Michael, staring after her as if she were leaving him forever.

———•———

She appeared in a drawing room filled with heavy Victorian furniture. It was all made of solid wood and upholstered in red. The walls were the same dark wood, and the carpet held the same rich reds. A fire burned in the fireplace, making the room too warm. It smelled of cigars and Emma resisted the urge to sneeze.

"I don't believe that whist is a game that was meant to be played by people with brains," said a female voice behind Emma.

She turned. All three Fates were sitting at a round wooden card table. They all had cigars in their mouths, and brandy snifters at their sides. They were wearing smoking jackets and trousers, and they had their hair cut so short that they looked like teenage boys pretending to be men.

"Excuse me," Emma said.

Lachesis took the cigar out of her mouth. "We're in the middle of a hand."

"Unless you know something of this game," Clotho said.

"What is it?" Emma asked, wishing she hadn't.

"Whist." Atropos set her cards down. "I really don't like these rules."

"You never like rules," Lachesis said.

"Shh," Clotho said. "That's not something we want out."

"It doesn't really matter," Atropos said. "I don't have to like them to make them."

Lachesis set her cards down as well. "I thought you'd be settled now. You've seen Aethelstan. I know you don't get along, but he'll be a fine teacher."

"If he isn't right for you," Clotho said, "I'm sure he'll find someone to help."

"You're a bit high maintenance, Emma," Atropos said gently. "Perhaps if you give a little, Aethelstan won't be so defensive."

"He should be even more defensive," Lachesis said. "After all he's done to this girl."

"It wasn't intentional," said Clotho. "We've given him trouble over that, but we know it to be true."

"All the more reason he'll be the best teacher for you, Emma." Atropos stubbed out her cigar. "He knows what happens when magic goes awry."

"He's afraid you'll do something equally as disastrous," Lachesis said.

"We're lucky you haven't so far." Clotho set down her cards. "You've come close."

"That restaurant could have been a catastrophe," Atropos said as she picked up a new cigar and cut off the end with her shears.

"How many times do I have to tell you not to do that?" Lachesis said. "You'll dull them."

"I agree with you about Aethelstan," Emma said. She felt overwhelmed by them as usual.

"You do?" they asked in unison. "Really?"

"Yes," Emma said, swallowing hard. The cigar smoke was making her light-headed.

"Then why are you here?" Clotho asked.

"Because I have a request," she said, trying not to sound too desperate. Her entire future rested on their responses and she had no idea what she would do if they said no.

—⁂—

The spell had been in Old English. Michael had recognized the sound of the words. Emma had told them to him before she left. He stood up and took the spell list out of his wallet. He scanned it until he found the one she had uttered.

She had gone to the Fates.

He cursed silently. What was she doing there? She had to be going for some kind of ruling, something that was out of the ordinary. He knew that much. Was she asking for longer life for him? Some way they could have equal footing?

Hadn't he been clear? He wanted to be with her no matter what. But maybe she didn't want to be with him.

She hadn't kissed like someone who didn't want to be with him.

He had a bad feeling about this.

He stared at the words on the page for a moment, wondering if they would send him to the Fates. There was only one way to find out. He cleared his throat and recited the spell, and waited.

Nothing happened.

Emma had disappeared in a matter of seconds, but he was still standing here. Well, the Fates weren't his governing body after all. He was just a lowly mortal who aspired to love someone who had had stories told about her for centuries. The Ghost of Christmas Present had been the original Merlin, and Aethelstan looked like some sort of Greek god.

Not to mention the fact that Emma was the most beautiful woman in the world. The Fates, everyone, would see Michael as an interloper.

He wasn't. He loved her, but he was willing to let her

live her life in the way she thought best. He just had to make sure she wasn't doing anything they would both regret later.

Still clutching the paper, his hands trembling, he went to the hotel phone. After struggling for a moment to figure out how to get an outside line, he dialed the number for Aethelstan's home. Voice mail answered. Nora, giving the standard leave-a-message line.

Then Michael called Aethelstan's cell phone and got another voice mail, this time Aethelstan's—quite charming and extremely personable. Michael hadn't had any idea that the other man could be charming, but then Michael was usually immune to things like charisma and charm.

Finally Michael dialed the restaurant, and after being abruptly dropped, then listening to clanging silverware and cursing cooks, he found out that Aethelstan had gone to inspect cilantro from a new supplier.

There had to be an easier way to reach magical people. Michael couldn't believe all that calling for them or using code phrases was completely made up.

Unfortunately, he didn't have time to find out. He didn't leave a message with the restaurant—that was too complicated. He toyed with calling Nora at her office, but he knew she couldn't do anything more than he could. If only he had magic. But wishes wouldn't do him any good, not without the power to go with them.

And then he turned toward the window.

Wishes. He smiled. There were magical white horses only two blocks away.

He stuffed his wallet back into his pocket and let himself out of the room, heading for the horses. He only hoped he made it in time.

"Well," Atropos said, setting down her shears, "get on with it."

"Yes," Lachesis said. "Being coy won't help."

Emma's heart was pounding. The room was stuffy, and the cigar smoke swirled around her. "I've been doing a lot of thinking about this. For the last few days especially. And I've made a decision."

"You're still being coy, my dear," Clotho said, tugging on the sleeve of her red smoking jacket.

Emma straightened her spine. "I want to give up my magic."

Atropos made a tsk-tsk sound. "You just don't want to work hard. Magic takes discipline."

"I have discipline," Emma snapped. "I learned how to speak half a dozen languages. I learned the history of the world. I learned how to function in the modern environment."

"Yes, and you wouldn't have had to do any of it if you'd only taken Aethelstan's catch-up spell," Lachesis said.

"No wonder you're burnt out, child," Clotho said. "Learning is difficult. You should have thought that through before making the wrong choice."

"The wrong choice?" Emma's voice went up. "It wasn't the wrong choice. Aethelstan's spell would have left me with a superficial knowledge of everything. My knowledge isn't superficial. It's real and it's mine. Do you know how important that is?"

"It's not important at all," Atropos said. "After a few thousand years, you'll wonder why you tried so hard to learn about things you'd only forget."

"I don't want to live another thousand years," Emma said. "I hate magic. I hate what it's done to my life. That's why I want out of this."

"You'll regret the decision," Lachesis said. "Your life will be terribly short. You won't have any recourse at all. You'll be—unremarkable."

"I don't think so." The voice was Michael's. Emma whirled. He was standing near the fireplace, holding a white horse on a lead. One of her special horses.

"Michael," she breathed.

"Great Caesar's Ghost," Clotho said. "It's a mortal."

"It's Emma's mortal," Lachesis said, sounding smug.

"That's why you want to lose your powers," Atropos said. "You feel sorry for the creature."

"I do not!" Emma said.

"You want to give up your magic?" Michael let go of the horse and came toward her. "Emma, you can't. It's part of you."

"No," she said, "it's not. I was just telling them that I hate it."

"You don't hate it, child," Clotho said. "You hate the inconvenience of it. A whole different thing."

"No." Emma clenched her fists. They had to understand this. "I hate magic. It's ruined my life and I just got it back. Don't you understand? I hate the loud crashes, the talking cats, the ghostly saviors."

"Oh, I thought that a unique spell," Lachesis said. "I saved it for future use. You have an immense talent, Emma."

"A talent I don't want to use."

Atropos sighed. "So dramatic."

"What are those?" Clotho asked.

Everyone turned. The room was filling up with white horses—and expanding to accommodate them.

"Oh dear," Lachesis said. "Your beggars are getting their wishes."

"Nothing bad, I hope," Emma said.

"Not so far," Atropos said.

Michael slipped his hand in Emma's. She held on tightly.

Clotho sighed. "We are going to have to deal with this."

"One problem at a time," Lachesis said.

Atropos had turned her attention back to Emma. "You know, Zeus once considered giving up everything for a mortal."

"He did not and you know it," Clotho said. "That's a myth."

"No, actually," Lachesis said. "I remember it. He had to be talked out of it."

"You can have relationships with mortals. Satisfying ones, too. But to give up your future for one just isn't something we allow." Atropos glared at Michael. "I hope you didn't encourage this, young man."

He glanced at Emma. She was watching him in confusion. She thought the Fates never spoke to mortals.

"I may have," he said. "Inadvertently. This morning, we were talking and I reminded her how different our lives were."

"And I suppose you said you couldn't live with her so young and you getting old and decrepit. You needed to at least look the part, perhaps even have your aging process slowed down." Lachesis leaned back in her chair. Her smoking jacket gaped at the bosom. Emma wondered if that was some sort of test.

"No," Michael said. "I told her I'd be with her no matter what."

"Really?" Clotho's voice rose in surprise. "Did he really say that, Emma?"

Emma nodded. She squeezed his hand. "That's why I'm here."

"Oh, dear, now I'm confused," Atropos said. "I would think there was no problem if he loved you no matter what."

"It's not about him and me." She squeezed his hand. "When he said that I realized that I could do what I want. And I want to be normal."

All three Fates rolled their eyes.

"You'll never be normal," Lachesis said. "Your thousand-year sleep guaranteed that."

"If it's children you're worried about," Clotho said, "we've checked with the Powers That Be—"

And with that all three Fates bowed their heads and spread out their hands in a reflexive movement, the way a Catholic might cross himself—

"They said you can still have children even though your magic has arrived. They warned us to warn you, however, that when your hormones go out of whack you might want to go into seclusion. They expect earthquakes, tornadoes, hurricanes. Things you'll be able to put right afterwards, but still, why have all that damage if you can avoid it?"

Michael was looking confused, but he didn't say anything. Six more horses appeared behind him.

"It's not about children," Emma said.

"Then what is it?" Atropos said.

"I like this century," Emma said. "I like the idea of spending the rest of my life in my neighborhood, teaching people, and writing books. I don't want adventures. I hate them. I don't want the responsibilities that magic brings. If I get pregnant, I don't want to worry about having a hormone surge that could wipe out the entire Midwest."

Michael squeezed her hand in support. She squeezed back.

"Please," she said, "if you look into my heart, you'll see how I feel. I appreciate the magical gift. I just don't want it."

The Fates were silent for a moment. Clotho swirled her brandy. Lachesis took a puff off her cigar. Atropos cut one of her cards in half.

Emma felt something pass through her, like several fingers touching her mind. Then they went away.

"How very odd," Lachesis said.

"Well, you can't be normal if you turn down magic," Clotho said. "Everyone wants some."

Atropos cut another card. Lachesis took her scissors away. Atropos didn't seem to mind. "If we do this, she'll end up with the mortal."

Emma bristled. Michael held her back.

"What's wrong with that?" Lachesis asked.

"He's trying to be a hero," Clotho said. "He even arrived on a white horse."

"That's my horse," Emma said. "It's really a wish. It should have vanished."

"Where do you think wishes go when they're done with their work?" Atropos said.

"It's really our wish," Lachesis said.

"Well, not *our* wish because we wouldn't have wished him here, but all wishes ultimately come from us," Clotho said.

"And all wishes return to us," Atropos said.

"Well," Emma said, "I wish to lose my magic. Please."

"It's a death sentence, Emma," Michael said. "What's fifty years when you could have thousands?"

She turned to him. This would bother him for the rest of their lives if she didn't explain it now. "It's better to have fifty wonderful years, Michael, doing exactly what I want, than a thousand miserable ones."

"There we go!" Lachesis said.

"The magic words!" Clotho said.

"Who would have thought the girl understood the essence of happily ever after?" Atropos said.

Emma was still looking at Michael. He pulled her close. "I hope you'll be happy with this," he said.

"Of course she will," Lachesis said.

"It's the prophecy," Clotho said.

"Strange that we were the last to see it," Atropos said.

"We weren't paying attention," Lachesis said.

"Young man, do you know how to play whist?" Clotho asked.

"Never tried it," Michael said.

"Don't," Atropos said. "It's dull and you only have limited time. Do things you enjoy."

Emma grinned at him. Michael grinned back.

"Emma," Lachesis said. "We'll return you to your life. Your magic will be gone, and so will your spells, although we will honor all those wishes."

"At least fifty so far," Atropos whispered.

"Fifty-one," Clotho said, "and not a nasty one in the bunch."

"As I was saying," Lachesis continued, "you won't ever be able to get your magic back. This is your last chance to change your mind."

Emma felt as if a huge burden were lifting off her. "I won't change it."

"Very well," Clotho said.

"We shower you with blessings," Atropos said.

"And send you away with love," Lachesis said.

"We'll miss you, child," Clotho said.

"I'll miss you, too," Emma said, but they had vanished. She was standing in the hotel room, Michael at her side. He was still holding her close.

"I can't believe you did that," he said.

"Why not? Because you'd keep the magic?" She had an edge to her voice. She was worried that he wouldn't be interested now. She was different, after all, not the special woman she had been before.

"No," he said. "I was thinking that it was an enormous burden."

"Then why can't you believe it?" she asked.

"Because I thought it was so much a part of you."

"That's because you've only known me since I had the magic." She studied him. "Will you miss it?"

"Your magic?" He pulled her down on the bed. "You still have magic, Emma. Just not of the snap-your-finger-and-turn-a-house-cat-into-a-lion variety."

"Professor Found, will you let me keep my job?"

He smiled. "Sleeping with your boss. That's a trick that's not recommended in business school. How about marrying him instead?"

"Can I keep my job?"

"You're quite focused, you know that?" His eyes twinkled. "How would it look if I fired my wife?"

"Tacky," she said, kissing his neck.

"That's right. We'll have to marry before we go home."

"I'm afraid now we'll have to drive back," Emma said.

"Two thousand miles with Darnell all over again?" Michael shuddered. Emma couldn't tell if it was a mock shudder or not. "How about asking Aethelstan to zap us back to Madison?"

Emma giggled. "I think he'll do it, after he stops yelling at me for making a major decision like this one without him."

"He'll have to get used to the fact that I'm the man in your life now," Michael said.

"I think he'll be relieved."

Michael started to kiss her, and then he stopped. She frowned at him. "What's wrong?" she asked.

"The Fates mentioned a prophecy. They said it just came true."

She thought for a moment. "I never paid much attention to prophecies. They even had to remind me about it."

"What was it?"

"You will find what you seek," she said, and then, suddenly, she laughed. She couldn't help herself.

Michael was frowning at her.

"Oh, Michael, it's perfect," she said. "Don't you see?"

"No, I don't see," he said. "What's so funny?"

"After this trip…"

"Yes?"

"I was Lost, but now I'm Found."

He grinned. "Those Fates are right. You'll never be normal. Life with you will be fascinating."

"I'm glad you think so," she said.

"Oh, I do."

He started to kiss her, but she put a hand to his mouth.

"I think I've been thoroughly kissed, Michael," she said. "I'm ready to move on."

"Oh, no, you're not," he said. "I've only got fifty short years with you, Emma. I've only just begun to kiss."

Then he lowered his mouth to hers. As she sank into the pillows, she realized that she was feeling joy for the first time since she woke from her thousand-year sleep.

So this was what happily ever after felt like. She liked it more than she could say.

Read on for an excerpt from

Charming Blue

He's lived through ages with the curse of attracting women…who end up dead

Once upon a time…he was the most handsome of princes, destined for great things. But now he's a lonely legend, hobbled by a dark history. With too many dead in his wake, Bluebeard escapes the only way he knows how—through the evil spell of alcohol. But it's a far different kind of spell that's been ruining his life for centuries.

How will she survive this killer prince charming?

Jodi Walters is a fixer, someone who can put magic back in order. She's the best in Hollywood at her game. But Blue has a problem she's never encountered before—and worse, she finds herself perilously attracted to him.

Coming September 2012
from Sourcebooks Casablanca

Chapter 1

NINETY-FIVE DEGREES IN THE SHADE, AND STILL THE magical gathered outside Jodi's office, pacing through the landscaping, huddling under the gigantic palms, pushing past blooming birds of paradise that she spent a small fortune on, and leaning on the fountain she paid some city administrator extra just so she could keep it running in the middle of the day. She needed that damn fountain, not because she liked flaunting water laws, but because any minute now a cell phone would explode, and its owner would throw it in panic.

Usually the magical would have enough presence of mind to throw an exploding cell phone *at* water, although she had learned over her long and storied career that using the words "the magical" and "presence of mind" in the same sentence could be a recipe for disaster.

She pulled her sporty red Mercedes convertible into driveway, waved at her current, potential, and former clients, and parked under the carport, dreading the next few minutes. She would have to thread her way along the curved tile sidewalk that she put in a decade or more ago, before cell phones forced her magical clients to stand outside (she *hated* it when cell phones exploded inside). Back then, she thought the smokers might be a problem, so she installed an antique upright ashtray that she bought at a flea market—one of those ashtrays, she had been assured, that had stood on the MGM lot back when Clark Gable roamed the premises.

The ashtray still got a lot of use, but mostly the cell phone users had pushed the smokers aside. And no matter how much she told her magical clients that the longer they used a phone, the more likely it was to explode, they never listened to her.

Of course, you really couldn't survive in Los Angeles without a phone. She bought hers in bulk. The manager at the phone store finally taught her how to transfer her number to a new phone, so she wasn't stopping in every other day demanding an emergency phone repair.

She grabbed her purse, today's phone, and her briefcase, stuffed to the gills with contracts, memos, and all that junk computers were supposed to replace.

By the time she waggled her car door open, she nearly hit four dwarves (of the Snow White variety), two selkies (clothed, thank heavens), and one troll. He was a sweetie named Gunther whom she used to find regular work for in Abbott and Costello movies, before he returned to the Kingdoms. Now that he had come back to the Greater World, she was having trouble placing him, which she thought was just plain weird, given the popularity of fantasy movies these days. But whenever he went to a casting call, he was told to remove his costume, and he couldn't, since he truly was tall, gray, stonelike, and glowery.

She hadn't figured out a way around that yet, but she would.

"I don't have time, Gunther," she said as she slung her purse over her shoulder and closed the car door with her foot. She hadn't looked, so she hoped she didn't catch one of the small magical in that move. Pixies in particular liked to get between cars and doors.

But no one screamed, so she was probably safe.

"I'm so sorry to bother you, Miss Walters," Gunther said slowly, ever proper. He had nineteenth-century manners, which was another reason she loved him. "But I do need a moment—"

"Can Ramon deal with it?" she asked. "Because I have an emergency."

She wasn't sure what the emergency was, but Ramon, her assistant, had called her out of a meeting with Disney and told her she was needed in the office. The Disney meeting was a bust anyway. For some reason the kid in charge, and he really was a kid (twenty-five if he was a day), thought she worked in animation. She couldn't seem to convince the kid that she *didn't* work in animation, so she was happy to leave.

Still, it was unlike Ramon to interrupt her at all. He was the best assistant she had ever had, which was saying something, considering how many of her assistants went on to manage Fortune 500 companies. Ramon knew how important the meeting was in Hollywood, even if it was a bust-deal with Disney.

"I *hope* Ramon can deal with it," Gunther said slowly. He was trying to keep up with her, which showed just how panicked he was. Trolls didn't like to walk fast. "It's the first of the month…"

She stopped, closed her eyes, and sighed. The first of the month. Of course. The rent was due. And Gunther couldn't get work, even though when he returned to the Greater World she had told him she'd have no trouble placing him. All the *Lord of the Rings* knockoff films, the Syfy Channel, the five fairy tale movies in development in three different studios—she had thought at least one of them would need a troll. A real, honest-to-God troll, not something CGI-ed. But so far, no takers, and Gunther was reluctant to go home and ask for more gold from his family so that he could pay his rent.

"Okay," she said. "Sit quietly in the waiting room. I'll have something for you after I solve this emergency."

Gunther nodded. It took him nearly a half an hour to smile, and the smile was never worth the wait. (In fact, it was a bit creepy.) So the nod had to do.

At least his bulky presence had dissuaded some of her other clients from approaching her. She smiled at them all, held up a hand, and kept repeating, "Make an appointment, make an appointment," as she headed to the front door.

Her office was in a 1920s Hollywood-style bungalow, which meant that it had been upgraded and expanded far outside of its original floor plan. The house had belonged to some important starlet before the Crash of 1929, and then purchased by an even more important starlet in the 1930s, "improved" by said starlet's second husband (a successful screenwriter) in the 1940s, and suffered a decline along with the studio system in the 1950s. An entire counterculture of hippies lived in it during the 1960s, and it was nearly condemned in the 1970s, until Jodi bought it, restored it, and "improved" it some more.

Now it had air-conditioning, a large pool for her mer-clients, a cabana, and four other side buildings. She had kept her office in the main building, the historic bungalow, even though she kept thinking she should move to the very back, away from the crowds.

And she had crowds, every single day. This client, that

client, this friend of a client, that enemy of an old flame. They made her head spin. She had hired help, but none of them had the organizational magic that she did. They had all been competent, but none were as good as she was.

She had come from a family of chatelaines, the people who kept the castles and great manor houses of the Kingdoms functioning. Her family had served—and still did serve—some of the greatest rulers the various Kingdoms had ever known.

But Jodi was a modern woman, one who did not want to waste her time managing someone else's household. She had fled the Third Kingdom in the early twentieth century, when it became clear that modernity would cause tensions in the Kingdoms themselves.

Until the late nineteenth century, the Kingdoms were isolated from this place, which folks in the Kingdoms called the Greater World. Sure, there was occasional crossover, mostly from literary types. Shakespeare stole half his oeuvre from his Kingdom visits, and Washington Irving had written down Rip Van Winkle's story damn near verbatim, only changing the name of the poor hapless mortal who had stumbled through a portal between the Greater World and the Fourteenth Kingdom.

The Germans were the worst. Goethe claimed his Faust stories were inspired by legends he had heard in a tavern in Leipzig, when actually he had found yet another portal into a Kingdom and barely escaped with his life. And the Brothers Grimm had gone into the Kingdoms on something like an archeological expedition, there to map the Kingdoms themselves, and returning instead with the stories of people's lives, stories the Brothers Grimm exaggerated and mistold to the point of libel—had libel laws existed between the Greater World and the Kingdoms.

Sometimes Jodi found it ironic that she had escaped her fairy tale existence to come to a place that took the Grimm Brothers' lies and exaggerated them even further.

But she wasn't the only fairy tale refugee in Los Angeles, as her front yard now showed. Hundreds of malcontents fled the Kingdoms over the years to come here and have a real life, only to be disappointed at how plain, monochrome, and *real* the lives actually were.

She pushed open the solid oak door and stepped into what had been the living room of the bungalow, now a gigantic reception area with arched ceilings and lots of comfortable seating areas marked off by large fake plants. The cool air smelled faintly of mint, a scent that soothed most of the magical (and most regular mortals as well).

Ramon had suspended two flat screen television sets from the ceiling, high enough to be out of what he called "the magical vortex," whatever it was that caused magic and electronics to intertwine. Ramon corralled all of the electronics here. He made everyone who entered drop their cell phones, MP3 players, and other gadgets into a basket on his reception desk. If the tech stayed near him, it didn't explode.

Ramon was pure magickless mortal, thirty-something, although he pretended he was twenty-five. He called himself Ramon McQueen, after Steve McQueen, the rugged 1960s icon, and some tragic silent film star whom hardly anyone had ever heard of and whom Jodi barely remembered. This Ramon was neither tragic nor rugged, but he was very pretty in a way that would have made him a movie star in the 1920s. He wore as much makeup as silent film actors did as well, accenting his sensitive mouth and outlining his spectacular brown eyes in kohl.

He was so good at organizing things that three weeks after she hired him, she looked into his aura to see if he had organizational magic. She could see auras—that was how she read magic. She should have trusted her instincts: he didn't have any magic at all. But his organizational skills were so amazing that she couldn't quite believe they had no magical component.

The waiting room chairs were filled with even more clients, potential clients, and former clients, mostly separated by type—human-appearing but magical; minor storybook characters; the enchanted; creatures; half-human creatures; spelled humans; shape-shifters; and little people of all species, races, and creeds. Not all were waiting for her. The creatures primarily went to her best assistant, and the extras (primarily the minor storybook characters and the little people) went to her next best assistant. She had a third assistant whose clients worked for the various theme parks, but they had a separate entrance (with a different receptionist) in one of the outbuildings so that they wouldn't contaminate the so-called Real Actors.

She had no one who worked animation. (Boy, that meeting still irritated her.)

The conversations were muted. She didn't allow discussion of magic or former fights or past conflicts, and the magical didn't like discussing their upcoming work with each other out of fear that someone else might get the job. So what few conversations happened were usually about things like apartment rentals, good deals on costumes, and which vehicles were built solidly enough that their computer components survived long-term exposure to magical fields.

Ramon had muted the two flat screens but had left them on all-news channels—one currently covering the fires in Malibu Canyon, and the other giving the latest lurid details of the case the media was calling the Fairy Tale Stalker case.

Jodi hated the case's name and wished she could get the media to change it, but she had become aware of the story too late to do anything. Usually she would have managed something. Theoretically, she was Hollywood's best magical wrangler (although the mortals simply thought she was a manager with some very strange clientele), but in practice, she had become the fixer for all of Los Angeles County.

If someone magical was in trouble, then Jodi usually got involved. Involvement generally didn't mean more than sending the magical to the organization, but occasionally she had to delve deeper. She didn't mind. She had been fixing things since she arrived here almost a century ago. Fixing had become as natural as breathing.

"What couldn't wait?" she asked softly as she opened the gate to let herself into the area behind the reception desk.

Ramon looked up at her. A black curl had fallen over the center of his forehead, and his makeup was slightly smudged. He had removed his suit coat, revealing a gorgeous purple shirt made of some lightweight material. Even that hadn't stopped a pool of sweat from forming along his spine.

Very unusual. Ramon was usually the picture of crispness, even in the middle of an LA summer afternoon.

"First of all, let me simply say, it is *not* my fault," he said in that precise way of his. "You made the appointment, and you wrote down the man's name instead of the company, for heaven's sake, and he's a newbie, and I had no idea he was with Disney—"

"That's fine, Ramon," she said. "It wasn't going well anyway. He had no idea who I was."

"—*and*," Ramon said, not to be derailed, "she *threatened* me."

That caught Jodi's attention. "Who threatened you?"

"That cantankerous little fairy. I rue the day you made it possible for me to see her and her kind," Ramon said. "If you could ever reverse that spell, I would appreciate it."

Jodi frowned. She had spelled Ramon so that he could see magical creatures normally invisible to the mortal eye. Only one type of creature fit into his current description. In fact, only one person—if she could be called that—fit.

Cantankerous Belle, better known as Tanker Belle, whom some believed to be Tinker Bell's older, meaner cousin. Whoever Tanker Belle was, she led a group of tiny fairies who had either divorced themselves from the human-sized fairies of Celtic lore or had never belonged to the group in the first place.

The magical weren't all from the Kingdoms. And not all of the magical seemed to have problems with electronics that the Kingdom magical did. One faction of the human-sized fairies, who had been involved in a power struggle for more than a century, had found a home in Las Vegas amidst all that technology, and they seemed to be doing fine…

Wickedly Charming

by Kristine Grayson

He's given up on happily-ever-after...

Cinderella's Prince Charming is divorced and at a dead end.
The new owner of a bookstore, Charming has given up on
women, royalty, and anything that smacks of a future. That is,
until he meets up with Mellie...

But she may be the key to happily-right-now...

Mellie is sick and tired of stepmothers being misunderstood.
Vampires have redeemed their reputation, why shouldn't
stepmothers do the same? Then she runs into the handsomest,
most charming man she's ever met and discovers she's going
about her mission all wrong...

"Grayson deftly nods to pop culture and offers clever
spins on classic legends and lore while adding unique
twists all her own."—*Booklist* starred review

"I love this take on an old story... Exceedingly endearing..."
—*Night Owl Reviews* Reviewer Top Pick

For more Kristine Grayson, visit:

www.sourcebooks.com

Utterly Charming

by Kristine Grayson

———

He could be her own personal Prince Charming if only dreams did come true...

Mysterious, handsome wizard Aethelstan Blackstone hires beautiful, hardworking attorney Nora Barr to get a restraining order to protect Sleeping Beauty from her evil stepmother. But if Sleeping Beauty is supposed to be his soul mate, then how come he's becoming bewitched by Nora?

And when Nora finds herself baby-sitting a clueless maiden from the Middle Ages, avoiding a very wicked witch, and falling hard for a man whose magic she doesn't believe in, she begins to think that love itself is only a fairy tale...

———

"Grayson uses smooth prose and humorous, human characters to create a delightful, breezy tale perfect for anyone who truly enjoys happy endings." —*Publishers Weekly*

"This is another fascinating tale! I love how Kristine Grayson adds twists to the fairy tales that we all know and love!" —*Bitten by Books*

For more Kristine Grayson, visit:

www.sourcebooks.com

Acknowledgments

Many thanks to my sister Sandy Hofsommer who helped me understand the nature of fairy tales and for remembering; and to my husband Dean for discovering the romantic heart of a short story that lead to *Charming* and now *Kissed*.

About the Author

Before turning to romance writing, award-winning author Kristine Kathryn Rusch edited the *Magazine of Fantasy & Science Fiction* and ran Pulphouse Publishing (which won her a World Fantasy Award). As Kristine Grayson she has published six novels so far and has won the *RT Book Reviews* Reviewer's Choice Award for Best Paranormal Romance, and, under her real name, Kristine Kathryn Rusch, the prestigious Hugo award. She lives in Oregon with her own Prince Charming, writer Dean Wesley Smith (who is not old enough to be one of the original three, but he is handsome enough) as well as the obligatory writers' cats. www.kriswrites.com.